The Glassfire Serpent: *Embers*

*for Rose.
Enjoy the Netherwarlde!*

Also By James Fahy

The Changeling series:

Isle of Winds *(book 1)*
The Drowned Tomb *(book 2)*
Chains of Gaia *(book 3)*

Phoebe Harkness series:

Hell's Teeth *(book 1)*
Crescent Moon *(book 2)*
Paper Children *(book 3)*

The Changeling series: Book 4

The GLASSFIRE SERPENT
Embers

James Fahy

LUME BOOKS

LUME BOOKS

First published in 2021 by Lume Books
30 Great Guildford Street,
Borough, SE1 0HS

Copyright © James Fahy 2021

The right of James Fahy to be identified as the author of this work has been asserted by them in accordance with the Copyright, Design and Patents Act, 1988.

All rights reserved. No part of this publication may be reproduced, stored in a retrieval system, or transmitted in photocopying, recording or otherwise, without the prior permission of the copyright owner.

ISBN 978-1-83901-415-4

Typeset using Atomik ePublisher from Easypress Technologies

www.lumebooks.co.uk

For my Dad.
I know you never read my books, because I never wrote a book about Spitfires or Lancaster bombers for you,
I wrote about dragons and magic, but that's okay. I know you were proud of me.
I'm proud to have had a father like you.
I miss you every day. I'll see you again.
Until then, this one's for you.
Tucker

1

A Yellow Knight

The sky above Trafalgar Square was the white hard flash of a frozen bulb. It glowed from within. The threat of snow hovered, but it refused to fall. Instead, it hung like a threat, glowering over London, a frosted bowl of cold promise. The British winter sun, which had not been fully seen for days, hid up there somewhere, coy behind its pale late December skirts, making its presence known only by ghostly shimmers in an occasional thinning of the skies. It appeared here and there in glimpses, a wan spectre, a high and tiny button pinned to a white sheet.

The large city square below was filled with only the hardiest of tourists, bundled in their parkas and bubble jackets, wrapped anonymously in scarves, hats, and gloves as they milled around, rustling their guidebooks and city maps and waving their selfie-sticks. The flagstones beneath the multitude of feet were ash grey and tinged with a tenacious frost.

Huddled by a vast, sky-piercing column of fluted stone and flanked by dark sculpted lions of enormous stature, two teenage boys stood, shivering and stamping their feet. Both leaning against low railings between the frozen bright sky and dark stone floors.

They looked as anonymous as any other in the cold crowds of the capital, wrapped as they were in dark hoodies and thick winter coats. However, both boys had the distinctive trait of not being human, which always sets you aside a little ... no matter how hard you try.

"How are you not cold?" one complained to the other, his breath coming before him in a small, frosted cloud through his chattering teeth. He was slight of build, with messy blond hair tucked under his hood.

Robin Fellows – Fae, Changeling, Scion of the Arcania and the last great hope of the Netherworlde – was losing feeling in his extremities.

His companion ignored him utterly. The second boy was taller by a head, with ashy grey hair tucked under a dark woollen beanie. He was wearing no coat, only a dark hoodie, and he leaned rather bonelessly against the chilly railings, the great lions of Trafalgar at his back, with his hands thrust deep into the pockets of his jeans. He was pale as milk, and scowling, although this was merely his default expression. Jackalope was a free Fae, something of a rarity in a time when most of his kind were enslaved or imprisoned, and this was his first time in the capital of the mortal world's England. He didn't seem impressed.

Robin kicked at him lightly, not taking his own hands out of his coat.

"Oi!" he snapped. "Earth to Jack."

The older Fae opened his eyes and gave Robin a sidelong glance. He reached up under his hood and removed his oversized headphones, letting them rest around his neck.

"What? Why are you kicking me?"

"I said, 'how are you not cold?'" Robin repeated. "We've been standing here for half an hour. I'm bloody perished. Shall we go and get a hot chocolate or something?"

"The Lady Irene instructed us to remain here and await her," Jackalope replied with grim sincerity. He glared around at the city square. "It's bad enough that all these … humans … are here." Robin noticed the sneer in his voice. "It would be even worse inside one of those tiny steamy cafés."

He pulled his hood tight to the sides of his head, still peering around the milling crowds with open suspicion. He was ensuring his horn stubs did not show. All Fae, save for Robin, had horns. Jackalope's had been sawn off long ago, in another world, deep in the prison camps of Eris, but the flat nubs of their roots still nestled in his grey hair. "And to answer your question, *this* is not cold. Try living a few years on the Gravis Glaciem. Then you'll be glad of your thermal briefs."

He reached down and flicked off his music, pale fingers dancing across the screen of his phone.

"Whatever, Beats-by-Fae …" Robin rolled his eyes, sulking slightly at his companion's stubbornness. He really did want a hot drink. "What are you listening to, anyway?"

"BTS," Jackalope replied flatly. "If you're bored, Scion, you should have brought a book. You like books."

It never failed to amaze Robin how quickly Jackalope had adjusted to life in the human world. When they had first met, the de-horned Fae had been a wild thing, living alone in a cave in the snows and dressed in ragged wolf furs. Solitary and practically feral. After only a month as a permanent resident of Erlking, he had seemingly morphed with considerable success into the archetypal moody teenage boy, avoiding Hestia the housekeeper's attempts at healthy and home-cooked food and instead frequently ordering pizza for delivery to the Hall, even if this meant sneaking all the way down the great driveway to the edge of Erlking's property line, to find a place where his phone would catch a signal. He had also, rather unexpectedly, with his grim and stoic nature, developed an unquenchable and unapologetic taste for chirpy K-pop.

Robin looked around Trafalgar Square, blowing out another arabesque of frosted breath and listening to the cars and trucks roar by in their endless bustling. The symphony of London, which never ceased. The traffic was a constant dull thrum, blood in your ears. It was like hearing the beat of the city's own heart.

Beneath his coat and the chunky sweater he wore, his seraphinite mana stone rested comfortably against his skin, jostling occasionally against the small silver horseshoe pendant that Aunt Irene had insisted they both wear for the duration of the trip.

As usual, the mana stone at least was warm. A small teardrop of cosy heat in the otherwise biting chill.

It had sounded like a fun escape when Aunt Irene first suggested it. A trip down to London, a rare chance for Robin to escape the boundaries of Erlking for once. Erlking was his home and his sanctuary. But while Eris ruled the Netherworlde, the Hall was also his prison.

He had visited the great city a few times with Gran when he was younger, but he had been so little, and it had been so long ago, that he only remembered snippets, shards of memory here and there. A ride on the London Eye. Running excitedly around mummies in glass cases at the museum. Having hot chocolate in a tiny café somewhere, surrounded by Christmas shoppers.

Maybe that was why he craved hot chocolate now.

But despite the uncharacteristic and welcome freedom this outing had brought, Robin was paranoid all the same. The agents of Lady Eris, dark Empress of the Netherworlde, were everywhere in both worlds, he was frequently told by pretty much everyone he knew. They were always searching for him. They were always on the hunt. That had been drilled into him so often since coming to Erlking that now, temporarily free of its bounds, he had spent much of the last two days visit looking suspiciously over his shoulder rather than enjoying the sights.

"You're just in a bad mood because she didn't let you bring Phorbas," Robin muttered to Jackalope.

Phorbas was a knife, haunted by the trapped and disembodied spirit of a satyr, Robin's first tutor. Jackalope, who had no mana stone himself, and therefore no magic, had become rather attached to it. He may not have the skill to cast, but his practical combat skills were second to none, and Robin knew that the older Fae felt naked and defenceless these days without the weapon constantly at his side.

"I don't see why he couldn't come." Jackalope rocked a little on the railings, feigning indifference with a dismissive shrug and a snort of air down his nose. His frown, Robin noticed, matched the carved frown of the great Trafalgar lion behind him quite well.

"Because he's a *knife*," Robin explained with emphasis, for the hundredth time. "This isn't the Netherworlde, Jack. You can't just stroll around town in the human world with a blade stuck in your belt. The police are very clear about that. It's one of their main rules. Knife crime is a real issue in London. You want to get tackled to the ground by an armed response unit?"

"I'd like to see them try," Jack sneered with a curl of his lip. He glanced up at the soaring, decorated column behind them, stretching off into the white sky high above the roofs of the tall pale buildings all around. Traffic hummed and blared continuously as the city moved around them. "What is this place anyway?" he asked. "There is a man on top of this pole. Was he a wise king? He is guarded by lions, so he must have been important."

"Nelson," Robin explained, following Jack's gaze and squinting into the harsh brightness of the white, snow-filled sky. "That's Nelson's column. It's famous. He …" Robin stumbled mentally. One of the downsides of being home-schooled at Erlking was that much of his curriculum comprised learning to harness the power of the elements, magical casting and combat. When you spend most of your time training to defend yourself from nefarious otherworldly evils, it leaves very little time for normal education such as British history (although Henry sympathised and shared his schoolbooks when he could. Often encouraging Robin to do his homework for him).

"He was an … admiral?" he stated, although uncertainly.

"That's a bird," Jack replied flatly, still looking up at the distant statue above. "So, he was a shapeshifter, then?"

Robin shook his head, causing his furry hood to wobble. "No, not that kind of admiral. I mean like, in the navy. You know … wartime."

Jack looked down, shrugging. "Yes, I know wartime," he said darkly. He scuffed his trainers against the cold and frosted flagstones beneath his feet, and an uncomfortable moment or two passed.

"Perhaps one day, Robin Fellows, when you have fulfilled your destiny, defeated Lady Eris and restored the Fae to their rightful place in the Netherworlde, they will show you the same honour, and put you on a stick also."

"Column," Robin frowned with narrowed eyes. "It's a column, not a stick."

He noticed the tiniest corners of Jackalope's mouth were turned up, as though he were trying hard not to smile. He was teasing. Robin had discovered that, despite all appearances, the grim older Fae did in fact have a sense of humour. It was just extremely well hidden. It was hard to tell when he was joking – or not.

"And I don't want to be on a column. I'd rather be in a café."

At least it wasn't snowing, he thought, peering up again at the bright silver sky. It hardly ever snowed in the city. No doubt back up north at Erlking, high on the wild moors, the Hall would be under several feet of white powder and Mr Drover, Erlking's handyman, would be busy shovelling a labyrinth of pathways here and there between the outbuildings like a rat maze.

"I wonder what the others are doing now," Jack said, ignoring Robin's not-so-subtle hint for warm beverages. "I imagine they are enjoying the peace and quiet of Erlking. There are too many humans in this city."

"You wanted to come," Robin reminded him. "You said you wanted to get out of the house."

"I didn't know there would be so … many … humans," Jack muttered, showing a distinct lack of understanding of how cities – and capital cities in particular – worked. "I wanted to see the buildings. I've seen them now."

"Well the others couldn't come, could they? It's not a school trip. Karya's still hobbling about on a cane after being stabbed, almost to death, with a spear last month; Henry refuses to leave her side because he's apparently turned into Florence Nightingale these days and Woad, well …" Robin shrugged helplessly. "Woad's blue."

"He could have used a glamour to appear human," Jack argued, reaching out and patting the flank of one of the enormous, dark lions at his side. "He has done that before."

"Woad in London would be … chaos." Robin smirked, sniffing in the cold. He could already picture the blue faun scrambling up Nelson's column and doing acrobatics on the top. "You and me? At least in comparison, the two of us don't draw too much attention."

Jackalope leaned over and jogged Robin with his shoulder, almost knocking him completely off balance.

"You are wrong. We are attracting attention, Scion. Those humans there have been watching us for some time. They're acting extremely suspiciously."

Robin's gaze followed to where Jack was indicating. Across from them, great steps led up from the square to the vast imposing façade of the National Gallery. Many people were sitting on the cold steps, drinking coffee in groups, bundled together for warmth, eating sandwiches and resolutely ignoring the signs instructing everyone *not* to sit on the steps.

"You see them?" Jack muttered out of the corner of his mouth. His long pale eyes were filled with distrust. "The female humans."

There was a group of teenage girls, all in hiking jackets, backpacks gathered at their feet, sitting on a low wall chatting together and flipping through tourist guides, clearly in the capital to see the sights. All four of them were indeed occasionally looking their way, whispering to each other through mittened hands and laughing in each other's ears.

Robin felt his face turn red, and suddenly everything about him, from his facial expression to his stance, felt incredibly awkward. Robin wasn't very suave around girls at the best of times. Karya hardly counted. She was basically family. And the only other girl he'd had any real regular contact with tried to kill him on occasion, when the mood took her. It wasn't a tremendous pool of experience to draw from.

"They seem interested in you," Jackalope said, louder than Robin would like. "Perhaps they are servants of the Dark Empress."

"Shut up," Robin said, thrusting his hands into his pockets, feeling as though he arms were suddenly comical and floppy, like great tubes of dumb spaghetti. He made a show of inspecting the large lion sculptures with great interest. "They're just regular girls. Don't *stare*!" He noticed Jackalope had folded his arms across the front of his hoodie and was now throwing a challenging and defiant glare at the girls, his head tilted to one side.

Girls were difficult enough one on one, Robin firmly believed. Girls in a group? That was just terrifying.

"One approaches," Jackalope said in an offhand way.

"What?" Robin whirled in panic. One of the girls had indeed detached from the wall and was wandering over to them, making her way across the cold and crowded December square, with wide eyes and a large smile. Her friends, Robin saw, seemed to be in fits of hysterics behind her.

"Hi." She gave both of them a little wave as she reached them. Her hands were encased in thick red woollen gloves. "Sorry! My friends are weirdos, ignore them." She looked back, grinning. She seemed perhaps a year older than Robin, but he couldn't really tell.

"We were just watching you guys hang out over here. We're over from Minnesota. Here to see Christmas in Britain. Are you Londoners?"

Robin shook his head, attempting to appear relaxed. His tongue felt like a dead and useless slug in his mouth.

"We are from distant parts," Jackalope said sternly, looking the girl up and down with open disapproval.

The girl, who Robin thought was quite alarmingly pretty, glanced at Jack, frowning a little in confusion, and then turned her attention to Robin. "My friends were having bets with each other that you guys are models. Told you they were idiots. But I said you look like you're in a band." She blinked, inspecting Robin's face carefully. "Oh, wow. I love your eyes. Are those contacts? It looks so real!"

Robin had one blue eye, the soft shade of a pale duck egg, and one eye green as emerald. Cumulative exposure to the various Shards of the Arcania over the past couple of years had taken a physical toll on him, and parts of him had become, it seemed, permanently Puck. He barely noticed it himself anymore.

"Oh … erm … ha!" He blinked, self-conscious, resisting the urge to cover his green eye with a slap of his hand. "No, it's … genetic, I suppose. We're not in a band, or … ha, models, no."

"Robin sings very well," Jackalope said, behind the girl's back. "I have heard him in the bath, although his taste in music is terrible."

She laughed and Robin shot daggers at the older Fae, who didn't seem to notice.

"What do you want, human girl?" Jack said, haughty and blunt as ever. "We are not models. We are real."

The trouble with being Fae in the human world, is that most Fae are blissfully unaware that to regular humans they appear quite beautiful. Even a Fae bundled in a heavy parka exudes a certain ethereal and unmistakable otherworldly elegance, whether they want to or not. Just as a burning candle cannot help giving off light. Both Robin and Jack were completely clueless about this. Had anyone at Erlking pointed it out, they would have been terribly awkward about it. But nobody did, because, frankly, none of them cared. When you live in a mansion filled with magic and mystery, there are far more interesting places to look than mirrors and far more exciting things to think about than appearance.

"She means like fashion models." Robin finally found his voice. "Not mannequins." He scratched his head awkwardly. "No, we're not," he assured the girl. "Models, I mean."

From the corner of his mouth, he hissed to Jackalope. "She probably just thought that because you're slumping about the place looking moody and pouting all the time like a poser."

"Oh well, anyway …" the girl said, leaning in towards Jack. "My friend back there, in the red coat … Tammy. She thinks you're like … *seriously* cute. She tried to stop me coming over." She laughed, and Robin couldn't tell if she was amused at Jack's confused face, or at the fun of embarrassing her friend, who, back on the steps, had hidden her face in her hood and was attempting to hide behind the other girls on the wall, all of whom were cackling.

"But … you know … we wondered if you want to grab a coffee or something?" She looked at Robin, grinning and looking a little shy and embarrassed herself for the first time since bounding over. "Both of you I mean, of course? Our treat?" She had thrust her hands into her pockets and was stamping her feet against the cold. "I'm Emilie."

Robin was now sure he was blushing from toes to eyebrows and was no longer feeling the December cold. He stammered to formulate a reply. One of the girls shouted something unintelligible, and their assailant turned her back on the boys momentarily to shout back amongst laughter.

"Make her go away," Jack hissed urgently to Robin, his silver eyes flashing. Robin looked helpless.

"Bring the lions to life or something," the pale Fae commanded. "Humans are so aggravating."

"I can't do that!" Robin hissed back.

He found it rather mortifying that he had faced centaurs, dragons and all manner of terrifying beasts, but in the face of the opposite sex, Robin was at a total loss.

"So?" The girl whirled around to face them again. "How about it?" She grinned, giving them a jokey double thumbs up in her mittened gloves and bouncing a little on her heels. "Free coffee for super cute guys? Sound fun? We don't bite!"

In the face of their silence, she looked from one boy to the other, clearly a little deflated by their lack of response. "Oh, wait ..." She pointed between them. "Are you guys a couple?"

"Would that make you desist?" Jackalope asked, still staring at her through hooded eyes.

"Huh?"

"Well, the thing is, we're kind of waiting for someone ..." Robin began to blurt, but Jackalope butted in.

"We are not really interested in your kind," he told her, in what Robin could only guess was Jack's best attempt at being civil. He gave a nod to Robin, as though to indicate that he had this whole situation in hand.

"Our ... kind?" The girl looked a little off balance.

Please don't say humans again. Robin screwed up his eyes.

"Your companion's interest in us is misplaced," Jack continued. "The people of Erlking have little to discuss with regul ..."

"What he means is ... um ... we ..." Robin stammered. The girl blinked at them.

"Oh, its fine!" she said suddenly. "I totally get it. You guys are *together*. Damn." She laughed to herself, folding her arms. "That's so not fair ... to *me*, I mean. You're both so pretty. You make an amazing couple."

Jackalope seemed to realise the potential escape route. Without warning, his hand shot out and grabbed Robin's firmly, lacing his cold fingers with the Scion's.

"We are two of a kind," he told the girl with great gravitas. "We are very much in love."

Robin tried in vain to twist his hand out of the other boy's grip, but Jackalope was far stronger.

The girl's hands went to her chest. "Oh my God! You guys are *so* romantic. That's adorable!" She clapped her hands together in the cold. "Well … I can take a little heartbreak on a winter afternoon," she grinned. "But hey, still get coffee with us okay? Wow, you look so glamorous together."

"No, we don't!" Robin hissed. "We don't look glamo …"

"We have to go," Jack nodded to the girl earnestly. "He is cold, and I cannot bear to see him in discomfort." He glanced over at Robin; his face as deadly serious as ever. "Such is my deep and abiding affection."

The girl started to reply, but Jackalope had already dismissed her and begun to stalk away, dragging Robin along with his vice-like grip. The Scion of the Arcania stumbled after him, struggling to keep his footing and wishing fervently that the ground would open up and swallow him whole.

"Oh … my … God!" he hissed when they were a few steps away, headed across the square to the gallery. "Could you *be* any less convincing? I feel like I'm being kidnapped."

"Well, I'm not going to kiss you," Jackalope replied tersely. "I don't do public displays of affection."

"You don't do *any* displays of affection!" Robin replied harshly. "And I don't bloody well want you to kiss me! Where are you dragging me?"

Jackalope pointed ahead with his free hand, still pulling Robin along as lovingly as he could convincingly manage in order to lose the mildly disappointed humans behind them. "Towards sanctuary from human attentions," he replied. "Look, our saviour has emerged."

At the top of the steps, a tall thin woman, elderly but with the regal poise of the habitually straight-backed, had emerged from the imposing doors of the art gallery. She was dressed in a long wool coat the colour of pearl, and her silver hair, coiled up into an elaborate bun, was fastened beneath an elegant fur hat. Aunt Irene, the guardian of Erlking Hall, peered down the steps at the two Fae approaching hand in hand. By way of greeting, she raised an envelope and an eyebrow.

"It is good to see you two getting along," she said, distracted, as they finally reached the top of the stairs. "I apologise for keeping you both waiting, but I have managed to achieve what we came here to do."

"You can let go of my hand now," Robin muttered, murderously.

"We were assailed romantically by strangers from Minnesota," Jackalope explained seriously.

"I could not be less interested," Irene smiled at them both, although her piercing eyes glanced over at the now distant group of girls, and she looked faintly amused.

"While you two have been turning heads, *I* have secured us invitations to the private showing. Shall we head inside now? Before the two of you bewitch any more innocent humans?"

Robin, Aunt Irene and Jackalope were not in London in chilly December merely for sightseeing. They had come with a singular purpose. Recently, Robin had been away in the Netherworlde, destroying Eris' most foul and secure prison, the Hive, freeing the woods of dryads from a scourge-dragon and winning the Shard of Earth. Meanwhile, Irene had been busy making her own investigations into the abiding mystery of the Cubiculu-Argentum.

Robin had explained to Jackalope, who hadn't been present for much of their investigations, that hints and clues had been discovered, piece by piece, ever since he first came to Erlking. Hints indicating that before the great shattering of the Arcania, at the culmination of the war and the downfall of their people, King Oberon and Queen Titania had put in place a great and closely-guarded mystery.

Before the leaders of the Fae had mysteriously disappeared, leaving the Netherworlde to be overtaken by Eris, the king and queen had used a network of agents named the Sidhe-Nobilitas – the knights of the Fae court as it were, and including Robin's own father – to construct something known only as the Cubiculu-Argentum.

Nobody knew what this was. A weapon of some kind? A great treasure? Whatever it might be, great pains had been taken to keep it secret and hidden. It was clearly important, and perhaps, Irene suspected and hoped, it could be crucial to the rebellion. Something they could use to turn the tides. To unseat and defeat Eris, once and for all.

Oberon and Titania had been extraordinarily thorough with their secrecy, however. A chance find within a puzzle box, which Robin had stumbled upon in an Undine's grave, had led them to a drowned tomb hidden deep beneath a lake … a tomb belonging to one of the trusted Sidhe-Nobilitas. This tomb had held a strongbox containing an enigmatic clue to the nature of the Cubiculum.

The clue, infuriatingly vague, had been a nothing more than a single scrap of paper. An old library stamp card, almost illegible and seemingly worthless.

Irene, reasoning that nothing so well hidden, however mundane in appearance, could be worthless, had enlisted the not inconsiderable expertise of Mr Ffoulkes, a Fire Panthea whose speciality was in antiquities and the identifying of lost things. But even with all his considerable expertise, Mr Ffoulkes had managed to shed only the smallest glimmer of light on what book this library card might relate to. He had surmised that, whatever book once housed this card, it had been last checked out in the 1920s, by a man – judging from analysis of the handwriting – whose name likely began with G.

This really wasn't much to go on at all.

They had all been understandably frustrated at the vagueness of the clues. Locating just one unknown book and understanding its significance to the Cubiculum, and how on earth this all tied in with the shattering of the Arcania in the first place, seemed, on the face of it, an insurmountable task.

But Irene of Erlking was nothing if not tenacious. While Robin and his friends were raising hell in the forests of the Netherworlde, driving Eris' forces from the woods and learning of the gifts once bestowed on the Netherworlde by each of the legendary Elementals, Irene had been diligently researching, following every lead, visiting every library. And what she had found, as Robin learned on his return, was that clearly whatever the mystery book was, the rebellious folk of Erlking were not the only ones looking for it.

Wherever Irene had looked, wherever her clues and investigations had brought her, each time another party had been there before her – someone else following the extremely scattered breadcrumbs, searching for the same prize. With difficulty and time, she had established the identity of this shadowy competitor. A London firm of high prestige: Sire Holdings.

Further investigations had revealed an insidious commercial empire, with tentacles snaking into every sector of life. Sire Holdings had investments in travel, property, finance, the arts, technology, scientific research. A regular controlling cabal, with very little public branding or face. Sire Holdings chose instead to shun the public, quietly working their influence into all aspects of life from the shadows.

Irene had attempted, on many occasions, to gain an audience with their CEO, but this was where the guardian of Erlking had finally hit a wall.

In the Netherworlde, Irene Fellows was a tremendously powerful Panthea, commanding respect and fully capable of decimating a battlefield full of centaur with one wave of her hand, should the fancy take her. She was the all-knowing steward of Erlking itself, the sole guardian of the last Fae bastion of magic and secrets. However, despite this impressive pedigree, in the eyes of the more mundane human world, she was still nothing more than an eccentric old lady; with plenty of money for sure, but with no real-world connections. Every attempt she made to secure an official meeting with the owners of the enigmatic Sire Holdings had been politely but firmly rebuffed.

"So, why are we at the art gallery?" Jackalope asked, as the three made their way inside, their footsteps echoing across the marble floors. "I know you said there was something in London we had to see, but I had imagined it would be a library, if it's a mysterious book you're looking for. Not an art gallery."

"We are here, Master Jack," Irene replied, as she led the boys at a swift pace through the calm and quiet crowds within, "not to look for a book at all, but to look for a person. Hurry along now, the exhibition event is open already. It is invitation only, and I had to use a little mental persuasion to secure even one ticket. Mental persuasion which will only last as long as my cantrip holds."

"One ticket?" Robin was confused, still massaging his crushed hand. "But Aunt Irene, there are three of us."

"Nobody will see the two of you," the old woman replied by way of explanation – although it wasn't much of an explanation at all.

They passed together through the quiet and impressive bowels of the gallery, from hall to hall and along wide corridors, headed, Irene told them, for the Wohl Room, a part of the gallery which had been rented out for the exhibition in question. It was wonderfully warm compared to the freezing air outside.

The tall Panthea strode along, flanked by a young Fae either side, trotting to keep up.

"This particular private gathering of the great and good," she told them as they walked, "is for an exhibition of rare books and early editions. Collectors, very exclusive ones, have come from all over the world … by invitation only, of course."

"And you think the book that we're looking for might be here?" Robin asked.

Irene shook her head, her silvery droplet earrings shining in the lights. "Not at all," she explained lightly. "That would be terribly unlikely. But what I do know, young Master Robin, is that this event is being hosted by Erasmus Knight, patron of the gallery, influential art and literary critic and above all else…" she glanced at them significantly, "current CEO of Sire Holdings. He has offices in the city, but I believe he holds a personal workspace here at the gallery, too."

"Our nebulous book-hunting rivals," Robin nodded, knowingly.

"Indeed, my young ward," Irene concurred, as they passed along a row of softly-lit Flemish artworks. "The ever-elusive Mr Knight has included in his invitation an opportunity for the esteemed guests to bring along something from their own collection, to be dated and valued."

"Bring your own old and rare book?" Jackalope mused. "So … he's fishing?"

"He would appear to be doing just that, yes," Irene agreed. "One can only assume that Mr Knight is hoping that, amongst his exclusive VIP guests, there may be one who bears the book that both he and I seek so fervently." She raised her eyebrows almost imperceptibly. "Highly unlikely, of course, but if nothing else, it shows that they are just as much in the dark as we are."

"So, you plan to corner this guy and confront him about the book?" Robin asked. "Find out why on earth a human company is interested in a tatty old tome that's tied up with another world?"

"Quite the opposite." Irene shook her head, chivvying them along. "I shall be doing no confronting whatsoever." She reached into her bag and removed an ancient-looking book in faded crocodile leather binding. "I am simply an enthusiastic collector, wishing to gain an appraisal of my second edition *In Memoriam* by Tennyson, that is all. I'm hoping it will hold his interest a while. You see, I shall require him to be ... distracted."

"Distracted from what?" Jackalope asked, as they turned a corner and were faced with ornate double doors, one of which was open. From beyond it, calming and elegant classical music emanated.

"From the two of you, of course," Irene replied lightly. "Breaking into his private gallery office and seeing what, if anything, you can discover."

She stopped in the shadow of a pillar, fishing a small vial from her bag as she tucked the poetry book under her arm. The vial looked like an ornate perfume bottle, covered in tiny carved dragonflies.

"Here." She passed it to Robin. "Please place two small drops behind your ears, both of you. Quickly now. I wish to head inside immediately. I detect canapés and it is a terrible crime to be the last to the appetisers, no matter how dubious the gathering."

Robin pulled out the stopper, sniffing at the contents curiously. Whatever the faint purple liquid within was, it had a strong floral scent, like honeysuckle and vanilla. He frowned at Jack.

"Perfume?"

"Liquid Inconspicuum," his great aunt replied. "A tincture of my own devising. It is made from a blend of crushed shrinking violets and the petals of the common wallflower, both prevalent in the Netherworlde. It will allow you to avoid notice."

Robin upended the bottle onto his fingertip and applied the cool drops behind his ears. "So ... like an invisibility potion?" he asked as he handed the bottle to Jackalope, who curled his lip at it with distaste.

"Nothing so vulgar," Irene replied. "It does not make you invisible as such, simply," she waved a hand in the air, "harder to notice. The eye slides away." She took the bottle back from Jackalope, who had administered the flowery tincture with ill grace. "And for full disclosure," she added, "it works only for social gatherings, so put from your mind immediately any thoughts of borrowing it later to raid Hestia's pantry for midnight feasts."

"I wasn't thinking that," grumbled Robin, who absolutely had been.

"You want us to sneak into his office while you keep an eye on him, this human-world CEO?" Jackalope rubbed at his neck, nose wrinkled against the smell of the Inconspicuum. "Sounds risky and a bit illegal. I like it. What are we looking for, exactly?"

Irene looked thoughtful. "I have no idea, to be honest. But anything out of the ordinary. I'm certain the two of you will know if when you see it. None have keener eyes than the Fae." She regarded the two of them seriously. "Do not be nervous. Keep your horseshoe chains on. And please remember, touch what you like, rifle and root, shake the place down if you must, but for heaven's sake, leave things as you found them, and don't take anything." She nodded to them. "Are you planning to hold hands again?"

Both boys glared.

"Very well," Irene nodded. "Then, if we are prepared, let us head into the belly of the beast. For intrigue … and canapés."

The Wohl Room was large and glitzy in an understated way that Robin thought Gran would have described as "terribly hob-nobbery". Soft green damask walls were covered in huge and heavily decorated gilt frames, each filled with a busy-looking Venetian Renaissance painting. Overhead was a spectacular glass ceiling, criss-crossed by repeating arches of white coving; each was emblazoned with gold filigree and reminded Robin of a very upmarket Victorian train station. Throughout this large space, there were countless waist-high display columns, atop which, in clear glass boxes, ancient-looking books rested on silk pillows, softly illuminated for display. Some books were closed to show off the original bindings, others spread open like pinned butterflies, their faded words on yellowing parchment glowing in the dim light. In one corner of the gallery, a string quartet was filling the room with restrained music, and everywhere people milled. A proliferation of humans, all in white-tie and sparkling dresses in the colours of jewels, mingled quietly, champagne flutes in hand as they threaded their ways between the books on display, talking merrily in groups or studying the artefacts with intensity.

"Everyone here looks wealthy," Jackalope noted in a whisper. "Diamonds and gold everywhere. It makes me wish I was still a treasure hunter."

It made Robin glad they were – to some degree – invisible. He and Jackalope would have looked quite out of place, dressed as they both were in a manner more suitable for a skate park than a high-class gala. Great Aunt Irene, of course, was regal by nature, and now led them into the room with the poise and assurance of a Russian countess from the time of the Romanovs.

She was making a bee-line for a small group of men and women near the centre of the room and the boys trailed after her, Robin noting with some satisfaction that not a single person so much as glanced at them; although one or two sneezed as they passed in a cloud of floral tincture.

Irene accepted a flute of champagne from a silver tray held aloft by a passing waiter; several were winding their way through the guests, and Robin and Jackalope both managed to swipe a handful of nibbles without the server batting an eyelid.

"Mr Knight," Irene said politely in warm greeting as she reached the back of a large dark-suited man. He turned to face her, with an enquiring look on his face.

Robin had expected the CEO of Sire Holdings to be an elderly gent with a powdery, frowning face – old businessmen always seemed to look like that – so he was quite surprised to find that the man who had turned, detaching himself politely from the group to greet his aunt, looked no older than thirty.

He was also remarkably heavy-set – wide and broad, his immaculate suit perfectly tailored over an ample stomach. His face was handsome, in a pale and rather jocular way, and his smile wide and friendly. Remarkably wide, in fact. However, his deep-set eyes, Robin noted, were not quite on the same page as the smile. They were cornflower blue and very intense. Those eyes did their best attempt to twinkle in a friendly manner, but somehow didn't quite manage it. Yet the most unusual thing about this man, Robin noted, was not his surprising youth for a CEO, or unexpected projection of warmth, but rather his incongruous hair. It fell atop his head in floppy waves, like some tousle-haired schoolboy, and was the lurid bright yellow of churned butter. It barely looked natural, almost glowing in the soft light.

"One and the same, my dear lady," he replied smoothly, looking her up and down so briefly that it was almost like the shutter of a camera. He raised his own champagne glass, which was dwarfed by his large fingers. "And you are?"

Irene smiled politely; her chin held high. Erasmus Knight was tall as well as wide, a commanding presence in his crisp, Saville Row suit. But she was also tall and commanding, and they now stood eye-to-eye.

"I am merely a collector." Irene shook his hand politely. "You have quite the collection on show here today. I must admit, I'm awfully impressed."

Mr Knight laughed modestly, the wide grin reappearing. For a moment, the yellow-haired man seemed to glance Robin's way, only to immediately slide his eyes back to Irene, blinking a little rapidly as though trying to refocus. Liquid Inconspicuum in action.

"Ah yes, would that I could take credit for it all," he said jovially. "However, many of the works here are on loan. Things of the past, preserved so well. Ancient things enchant me. My mission in life is in restoration. Bringing them back to life. They are articles of beauty, are they not?"

Irene glanced around thoughtfully. "Age does not inherently confer quality, I think," she said. "I am an old person, so believe me, I know. I think the value of their beauty, for myself, would depend entirely on the words to be found within."

The man nodded graciously in agreement. "An astute observation, indeed. It's wise to remember to see past the surface. Things so often differ from that which their appearance would suggest." He gestured towards the book in her hand with his champagne flute. "And what have we here? You have brought a little something for me to verify and value, perhaps?"

Irene smiled and presented the volume of poetry. "Tennyson," she said, and nodded. "The greatest love letter ever written. It has been in my family for time beyond time. I've honestly no idea of its origins or value."

Mr Knight's eyes lit up. "I must assist, then!" He nodded. "What a rare and wondrous thing." He offered his arm, which Irene linked with perfect ease and grace. "Wear and tear and tattered around the edges to be sure … but enough about me." He laughed politely at his own joke. "Even in something so original and beautiful in design, I feel there is always room for improvement. Shall we take a seat and look through it together?" he suggested. "I would bring it to my office, but alas, I have a speech to make in …" he glanced down at his watch, rather affectedly, "ten minutes' time, and am needed here."

As he led her away into the crowd towards one of several sofas lining the walls, Irene discreetly flapped a hand behind her at the near-invisible boys. The message was clear. Ten minutes. The larger-than-life Mr Knight would be kept busy, so they were on a timer.

It didn't take very long to find the curator's office. Jack and Robin, dodging the milling party guests, slipped through a side door of the

Wohl Room and beneath a velvet rope, upon which hung a sign politely stating *Staff Only*.

Beyond this, away from the classical music and chatter of the exhibition, they found a series of empty and silent dim hallways, lit with only low security lights. This was backstage at the gallery, Robin supposed. As they padded hurriedly along the corridors they passed some doors marked for storage, and others bearing little silver nameplates. Clearly the workspaces of the permanent staff.

Jogging as silently as they could on the marble floors, and feeling like cat burglars, they flattened themselves against the wall and held their breath as a trio of waiting staff passed by hurriedly, carrying silver trays of nibbles and wine.

But before long, at the turn of a silent and deserted corridor, they found what they were looking for. A closed office whose nameplate read *Knight, E – Humanities*. A gentle rattle of the doorknob confirmed that the gods of nefarious espionage were smiling on them. It wasn't locked.

Robin and Jackalope slipped silently through the door, the older Fae closing it softly behind him.

"Did anyone see?" Robin hissed. Jack turned from the door and shook his head, glancing around the dimly-lit office.

"No-one's seen us since we got here," he whispered. "I only hope this perfume isn't permanent. We smell like Hestia's poopery."

This brought Robin up short. "Hestia's *what*?" He stared at Jackalope.

"You know, those little bowls of dried flowers she leaves all over to make the rooms smell better. They make me sneeze." Jackalope sniffed.

Robin breathed out. "Oh my God, Jack. Potpourri! It's called *potpourri*. Give me strength!"

His companion shrugged. "I don't think anyone saw anything, though. They're all watching that strange fat man hold court and waiting for his speech."

Robin made his way deeper into the still and silent office. It was exactly as he expected a museum curator's workspace to look. A desk cluttered with various academic bric-a-brac, sheaves of papers and ring binders, shelves filled with books and small classical statues – and everything in pools of soft illumination from the desk lamp. He wasn't altogether sure what Aunt Irene expected them to find in here.

"I feel like a spy," he said in a self-conscious whisper, moving to the large desk and glancing over the files and paperwork that covered its dark, polished surface. The room smelled of beeswax furniture polish. There was something that looked like a half-drafted thesis, presumably something of a passion for Mr Knight: *The Alchemy of Improvement, Ancient Works for Modern Use.*

"This all just looks like professory book stuff to me. Paperwork about the gallery exhibition. Nothing special."

"Try the drawers in the desk," Jackalope suggested, walking to a window and peering out suspiciously. Outside, it had finally started to snow, and the light was apparently fading, although that could have been simply the effect of the glowering December skies. In wintertime England, with short days and enough cloud, twilight could begin anytime in the early afternoon.

"If Lady Irene believes that Sire Holdings is after the same mystery book that we are, there might be something on it here. Something more than we've currently got to go on, anyway." He stared out at the snowflakes, their tiny shadows passing over his face through the glass like a cloud of silent gnats. "Which is practically nothing, let's face it."

Robin smiled a little to himself as he tried the drawers. Hearing Jackalope say "we" was still surprising to him. He seemed to have finally become a member of the Erlking resistance, despite his protestations.

A drawer in the large and ornate desk rattled in Robin's hand, but did not open.

"It's locked," he whispered, glancing up at Jack.

"Well, that's suspicious," the older Fae observed. "Clearly, the smiling, champagne-sipping Mr Knight wants to keep something under lock and key."

"You think *everything's* suspicious." Robin rolled his eyes. He rattled the drawer again, and in doing so made a small bust of some long-forgotten Roman dignitary wobble on the desktop. "I forgot my super-spy lock picking kit," he muttered sarcastically.

Jackalope had folded his arms and was now leaning against the windowsill, staring at Robin scornfully. "For the sake of the fates!" he said. "Have you forgotten who you're supposed to be? You're the Scion of the Arcania, right? Open the drawer."

"Ah … right," Robin stammered, feeling a little foolish. He knelt in front of the drawer, one hand seeking out the smooth hard weight of the mana stone around his neck. The seraphinite felt warm and reassuring in his hand, like a paperweight. He lined his lips up with the ornate lock and blew, pushing air inside and casting a gentle featherbreath cantrip at the same time.

He felt the tiny cyclone of air swirl around the inner mechanisms of the lock, and the weight of tiny tumblers clicking and falling.

The drawer popped open.

"See, you just needed to blow it a kiss," Jackalope sniggered, coming over to join Robin as he pulled the drawer open. "Anything there?"

There was indeed. Robin reached inside and pulled from the drawer a thick notebook, bound in what appeared to be old calfskin and wrapped all around with lengths of cord. It looked like an ancient artefact.

There was a brief moment of excitement, as he laid it out on the table, when both boys considered the possibility that this may be the fabled and much sought-after mystery book they were all looking for. But that made no sense. If Sire Holdings already had the mystery tome, what would be the point of holding this event?

It turned out to be something quite different. This was not a book that had ever been in a human public library. It was something altogether more personal.

"A journal?" Robin asked aloud, flipping through the pages. They were old, yellowed and thick waxy paper, covered busily in handwritten scrawl of a deep maroon ink, which had dried like brown blood – spiky lines and ink blots on every page. Whatever it was, it wasn't in English. He couldn't read a word of it.

"This is the high tongue," Jackalope said with surprise and interest, peering over Robin's shoulder.

"Can you read it?" Robin asked, glancing at his companion. Jack shook his silver head, looking slightly abashed. "I recognise it, but I never really learned to read. Other, more important things to do, like, you know, skin rabbits and not starve to death in the wild. My brother could read. He was the clever one."

Robin flicked onwards through the pages, one ear listening for any sounds from the doorway, painfully aware that they could be interrupted and discovered at any moment.

Every page of the strange book was filled with writing, many also had hand-drawn doodles, sketches or illustrations.

"What I want to know," Jackalope said, "is what jolly Mr Erasmus Knight of Suspicious Human-World Conglomerate Inc, is doing with an arcane and otherworldly journal in the first place? How did it come into his hands?"

Robin shrugged. "Well, he is a collector I suppose," he mused. "Here, what do you make of these?" He jabbed a finger at several illustrations as they flipped through the pages. The paper glowed softly in the light of the desk lamp. One image, sketched in red ink, showed twin snakes – one dark, one pale – entwined in an elaborate pattern, circling upwards like a Celtic knot tattoo. Where their heads met at the top, they held something between them that looked like a roughly-hewn heart-shaped jewel. Another sketch on the opposite page showed what appeared to be a family crest, filled again with scales and fangs. Another enigmatic sketch seemed to depict a long serpent, burrowing beneath the ground, stylised mountains above it as it moved through the dark.

"No idea," the older Fae shrugged. "Someone likes drawing snakes, I guess. Snakes holding jewels, snakes on shields. Burrowing snakes. What's this one?" He jabbed a finger on the page, stopping Robin's incessant flipping back and forth. This sketch had no snakes. If anything, it looked like a birds-eye view of a circle of trees; it reminded Robin of a Janus Station, a pathway between the worlds. Those were often a Stonehenge-like ring of stone. There were seven trees in the circular picture, each drawn roughly from above, and with tiny footnotes that neither boy could read peppered around them in swirls. Something had been drawn in the centre of the trees. A rough oval, like a pool or a puddle.

"It looks like ... a design for a garden feature?" Robin shrugged helplessly. "How do I know? Maybe this guy is into landscaping on the side."

Jackalope angled the book towards himself and flipped back a page or two, to the picture of the intertwined snakes holding the heart-shaped jewel, and indicated some scrawl. "I know this word," he said grimly. "*Frater*. It means brother. I know that much." He looked uncomfortable. "It's the only word I ever thought important enough to learn to read."

Robin didn't reply immediately. He knew how much Jackalope had been through, losing his brother in the war. The boy had tormented himself for much of his life, convinced his brother's death had been his fault. Of the many scars carried at Erlking, it was perhaps the deepest. A cloud, which shadowed the boy still. Jackalope's face was difficult to read in the gloom of the dark office, as his fingertip brushed the word in the book, written in ink as brown as old blood.

Robin looked back to the page. There was a similar font on the opposite side of the entwined snakes.

"*Soror*," Robin read aloud, a little hoarsely. He shrugged. "Sister?" he guessed. "Snake family, huh. Call me Captain Presumptuous, but as far as I can see, none of this has anything to do with a missing super-secret book. This is something else entirely."

Further along in the crowded journal, Robin was surprised to find maps. Not ancient treasure maps, but modern, real-world maps. They looked as though they had been torn from an Ordnance Survey publication and sellotaped into the journal.

"There are human cities and towns," he said, his curiosity deepening as he flicked through them. "Liverpool ... York ... Whitby ... Harrogate ... look here, there are circles and question marks all over them. Someone is looking for something. *Puella Perdita*. Look, that's what's written at the top of every single one of these maps."

"We cannot take this with us," Jackalope said. "Your great aunt was very clear. We were to leave everything as we found it. No trace of disturbance." He sounded frustrated. "If only there was some spell or cantrip to record its likeness. What use are air, water and earth tricks? Could you not have learned something useful like this by now, Scion?"

Robin glared at him. But then inspiration struck. "Actually, no need for magic, broody McGrudy," he said. "Give me your phone."

Jack looked immediately defensive and alarmed. He guarded his haunted box jealously.

"Why?" he spluttered. "Why should I? It's mine. It's my ..."

"Precious?" Robin flapped his hand impatiently. "Just give it to me, will you? I don't have one. We don't know how long we've got."

Reluctantly, Jackalope gave up his prized mobile phone, Robin almost having to pry it from his fingers.

"Hold the book flat for me," he instructed, opening the camera function. We can't take the book with us, but we can pirate the heck out of it,"

"Don't *swipe!*" Jack muttered angrily. "Just take the damned photos!"

"Why are there so many selfies?" Robin sniggered, flicking through Jackalope's image gallery. "Are you ... trying out new hairstyles? Don't your shirts show up on camera?"

Jackalope angrily snatched the phone back from Robin, high pink spots of colour on his pale cheeks. "I was *trying* to find a way to cover my horn stubs!" he said. "Forget it! I will take the photos. You hold the page."

"Okay, okay … I'm only teasing," Robin sniggered, but he held the pages down flat as instructed.

Jackalope snapped picture after picture, Robin listening intently for any footsteps at the door, but hearing only the snow fall softly against the windowpanes and the distant, muffled murmur of the exhibition outside.

"Whoever owns this journal," the Fae murmured, the pages rustling and whispering as the camera clicked, "they have been looking for something, or someone. All these maps, all these clues, and snake and serpent motifs everywhere. I think Mr Knight might be doing more than just trying to track down some old and mysterious book. I think he's a man of many projects."

Robin nodded but kept glancing nervously at the closed study door. A thin letterbox of light shone beneath it, a slice of the corridor beyond. He was watching for any passing shadow, any indication that someone might be approaching. Surely it had been more than ten minutes by now. Was Aunt Irene still keeping Mr Knight distracted? Indulging the man's passion for the restoration of things old and lost?

"Well, he definitely knows something about the Netherworlde, that's for sure," Robin agreed. "You don't just stumble on coded diaries full of snakes every other day."

"Wait … what's this?" Jackalope stopped, the page he had just flipped having revealed something wedged in the pages, close to the spine of the book. It looked like a thin stick, perhaps being used as a bookmark; jet black and no thicker than a pine needle. Carefully, he lifted it from the pages and held it up to the lamp for a closer look.

"It's very light, whatever it is. It barely weighs a thing."

It was twice as long as his hand, a slim spike, hollow and slightly translucent. "I can't figure out what it's made of." Jack gave it a gentle shake, passing it to Robin.

As the odd smooth spike fell into his palm, a strange and unexpected frisson passed through Robin. It was as though Jackalope had just dropped a live electrical wire into his hand, sending a flicker of current coursing up his arm. Surprised, Robin blinked, closing his fist around the object, and a great swift darkness rolled like smoke across his vision.

He squeezed his eyes closed hard, feeling as though his head had just suffered a great blow, a seething migraine, and behind the dark canvasses of his eyelids, images rose, fractured and unbidden, flickering across his mind, like someone else's memories.

Wings, dark as soot, vast against the night sky full of stars, glossy and black. A screech, as of some great avian creature, echoing from snowy mountaintops. Wings on fire, a sky full of them. The sun glinting from countless windows of a many-towered castle nestled in a jagged snowfield. A glittering crystal castle filled with books and treasures.

The images came faster and faster, rolling across Robin's mind as a fractured kaleidoscope. A land of lava and glossy black glass, sky filled with crimson birds, and next, a circle of burned and blackened trees surrounding a murky pool in a dead garden, skeletal branches like smoking charcoal. A garden high up somewhere, hidden on a terrace in some terrible, sprawling city. Robin smelled fire and smoke, felt the chill of cold mountain air and the crackle of burning wood. A dizzying sense of height and speed, and a feeling of great power, barely contained. The images and sensations flew by, one after another, a flickering film reel. Almost too fast to make sense of. The shadow of a great bird passed over the blasted, skeletal grove once again, and the dead trees surrounding a churning pool began to leaf and bud. As the image faded, Robin noticed with horror, even while watching the dead trees bloom back into life in their strange and ominous circle, that the branches were filled with spiders' webs. Hundreds of them, threading thickly between every branch. Tiny black spiders crawled in their thousands through the branches and across the grove. There was a final rush of heat to Robin's face, as though he had just opened an oven door, and he dropped the slim needle, his eyes flying open.

"What just happened?" Jackalope was staring at him with undisguised shock. "Scion? You seemed in a trance. You ... Pucked out, right in front of me."

Robin blinked rapidly, feeling drunk and watery on his feet. He steadied himself on the desktop, shaking off the strange images and sensations as he felt his heart rate slow. His nose was still full of the odour of smoke and his body crawling with unseen spiders.

"I think ... I think I had a vision." He noticed that Jack had caught the strange glossy thing as he dropped it. "This thing ... it spoke to me. Showed me ..." He shook his head to clear it. "I don't know. Heat and fire, and height and snow. I think it was talking to the Puck."

"You *are* the Puck," Jackalope reminded him, grabbing Robin by the arm as he swayed a little.

Robin rubbed at his eyes, feeling the world return to normal. "I know, I know. I mean ..." he stammered. "I don't know what I mean. I saw places ... I think. Places that I should know. But they're nowhere I've ever been. I saw ... dead things come to life, but everything was tangled in webs ... controlled. Something controlling the power? I don't know ..."

It was the frustrating feeling of waking from a dream and having it fragment, slip through your fingers and lose all form and meaning.

"We must leave," Jackalope said, nodding. "You look like you're going to faint, and I'm not carrying you."

"I'm not going to faint," Robin argued defensively, though he did feel very light, as though he might float away at the slightest breath. "Have we captured the whole book?"

Jack nodded, shaking his phone in mid-air. "All in the magic box. We're getting out of here now," he said. "Lady Irene said to ensure we leave no traces, and I think a big puddle of post-vision vomit counts as a trace. Let's go." He wrapped up the book, carefully replacing it in the drawer and sliding it shut, as though no-one had ever been there.

Robin nodded. His mana stone felt like a hot coal against his chest, as though it had received a huge charge. He still couldn't shake the sensation that he was crawling with spiders, tiny fat-bodied black things. Robin leaned past Jackalope, blowing a second featherbreath and locking the drawer once more.

Checking the room one last time to ensure it appeared as they had found it, the two boys padded towards the door. Robin was just reaching for the handle, when, to his horror, he saw it turn. His eyes widened, and he exchanged a silent, panicked look with Jackalope, who, thinking quickly, pushed the Scion to one side, flattening them both into the shadows.

They held their breath, trying to be as invisible as possible, as someone entered. Mercifully, whoever it was did not close the door behind them, but left it open wide, shielding the interlopers behind. Robin heard footsteps in the room. There came the sounds of someone shuffling through papers on the desktop, and then the click and scrape of drawers and cupboards opening. Risking a glance, Robin peeked out from behind the door.

He had expected to see the large frame of Mr Knight. This was his office, after all. But to his surprise, the interloper seemed to be a girl or young woman, slim and slight, dressed in smart business clothes. She was facing away from them, looking over some paperwork on the desk, so Robin couldn't see her face, only the back of her head. Her hair was a dark copper colour and wound tightly around her head in an elaborate knotted braid that looked both elegant and severe.

Jackalope grabbed at Robin's shoulder, trying to pull him back into the shadows and the safety of their hidden doorway nook, but Robin shrugged him off. The girl had lifted the old-fashioned landline telephone on the desk. He watched her dial, swiftly and efficiently, and a moment or two later, she spoke.

"Mr Knight? Yes. I have checked as you instructed," she said. He saw her shake her head a little. "No, nothing seems out of place. All is as it should be. Do you wish me to remain here? Or shall I return to the exhibition?"

Mr Knight must have taken some time giving the girl, who Robin could only assume was his assistant, further instruction, as she stood stock still, like a soldier awaiting command, the telephone held to her ear. Occasionally she nodded. "You do not wish me to search the rest of the museum?" she asked after a while. "If security has been breached as you suspected then ... no?" She nodded, listening. "Very well. As you instruct." She sounded both chastised and obedient. More like a servant than an employee, Robin thought. But the strangest thing of all, was her voice. There was something so *odd* about it.

Jackalope nudged him, indicating with a raise of his eyebrows and a flick of his head, that this was their chance to slip out, while her back was turned and the door wide open. Robin swallowed and nodded. His curiosity was overwhelming, but the older Fae was right. They were two buzzing flies who needed to leave the spider's parlour, especially if Mr Knight somehow suspected there were people snooping around and had sent his staff to check. They would simply have to hope that the little information they had obtained would be worth something to Aunt Irene.

As silent as shadows, both keeping their eyes locked, hawk-like, upon the girl. She remained standing at the desk, phone clutched to her ear as she peered emptily into the darkness, oddly robotic. They slipped around the door, praying for a lack of squeaking floorboards, and out into the corridor beyond.

As soon as they were clear of the room, the two boys padded away as quickly and quietly as they could, fleeing the office and desperate to get back to the exhibition, where they could blend unseen into the crowds thanks to Irene's cantrip.

"Knight knows," Jackalope hissed as they hurried along the corridors. "He knows someone was snooping. Why else would he send one of his people to check his office?"

Robin nodded in agreement. His only thought was getting back to Irene and them making their excuses and leaving while they could.

"That girl," Robin said, still shaking off the strangest sense of familiarity. "There was *something* about her. Her voice, I think." He couldn't be sure if the odd feeling was real, or a hangover from his recent strange visions.

"You're telling me," Jackalope agreed. "Don't tell me you didn't notice, Scion?"

Robin blinked at him enquiringly as they pushed through double doors at the end of the corridor and emerged gratefully back into the noise and bustle, the safe anonymity of the Wohl Room and the exhibition space.

Jackalope's grey eyes had narrowed and filled with a wary curiosity. "She sounded exactly like Karya."

They wound their way back into the still-milling crowds, dodging several times to avoid collision with rustling skirts and champagne-quaffing guests. It was a dance just to avoid being walked into or stepped on. Clearly the tincture they wore was still in effect, as every eye in the room slid off them.

Almost every eye. Both boys jumped as a hand descended upon their shoulders from behind. There was a moment of panic as Robin imagined turning to find himself under the grip of Mr Knight, but to his relief, it was Aunt Irene who had stopped them, materialising from the crowd like a serene and composed spirit.

"I was considering coming to look for you two," she said, calmly and quietly. "Our eminent host finished his address to the crowd, and I could only hold his attention for so long. He seemed rather ... distracted." She smiled tightly. "I trust you two had an illuminating investigation."

Jackalope nodded. "Nothing we expected to find, but plenty of strangeness." He tapped his jacket pocket, where his phone was. "We have captured images of our findings, to study later."

"I think Mr Knight knows something's up," Robin said. "Though I don't know how he would. He sent some girl to check his office. I think he knows someone was in there."

Irene looked thoughtful, her grey eyes casually flicking around the room as she guided the two boys by the shoulder towards the exit of the exhibition space. Not too directly of course. Making a beeline for the exit might draw unwanted attention.

"My little cantrip fools only human eyes," she said to them, glancing up at the corner of the room, where CCTV cameras were discretely concealed. "Not electronic ones. I did not buy us invisibility, only a head start. I believe it's time we left. We can discuss everything once we are back amongst friends. Something we most certainly are *not* right now. The hospitality of Sire Holdings is the hospitality of wolves."

Robin wanted to mention the girl, and the strange splinter of unknown material they had found, the book full of serpents and maps, and the odd visions, but he understood. Whatever Sire Holdings were, they were certainly not simply the benevolent conglomerate they seemed, and as polite as Mr Knight had been, Robin didn't trust him one bit. Even a brief meeting with the corpulent man had made him feel uneasy.

"Leaving already, dear lady?"

Irene had ushered the boys all the way to the entrance, where the museum lay before them and the snows of London beyond, when the voice, deep and smooth as silk, piped up suddenly behind them. In a move that was both effortlessly graceful and quite deliberate, she turned, somehow tucking both Robin and Jackalope behind her and giving them a gentle push out of the room and into the darkness of the exit corridor beyond.

Mt Knight stood, champagne flute still in hand, with his free arm tucked up into the small of his back like a regency gentleman at a country ball. He was smiling warmly, his eyebrows raised in polite enquiry.

"I'm afraid so," Irene replied politely with a courteous nod. "At my age, I find I don't have the stamina I once did. Evening falls and I hear my bed calling. Such a shame not to stay longer, but such are the ravages of age."

Mr Knight offered her a smart toast, his glass glinting in the soft lighting. "Oh, I doubt that entirely," he smiled. "You do yourself a disservice, madam." His eyes twinkled merrily. "I am sure you are filled with secret reserve. One must never take things at face value, don't you agree?"

"Oh, I never do," Irene replied. She gave a small and formal bow. "But I mustn't take up any more of your evening. It has been an interesting exhibition, even if we didn't manage to value my book."

"I trust you still found it informative?" The tall man sipped his wine, nodding his head forward, which made several of his chins bunch up above his perfectly-starched shirt collar.

"Indeed," Irene stood very straight; her head cocked slightly to one side. "*How* illuminating remains to be seen. But I have always been inclined to shine a light into dark corners. Professional habit."

"Dark corners are my absolute speciality," Mr Knight said. He cast an arm at the exhibition, at the many old and unearthed books on display. "The seeking of things ... lost."

"Of that I have no doubt," the old lady replied. "If you'll excuse me, I really must catch a train."

The yellow-haired man nodded with excessive decorum. "It's a shame we couldn't talk more," he smiled. "But I suppose I cannot force you to stay."

"No," replied Irene, quietly but firmly. "I think you would find that ... unwise."

She nodded in farewell and turned her back on the CEO of Sire Holdings, ushering Robin and Jackalope ahead of her. Robin was oddly grateful that he was still, for all intents and purposes, invisible.

"You have my card, should anything of interest come into your possession for which you require a valuation," Mr Knight called after her jovially. "And I of course shall contact you, should I find a potential buyer for your Tennyson. I know, after all, *just* where to find you."

Irene stopped in her tracks for a second. She looked back, her face still calm and unruffled. "You do indeed, Mr Knight, I'm certain of that. And my door is always open ... to those who can enter it. Should you find yourself in my locale in the future, you are welcome to call." She looked thoughtful for a second. "Of course, do telephone ahead. To receive guests without prior warning is a grim business indeed."

Mr Knight laughed at this, his alarmingly wide smile revealing large teeth, and toasted her again, turning away and back to his exhibition.

"Indeed. Have a safe journey home," he called, as he turned to melt back into the crowd. But he had not quite finished.

"And a message, if you will, to one of the little lambs in your care." The timbre of his voice had become almost imperceptibly more aggressive. Staring at his back, Robin could not see the man's face, but he was quite certain the smile had gone. "The wolf … is hunting." He waved casually over his shoulder without looking back. "I'm quite certain we'll meet again. *All of us.*"

Irene didn't speak or stop until they had made their way through the winding vaulted corridors of the museum and out into the blessed fresh air, freedom, and safety of Trafalgar Square. December afternoons are short and night had fallen almost completely now. The city twinkled with lit windows and the jewel-sparkle of traffic headlights threading the roads. There were still crowds, bundled against the night, and the snow was falling softly. Chatting to tourist girls about hot beverages seemed like a million years ago, given the subsequent strange encounters, discoveries and visions in the gallery.

"We must return to Erlking immediately," Aunt Irene told them. "Horseshoes will only protect you two so far, and we would be wise to put some distance between ourselves and that man before he realised that something of his has been taken."

Robin frowned up at her as they made their way into the crowds of Christmas shoppers, melting away into the anonymity of the city as they left Trafalgar Square behind. "But we didn't take anything," he said in confusion. "Except photographs, I mean. Did you hear what he said? About seeing us again? All of us? I think that guy could see us."

Irene nodded. "He has keen eyes, that one. Sharp as daggers and just as deadly, I'm sure of that much." She had raised a hand, hailing a taxi. "A seeker of things lost, a collector of old treasures. The man is a magpie, and a magpie always notices if trinkets are taken from its nest."

She held out her hand, expectantly. "Let me see what it is that you felt was important enough to disobey my instruction," she commanded.

Robin stammered: "No, really, we didn't steal anything, we just looked around!"

Irene's sharp eyes flicked to Jackalope, and she curled her fingers in beckoning, a little impatiently. Robin saw the older Fae sigh, a small cloud of breath escaping his mouth in the cold dark air. He fumbled in his pocket, and a second later dropped something into the old lady's hand.

Robin stared. It was the strange twig-like splinter. He glared at Jackalope, who looked away shiftily and shrugged.

"I'm a treasure hunter," he muttered. "I couldn't help it. Seemed important. It gave the Scion conniptions."

"You're a thief," Irene said, though not unkindly. "Which is *exactly* why I brought you along. You have a discerning eye." She held up the strange splinter, examining it. "Do you know what this is?" she mused, as a black London cab pulled up, its brakes squealing, shining in the darkness like a fat mechanical beetle.

Robin and Jackalope both shook their heads. Irene pursed her lips, thoughtful for a moment, and then opened her purse and dropped it inside, closing the clasp again with a snap.

"It is a feather," she said smartly. "A feather from which all the quills have been removed. Burned away. The hollow spike only remains. Do you know what this means?"

Both boys shook their heads again, staring expectantly at her as she opened the car door, taking one last look back across the square to the brightly lit gallery. She blew air down her nose, lips pursed.

"Neither do I," she admitted, with reluctance. "But one at Erlking may. Let's go home."

2

Mistletoe and Memory

Erlking Hall stands high on a hill above the small and sleepy village of Barrowood. Its ancient stone wings and gables are hidden from prying eyes by thick woods and high walls, which are in turn nestled within rough peaks of rugged moorland. A lake glitters in its grounds, catching the sun and reflecting the white clouds of the wintry skies above. In summer, these woods of Erlking are alive with birdsong, dappled light shimmering like mirages with pollen drifting in the air, golden motes of glittering dust. The manicured gardens and grounds unfurl around the buildings, a verdant grass skirt, rolling down the hill toward the distant smoky rooftops of the village below. In autumn-time, the estate of Erlking sits in a nest of gold. The forests aflame with papery leaves the colours of rust and blood, sharp honey-light pooling here and there in the hollows, and the towering moors surrounding it are ablaze with great seas of bright purple heather under skies of crisp fire.

But now, here in late December, amidst the deep and sleepy reaches of winter, Erlking Hall stands fast; silent and still in a landscape of snow. The hills and grounds alike are a blank, crisp canvas of purest white. The leafless trees of the forest are a tangle of bold charcoal sketches against the pale backdrop. The crystalline sky seems to drift down from its heights to rest in silent, rolling banks of icy fog against the moor-tops, providing a lowering and cosy roof for the world. Erlking in winter becomes a hushed and secret confection. Still and hidden in freezing fog through which the pale sunlight glows like mother of pearl. And all is hushed and expectant. No movement, save for the occasional, red-breasted robin flitting industriously from branch to branch, dislodging powdery snow with its fussy flutters, or the swift, dark smear of a hare racing across open ground, darting from treeline to treeline.

But Erlking at Christmas is not unwelcoming. The many leaded windows are lit with a cosy, buttery light. Grey wisps of smoke rise lazily from every warm chimney, curling up and away into the falling snow like peaceful ghosts.

Shortly after the incident at the gallery in London, with all its strange encounters and discoveries, Christmas was coming to Erlking, and with all residents finally home, the last bastion of the Fae resistance was determinedly decking the halls.

Mr Drover, Erlking's dedicated groundsman, had cleared the driveways with his enormous shovel, a thick black iron affair that looked more a mediaeval weapon than a tool. He had felled a great fir, deep in the woods, and now it occupied its customary place in the great entrance hallway, rich and fragrant green beards of winter soaring upwards, past the sweeping open staircase to the balcony above. As was traditional, the other Erlkingers were currently taking bets on how Mr Drover had actually got the tree from the forest to the house alone. Henry suspected hired redcap labour, whereas Woad favoured his own conspiracy theory, which was that the trees were sentient, and quite happy to take turns each year to walk inside, get warm and bling it up a little.

Calypso, water nymph and tutor of the Scion, had set to work with the decorations. The concept of Christmas, or indeed celebration, was alien to her nature, but with some patient explanation and encouragement from Mr Drover and Aunt Irene, she had been persuaded to put her considerable skills in the Tower of Water to use. The vast tree was strung with garlands of multi-coloured icicles, jewels that never melted or dripped. The windows of the Hall were likewise decorated in swirling patterns of fern frost, and every chandelier sparkled with shimmering ice, so that much of Erlking resembled a geode cracked open and laid bare. Glitters of light split into countless diamond facets.

Erlking's newest resident, Mr Ffoulkes, had been inspired by the efforts of the others, and had taken it upon himself to oversee the remainder of the decorations. To everyone's quiet but politely-unspoken horror, not a surface now remained anywhere within that was not, in some fashion, tasselled with gold or draped in velvets of red and green. Subtlety and understatement were not the style of Mr Ffoulkes. He seemed determined to drown the Hall in as much fussy brocade as appeared within his seemingly inexhaustible supply of waistcoats. In fact, much to the surprise of the other residents, Ffoulkes seemed to have embraced the spirit of the season entirely. He had taken, in the last few weeks, to wearing a red Santa hat, complete with fur trim and pom-pom. Had his beard been white rather than fiery red, he could have passed for a very neatly-finished Father Christmas – although his attachment to the hat, many guessed, had more to do with its ability to conceal his bald head than any inherent joviality.

The Hall may well have been visually dressed for the season, but this was not the only pleasant assault on the senses.

The halls, parlours, corridors and stairwells of the rambling old house were filled with a constant stream of good smells, as Hestia – Erlking's cook and housekeeper – prepared an endless procession of festive feasts and dishes. Mulled wine and spices, roasting ham and turkey, the sizzle of crisp roast potatoes and the soft warm smells of maple-glazed parsnips led you from room-to-room by the nose on a daily basis.

Aunt Irene voiced more than once her opinion that Hestia's sudden obsession with endless cooking was her own personal way of coping with the season. If she kept herself busy in her kitchens it left less time to be horrified by the opulent chaos of Mr Drover, Calypso and Ffoulkes, as they covered her precious and orderly Erlking in flippant and haphazard ornamentation.

Before Robin had first come to Erlking, the rambling mansion had been often quiet. A sedate and lonely place. Now, with the ever-swelling ranks of the resistance, the house was alive with commotion.

In fact, the only person who did not seem much involved in the festive preparations was Aunt Irene, who had taken to spending much time alone in her study. Upon their return from London, she had taken the denuded quill that Jackalope had stolen, along with the many photographs of the strange book, and had announced to all that she needed time to make sense of things. Other than at mealtimes, she had rarely been sighted since, though this, in itself, was not too unusual. Irene had always been a busy woman.

* * *

Despite the many preparations for the festivities soon to come, there was still the usual round of chores to be completed, and with all lessons on hold for the festive period, many of these fell to Robin.

He may be the Scion of the Arcania and prophesied saviour of the race of the Fae, Mr Drover had told him firmly, thrusting a shovel at him as he buttoned his parka against the cold. But horses will need mucking out, no matter what.

And so Robin found himself, on the morning of Christmas Eve, away from the festive main Hall of Erlking, some distance across the grounds and down at the stables, ankle deep in loamy droppings and old straw, which clung to his wellington boots in clumps. Meanwhile, two horses snorted and chuffed in their shadowy stalls, imperiously ruffled by the young Fae's intrusion to their territory.

Henry, Robin's best friend and son of Mr Drover, had come along to lend a hand. His school, down in the village of Barrowood, had long since closed for the holidays and he and his father always moved into Erlking full-time over winter. Robin looked forward to this; it was like having a brother live with him. Although, he mused, as he lifted another heavy shovelful of pungent straw in the must stables, perhaps not the most energetic or helpful one.

Henry had become bored of cleaning within five minutes of their arrival at the stables, tracking twin lines of footprints through the deep snow which crunched and crumpled under their feet. The lanky boy, his messy brown hair so long overdue a trim that he had begun to resemble a feral wood spirit, was now sitting on a square bale of hay, kicking his heels against it and sending up small flurries of spores as he watched Robin work.

"Can't believe the old bird's got you on mucking out duty," Henry sniffed, wiping at his red nose in the cold. "I mean, after everything you said happened down in London? Shouldn't she be consulting with you about your freaky visions and stuff? I mean, you're the Scion, right? This …" he indicated the dark and draughty stables, blowing out a plume of breath as Robin did his best to ignore the complaining, "shovelling muck, well, it's a load of horse …"

"It would go a lot faster if you actually mucked in," Robin cut him off with a smirk, dropping a load of manure from his shovel into a rusty old wheelbarrow. "I know you're doing your best to keep us both warm, blowing a lot of hot air, but the sooner it's done, the sooner we can get back inside."

Henry stared up at the dark graveyard for spiders' webs that filled the distant rafters. They creaked and swayed above the two boys. The stables were more than a little run down and every gable seemed to creak and groan as if haunted, shifting slightly like a ship at sea. The icy wind blew its way inside at a million places, pushing cold invisible fingers through knotholes everywhere.

"I haven't been down here for years," Henry mused, ignoring Robin. "Never really trusted horses, to be honest. Kickers, every one of them. One bit me on the shoulder once. Not hard like, but still. Makes you wary. I used to call these the *unstables* because they sway about so much. I'm sure it's only Irene's willpower that stops them from falling down altogether."

Robin planted his shovel in the ground, leaning on the handle. "I didn't even know there were stables here at all," he admitted, looking perplexed. "How long have I lived here now? How did I not know we had stables? I've been over every inch of Erlking."

This was a bald lie. It wasn't *possible* to go over every inch of Erlking. It seemed to shift around sometimes, like a kaleidoscope of corridors and rooms. Places you found one day, you might never see again.

Henry shrugged. "Dad usually looks after the horses. There's only these two left now. We used to have more when I was little, I'm sure I remember. People were always coming and going and leaving them here. I suppose a lot of people were Netherworlders. Passing through, either from here to there, or the other way around. Like those three spooky women who came with Ffoulkes. We used to get a lot more … traffic." He glanced at Robin. "Reckon Irene's choosier about who sets foot through here these days, now that you're here. Got to protect the Scion, after all."

Erlking was the only Janus Station – passing place between the two worlds – that did not fall under the jurisdiction of Lady Eris, dark ruler of the Netherworlde. It was, therefore, the only port with no passport checks. A way to cross the borders unseen.

"Well, these two horses look well cared for anyway, even if they are the only ones left," Robin observed.

They were indeed a handsome pair. Friesians both, with glossy black coats like polished oil and thick curly manes and tails. Tall and sturdy looking, but both seemed nimble and light on their feet, dancing back and forth whenever Robin approached them. One was pure black, the other had a slight blaze on its forehead, almost like a crescent moon.

"What are they called?" Robin asked.

Henry cocked his head. "Horse one and horse two?" he guessed. "Don't ask me. Those two have always been here. But enough about bloody horses, what about this evil CEO?"

Robin had already been over the events at the museum a hundred times since their return. He and Jackalope had been pressed for every detail over and over again. The only thing they hadn't mentioned, at Aunt Irene's request, was the strange girl who had reminded them both of Karya.

"Until we know more," the old lady said during their train ride back north, "it does not do to speculate on certain matters, not when we hold only one card of a whole pack. We will get to that in time, but for now, Karya is still … recovering. I do not wish her to be further concerned until I have drawn my own conclusions."

As always with Aunt Irene, it had been a strict command issued in the form of a light suggestion, and although Robin didn't like holding back information, he trusted Irene's judgement above all else.

"There's nothing more to say about the evil CEO," Robin insisted. "I've already told you everything. He was just a weird posh guy, massive, very polite and creepy as hell. And we should stop calling him the 'evil CEO'," he added.

"Yeah, but …" Henry raised his eyebrows. "He *is* though, right?"

Robin nodded, unable to suppress a smile at Henry's poking. "Oh, totally. Evil corporate vibes all round. He and Aunt Irene didn't like each other one bit. And he knew where we were from, and I reckon he knew Jackalope and I were there, even if he couldn't see us."

"He's definitely from the Netherworlde then," Henry concluded. "I don't get why a Netherworlder is running a huge shady company here in the human world though."

"Lots of Netherworlders live in the human realm," Robin reminded him. "Plenty of them fled here to escape the war. Look at Ffoulkes, for instance. He ran an antiques business in London for years."

"Yeah, but Ffoulkes isn't evil," Henry insisted. "*Annoying*, yes, but not *evil* evil."

Robin piled the last of the old straw into the wheelbarrow. "I don't think people are as simple as good and evil, Henry. No one wakes up in the morning cackling about how many wings they're going to pull off flies. People are just ... people. Who do good things or bad things."

"Like how Hestia boil-washed all my jeans the other day?" Henry glowered. "And now I can't bend them at the knee. Or like Ffoulkes insisting we all gather around the piano *every night* and listen to his carol recitals. Both, you have to agree, evil things."

"My point is, good people can do bad things, and bad people, well ... sometimes there's hope." Robin shrugged. He was a little unsure what he was getting at himself, but Henry saw things in black and white, and after everything he'd experienced, Robin no longer felt that was a safe way to live.

"Name one bad person who's done a good thing," Henry challenged him. "And don't say Strife, or I'll kill you. Yeah, yeah, he helped us get through the labyrinth and into the Hive last time we were in the Netherworlde, but that was nothing to do with us at all and everything to do with helping himself. He just wanted to knock his little sister off her perch and deliver us gift-wrapped to bloody Strigoi."

"What about Peryl?" Robin said lightly, poking at some straw with a shrug.

Henry blustered. "What about that psycho? She's a maniac!"

Robin bristled. "Well, she brought Jackalope to Erlking, didn't she? She could have let him die, but she didn't. She healed his wounds and brought him here, where he'd be safe."

Henry glowered again. "Only you, of all people, would think Jackalope at Erlking was a good thing." He sulked a little. "Pouting and frowning all the time. He's a poser. You Fae lot, with your silky hair and sparkly eyes." He rolled his own, resolutely un-glittering eyes and Robin suppressed a snigger. He suspected Henry's issues with Jackalope stemmed mainly from the Fae taking up so much of Karya's attention. An ability the Scion had noticed was a commodity Henry seemed more and more desirous of these days.

"And if Angsty-Biceps isn't a pain all in his own right, just to remind you, the screw-loose Miss Peryl also planted a gloomoth inside him and was actually spying on us all the whole time," Henry pressed on.

"Yes, but ..."

"*And* she almost killed Karya," Henry said hotly. "Or have you forgotten our friend getting run through with a spear and almost dying? It was only a month ago. She's still not right. I don't even know if she's getting any better. That was Peryl!"

Robin swallowed. He'd been over and over that moment in the Hive in his mind. How the guard had launched the spear, how Peryl had flung out her shadow mana as it hurtled towards Robin. He didn't think she'd been steering it. He thought she had been trying to deflect it. Trying to save him. Unfortunately, in doing so, it had been directed onto Karya, who had been run through.

In his mind's eye he saw Peryl losing her footing and falling away into the great darkness below. It was the last they had seen or heard of her.

"Well," he said. "You're getting off the point, anyway. We were discussing the CEO. I think, evil or not, we all agree that Sire Holdings is up to something and it's more than just looking for the same book as Irene. All this other stuff about snakes and serpents, all those maps."

"So why has the old battleaxe got you out here, looking after horses?" Henry wanted to know. "You should be being trained, you have a fire tutor now, even if it is awful Ffoulkes. We should be looking for a way to get into Dis. That's what we agreed on, isn't it?"

Robin shushed him urgently. Following Karya's injury, they had indeed agreed that if they were ever to get any answers about her, they would need to go to the capital city of the Netherworld, right into Eris' domain, where Karya had originally come from. They had also made a pact to keep this dangerous intention secret from the adults. Irene would never allow it, not in a million years, and it was no simple task to consider.

"Keep it down," Robin said. "We need a better plan than we have for that. It's not like we can just stroll up to Eris' front door and knock, is it? And from everything Karya's told us, the city is a fortress. Absolutely impregnable." He sighed a little. "Anyway, we're going nowhere until she's back to full strength, and she's far from that, at the moment."

What Robin said was true. Karya's wound, which would have been fatal to most, had healed itself with alarming speed. This had only raised more questions amongst the Erlkingers as to her nature and origin. Woad, Erlking's resident faun and the one amongst them who had known Karya the longest, had confirmed that even he had never heard of any Panthea with healing skills that worked so fast. But then, Karya was neither Panthea nor Fae. They didn't know *what* she was. That was part of the problem.

The girl herself had admitted that her own memories were fractured. She wasn't entirely sure where she had come from. All she had ever revealed was that she fled from Eris after seeing a vision of Robin, long before even he knew he was the Scion himself.

"She's on the mend," Henry said stubbornly, sounding as though he was trying to convince himself as much as Robin. He was oddly protective of Karya, a girl who had proved time and again that she needed precious little protection from anyone. "She's up and about, walking … a bit … just like she said she would. She was so determined not to be bedridden at Christmas."

Robin couldn't argue with this, although he put Karya's convalescence down more to her stubbornness and sheer force of will than anything else.

"She might be walking, but she's still weak," he insisted. "Her mana, I mean. Fates alone know how much of her mana she used up dragging herself back from the brink of death. She's said herself, she doesn't feel like she has any left over. I haven't seen her cast so much as a cantrip in weeks, let alone anything impressive like tearing between the worlds." He looked over at the two horses, who seemed to be following their conversation with quiet interest. "It will take time for her to build her stamina back up. In the meantime, we're just going to have to hope she gets better and not worse." He forced brightness back into his voice. Christmas Eve felt no time for dark and worrying talk. "Hestia is certainly forcing enough chicken soup down her to feed a small army, anyway."

Inwardly, Robin was still very shaken by the events of autumn. He had come so close to losing a friend for good. Someone had almost died, because of him. He wasn't blind enough not to realise that being part of the resistance against Eris came with such dangers. Of course it did. But he was determined. No one was dying on his watch. Not for him. To hell with any great prophecies and destinies. Erlking was his home and his family, and more and more, it felt his responsibility to protect them all. His duty.

Henry wanted to go and visit Karya in her rooms, once the stables and their two dark and snuffling residents were finally in order, but Robin pointed out that by then it was close to dinnertime. Hestia would have produced one of her seven-course festive feasts, and everyone would be gathering in the dining room, save for Karya. Exhausted by noon, she had taken to napping in the early afternoons.

As an alternative, Henry grudgingly agreed to help find Woad and Jackalope instead. Jack was most likely in the walled rose garden, which was barren and bare in this season, a maze of thorns and dried grass – but a useful space nonetheless that he had adopted and filled with wall mounted targets and bullseyes, where daily he honed his knife-throwing skills. Jackalope had a deadly aim. Never more so than with Phorbas, his favourite blade. The shining silver knife never seemed to miss its mark. It did, of course, have the slight advantage of being sentient and possessed.

Woad, on the other hand, they guessed would be foraging. All the squirrels, his natural enemies, were asleep for the winter and, denied the sport of the hunt, the small blue boy had instead taken to a rather experimental form of hedgerow botany. Bringing home endless handfuls of berries, roots, leaves and spores to determine what was edible, what was poisonous, and what, not being quite either, had the most hilarious side effects.

This being Erlking, seeds blown through the rift between the worlds had taken root here and there in the mortal-world woods and forests, which meant that the faun, on his frequent hedgerow expeditions, encountered more than mere dandelions and nettles. A particular clump of muddy mushrooms he had gathered (once verified by the knowledgeable Hestia that they were not likely to kill him on the spot if ingested) had been made into a dubious-looking soup of the boy's own devising. A bowlful of this had the curious effect of making his hands and feet swell up to more than three times their usual size. It wasn't painful, Woad had insisted happily, just incredibly comic, and he spent the remainder of that particular day down by Erlking's front gates, stomping around in the snow and leaving enormous footprints, his fiendish plan to make the villagers of Barrowood believe a yeti might live at Erlking. Henry had pointed out that a faun would be fantastical for enough regular humans, but the blue boy would have none of it. "A yeti is make-believe and scary!" Woad had replied, as though Henry was an idiot. "Fauns are very real and magnificent!" And with that he had been off with a swish of his blue tail, his huge, oversized hands waving surreally in the air above his head as he darted off across the grounds on great flopping feet.

Robin and Henry, still smelling faintly (though not unpleasantly) of horse droppings and fresh straw, followed rabbit tracks in the deep snow around the corner gables of Erlking. Their hands were thrust deep into their thick coat pockets against the cold, and they wondered to one another what state they might find their friend in today. Dry and leafless creeper covered the stonework, verdant in summer, now nothing more than a rattling spiderweb of dried sticks, hugging the cold stones in a brittle membrane, every twining branch covered in a shimmer of frost.

The rabbit prints stared up from the white snow before them, a series of imprinted shocked faces decorating the powder. Into these depressions, made by hasty paws, the white snow-light fell and turned to pools of lightest blue.

They found Woad not far around the corner of the east wing, in the garden of decorative raised beds, filled at this time of year only with tiny winter blooms, frosty white and blood red against their boxes of bare earth. The faun was asleep on the lip of a fountain from which a life-size statue of a satyr sprang, head tilted to one side and eyes permanently closed as it blew into carved pan pipes. The statue was crusted with a glittering sheen of frost, and Woad was snoring loudly in its shadow. It loomed over him like a guardian.

Robin wondered for the millionth time since they had met, how hardy the small creature must be not to feel the cold, dressed as he was in only his usual pair of ragged brown pants. Bare chest and bare feet exposed to the December air, but seemingly none the worse for it.

"His tail is going to freeze and fall off, one of these days," Henry muttered into his scarf, which was wrapped up tight against his mouth. "Look at him, dead to the world. It's like some horrible mixture of Peter Pan and Papa Smurf."

Woad reminded Robin of a cat more than anything else. He certainly had a habit of coming and going whenever he pleased, pushing things off tables for fun, and, as evident here, could sleep soundly absolutely anywhere.

As they reached the fountain, Robin glanced up at the old statue looming over his little blue friend. It was in poor repair with one horn snapped clean off, and was covered here and there with a thin, stringy moss. It was funny, he considered, that most humans grouped satyrs and fauns together as one thing. Having spent time at Erlking and in the Netherworlde, Robin knew better of course. Satyrs, like the stone one here, were a noble Panthea, half man, half goat, and known to be excellent scholars. Keepers of secret knowledge, seers and prophets, and masters of the Tower of Air. He had read in Hammerhand's *Netherworlde Compendium* that they still guarded knowledge in some great library hidden in the Netherworlde. They were also believed to have been largely responsible for moving a floating mountain far out to sea, back when the war had started; the Isle of Winds. Robin had visited it when he first went to the Netherworlde two years ago. He'd just turned thirteen at the time and had been very out of his depth. A lot had happened since then.

Fauns – he glanced down at the creature sprawled beneath, open mouth lolling and snoring quietly, snowflakes settling peacefully in his eyelashes – were as different as could be. Wild and untamed things. Tricksters and troublemakers and jacks-of-all-trades when it came to harnessing the powers of the Arcania.

Woad had been Robin's very first non-human friend. Robin noticed for the first time that since their initial meeting, the faun did not appear to have grown or changed. Both Robin and Henry were taller now; Henry was practically a bean sprout, his voice at that hilarious stage of cracking alarmingly every now and again. But Woad appeared just the same. Perhaps fauns aged more slowly than humans and Fae, he reasoned. There wasn't a tremendous amount of lore on them.

Robin gave Woad an affectionate tap with his foot to wake him up, startling the creature so that he fell into the bowl with a yelp. Jerking awake, he leapt to a crouch like a startled animal, which made both Robin and Henry laugh.

"Never, never startle a sleeping faun!" Woad admonished them, blinking away sleep. "That can be a very dangerous thing to do! Better to kick a sleeping tiger – safer, too!"

"Well, as cosy as you seemed there, Woad mate, looking like some frozen corpse found on Everest …" Henry's muffled voice came through his scarf, "it's getting on. Hestia will be ringing the bell any minute and you know she has a fit if anyone's late for a meal. Especially a Christmas Eve meal."

Woad leapt nimbly out of the stone bowl of the fountain, landing so lightly on the snow that he barely made an imprint in the deep powder.

"Being late for a meal is not in the nature of *any* self-respecting faun." He shook snow out of his hair. "Even if it is suspect and untrustworthy human-world food."

The three of them began to make their way back across the white canvas of the gardens and towards the inviting warmth of the house, where yellow lamplight spilled from mullion windows to cast fish-net shadows on the cold ground outside. "Well, it's a feast day," Robin reminded the faun. "So, human-world food or not, old Hestia's likely pulled out all the stops. There's bound to be something even you like. You like mashed potatoes, right?"

"Not the taste," Woad muttered loftily.

"He only likes that he can sculpt it into various scandalous and offensive shapes," Henry sniggered. He shrugged after a moment's thought. "Me too really, if I'm honest."

"This Eve of Christmas ..." Woad spun, walking backwards and keeping pace with the others so he could look at Robin with his flashing yellow eyes. "It's the time when the old man comes, humans believe, isn't it? The bearded one who breaks into houses when everyone sleeps."

Robin grinned, sniffing in the cold air, which seemed to have frozen inside his nostrils. "Father Christmas, yes. The kindly old saint. It's not so much breaking in, really. Everyone wants him to come ... you know, for the loot."

Woad nodded sagely, still walking backwards, clearly considering himself an expert in human-world traditions. "And beneath the furry tree, the bearded intruder leaves pheasants for all."

"Presents," Henry corrected him, as they reached the great wooden door which led from the courtyard kitchen to the back rooms within.

Woad looked quizzical. "Oh ... I suppose that makes more sense," he decided. "I mean, I'd be happy with pheasants. There's some nice eating on a pheasant, though I admit I was wondering how he convinced them all to stay under the tree until morning. Try putting a brace of birds under a furry tree usually and you don't wake up to magical whimsy, you wake up to your living room destroyed and bird poop everywhere."

As Henry opened the door, tugging his scarf down off his face and shaking his head in mild bewilderment, the toasty warmth of the house flooded out to greet them, and he was brought up short by Jackalope coming the other way, the two almost colliding.

"Scion." The tall Fae glanced at them, looking put out. "I was just sent to look for you three. Hestia doesn't like being kept waiting, you know. She puts a great deal of effort into her meals. Your absence would bring her dishonour."

"You, scowly McMisery." Henry jostled past him into Erlking, "are such a bloody housekeeper's pet. Honestly. What with her sweet and loving temper, and your sense of joy and fun, you two are made for each other. She'd adopt you if she could, I reckon."

Jackalope visibly bristled as they all bundled inside. Robin had to agree with Henry's assessment. Their old housekeeper, who seemed to regard every other child in the house as an inconvenience or nuisance at best, did seem to have taken a shine to Jack. He always got extra helpings at dinner, and Henry never once failed to comment on it. Robin found it more endearing than annoying. After all, Jack had lived on not much more than moss and mushrooms in a frozen cave for years and had come to Erlking emaciated and cold. Robin secretly suspected that beneath her veneer of brittle waspishness, Hestia might actually be quite a decent person.

Henry disagreed. "Beneath that layer of bitter onion," he had told him loftily, "is another layer of bitter onion."

Shrugging out of their coats and hanging them on a row of pegs as their boots dripped snow into puddles around their feet, Robin couldn't help but notice that Jackalope looked a little concerned. He wasn't simply put out at having been sent on a fetch-and-gather errand.

"What is it?" Robin asked, stamping more snow off his boots onto the stone floor, while Woad at his side shook himself like a dog, dislodging a flurry of snowflakes.

"Well … it's a special evening, apparently," Jackalope began. "Your aunt says that humans traditionally have games and diversions. Ffoulkes just jumped on this, I overheard them all talking in the dining room. He expects us all to play something called shar-ards?"

"Charades, you mean?" Robin smiled. "Yeah, I like that. It's kind of daft, but it's not Christmas without charades." He could see that Jackalope, who had clearly never played a game of anything in his life, looked wary and worried. "You have to guess something," he explained. "Like the name of a book or a movie, just by someone making shapes, you know, with your body, no talking. It's fun, you'll see."

The Fae's grey eyes widened and his jaw clenched. "In front of other people? We are expected to show and prance? For fun?"

"Yeah, fun," Henry said with a grin. "You might want to try it sometimes. It won't kill you. Honestly, mate, sometimes I reckon if you were any grimmer, you'd be, well ... a Grimm."

Jackalope shot Henry a look of daggers, and then turned earnestly back to Robin. "One could be excused from this duty, however?" he asked, with just a hint of desperation in his voice. "If, for instance, one was wounded accidentally with his own dagger?"

Robin turned Jackalope around by the shoulders and marched him down the corridor after Henry. "Don't be dramatic," he said. "It's only a laugh. It's Christmas, and no one's going to make fun of you. You're amongst friends."

"I might make fun of you," Henry called back cheerfully over his shoulder. "Just for full disclosure. It's entirely likely."

"Me too!" Woad cackled.

The dining room was as bedecked with Ffoulkes' smothering festive cheer as the rest of Erlking, with every available inch of every available surface glittering and shimmering with frosted holly and flickering candles. The perfumed scents of myrrh and frankincense drifted through the cosy glow, and Madame Calypso had, in an uncharacteristic display of whimsy, agreed to cast a significant cantrip which caused soft flakes of snow to fall continuously from the high, vaulted ceiling, melting away to nothingness just before they reached the heads of the diners, each flake catching and spinning in the candlelight above their heads like glitter.

Robin was delighted to see that Karya had heroically made the journey from her room upstairs, determined not to miss out on the Christmas Eve feast, even if it meant hobbling slowly and laboriously along Erlking's long and twisting corridors on a pair of cumbersome crutches. She had barely left her room since they had returned to the human world, taking all of her meals in bed, and her recovery had been firmly policed by Hestia. It was hard to believe that just a month ago she had been run through with a spear in the Elderhart Forest. Nobody could blame her for having a bad case of cabin fever, even if Hestia did tut and sniff disapprovingly as she brought out the first course of food, slamming the girl's plate down in an obvious slight at her disobedience.

The snow was falling in earnest outside the windows as they sat down to eat, so thickly that the eager December night seemed to slide up to the glass early, pressing its shadowy face against the pane to watch with interest those gathered around the feast within. Chattering and talking happily, passing plates and salt and gravy, everyone taking turns to encourage Woad to remain in his seat.

Robin, at times such as these, felt a strange duality of emotion. As he looked around the table, listening to his companions, both young and old, chatter and eat their way through festive dinner, he was filled with a deep contentment, a stable sense of home, which felt as nourishing and warming to him as the plethora of food laid out before them. This cosy room, grand and sparkling, filled with quiet magic and sumptuous celebration, spiced with the particular sense of anticipation and excitement that only Christmas Eve can bring. It contained, for want of a better word, his family. Each in their way as dear to him as his adoptive Gran had been. He watched Aunt Irene, quiet, calm and grand as the Hall itself, deep in conversation with Henry's father, Mr Drover, who had gone all out for the occasion and swapped his habitual battered old tweed jacket for a highly questionable dinner suit of deepest maroon. Whether they were discussing the fate of the universe or when to begin planting spring bulbs after the frost, Robin couldn't have guessed. She had the bearing of an elegant dignitary, and he the blustering everyman – but Robin had never seen the two exchange a single cross word or seem anything but perfectly comfortable in each other's company. The firmest of friends. Beside them, Calypso pushed her food around her plate, peering at it in a daydreaming kind of way, as though she might discern the secrets of the universe from honey roast parsnips as a sage would read the future in entrails. The nymph's hair flowed softly about her shoulders, constantly in motion as though under water. Robin recalled her initial reluctance to come to Erlking at all; she had arrived under sufferance to repay a debt. These days she wore Erlking like a comfortable and familiar robe, floating through its hallways unbidden by anyone. His tutor, like all of them, had made the place her home, a sanctuary from her troubled past – and the only thing in it that seemed to irk her was the man at her side.

Ffoulkes talked continuously, of course, to everybody and nobody in particular at the same time. Popping and hissing merrily like a campfire. Never had Robin met anyone so much in love with the sound of their own voice as this man. The Fire Panthea was Erlking's most recent resident and here only to repay his past misdeeds as best he could by tutoring Robin in the Tower of Fire (although, much to Robin's irritation, they had not yet had a single lesson).

Robin knew that Aunt Irene had her own reasons for keeping the man around. He was something of an expert in antiquities and the origins of old things. Without his input, in fact, they would know even less than they did about the mysterious book so sought after by the enigmatic Sire Holdings. Since their return from London, Ffoulkes had been given the photographs from Jackalope's camera roll to decipher – though if he had discovered anything about their meaning yet, Robin certainly hadn't been informed.

"Are you feeling okay, Scion?" Karya asked from his left, jogging him lightly with her elbow. "You look like you're a million miles away, off in Cloud Cuckoo Land. Snap out of it, will you? It's the eve of the Christmas. There'll be glowing moose on Erlking's roofs tonight."

Robin glanced at her, snapped out of his musings. "It's reindeer, not moose," he corrected her with a smile. "And it's only one of them that shines." He held his soup spoon up to cover his nose. "Just this bit."

Karya rolled her eyes, as scornful of foolish human-world things as ever. "Well naturally, because that makes much more sense, doesn't it?"

"It should be us asking if *you're* okay," Henry said to Karya from Robin's other shoulder, leaning in across the candles. "You look pretty pale and awful. Are you sure you should be downstairs?"

Karya narrowed her eyes at the tall, messy-haired boy. "Thank you, Henry, for that lovely assessment. I'm fine. I'm not helpless. What am I going to do upstairs on my own on Christmas Eve? Pull a cracker with my shadow? I feel like the princess locked in the tower, stuck up there on my own all the time." She stuck a fork viciously into a tiny sausage wrapped in bacon. "I'm not the princess type."

Henry cast a sly glance at Hestia, who was clomping around the table doling out drinks, and whose single concession to the festive period was a twist of thin red tinsel around her tightly-drawn bun of hair. Her face was as dour as usual. "And there's the wicked witch holding you prisoner, eh?" he said quietly. He then put on a dramatic conspiratorial voice. "Her hair might say 'ho, ho, ho,' but that face says 'bah humbug'."

Robin couldn't help snickering.

"Hestia is dutiful," Jackalope said sharply to them all, seated on the far side of Karya and trying his best to look disapproving and aloof – which, to his credit, was no mean feat in a purple paper crown. "Karya was grievously wounded, almost killed. You should not mock those doing their best to speed her recovery."

Karya held her hands up. "Will you stop bickering?" she moaned. "For the millionth time, I'm fine. I'm feeling much stronger."

Robin wasn't convinced. She didn't look stronger. But he kept his counsel.

"You still haven't done any magic though, boss," Woad piped up around a mouthful of mashed potato. He didn't look up from his plate, such was his concentration on his food, but his matter-of-fact statement made everyone a little uncomfortable.

It was true. Karya was a master of the Tower of Earth. It seemed to come as naturally to her as breathing came to others, but since her near-death experience, the few times she had attempted even a simple cantrip, results had been less than spectacular. She glanced down now at her bracelet, her mana stone, which circled her wrist. Usually a fiery glowing amber, the stones were dull, almost as black as jet.

"Well ... I didn't say I was a hundred percent yet," she muttered moodily. "These things take time. I just have to build my strength up, that's all."

"Hear! Hear!" Woad agreed cheerfully. "And 'here' as well." He scooted a large platter of golden roast potatoes down the table towards her. "Nothing builds up strength like lots and lots of yummy food. Eat up, boss!"

Robin watched Karya smirk at Woad as she dutifully dug her fork into the plate, but he was still worried, despite her reassurances. The girl's eyes, usually a bright gold, the colour of tree sap caught in sunlight, had seemed paler than ever lately. Washed out. It was frustrating. They could hardly take her to a human-world hospital. They just had to take things slowly here at Erlking and hope for the best.

The trouble was, Robin considered as his friends chatted amiably around him and the Christmas Eve feast moved eventually onto pudding, they didn't have the luxury of taking things slowly, did they?

The five of them had discussed it countless times over the last month, gathered around Karya's bed like a council that was half war-meeting, half sleepover. The fact remained that Robin had destroyed the Hive.

He had freed the entire race of dryads, and Irene had decimated Eris' army of centaur and scourge. It was no longer a case of hiding away and becoming strong enough to face the darkness. It was now open war. The darkness was coming. Even Aunt Irene had admitted that Eris would be out for blood. For a proud ruler without mercy, to be humiliated and beaten back as she had been; to have the Earth Shard snatched from under her nose and her plans brought to ruin – how could it be otherwise? There was very little chance of her letting *that* slide. Erlking had to act, they had to prepare themselves for her next move. And what frustrated Robin most of all was that instead of doing so, they were going to gallery exhibitions and rubbing elbows with some human-world corporation, while Karya, one of Erlking's strongest assets, seemed to be getting weaker by the day.

"Scion," Karya whispered to him, laying a hand discreetly atop his at the table. Robin hadn't realised that he had zoned out again while tremulously holding a spoonful of plum pudding dripping in custard before him. He glanced at her. The others were all chatting away, lost in the festivities, but Karya had always been coolly perceptive. She narrowed her eyes at him. "I know your mind is busy," she said, not unkindly, and quietly enough that the others didn't hear. "You're the changeling. The saviour of your race, I get it … I do. No days off. But for tonight, don't be the Scion, don't be Puck." She glanced around at the company, at the enchanted snow falling over the lively conversation and clinking of glasses as the fires cracked and popped merrily in their decorated hearths. "Tonight … just be Robin," she said firmly. "Enjoy the evening. Dark times might be coming at us like a wave, but right now, the beach is calm. Enjoy the night. This may be the last Christmas Erlking gets to celebrate like this, with everyone here."

Robin felt self-conscious as she took her hand away. "Sorry, I just keep worrying. I know, you're right." He gave himself a mental shake. "Tomorrow is a problem for future me, right? I just have busy brain." He looked around as Hestia cleared up the plates and everyone began that part of a great feast where belts are loosened from too much indulgence. "You're right, of course. All we have is now."

She smiled, still looking tired, but bearing up well through the fortifications of five courses of stodge. "Always," she agreed. "Don't miss it."

Henry's head suddenly popped between them like an errant mahogany dandelion.

"Oi, what are you two conspiring about? Muttering in dark corners? Looks fishy to me," he huffed.

Karya rapped him smartly on the side of the head with her spoon. "Grown up talk," she sighed. "You wouldn't understand, you great shaggy idiot."

Henry flinched away but was unable to maintain his frown. "Did you see that?" he said to Robin. "She hit me! That's assault. Well, Scion of the Arcania, aren't you going to pull rank? She should be confined to her room again like that mad woman in *Jane Eyre*. She's clearly dangerous."

"You bring it on yourself with your eavesdropping," Robin laughed. "I think we should all be more concerned about the fact that Woad over there has been quietly eating an entire sherry trifle on his own."

Jackalope, seeing that Henry had left his place at the table to harass the others, took this as his opportunity to rise. "If there's nothing else …" he muttered, his chair squeaking backwards on the floorboards. "I think I'll just … turn in for an early …"

He was cut off by the loud tinkling of a spoon against a wine glass. Ffoulkes had also stood up and was now rapping his goblet musically to gather everyone's attention. He looked a little pink in the cheeks from overindulgence. "A fine feast!" the man cried merrily. "All honour to our most gracious lady of ceremonies, Hestia, for such a triumphant celebration!"

There was a smattering of polite applause, during which Ffoulkes took a little bow, as though it was partly directed at him.

"And now," he continued with a twinkling grin, "might we all retire to the parlour adjacent, for a smashing game of charades?"

Robin caught Calypso looking heavenwards with resigned despair. The nymph poured herself a large glass of Baileys. He heard Jackalope mutter under his breath: "Damn."

"Nice try, Silver Top," Woad giggled loudly at the sullen Fae. "No escape for any of us." He hiccupped, his entire head buried in the now-empty glass trifle bowl, making his chuckles a menacing echo.

The night wore on with much merriment and few real casualties, although the game of charades was by far the strangest Robin had ever played. It was difficult when almost none of the participants had any knowledge of real-world popular culture. They could hardly guess recent movies or books, and Robin wasn't sure there had ever been a working television in Erlking Hall, and so instead, categories such as "deadly herbs of the Netherworlde", "ballads of the dead" and "famous underworld locations" left Robin and Henry trailing in points behind everyone else.

By eleven that evening, the snow had finally stopped falling outside the cosy parlour and the countryside beyond the leaded windowpanes was a still and glittering sculpture of white powder and clear black sky, with not a breath of wind to stir the tree branches. The icy air was still. Within, things had also calmed. Hestia had taken herself off to bed, and the remaining four adults were gathered around a card table in the cosy glow of a bay window, engrossed in a game of bridge while they enjoyed a nightcap together.

Robin and the other Erlkingers sat across the room, near large patio doors of stained glass. They were lounging on sofas and chairs that had been dragged up into the small island of light cast by the embers of a long-untended fireplace, talking now and then amongst themselves in a lazy, amiable way of everything and nothing. What Gran would have called a "cabbages and kings" conversation. Woad had curled up on the hearthrug in front of the fire, his hands laced across his stomach as he fought the urge to submit to the sweet call of sleep while he digested the huge amounts of trifle he had consumed. They were all taking care to speak in low tones, hoping that the adults of Erlking had completely forgotten their presence and thus to avoid being sent to bed. When Karya and Jackalope seemed deep in murmuring conversation about the oddness and impenetrable nature of humans' festive customs, Henry tugged at Robin's sleeve surreptitiously.

"What are you scrabbling at me for?"

Henry looked half devious; half panicked. "Shh!" he hissed, nodding his head towards one of the long sideboards beside the fire. It was all polished walnut and topped with glittering candles, and stood at some distance from the others. "A word, in private?"

Frowning with intrigue, Robin heaved himself out of the deep and comfortable sofa he had curled up in, shaking off pins and needles – one of his legs had begun to go to sleep – and followed the suspicious boy away from the glow of the fire. He glanced back at Karya and Jack, but being deep in quiet conversation, neither seemed to notice them slipping away. Henry stepped lightly over the now sleeping Woad, and practically dragged Robin to one side.

"What's gotten into you?" Robin asked. He found himself whispering, drawn in by Henry's cloak and dagger manner.

"Keep your voice down!" Henry looked odd; a bit flustered and nervous. Even in the dim and cosy candlelight of the parlour, his ears were clearly pink. He shuffled from one foot to the other.

"I need your advice a bit," he muttered. He was fumbling for something in the back pocket of his jeans. Robin looked at him curiously.

"My advice? About what?"

To his surprise, Henry produced a clump of leaves and berries, holding them up so Robin could see, as if he were displaying a rare treasure. Robin blinked.

"Is that …?"

"Mistletoe," Henry nodded fervently, still looking a little wild-eyed. He glanced over Robin's shoulder, haunted and afraid. Robin turned and followed his stare to where Karya and Jack were still sitting.

"What do you reckon?" Henry grinned.

Robin took a moment to regard his friend carefully, wondering if he'd gone quite mad. He glanced back at the sprig of mistletoe the taller boy held clutched in his fist like a crucifix to ward off the undead. It looked a little wilted and squashed, which was no surprise since he'd presumably been carrying it in his pocket all evening.

"Well," he stuttered. "I mean … it depends …"

Henry stared nervously at him. "It depends? On what?"

"Well," Robin faltered. "I think if you're looking at Jackalope, you'll need a stool or something to stand on. He's taller than you. And if you're thinking Karya … I'm going to retreat to a safe distance."

Henry hit him on the arm, making Robin wince.

"Stop it, moron!" he hissed. "Of course I mean Karya." He cleared his throat a little self-consciously. "I mean … just as … you know … a prank, a joke, kind of thing."

Robin was staring at Henry with fresh eyes.

"You're actually serious, aren't you?" he said in wonderment. "You want to …"

"Just 'cause it's Christmas!" Henry said defensively. "And you know, tradition, and I thought it would be ... funny." He pursed his lips, seemingly aware that he was babbling and forcing himself to slow down. "You don't think ... it would be funny?"

Robin considered this carefully for a moment.

"I think she would kill you," he decided. "And I don't mean figuratively. I mean actually kill you. Reduce you to a smouldering pile of dust with just a glare." He covered the mistletoe in Henry's hands as though staging some kind of intervention. "Look, Henry ..." He took a breath, still finding this turn of events a mixture of shocking and hilarious. "I'm only concerned for your safety, as a friend. But of all your pranks and cunning plans since we met, this one is ..." He cast around. "Suicide."

Henry looked terribly deflated.

"I mean, I know you've been spending a lot of time with her, Jack and I were only saying before that you're the fussiest nurse there ever was, but ..." He considered how to phrase it. "Henry, are you telling me that you actually *like* Karya?"

Henry snatched his hands away, looking ruffled. "Of course I like her," he said gruffly. "She's an Erlkinger."

"No, that's not what I mean. I mean ... LIKE ... like." Robin pressed on. "Because I remember when she first came here, and you kicked up such a fuss about there being a girl in the house. And to be honest, you two have kind of been at each other's throats ever since."

Henry looked embarrassed. He stuffed the crumpled plant back into his pocket. "Just forget it, then." He rolled his eyes, as if to mock Robin's earnest tone. "Don't take things so seriously. It was just a joke, that's all. I thought it would be a laugh, get a reaction."

"The reaction being her kissing you?"

Henry narrowed his eyes at Robin. "Shut up. You're getting nothing but coal tomorrow. I wish I'd never said anything now."

"Sorry," Robin said. Everything about this felt both funny and awkward at the same time – as if the group dynamic Robin had come to rely on was suddenly shifting, like sand beneath his feet. He didn't really know how to react. "I just, I didn't know if you were teasing, or serious or ... to be honest, I still don't," he admitted. "I've never thought of Karya that way. You've never looked at her that way either. I don't think she'd be amused if ..."

"People can change their outlook, you know," Henry said. "If they want to. When you get to know people, even if they're bad tempered or insufferably bossy, sometimes they … grow on you, right?" He leaned back against the sideboard, looking glum and embarrassed. Robin was sure that he wished he'd never brought it up at all.

"You don't know what's right in front of you sometimes, until you almost lose it."

Robin was trying to imagine how the scene would have played out. Whether Henry envisioned it as a silly prank or whether he meant it in earnest, try as he might, Robin could not see things ending in anything other than total destruction. Karya, even in her current weakened state, would surely slice Henry to ribbons with words alone. She seemed barely to tolerate his presence at the best of times.

Henry coughed, leaning nonchalantly on the sideboard and assuming an air of indifference as he took in Robin's alarmingly thoughtful expression. "Wow, Rob. You take everything so seriously. Just forget it, deep thinker. It was just a daft idea for a bit of fun, that's all. Maybe not my most well thought out plan anyway, I admit." He grinned. "But … you don't reckon she'd be moved? I mean, I'm a big strapping lad, you know. A lot of girls at school say I'm quite the catch."

"Yeah, I'm sure you knock 'em all dead." Robin shook his head helplessly. "Who could resist your chunky shapeless knits and that majestic tangle of hair?"

Henry grunted, sneering at him.

"I'm just not sure …" Robin glanced back towards Karya and Jack. "Even if you were serious …"

"Which I'm not," Henry specified quickly.

"Which you're not, yeah, got it," Robin said, supportive as only a best friend can be. "I'm not sure you'd be her … type."

Henry glared past Robin back towards the group of sofas pulled up by the fireplace, his lip curling. "Yeah, yeah," he sneered, looking at the shadowy figures in the firelight. "Well, I'm not going to apologise to the universe for not being Mr Six-Packalope over there." He actually tutted. "Look at them, thick as thieves. She's always been a bit mooneyed over him, hasn't she? What's he got that I haven't, eh? That's what I want to know."

Robin shrugged. "A comb?" he suggested.

Ffoulkes let out a harsh laugh of triumph, and Robin glanced over to the bridge table where the red-bearded man had clearly won a game, or a round, or a hand (Robin didn't have the faintest idea how card games worked.) The Fire Panthea was looking very smug and was clearly celebrating with little grace. Opposite him, Calypso was lolling in her high-wingbacked chair, having sunk so low she may as well have been lying down, and was staring at him with lazy disapproval while the ice in her drink spun in little circles, stirring her cocktail unaided.

"Oh well, *that's* just great!" Henry spluttered, drawing Robin's attention back, away from the adults. Robin followed Henry's gaze to see that Jackalope had left the room, stepping out through the patio doors into the moonlit snow of the gardens beyond. Karya, Robin saw, had followed him and the two were rapidly moving out of the small pool of light and into the darkness of the night. A chill breeze entered the room where the doors had been left open, making the fire crackle and waking Woad from his slumber. The baggy-eyed faun looked around suspiciously, as if to check that nobody had caught him napping.

"Where are those two off to?" Robin wondered with a confused frown, watching their shadowy figures recede and blend into the night, like ink.

"Jackalope got up and went out," Henry said, still spluttering in indignation from his roost at the sideboard. "Dunno why, just stalked off, probably to go and be moody and mysterious in the moonlight, and Karya just leapt up after him."

Robin, curious, made to head out after them, but Henry grabbed his arm.

"Oh, leave it," he said. "Let them have their secrecy. I'm not following after like some lost little puppy and neither should you."

"Henry, I ..."

"You know what they're like, both serious and broody. They're probably discussing the great and powerful workings of the universe and Netherworlde politics out there. What use are us mere mortals in that kind of discussion?"

He glanced at Robin, narrowing his eyes. "Well," he corrected himself. "*I'm* merely mortal, anyway, you're a magic ... fairy, prophet, saviour, or whatever you are." He shook his shaggy head. "But that's not my point. My point is, clearly, *we're* not invited to the sombre, serious midnight stroll in the snow."

Robin thought Henry was being a little unreasonable, even if he was upset, and he was just opening his mouth to say so, when Woad piped up from his seat on the hearth rug, making things ten times worse.

"It's a magical night for Christmas romance in the shadows. Maybe you could lend them your mistletoe, Henry boy?" he suggested, helpfully.

Henry's ears were now very red. He thrust his hands into his pockets.

"Right," he said decisively. "That's it. That's me for the night. I'm off to bed before Santa turns up. See you all on Christmas morning."

"Henry, don't be like that," Robin urged as the older boy turned to leave. "You can't be mad on Christmas Eve. I'm pretty sure it's against the law or something. Anyway, I think Woad's got the wrong end of the stick…"

"Fauns never mishandle sticks!" Woad said, offended. "When it comes to handling any tree parts, fauns are experts! Be it a reedy twig or a mighty cudgel, nothing is more deadly than a forest-wielding faun."

"*You're* a reedy twig, you little blue nutter," Henry grumbled in a half-hearted but at least friendly manner, which Robin took as a positive sign. "I'll give you a mighty cudgel around the ear in a minute."

Robin saw Woad's hackles rise.

"Fauns," Woad said, a little louder, "are perfectly proportioned in every way. Built for maximum efficiency, with no wasted energy directed to long, lolloping limbs, like some ungainly humans I could mention."

Robin shot the little blue boy a look of death, willing him to shut up. Henry had already stalked off and was headed for the large double doors leading back through to the dining room.

Robin tried to think of something to say to make him stay, glancing back at the French doors and the soft glow of the snow beyond, shining in the blue-black shadows. He could just make out the dim forms of Jackalope and Karya outside, but before he could decide whether to follow Henry or rush out to them to see what on earth they had sneaked away for in the first place, Woad, whose eyes were keener than anyone else's, cried out.

"He has her in his arms!"

Henry, his hand still on the door handle, whirled around in shock at this, his face flushed and caught between panic and scowl, but Robin barely noticed his scandalised friend. His attention had been drawn to the card table, where Aunt Irene had stood up so quickly it was a wonder her chair hadn't toppled over backwards. Her hand of cards fell to the tabletop, discarded and forgotten, and her sharp eyes were trained over the heads of the boys and out into the darkness beyond.

Her playing companions were all staring at her in confusion, the hard and very stern set of her face trained on the gardens.

"Something is wrong," she said, quickly and quietly.

Robin followed her gaze and saw finally what Woad had seen before his dramatic yelp. Jackalope and Karya were not having any kind of mistletoe moment out there in the privacy of the dark gardens, despite Henry's fears. The silver-topped Fae was in fact staggering back towards the house, carrying before him the limp body of the girl, her arms dangling loosely and swaying with each step. Her head was lolling against his chest.

"He has her in his arms!" Woad repeated, leaping to his feet and rushing to the door. "Boss! What happened? What have you done to …"

"Robin," Irene said sharply, issuing commands at once. "Help Jackalope inside." She glanced at Mr Drover, who was getting to his feet, looking alarmed. "Go and fetch Hestia at once," she instructed.

Henry's father nodded, looking rattled, and Robin and Henry had crossed the room to the glass French doors without even realising they had moved. The cold air outside was bitingly cold against their faces.

"Help me with her!" Jackalope grunted. "She's small, but she's heavy as lead." He looked shocked himself, as Robin and Henry clumsily helped him bring the unconscious girl back into the light and warmth of the parlour.

"What happened?" Henry babbled. "What did you …"

"I didn't do *anything*," Jackalope replied through gritted teeth. He had his hands under Karya's arms now, and Robin grabbed her legs as they staggered into the room. "We were just talking and then …"

Madame Calypso was suddenly by their side, looking calm as ever amidst the sudden panic. With a simple swish of her hand and the silvery flash of a waterwhip cantrip she flicked a barrage of heavy scatter cushions off the sofa by the fireplace, sending them rolling to the floor.

"Bring her here and lay her down," she instructed quietly, looking far more curious and interested than worried at the collapsed and pale form of Karya.

As the two boys lay the girl on the sofa, with Woad and Henry dancing about them agitatedly, Robin was far more concerned than his tutor. In the lamplight, Karya was whiter than he'd ever seen her. Her lips seemed utterly drained of blood, her cheeks were pale and her eyes seemed to be moving back and forth behind her eyelids. Nothing showed of them but thin slits of white. Her hands were twitching and her lips moved silently.

"And then what?" Henry demanded to know, staring from Karya to Jackalope, who was still looking flushed and out of breath from carrying the girl through the snow. "You were talking and then …?"

Jackalope ran his hands through his hair, dislodging flakes of snow that tumbled to the floorboards. He looked as surprised as anyone else. "She just … her eyes were strange. She started saying odd things, nonsense words … I thought she was being foolish, but then she fell, like a puppet with dropped strings."

Irene ushered them all back as Calypso knelt by the sofa, hovering her long and thin fingers over the unconscious girl as though testing the heat of a stove.

"Give the girl some air, please," the old lady said sharply. "Noble intent or not, it will not assist her returning to her senses to have four shouting boys all suffocating her, will it?"

"She has not fainted," Calypso said, in a manner that was almost offhand. "She appears to be in a fit of some kind."

"A tot of brandy, perhaps?" Ffoulkes suggested from the card table. He was the only person who remained seated, and although he had folded his cards, he held them in his hand, tapping them thoughtfully against the tabletop. "Brandy always does the trick if one is feeling a little light-headed." He barked a little laugh. "Or if one is wishing to feel a little light-headed, now I come to think of it, aha!"

Calypso and Irene ignored him completely. The nymph regarded the old woman as she peered down at Karya's still twitching form.

"Is the child prone to this?" she asked with a detached, scientific tone of interest. "Or perhaps she is still weaker than we thought."

Irene, who clearly had little notion of Karya's predisposition to fainting and fitting, glanced at Robin and the others in a silent question, her sharp grey eyes resting longest on Woad. He had, after all, known the girl the longest of all of them.

"She's never done this before." Robin shook his head. "Not since I – we – have known her, anyway."

"Boss sometimes goes away in her head," Woad said, still looking shell-shocked and worried. "When she has some of her memories from the past, or the future. She can say strange things when that happens. But not for a long, long time. And it's never made her crumple like a lamb unsure of its legs before."

"Is she having a vision?" Henry asked, looking fraught between the faun and the girl.

"She was speaking nonsense," Jackalope nodded. "Making no sense."

Karya, Robin knew, came with a host of oddities and contradictions. She had told him when they first met that her memories were not always her own. There was no way they could be, as she seemed able to recall things from long ago, much further back than she could ever have been alive. And sometimes she saw glimpses of possible futures. One such vision, that included Robin himself, had been the catalyst for her flight from Eris and her coming to seek him out in the first place.

Mr Drover returned with a livid Hestia, who burst through the doors of the parlour like a fury unleashed, her small, black hedgehog eyes swiftly taking in the scene, her puckered mouth set in a tight line. She would have appeared fearsome, were it not for the fact she was wearing a quilted peach bed robe and her hair was done up in tight overnight curlers beneath a hairnet.

"Out," she said curtly, shuffling across the room in her slippers. "Too many people, especially the children. Give Hestia room and peace, and she will see what is to be done. No peace where little horrors flap their arms and lips."

Irene gestured to the corridor. "Hestia has a point," she said calmly. "You four, upstairs. A circus is of no use when nursing is to be done."

"If you think we're leaving, you've got another think coming!" Henry spluttered, forgetting, in the heat of the moment, whom he was talking to.

Irene raised a single eyebrow.

Then, Mr Drover was suddenly at their elbows, jostling and herding Robin and the others from the room, despite their protests. "And if *you* think Lady Irene was asking," he blustered through his copious moustache, "then you're more confused than I figured, my lad. Come on. All of you, up to Robin's room, lads. Let our Hestia see to things here, you're only underfoot. She knows what she's about."

Robin glanced back as they were manhandled gently but firmly from the room. Irene, Calypso and Hestia were gathered around the still unconscious girl, backlit in the firelight like shadows. Snow had begun to blow in through the still-open patio doors, which Ffoulkes, at something of a loss for anything better or more helpful to do, was fussily closing against the dark night.

Hestia looked intent but quietly furious. Karya, Robin guessed, was going to get the lecture of her lifetime about defying bed rest orders, once she came to.

It had been a good hour, with no news from the house below, and Robin and his companions were practically crawling the walls of his circular tower bedroom. Robin stood in front of the fire, jabbing it occasionally with the poker. Jackalope was leaning out of the open window, elbows resting on the sill as he glared out into the snowy night, while beside him, Woad was doing handstands against the wall.

"Woad, will you give over with that?" Henry asked. "You're absolutely doing my nut in."

"You're no better," Robin said. "Pacing up and down like that, you're going to wear a groove in my floorboards, Henry. Can you not just sit down for a minute?"

"I like handstands," Woad muttered. "They help me concentrate. They get all the blood to my brain."

"I don't know how you can ask me to sit down, when one of our own has collapsed in the snow." Henry reached the wall and spun on his heel, pacing back across the creaking floorboards for roughly the millionth time in the last hour. "To be honest, I don't know how you can be so calm about it."

Robin gave the coals another jab, sending a cloud of firefly sparks up the chimney and into the cold air beyond. He certainly didn't feel calm, despite what Henry assumed. He felt worried sick.

"Getting all worked up is not going to help, that's all," he said, feeling very worked up himself, but determined not to let it show. "Karya's in good hands. Hestia is the best nurse in either England or the Netherworlde. She knows how to look after people. It's what she does."

"It's *all* she does," Woad agreed, his voice slightly gurgly due to his being upside down. "It's what she is."

"I agree with the Scion," Jackalope said from the window, without turning to face any of them. "Karya survived a direct hit from one of the Grimms back in the Hive. She's stronger than the rest of you put together."

"No one asked you," Henry sniffed, a little sharply. "And anyway, she's clearly not back to full strength yet. If this *is* one of those visions she was always telling us she got, it's knocked her off her feet. She's running on low batteries."

"Why *did* you two go outside anyway?" Robin asked. He saw Jack's back stiffen.

"I wanted some air," he muttered. "I didn't ask her to come with me."

"Who wants 'air' in the middle of the night on Christmas Eve?" Robin wondered. "What were you talking about, anyway?"

Jackalope sighed. "This and that." He gestured around at the room, finally turning from the window. "This place, Erlking. How you all call it a family. Your strange human traditions. Family at Christmas." He shrugged. "She doesn't like the idea of family. She told me hers was Eris' twisted lot, or at least that's as close as she's ever had to one. Can you imagine your nearest and dearest being the Grimms?"

"She has a better family here now," Robin said firmly. "All of us do."

"Well, I didn't like talking about it," Jack crossed his arms. "Mine is gone. Mine was taken away. It made me ..." He faltered a little, breathing in carefully. Even Henry stopped pacing. "I don't know, it made me think of *him*, and then suddenly the room felt too noisy and full of strangers to me." He shrugged in defence. "I needed some air. It's not a crime."

Even Henry seemed to soften a bit, if not much. "If your brother was still around, he'd think you were a prize idiot," he said bluntly. "Room full of strangers?" The boy snorted. "We might be a strange lot, but you're even stranger."

"No one is as strange as you are," Jackalope glared, his eyes flashing in the moonlight from the window. "You're the noisiest human I ever met. You hiss and puff and spit like a kettle forgotten on a stovetop."

Robin thought he understood Jack. He still missed his Gran. Things got better as time went on, easier to deal with, but it never really went away. Loss wasn't so much a wound that healed, as a permanent bruise that you simply learned how to nurse over time. You learned how to avoid knocking it and took care not to bump too hard into things that might remind you it was there. But every now and again – like tonight, in a house full of safety and new family – an offhand comment, the smallest thing, could be like a jab deep in the ache, reminding you that it was still there, forever freshly sore. He didn't begrudge Jackalope getting some air for a moment, in the privacy of the dark, to collect himself.

Sometimes, you had to take a moment to be alone with the bruise, and the person it was for.

"She followed you out because you were upset," Woad said, in his blank and often tactless way. "She likes you. She doesn't like that you're sad all the time behind your angry face."

"She does *not* like him!" Henry blustered.

"I am *not* sad all the time!" Jackalope snapped.

Woad shrugged, still upside down, sliding down the wall into a lazy crumpled heap, smiling as though everyone in the room was an idiot except for him.

"What *did* you guys talk about out there, then?" Robin asked.

"That's private." Robin wouldn't have believed it if he hadn't seen it with his own eyes, but Jackalope looked even more defensive than usual. The boy could make a clam look open and welcoming.

Woad sniggered. "He likes her back."

Everyone ignored the faun. Wilfully and pointedly. A knot of wood in the fireplace popped like a muffled gunshot.

"But she just started, what? Talking nonsense? Out of the blue?" Robin pressed.

Jackalope nodded, his head a grey halo in the moonlight, framing him from behind. "Her eyes rolled back, and she grabbed onto me, my shoulders. I thought she had slipped in the snow. Then it was all garbled. Then she collapsed."

He stepped away from the window as Robin set the fireplace poker down in its holder. "But I could pick out one thing, before she went down for the count."

"What did boss say?" Woad sat up to attention, suddenly interested.

Jackalope shook his head, clearly confused. "She said 'half a heart … they've got half a heart … hiding … the secret sister'." He looked around at them hopefully, clearly baffled. "If this means anything more to any of you than it does to me, please say so."

But it didn't. It was equally confusing to all of them. Robin said nothing out loud but a small part of his mind couldn't help but flick back to their encounter at the gallery in London, in the office of Mr Knight. When they had glimpsed the girl who had reminded them so much of Karya.

They were resolved as a group to question her when she awoke, but frustratingly, this was not to be. It was well past midnight when a knock finally came at Robin's bedroom door, and Mr Drover popped his head in to reassure them all. Karya was fine, he told them. Awake but tired, and she didn't really remember what had happened, only that she had felt dizzy. All four of them demanded immediately to see her, but Mr Drover would not be moved. Karya had been taken off to bed by Hestia, he told them, sticking his chin out beneath his bristling moustache with an air of determined authority. She needed a good night's rest, and there would be plenty of time to talk in the morning. But they could all stop worrying. It had been a funny turn, and nothing more than that.

"And … in case any or all of you bright sparks are thinking of sneaking around the shadows in your socks tonight," he added, wagging a finger at them all, "I'd strongly caution against it. Hestia reckons Karya needs a watchful eye, just for tonight, so she's camped out right at her door. You'd as soon get past a sphinx with no eyelids and into the underworld than you would get past our dear old housekeeper, and she likely bites harder, too." His expression softened, looking at the four of them. Their worry for their friend was genuine. "So, off to bed and all's mended by morning … *all* of you."

Henry reluctantly followed his father out of the room when beckoned, visibly relieved that the news was not more serious, but frustrated that Karya had been "locked away like a bloody inmate in the Tower of London," as he muttered murderously.

At least due to Christmas, the Drovers, senior and junior, were only off to their own rooms, not all down to the village, so at least Henry wasn't going far. That was some small comfort.

Woad had already curled up like a cat at the foot of Robin's bed, clearly determined not to return to his own room tonight. The faun would never admit it of course – he was a ball of solid bravado – but Robin suspected he had been far more worried about Karya's episode than he let on.

Robin turned to Jackalope as he went to leave, his hand already on the door.

"Hey, erm ..." he began. The older Fae looked back.

"Just ... don't take Henry to heart, that's all I was going to say. It's not you he doesn't like."

"I'm fairly certain he does not like me, and I could not care less about it," Jack replied with a careless shrug.

"No, I mean. He's prickly around you. You're still newish. I don't know. He was the same with Karya when she first came here. Kicked up a huge stink about having an untrustworthy girl in the house. Henry gets kind of defensive and, well, territorial."

Jackalope considered this. "The girl is not his territory," he replied. "She's her own. He would do well to realise that."

"Just be patient with him, that's all I'm trying to say," Robin said. "Henry has a good heart. He's my best friend for a reason. He could be yours, too, if you stopped butting heads."

Jackalope considered this. "Friends?" He rolled the word around his mouth like an unfamiliar taste, glancing between Robin and Woad. "I'm still not even sure what that is, really."

"It's someone you protect," Woad said, from somewhere in the blankets. "Someone who keeps your secrets and watches your back. Someone who matters to you, dull diplodocus. Someone who cares if you're happy or sad."

"If you want, you can stay with us tonight." Robin gestured to the floor. "I can make up a camp bed on the floor. You can take the bed, you know, if you don't feel like being on your own. It's Christmas Eve, after all."

Jackalope seemed to consider this for a moment, looking from the floor to the fireplace before looking back to Robin. This was a surprise. Robin had been fully expecting the boy to reject the idea out of hand immediately from sheer habit.

Eventually, Jackalope smiled a little. "A kind offer, but I'm comfortable enough. And besides, you two both snore. I can hear you from the floor below." He opened the door. "We should all sleep. It will be morning soon and a celebration day, and we all have questions." He nodded to the ancient carriage clock which stood on the mantelpiece in Robin's room. "Besides, it's past midnight, which means it's Christmas Day."

Robin hadn't realised this. Snow was falling thinly again outside the window, as one day had slipped into the next like silent magic.

"As I understand the tradition, the fat elf of jolliness will not bring the gifts and offerings until I am asleep. Merry Christmas, Scion and faun."

He slipped out, closing the door softly behind him.

Robin, exhausted by the night, clambered into bed in his pyjamas. The events of the evening had just stopped swirling around his head, and the sweet numbness of sleep had finally started to bleed into the corners of his mind, when, from the darkness, Woad piped up. "If it's after midnight, does that mean we can open our presents now?"

3

Hextra Credit

Christmas at Erlking was always a magical time. The Hall was alive at sunrise, and as ever before, Robin and company gathered beneath the huge tree in the entrance hall, supervised by a very bleary-eyed and sleepy Mr Drover, still bundled in his dressing gown, his hair and moustache bristling and unkempt, giving him the appearance of a startled hedgehog. They dug through the large landslide of presents that had appeared beneath the huge tree, as though by magic, overnight.

Aunt Irene made an appearance roughly halfway through the chaos of unwrapping, having made her way quietly down the stairs. She wore a long gown of festive fir green and unlike Mr Drover, she didn't seem remotely sleepy. Robin could not, in fact, recall a time he had seen his great aunt look anything other than sharp as a pin. He rarely even saw her blink.

They were all relieved to see that Karya had been released from the watchful guard of the old housekeeper, who had begrudgingly allowed her to come downstairs and join in just as the bright morning sun lit the windows on fire, blazing in the frost. Robin had worried she might be confined to another month of bed rest and miss all the fun. The wiry girl looked a little grey and worn out, but happy to be up and about. Nobody mentioned the strange trance. Not yet. They were all under strict instructions from Irene not to. "It is Christmas Day," she had instructed them firmly before the young girl had joined them. "Pleasure first, business later. There will be a time to discuss everything. But now is a time for fun. While there is still fun to be had, and still time to have it in."

Robin's tutors, Calypso and Ffoulkes, were helping to arrange the breakfast table, and both were gladly avoiding the chaos of the gift unwrapping which was underway in the hall. Calypso was happy to miss the unfathomable appeal of tearing paper, and Ffoulkes eager to show off his peerless aptitude in the kitchen. At any other time, it would have been unthinkable for Hestia to allow anyone else to lift a finger to help her with her chores, but by all accounts, the housekeeper had been awake all night by Karya's bedside, and her small, dark eyes were graced this morning with dark and grumpy rings, and so she accepted the help of the tutors, albeit sullenly.

"How's the haul this year, Scion?" Karya asked from the seat she had claimed at the foot of the staircase, just beyond the boundary of the sea of torn wrapping paper that was spreading like a slush pile from beneath the sparkling tree. She wore a large flannel robe, likely a cast off from Hestia. It was salmon pink, faded with age like an old rose, and she hugged it cosily around herself, stifling a yawn. Her brown mass of tangled hair was that particularly careless mess one only seems to be able to achieve properly on Christmas morning.

The haul, as it turned out, was good. For everyone, it seemed. Robin had received new cantrip books on air and earth magic from Karya, some of them very rare and difficult to come by. *The Satyrlore of the Skies* by Panadrus Brushtail and *Root, Sap and Bark : 101 Ways with Sylvan Fancies* by the Brothers Redrust. Each was thick and bound in dyed leather of lightest duck egg blue and deepest fern green respectively, and embellished in gold with stylised puffs of air and curls of ivy. The filigree swayed and squired around the covers, as was the wont of all magical books of Erlking.

She had even managed to get her hands on a tattered scroll of water cantrips, a Tower notorious for having very little written lore. Nymphs were not known for having the presence of mind to record their musings. Undine even less so. Robin was very impressed.

Woad's present to Robin continued the bookish theme. The small blue boy had presented his friend with a very heavy tome, emblazoned with the title *Fruits of the Nether: What Does Not Kill You, Makes You Stronger (or Very Sick at the Very Worst)* by Nausietta Reflux. Unlike Karya's offerings, which were refined and elegant, Woad's book seemed rather more garish, like a pulp horror paperback, with a cartoonish cover that appeared to depict a botanist foaming happily at the mouth while gathering a basketful of violently yellow berries in a forest glade.

The faun explained, with barely contained excitement, that it was a comprehensive guide to all the plants (both magical and non-magical) in the Netherworlde, with everything from their uses in poisons and spell-casting to delicious recipes. "From combustibles to constipation!" he crowed merrily. Given Woad's recent obsession with foraging and hedgerow gardening, Robin suspected that this was, in truth, a gift from Woad to Woad, but it was better than a dried and cured squirrel-skin hat, which was what he had been expecting, so he accepted it graciously, noticing the pages had already been well thumbed and several were stuck together with glam-glam jam.

"Open mine, open mine!" Henry jabbered impatiently, as Woad burrowed into the ever-deepening pile of wrapping paper with Robin's new book all to himself, having swiped it from him at the earliest moment possible. "These Netherworlders and their books. Honestly Rob, who gives books as presents?" Henry joked.

"I like books!" Robin insisted, smirking at Karya, who rolled her eyes at Henry. He took the small package Henry was insistently and repeatedly thrusting under his chin. "Alright, alright, don't shove it down my throat," Robin laughed, tearing off the paper.

A thick gold object fell out and into his palm. At first, he thought it was a heavy old pocket watch. The full-hunter type that flicks open like a metallic clamshell to reveal the clock face inside. But as he turned it over in his hands, frowning with curiosity, he saw the face had only one hand, which looked like a thick needle, coloured silver at one end and black at the other. It was spinning wildly back and forth, dashing to different points on the circular face, and all around the rim of the circle, countless minute faces with caricature expressions were carved. There must have been a hundred tiny faces comprising the outer circle, no two of them exactly the same.

"It's ... pretty," he said, more than a little confused. "What on earth is it?"

"It looks like a compass." Karya leaned forward with interest, rubbing sleep out of her eyes. Much like Robin, he suspected, she had likely been expecting Henry's gift to be some football stickers or a whoopee cushion.

"It's a moral compass!" Henry beamed proudly. "Pretty rare old bit of kit, that. It's supposed to help guide you, figure stuff out, whenever the figuring out of stuff gets tough."

"Where in the Netherworlde did you buy something like that?" Karya asked, surprised.

Henry glanced up rather sheepishly at Aunt Irene, who was standing unobtrusively to one side, surveying the proceedings while sipping tea from a small cup.

"I didn't exactly buy it," he said, a little awkwardly. "I found it, a while back, up in the attics. Lady Irene said I could keep it if I wanted to."

Irene nodded, with thoughtful eyes. "Erlking gives up its secrets only when it wishes to," she said. "And only to whom it chooses. At the time, I felt perhaps you may have needed some moral guidance. Heavens know, don't all boys? And girls, for that matter."

"Nah," Henry grinned. "I like to sail the seas of life without a map, I do. The seat of my pants are my only sail. But poor old Robin here, well …" He clapped a hand on the boy's shoulder. "He needs all the help he can get, right? He's always wringing his hands."

Woad sniggered from somewhere in the slush pile, making the wrapping paper shudder.

"It's great, thanks Henry." Robin looked down at his gift. "Why is it spinning like mad though?"

The needle of the ornate compass face was indeed making endless swift circles, round and round.

"It will take a little while to attune itself to your own personal mana, to your sensibilities," Irene explained. "It's been in young Master Drover's keeping for more than a month now, so the poor thing is undoubtedly both confused and exhausted," she added dryly, eliciting a stifled harrumphing laugh from Mr Drover.

Henry shot his father a dark look.

Eventually, Mr Ffoulkes emerged into the hall from an archway, a kitchen towel slung casually yet artfully over his shoulder. He was covered with a light dusting of flour, suggesting that his breakfast preparations, if not professional, were at least enthusiastic. His beard was also slightly singed.

"Merriest salutations of the season, young Master Robin, ahahahah," he trilled jovially with a flashing smile. "You shall find a small token from myself in this maelstrom too, I shouldn't wonder. I think you'll discover it to be as tasteful and practical a gift as one would expect."

"Gods help you if that's true!" Calypso's voice floated quietly from the room behind the man.

Robin's eyebrows shot up in surprise. He'd never had a present from a tutor before. Phorbas was a knife, after all, with limited gift-giving options other than the occasional nick of the thumb, and as for Calypso, well … it had never really occurred to her to bother.

"Found it!" Woad erupted from the present pile like a small volcano, holding aloft a compact square package in elaborately brocaded wrappings. He scuttled over to Robin, presenting it with an overly dramatic flourish which somehow managed to convey an imitation of Ffoulkes perfectly.

Beneath the wrappings, there was a golden drawstring bag. It was quite heavy and from it, Robin tipped into his palm a jewel. It was faceted like a diamond, big enough to fill his palm and completely clear. He turned it this way and that, watching the light catch and sparkle on its many polished faces.

"It's a gem?" he asked, surprised by the Fire Panthea's generosity.

Ffoulkes shook his head. "Not as such no, aha. What manner of tutor would I be, after all, if I neglected to gift you something to aid in your studies?"

"That's a cubic cornucopia, isn't it?" Karya sounded a little astonished. "They're very rare old things."

"A koobie corny whatsit?" Woad frowned, peering suspiciously at it. He sniffed it with curiosity.

"Ah! A keen eye, that girl!" Ffoulkes nodded proudly. "It is indeed a cubic cornucopia, and, my dear, rare and precious are my bread and butter, remember?"

Robin looked from Karya to his new tutor, still none the wiser. "But what is it, whatever it's called? And what's it got to do with my studies?" His heart leapt a little. "Does this mean we're going to actually start learning the Tower of Fire? At last?"

Ffoulkes shot a brief look across the hall at Aunt Irene, who nodded almost imperceptibly, sipping her tea.

"Indeed it does. No time like the present! We begin tomorrow. Give you time to let your Christmas meal digest first, eh?" He patted his own stomach, sending up a small cloud of flour from the rich embroidery of his waistcoat. "As for the prize you hold, its designated and solitary purpose is to contain an element. Fire, in this case. Think of it as a handy little bucket, capable of carrying fire for you without a drop spilled."

"A bucket …" Robin looked down at the glittering gem, still confused.

"All will become clear in our first lesson, I assure you. Pop it somewhere safe for now, and for goodness sake, don't drop it. It is … aha … *charged*, as it were." The red-bearded man smoothed his lapels fussily. "It would rather ruin the festive mood, I fear, should this fine tree become a crackling inferno."

Robin placed the innocent-looking little jewel very carefully back into its bag.

"I can look after it!" Woad suggested happily.

"No!" Karya and Aunt Irene said in unison, a little urgently.

Jackalope sidled over towards Robin, kicking aside drifts of torn wrapping paper, his hands thrust into his pockets. He had been almost silent throughout the Christmas morning chaos, being unfamiliar with the hubbub and traditions.

"The magic jewels, magic compass, books on magic. You really have a theme going on, Scion," he muttered. "It will make this look poor in comparison, but here, anyway." He dropped a small oblong unceremoniously into Robin's hand. It wasn't wrapped.

Robin was taken aback. He hadn't expected anything from Jackalope at all.

"Is that a cassette tape?" Henry craned his neck, incredulous. "I've never actually seen one in real life. Where did you get it from? Nineteen eighty-five?"

"There's an old player upstairs," Jackalope growled. "I wasn't sure how else to collect music, except on my phone. I'm still getting used to some human-world technology. But I saw someone fashion it this way in a movie." He nodded at Robin. Jackalope had been watching a lot of movies. "There are few things in the human world I find better than in the Netherworlde, Scion. But the music here, I admit, is very interesting. I have imprinted on this device some of my most impressive findings. You can educate yourself at leisure." His face, as always, was deeply earnest and serious, as though he was handing Robin a survival kit.

"You made me a mixtape?" Robin grinned. "That's kind of awesome, Jack. I think we're finally thawing you out after all those years on the Gravis Glaciem."

Written across the ancient cassette, in Jackalope's rather childish and chunky handwriting, was: *To the least of my enemies.*

"Still not quite mastered the word friend, eh?" Robin laughed.

"Take it or leave it." Jack shrugged. "Makes little difference to me. Karya wrote the words out for me, I just copied the shapes." He looked over to Hestia, who had appeared in the dining room doorway, her lip trembling ever so slightly from having borne witness to whatever Ffoulkes and Calypso had done to her kitchen.

"Much more importantly," he said, brightening at the sight of the housekeeper, "I think the food is ready."

Christmas Day passed, as Christmas Day will, with much making of merry, a degree of festive exhaustion and far too much good, rich food. Everyone else opened their presents. Outside, snow fell and pale rabbits darted across the lawns toward the lines of frosted trees. Carols were played on what Mr Drover still insisted calling "the wireless". Hestia served eggnog. Woad ate a pine cone from the tree on a dare from Henry. The day passed well.

It was not until late in the afternoon, when Henry's father was merrily snoring in an armchair beneath a paper hat, sleeping off plum pudding, and Robin's aunt and tutors were otherwise engaged, that the merry band of Erlkingers finally had a chance to meet in private.

Under the pretence of testing out a brand new quiver of arrows, which Robin had gifted Henry for his bow, all five had bundled themselves up in layers of coats, scarves and woollen hats, and now were gathered outside under a bright gunmetal sky, in the walled rose garden, bare and barren in the depths of winter. The snow crunched satisfyingly beneath their boots and their breath came in small collective puffs of white. Everyone shivered a little, except for Woad, who was as immune to the elements as if he'd been coated in Kevlar. He was still carrying the botany book, looking up only occasionally at the others making merry sport with the bow.

"So, are we going to talk about what happened last night?" Robin asked, gloved hands thrust deep into his pockets as he watched Henry and Jackalope setting up straw archery targets against one frozen and thorny wall. "I'm surprised Hestia allowed you to come outside at all, Karya. She's treating you like you're made of glass these days."

Karya, who wore her customary coat of tattered furs and hides, shrugged a little. The cold bit at her face, raising pink crescents on her paler-than-usual cheeks.

"I know this is going to sound unusual to all of you," she said, sounding irritated with herself. "But the vision, everything I apparently said, I don't remember any of it."

Woad was sitting cross-legged in the snow; having finally set aside his botany book he was now patiently building a small arsenal of snowballs. He frowned up at her, his bright yellow eyes flickering with unusual concern.

"That's not like you, boss," he said. "Whenever you remember the future, or see things we don't, it's always clear as ice."

Karya shrugged, stamping her feet in the powder. "I know," she admitted. "I won't pretend it's not a little concerning. But the last thing I remember was walking outside with Jack. Then ... I was in my room, with Hestia looming over me, like the angriest nurse I've ever seen." She blew air down her nose, clearly at a loss. "Maybe being run through with a poisoned evil spear has affected more than just my natural grace and poise. I need more time to heal."

"You said something about half a heart," Jackalope said, striding back towards the others while Henry tried in vain to nock an arrow to his bow with numb fingers. "And about a sister hiding. That doesn't ring any bells?"

Karya shook her head, frustrated. "No clue," she admitted. The girl regarded each of them, taking in the concerned looks of her friends.

"There's no need to stare at me as though I'm losing my marbles completely," she huffed. "I *know* there's something wrong. Everyone's noticed it, and you're all being so terribly careful and nobody's saying it, so I will."

She sighed. "I've barely used the Tower of Earth since I got back from the Hive. My mana feels ..." she glanced down at her darkened and lifeless bracelet, "depleted, somehow. Like an empty glass. I don't think I could make a leaf fall at the moment, let alone tear between the worlds. It feels as though I used up all of my energy in not dying, and it's ... I don't know, *undone* something ... deep inside."

"When we got back to Erlking," Robin said, looking around at the others, "after the Hive, we all agreed we needed to get to the bottom of the eternal mystery that is Karya, remember? We said we had to go back to your past. That's the only way we can figure out what's ..." He halted. He had been about to say "what's wrong with you", but the challenging look in her eyes stopped him. "What's ... going on with you," he finished lamely.

"Rob, darling Rob. We've been over this a million times," Henry sighed wearily. "It doesn't matter if you got two and a half Shards of the Arcania. It doesn't matter that you killed a dragon, or smashed Eris' prison to bits. Your loveable yet terrifying and nutty aunt is never, never *ever*, going to agree to let you, or any of us, go to Dis on a fact-finding mission."

"It would be suicide anyway," Jackalope nodded, his face grim. "Karya may have come from Dis, but it is the heart of Eris."

"You're too important to risk throwing into the lion's den, Pinky," Woad sighed, tossing up a snowball and catching it. "The old lady Irene is more likely to throw a surprise party for Strife himself here at Erlking and leap out of a cake waving sparklers, than let you, the precious Scion of the Arcania, go to that city."

"Then we don't ask!" Robin snapped, a little more sharply than he'd intended. "I understand. I really do. It's dangerous. It's walking right up to our enemy's door. I'm not stupid, you know. But what use is it being the bloody 'precious Scion', if all I do is sit about in this safe little sanctuary having lessons? What good is it if I can't even help a friend?"

Karya looked a little uncomfortable. "I never asked for help," she said folding her arms. "I survived just fine long before I met any of you lot, you know. I can find my own answers."

"What, in between fainting and not being able to do any magic, you mean?" Henry sighed and loosed an arrow, which whistled through the air with a hiss and landed square in the centre ring of the distant target with a satisfying thunk. He slung the bow casually over his shoulder, looking uncharacteristically heroic for a moment. "I agree with Rob. We should go to Dis, and we shouldn't ask. Better to ask forgiveness later than permission first, right?" He shrugged. "It's always worked for us before."

"I don't think you fully understand what you are proposing, human boy," Jackalope said, folding his arms and staring at the near-perfect shot with grudging admiration. "Dis is not your Disneyland. You can't just walk in."

"Jack's right," Karya said. "The capital city of the Netherworlde, as well as being a heck of a long way away, is completely impregnable. The only – and I do mean only – way in, is through the one outer wall gate, which is heavily guarded. There is no sneaking through. If we even try, we may as well tie a big pink bow around your head and deliver you to Eris as a late Christmas present. The gates are always locked, always watched, and Eris' eyes are always on them. As much as I agree that if there are any answers to be had about my ..." she glanced at her own hands, "*condition* ... then they lie somewhere in that city, but I don't see any way to get there. It's not even a case of getting permission to go. There's no real way *to* go."

Robin kicked at a lump of snow in frustration.

"Aunt Irene is so distracted with trying to locate this fabled book and unlocking the mystery of the Cubiculu-Argentum," he fumed. "What are we supposed to do in the meantime? Watch you get weaker by the day instead of getting better? All this business with Mr Knight and Sire Holdings, it's ... it's just a distraction. We should be focussing on you."

"I'm fairly sure your aunt knows what is and isn't important to focus on," Karya said diplomatically. "That book could be the answer to everything. The answer to the war, freeing the whole Netherworlde. I'm just one person."

"It could all be connected, anyway," Woad mused lightly, tossing his snowball from one hand to the other. The others looked down at him, sitting happily in the snow. "Boss' vision last night, the museum guy, the half-a-heart, burned-up feather and weird journal you guys found." He shrugged. "Maybe it all ties together, like ... a big knotty knot."

"Better for now to focus on your new lessons, and see what comes," Karya insisted, nodding at Robin. "For the time being. You'll be learning the Tower of Fire, after all. With a robust and level-headed tutor like Ffoulkes, what could possibly go wrong with that?"

Robin opened his mouth to answer but was cut off as Woad lobbed a snowball directly at his face.

As the following week passed, Christmas fading and one year slipping softly into the next, Robin was to discover that the answer to Karya's question was "quite a lot".

His first official Tower of Fire lesson took place in a large room, somewhere deep in the bowels of Erlking. It did not surprise him in the least that it was a place he had never stumbled upon before. Much like the hidden stables outside, the Hall was like that everywhere. Folding its corridors carefully like architectural origami, so you might miss altogether whole rooms, corridors and hallways, which lay hidden in the seams and only opened up when the situation demanded. The room, which Ffoulkes referred to as the necessarium, was wide, barren and funnel-shaped. A towering cinder cone soared around him, with plain stone flooring of dark shadows, and one encircling wall that stretched upwards and upwards for several storeys, windowless and twisting in dark stone before opening high above in an oculus window that lay open to the cold skies above.

It was a little like taking a lesson inside a great chimney, the kind you saw dotting the landscapes attached to old factories, run down and abandoned skeletons of the old industrial England.

Except no factory chimney, no matter how wide, was ever so oddly sculpted as the interior walls of the necessarium. The brickwork was fluted and it swirled in great arcing designs, which were carved into the encircling wall as it spiralled up above them to the open sky beyond, catching the light in curious ways, polished and glossy obsidian throwing shadows into its own sculpted grooves like the wrinkles of a brow. It was as though some strange force had gouged the stone. Here and there, scattered up along the tube of the chimney, clumps of spiky crystal, phenocryst, glittered in the darkness like stars.

In the midst of this frozen, windowless tornado of stone, Mr Ffoulkes stood. His hands were clasped behind his back, and a sly smirk, which no doubt he considered dashing, played on his face.

Robin thought the man was a little overdressed.

His tutor had foregone his customary embroidered suits in favour of a heavily ornate robe of deepest crimson, overlaid with a filigree of gold. He wore a tall, brimless hat, also red, which reminded the boy of something from feudal Japan.

"Come in, come in!" the Fire Panthea called with gusto as Robin closed the door firmly behind him. The heavy thud of the door in its frame echoed many times around the dark and ruffled walls, the sound being funnelled upwards like a pinball rolling in a groove.

Ffoulkes regarded Robin rather critically. "A tad underdressed, I see, for formal learning. A t-shirt and … whatever those things are."

"Sweatpants?" Robin offered.

"Indeed." Ffoulkes looked rather let down. "Well, at least *one* of us is prepared to school in the Tower of Fire, as all young Fire Panthea do." He indicated his own getup with a flourish of his incredibly wide sleeves. "This, my earnest pupil, is the official regalia of the Black Hills. Every young lord and lady of my fine people faced a tutor dressed in the traditional casting garb of the first manipulators of the Tower. And so indeed shall you."

"You look like a wizard from a children's party," came a voice from somewhere high above them.

Robin glanced upwards, following his tutor's gaze as he crossed the blank and empty floor, his footsteps echoing. About halfway up the tower's insides, reclining between the striations of spiralling stone, Woad was perched like a nesting bird. He always enjoyed Robin's lessons and had clearly come to spectate.

"It would be ill advised for the faun to squat so, here in this room," Ffoulkes said to Robin, sounding a little ruffled as he frowned up into the darkness. He smoothed the front of his busy robes lovingly. "The carvings and patterns of the necessarium are not merely for decoration. They are a funnel, to carry away both heat and fire."

"Woad, you had better come down." Robin waved up to his friend, who seemed unconvinced.

"Curiosity may well have killed the cat," Ffoulkes warned, "but fire fricasseed the faun."

"Fauns aren't afraid of fire," Woad called down to them in dismissive tones. "Fauns command Skyfire, don't you know? Everyone knows that."

Robin had no real idea what Skyfire was, but he certainly hadn't ever seen Woad command anything, at least not on purpose.

"You carry on with your fancy dress show," the grinning faun cackled. "I don't want to miss it."

Ffoulkes snorted down his nose. He made a quick hand gesture, flipping his hand out and uncurling his fingers as he swung his arm in the direction of the wall.

There was a soft *whump* and a bright yellow ball of fire erupted from his hand, the sudden light stinging Robin's eyes. It hissed through the air, spinning like a liquid firework, before smashing into the glossy wall at head height.

Sure enough, as it hit the carved stonework in a phosphorescent splash, the fire was caught in the grooves and flooded upwards, spiralling around them so that the walls of the necessarium became quickly veined with liquid light. At the very last second, Woad somersaulted from his perch, narrowly avoiding losing his tail as the streak of corralled flame whipped past him with a roar.

He tumbled down to the ground, spinning and landing softly on his bare feet like a cat. All three looked upwards as the fireball, channelled through the grooves, was finally spat harmlessly through the open oculus above, briefly brightening the grey sky outside.

"As ..." Ffoulkes said with some satisfaction, "so."

He blew on his hand, more for dramatic effect than anything, and smirked at Robin. Woad folded his arms with studied insouciance, discreetly flicking a smoking and singed tail.

"Are you going to teach me how to do that?" Robin asked. Truth be told, fire was the Tower he was most nervous about, but Ffoulkes' demonstration had been pretty impressive.

"When you are ready to be taught, indeed," the man replied. "The Tower of Fire is no trifling matter, little lord of Erlking. Fire is not languid like water. It resists shaping, unlike ice. It cannot be bossed around like earth, and you cannot think your way around it as you do with air." He nodded towards Woad, who smelled slightly singed. "Fire, as you can see, is hungry in and of itself. It wants to *live*. It wants to dance, to move, and to consume. And without control and understanding, it will do so regardless of your intent. It is volatile."

He cracked his knuckles, looking very self-important. "And it demands respect."

Robin nodded, swallowing a little thickly.

"And so, for our next session, please dress more appropriately," Ffoulkes continued. "Not as though you are about to jog your way around a banal athletics track for thirty minutes."

"This room is clever though, I will admit," Woad said, running his hands over the walls. "The way it sucks up the magic like a reverse lemon squeezer and spits it out up there, not in your face or on your tail, I mean."

"Many parts of Erlking Hall are built for one purpose and one purpose alone," Ffoulkes told the pair. "You must remember, children, that in the Netherworlde, this was the great bastion of the king and queen, the home of their loyal knights, the Sidhe-Nobilitas, and more importantly, where they honed their considerable skills. A friend of your own father designed this room, if my history is correct. A place to spar safely. A genius he was, by all accounts, quiet as night and full of quick cleverness. I believe, young Master Robin, that the two of them, this Fae architect and your father, used often to cross swords and enchantments here where we now stand."

Robin felt strangely reassured, knowing he was learning a whole new element in the space that his own father had once stood in.

"It is good that we are beginning your tuition now, especially with the eclipse coming up," Ffoulkes observed.

Robin frowned. "The what?"

"The solar eclipse," his tutor said with a smile. "Not far off now. No greater fire than the sun, after all. Always a special moment, whenever it occurs."

Robin didn't watch the news. It was difficult to do so here at Erlking, but he borrowed Mr Drover's newspaper every day, once the old groundskeeper had finished with it. He liked to keep abreast of the comings and goings of the mortal world, even if he was sheltered from it here. The boy felt certain he had heard no reports of an upcoming eclipse, and said as much to his tutor.

"Well, of course it wouldn't be on the *human* news," the bearded man scoffed. "Why would it, when the Netherworlde is the place due to have the eclipse? It won't be visible from any corner of England except here, in the skies over Erlking's grounds."

"If it's a Netherworlde eclipse, how would we see it from here?" Robin asked.

Ffoulkes gave him a wearied look, as though he were being deliberately troublesome.

"So very sure of where you stand, aren't you, little lord. Tell me, does Erlking exist in the human world or in the Netherworlde?"

Robin considered this for a moment.

"Both," he said.

Ffoulkes nodded. "And when you pass from room to room within these walls, are you in Erlking of the human world, or Erlking of the Netherworlde?"

Robin regarded the strange and unearthly chamber they found themselves in. "Well," he began, with limited certainty. "I thought the human world ... at least most of the time. Depending where in the Hall I am. I suppose I'm not sure."

Ffoulkes nodded briskly, as though this settled everything.

"And nor is the sky sure," he said. "Which is why sometimes it rains in the village and is sunny here. It's why you can drive back up the hill after watching a sunset, and sometimes see the sunset again, once you're in Erlking's grounds."

"Overlap," Woad said absently, inspecting his nails as though this was all obvious.

"And so as I was saying … the eclipse is due in the Netherworlde at some point soon. There's always something of a time lag. The worlds are out of step like a clumsy waltz, though it wasn't always so. We will see it here." He pointed upwards towards the open oculus above and the grey January skies outside. "And by the time it comes, I may not be the only one to throw a ball of fire at a nearby faun."

"Oi!" Woad shot the man a furious look, sticking out his bottom lip.

"Are you afraid of fire, Robin?" Ffoulkes asked, lightly but suddenly, as though hoping to catch his student off guard.

Robin considered this for a moment, and decided honesty was the best policy. "I think wary is the best word," he admitted. "I mean, air, water and earth – learning those, the worst that's going to happen is that you're going to get knocked over, soaked or muddy, right. But fire …"

Ffoulkes nodded, indicating that Robin should remain standing where he was while he himself strode loftily to the very centre of the room.

"Indeed! Respect! Respect and … ahahah … understanding." He held up his hands, fingers splayed. As he talked, small blue flames flickered into life at the very tips of his fingers, one by one, wavering and glimmering like Christmas lights.

"Think of the elemental Towers as music, perhaps." Ffoulkes moved his hands around slowly, the blue flames leaving traces of light in the dim and silent room. It was quite hypnotic. "Air is chamber music. Very precise, very careful and structured, mathematical and calculated." He began to move his arms in larger circles and shapes, as though performing tai chi. "The music of earth is simple and strong. Your stomping Russians! Drums, percussion and heartbeats, a solid and simple march."

The flames at the end of his fingers had elongated now, still blue at the tips, but tapering to a bright buttercup yellow where they stretched away from him, a ribbon dancer, following his movements and sliding softly through the air around him.

"Water? Well, the Tower of Water is jazz. All improvisation. Feeling more than thought, instinct and fluid motion, bubbling in and out of sense. But fire?"

He paused in his strange, dance-like gestures, the floating curls of fire ribbons all around him, trailing jellyfish tentacles of light, ever in motion like a floating web of illumination.

Ffoulkes' eyes glowed merrily. "Fire is a symphony!"

He threw his arms upwards, long, billowing sleeves falling back to his elbows. The ribbons of firelight cracked upwards, multiple whips, swelling as they did. Ffoulkes' mana streamed from the ends of his hands like flamethrowers.

The snakes of fire coiled and danced around one another in the air above him, merging, combining and growing bright enough to flood the room like the interior of a volcano. It turned the floor beneath them to a shining mirror. It chased the deep shadows of the fluted walls away, their flickering motion making it seem as though the interior of the necessarium rippled, suddenly alive.

Ffoulkes threw his arms back and forth, casting the ever-growing coils of flame around the air. They flickered and dripped, liquid ropes of bright lava as thick as tree trunks, great striking cobras twining around one another in a roaring dance that seemed made for dragons.

Robin shielded his face from the heat of it, the busy whirlwind of flame soaring in endless loops and knots above them. They were alive. Bright and hungry, hissing through the air and ecstatic in their own movement. Robin had always thought of fire as simply destructive, a destroyer and ruiner of things, but the mana pouring out all around them, the light, the heat, the motion … it was quite the reverse. This fire wasn't just alive, he felt. This fire was life itself.

"Every note, every weaving melody!" Ffoulkes yelled to them over the roar of the flames roiling in the air and twisting along the walls. "The beat and cadence, the rise and fall, the soaring conflagration of the music of fire! And you, Scion, play no instrument. Fire cannot be played, not by Panthea and not by Fae. It is the entirety of the orchestra, and your role is …"

With a flourish of his arms and a complicated gesture, he threw his hands wide.

"To conduct it!"

The great serpentine whorls of living fire crashed against the walls, exploding and showering all below with a rain of bright sparks like falling stars. Ffoulkes dropped his hands, his sleeves smoking slightly, as the fire mana poured into the walls and funnelled upwards, dancing through the spiralling stone and making the walls a blinding kaleidoscope for a few heartbeats.

The fire roared from the open roof, a great cloud of orange yellow sparks and embers erupting into the sky outside ... and was gone.

Blinking in the sudden gloom and quiet, no one spoke.

Robin was a little aghast. Even Woad, famously never lost for words, seemed impressed.

Ffoulkes had beaded sweat on his brow. Such was the demand on a natural performer.

"Of course," Ffoulkes said, getting his breath back as he made his way over to the boys once more, "you are not yet expected to conduct the orchestra when you yourself can barely carry a tune." He patted his sooty hands together briskly. "Best, I feel, to start you off with a simpler task. Think of it like mastering the musical triangle, ahaha."

From within his robes, he fumbled for something and tossed it carelessly to Robin. A fat cylinder bobbing through the air. Robin caught it, looking down in confusion. His face still felt hot from the fire show. He wondered if he still had eyebrows, but his heart was racing.

"A candle?" he asked.

Ffoulkes nodded, patting Robin companionably on the shoulder. "I've never been one for structured learning plans," he said jovially, as Robin stared at the thick church candle he had just been given, a look of bemusement on his face. "This is your first task. Light the candle."

Robin looked up at him. "Light the candle?" he repeated. "What, you mean like, with my mind?"

"With your mana!" Ffoulkes tapped the side of his own nose, waggling his red moustache. "There's a jolly good fellow. You'll find books in the library concerning fire, I imagine. Heaven knows I haven't time to look myself, but I shouldn't be at all surprised if you might find something useful there. When you light it. come back to me, and we'll press on further."

"But I don't know where to begin," Robin stuttered, holding the candle at arm's length in protest. "Aren't you supposed to *teach* me how? Isn't that the point of lessons?"

Ffoulkes was already at the door: clearly the lesson, such as it was, was already at an end. "And how, dearest boy, does one teach another how to listen to music? You have your candle, that is precisely where you begin.

I, on the other hand, am rather parched, and in dashed need of a decent G and T."

Robin was soon to discover that a small stub of candle could become his worst enemy. All day he tried focussing on it, sitting in his room with it perched before him on the table, his head level with its wick as he focussed all his will and mana, urging it to spontaneously combust by sheer bloody determination. Hours later, his only achievement had been to give himself a bad headache and watering eyes.

The following day, he enlisted Henry's assistance to raid the library for books on fire lore, but even with the help and guidance of Wally, Erlking's enchanted, stag-headed suit of armour, reading material was thin and hard to come by. There didn't seem to be any actual books on fire mana, just a few slightly singed scrolls, tightly-rolled waxed paper trussed up in red string and smelling faintly of gunpowder.

"What about this one?" Henry, sitting on a cold and sunny windowsill in the library, unfurled a crackling scroll hopefully. He read aloud: "*A Match made in Heaven. Ten Tricks to Heat Up Your Romance with Fire Magics* ... nah." He tossed into onto the floor, amongst several others which after some time of fruitless searching, were beginning to pile up around them.

Robin shook his head, unrolling a scroll himself. "*A Treatise on the Safe and Efficient Transportation of Magma: The Invention of the Lavabucket.*" He groaned wearily. "These are all useless. This one's all concerned with a legal row over patents." He rolled it back up again, sneaking a resentful sideways glance at his candle stub, perched obstinately on a nearby tabletop. "We've been through everything the library has and there's not a *single thing* telling me how to make fire." He blew out his cheeks and stared down at the floor beneath Henry's swinging feet, and the growing mound of old scrolls there.

"*Spice and Flame for Slow Cooked Chalpie Dishes,*" he rattled off from memory. "*Thick Walls, Light Roofs: An Adventure in Explosive Architecture ...*"

"*My Forbidden Salamander Lover.*" Henry kicked a scroll lightly with the tip of his shoe. "That one sounded quite funny."

"Not useful, though," Robin said. "Why is there so little info on fire mana? I thought water mana books were hard to come by, but at least I understand why. Water doesn't really work on written lore. But clearly, fire does!" He shook the tightly-rolled scroll in his hand. "So why doesn't Erlking have anything remotely useful on it?"

Henry shrugged. "My dad was very cagey about it when I asked him, to be honest," he said. "Apparently there's not a lot of fire magic allowed in the Netherworlde. Some kind of ban outside of the Black Hills. It's like, only used by nobles, the lah-di-dah hob-nobbery. And anyway, all the nobility of that region had a bit of a scandal, someone falling out with someone else. Families at war, that kind of thing. Some bun fight between two kids over an inheritance."

"So, it's like commoners wearing purple then?" Robin wondered aloud. "Not really permitted. It used to only be a royal or wealthy person's colour, right? Like a status symbol. Here in the human world."

"Yeah, I remember hearing about that at school, I think." Henry nodded, not looking very interested. He was inspecting another unfurled and charred scroll. "Of course now, these days, everyone wears it. Purple, I mean. Mainly game show hosts, to be fair."

"But Ffoulkes uses it," Robin said. "Fire, I mean, not purple ... and he's not hob-nobbery is he? I mean," Robin lowered his voice on the very slim chance that his tutor was anywhere within earshot "he makes out that he's well-bred, but ..."

"Yeah, he's more the used car salesman type, I agree," Henry said. "But he doesn't really strike me as one to follow rules or do what other people think he should. Did he say you had to actually use mana to light this candle? I mean, couldn't you just get a match? Maybe it's one of those zen, think-outside-the-box exercises?"

"I doubt it," Robin glumly replied. "I don't think mastering the Tower of Fire starts with mastering a Zippo lighter. I think he just doesn't really want to teach me anything. He's only agreed because he doesn't want Aunt Irene to kick him out of Erlking."

Truth be told, he didn't have a huge amount of faith in Ffoulkes at the best of times, but now not only did he seem to be approaching tutoring quite half-heartedly, but he was also dragging his heels in making sense of the photographs and feather they had recovered from the gallery down in London. Irene had given him the task of deciphering their meaning, and so far all he had said, while theatrically stroking his beard as thoughtfully as possible, was that he would need "to muse on it."

With the library and Henry of little real help, Robin shut the candle away in his bedside drawer, frustrated by the lack of guidance.

It was long after midnight, the darkest and quietest time in a deep crisp night of the type one only seemed to get in January, when help – of a kind – came from the most unexpected quarter.

The moon was trailing long silver fingers on the dark floorboards of Robin's bedroom as he lay on his stomach on the comfortable old bed, a copy of Hammerhand's *Netherworlde Compendium* propped up against the headboard as he sleepily browsed the chapters on Fire Panthea (scant information at best). The old house sighed and creaked around him in the darkness, and the soft glow of his bedside lamp wavered, so that Robin was beginning to nod on the cusp of sleep when he first heard the noise.

Initially, it sounded like a moth trapped somewhere in the room. Without giving it much thought, Robin's mana stone flashed and he cast a brief featherbreath, opening the creaking window across the room to let the lost creature out.

The chill night air poured in, a crisp invisible gust that briefly made his lamp gutter and the waxy pages of his book flutter at the corners.

The soft sound persisted.

After a few moments, shivering slightly, Robin rolled over onto his back and peered up at the high dark ceiling with a small frown at the inconvenience.

The papery fluttering didn't seem to be coming from up there. He couldn't see anything fluttering around in the shadows. He considered turning on the lights, but that would involve getting out of bed and padding across the cold floor to the light switch, which was located, very inconveniently, by the door.

Then he realised that the noise was not coming from the shadows above. It was coming from his side.

Robin sat up, making himself as still as possible, listening, his curiosity now piqued.

The fireplace was dark, a black mouth in deeper shadows. It wasn't coming from there, but from somewhere closer.

As his lamp guttered once more, he realised this was not from the breeze he had let into the room. The nightstand by his bed, atop which the lamp stood, was rattling slightly, making the lamp wobble.

There was something trapped inside the drawer!

Frowning, Robin slid out of bed and knelt on the floor in front of the bedside table. Was there a moth inside? Had it flown in somehow through the tiny keyhole and now was unable to escape? It didn't seem likely. The tiny, ornate keyhole in the dark wood of the drawer, to which Robin had never seen any kind of key, was far too small, and the quiet but urgent battering noises he could hear within sounded too big.

He pressed his eye to the dark hole of the lock, but to no avail. He could see nothing. With curiosity and trepidation, he grabbed the drawer's handle and tugged it open quickly. Robin half expected something to fly out; some outlandish night butterfly perhaps, or one of the monstrous but bejewelled dragonflies that skimmed the surface of Erlking's lakes in summer.

What he found was something quite different. The drawer was cluttered, as are all drawers used by teenage boys. The shiny moral compass he had been given for Christmas glimmered in its depths, nestled amongst graphic novels and manga, a half-eaten bag of Haribo sweets and a small notebook that he had been filling for months with cantrip notes. Atop all of this, a single piece of yellowed and waxy vellum, neatly folded once, was fluttering as though caught in a high wind.

"Hex message?" Robin whispered aloud to himself, lifting it gently out of the darkness. The paper flitered between his fingertips, a panicked bird beating its wings against the palm of his hand.

The last time the Erlkingers had explored the Netherworlde, they had each possessed a scrap of enchanted paper, on which they could send messages back and forth. A useful tool, as mobile phones worked only erratically within the Hall. Robin had lost his sheet back at the Hive. He had used it to send one final message back to Aunt Irene as Eris' great prison had crumbled around them. That message had called for aid.

Henry had since cut his own sheet in two, giving Robin half so that he could still be in the group chats that flittered between them all; these were usually late at night and often nonsensical. Robin hadn't used it in a while, though.

Sitting cross-legged on the bare boards of the room and leaning back against his bed, Robin now unfolded the fluttering paper, fully expecting to see written there some late night joke from Henry, a rude poem Woad may have sent everyone during a bout of creative insomnia, or perhaps a complaint from Karya about being mollycoddled by Hestia.

But he didn't recognise the handwriting.

It read simply: *Can you help me? I can help you.*

As Robin peered in confusion, the paper stopped flapping and the words, finally read, faded away. The ink sank invisibly into the paper until the sheet was clear.

He had no idea who the message was from, or how long it had sat in the drawer, waiting to be read, its contents growing ever more urgent until that urgency had led the parchment to flutter its way to Robin's attention.

He scrabbled around on top of the bedside table until his fingers found a biro and, after a moment's hesitation and with the cold air from the open window raising the hairs on the back of his neck, he wrote:

Who is this?

He watched his words disappear almost immediately. Well, whoever had written to him had clearly read his reply immediately. He waited. After a few maddening, seemingly endless moments, a reply appeared.

A friend. And underneath:

Someone stuck where you want to be.

Robin considered this. All of his friends were here, at Erlking. Almost everyone who knew him was here, come to think of it. Unless the message was from the Fae, Hawthorn, or Princess Ashe of the Dryads, or – even less likely – Flumenesqua the Undine.

Where do I want to be? Where are you?

There was a longer pause this time. The cool breeze rattled the open window in its frame. Somewhere, deep outside in Erlking's woods, an owl hooted, sounding lost and alone and very far off.

The word, when the reply bled into being on the parchment, was all in capitals:

DIS.

Robin sat up straighter, his eyes wide. The word was already fading as he stared at it, as though it had risen from a murky depth and was now receding. A shiver ran unbidden through him that had nothing to do with the chilly air.

Robin scrawled urgently: *I don't have friends in Dis.* If this was some kind of prank, it was a poor one. Receiving a message from inside Lady Eris' capital city was too surreal, and far too unlikely, to be funny.

I never said I was your friend. The letters were scratchily formed, as though the writer was scribbling quickly, was impatient. *Stop questioning and listen.*

The words faded, but before Robin could raise his pen to reply, more formed.

Little time to talk. Not alone here. Ever. Know what you're looking for, Scion. Even if you don't yet.

Robin swallowed. How did this mysterious stranger know that he and the others were secretly thinking of ways to get inside Dis? How *could* they know? He wrote as much.

Wrong question. came the response. *Wasting time. You want a way into the city. I have one.*

Could this mysterious messenger really be offering Robin a way to get inside Dis? If so, they could find out more about Karya. Maybe fix whatever was – increasingly – wrong with her.

And what do you want? Robin was suspicious.

A way out. The sentence was short and blunt. The letters, when they formed on the page, seemed deeply imprinted, as though whoever wrote to him was leaning heavily on their own sheet of paper. *Trapped. You're the Scion. I show you how to get in, when to get in. You get me out.*

When? Robin did not really understand.

The reply came almost immediately. *Pyrenight.*

The table lamp flickered oddly, making shadows and light jitter like flames across the yellowed sheet.

Lots of crowds. Plenty of distractions, his unnamed correspondent told him. *Even so, still only one way in for your kind that isn't chains, and that's the serpent.*

Robin hadn't believed he could be more confused than he already was, but he was now barely following the conversation. The words faded away as he read them.

Explain yourself properly, he wrote back in frustration. *Are you a Fae? Are you held captive? How are you messaging me this way?*

No time! The response was written with such swift fury that Robin could almost hear the scratching across the parchment as the letters formed hastily. *Not much left to write with. Hurry. I get you in. You get me out. Me and my kin. Deal?*

Robin considered. There was no time to consult with the others. By the time he had made his way to anyone else's room, whoever was anonymously offering him a way into Dis might take his lack of response as disinterest. Might disappear forever. He had to respond to the ultimatum now.

Deal, he wrote. He lifted his pen to write more, but the response came quickly, appearing even as his own words were still in the process of fading.

Good. And hurry. Seek out Luna at the agora. She can set you on the path to the serpent. Have to go. They're coming.

Robin read this urgently as a further message appeared below: *Will contact you again. Do NOT contact me. If they find this on me, it will be the end.*

There was nothing more.

The page remained blank. Robin waited a couple of minutes, silent in the dim lamplight, desperate to respond but afraid to. If this was indeed a message from someone trapped within the city of Dis, then surely they had put themselves in terrible jeopardy just by attempting to contact Eris' most sworn enemy. They must be desperate indeed to risk such a thing right under the empress' nose. If Robin were to respond and the message was seen by the wrong eyes ...

He eventually folded the paper and rested it back on his nightstand, mulling over the unusual conversation. What on earth was Pyrenight? And that nonsense about a serpent and an agora?

Not much left to write with, his correspondent had said. That was why they had kept things brief. That, and clearly a fear of being watched or discovered with the scrap of hex message paper.

The words that had formed on the page each time had been dark and blotted, like those created with a fountain pen. Most unlike Robin's biro-scrawled replies. In all of the anonymous author's replies, the ink had been rusty and brownish. Robin swallowed.

Whomever he had just been talking to, this friend who was not his friend, he suspected they had been writing in the only medium available to them. Blood.

4

The Darkest Day

"What even *is* Pyrenight?" Henry asked. He was squinting at Robin with his hand shielding his eyes, largely due to the bright winter sun glittering and refracting as it bounced from the surface of the lake up into his face. Clouds covered much of the sky, but they were shredded like torn wool, and the sun slashed through them, falling in straight beams which glanced off the water.

It was the following morning, the day of Erlking's predicted eclipse, and they were all gathered on the snowy banks of the water for Robin's next lesson in the Tower of Fire. He had, of course, told the others all about the strange hex messages, first thing over breakfast, as soon as the adults were out of earshot.

"More importantly," Woad said, sitting on the snowy bank and splashing his bare feet in the water, "when did we start trusting people who send messages written in blood in the middle of the night?" The frigid water didn't seem to bother the faun as he wiggled his blue toes. "I mean, even by the bravest faun standards … that's a tiny bit of a red flag, right there."

Karya, standing beside Robin and Henry, pulled her thick coat of animal skins more tightly around herself, looking tired as they watched the faun splash. The girl still appeared not to have slept for days, when in truth she'd been doing little else.

"Good point," she agreed. "Just because this withheld number claims to be able to help us get inside Dis and find out why exactly I'm running on fumes, doesn't mean they're telling the truth." She sighed. "Or at least, not the *whole* truth." She looked at Henry. "Pyrenight is a celebration night," she explained. 'In the Netherworlde. Kind of a feast day, I suppose." The chilly wind ruffled her furry coat. "Large fires, fireworks, lots of games and distractions and feasting. Speeches and parades."

"Sort of like Bonfire Night, then?" Henry clapped his hands together, rubbing them briskly in the cold. "Or the Fourth of July over in America? Sounds fun!"

"Hardly," Jackalope muttered, standing a little behind the three, hands thrust into his pockets as he peered out across the icy surface of Erlking's lake. "Eris marks her victory over the Netherworlde with Pyrenight. It's a celebration of when her rebellion 'liberated' the world from their oppressive and cruel Fae overlords. It's a day that marks the death of the king and queen and the enslavement and genocide of our race."

Henry looked a little abashed. "Ah," he said, a little awkwardly.

"We don't *know* that they're dead," Robin pointed out, sounding much less hopeful than he'd intended. Jackalope gave him a sneer. Robin couldn't really blame him. If the king and queen really were out there somewhere, where did they go, and why? Why just disappear? And why didn't they return to stop Eris?

"Traditionally on Pyrenight, there's a large festival within the city of Dis," Karya told them, looking between each of them seriously. "The bonfires, which line the streets or squares, are largely symbolic now, but they represent the original pyres on which the Fae criminals were burned."

"Like witches at the stake," Woad said, nodding. "Except of course you can't burn a real witch. They're far too clever to burn, and usually quite damp too. You *can* burn innocent prisoners of war, though. Sets an example for the others ... if you're a heartless, evil megalomaniac, that is."

Robin was horrified. Lady Eris ruled the Netherworlde with fear. Marking the anniversary of mass immolation of your enemies with feasting and fireworks sounded barbaric. "But it's possible to get inside the city?" he asked, hope in his voice. "Into Dis from the outside, during this festival?"

Karya shook her head. "Not remotely, not for us," she said, blunt as ever. "That's why I think this midnight scribbler of yours is writing nonsense. The gates of the city do open, yes, but they're still heavily guarded, and those from outside Dis are only allowed in for Pyrenight if they hold an invitation. Those people are scrutinised beyond belief."

"Invitations to the actual celebrations are something only the very, very elite and highest classes of Panthea who don't already live in Dis will have," Jackalope agreed. "And even then, only those who have proven themselves unshakably loyal to Eris. I suppose the only benefit of Pyrenight is that the city is in festival, so one could blend into the crowds more easily than usual. But there's still no getting inside."

Robin was staring out across the frozen lake, deep in thought. The far shore was lined with skeletal trees, their dark branches reflected upside down along the shining grey surface like thin fingers reaching down into the depths. In his hands he rolled his still-unlit candle stub from palm to palm, back and forth. It had been days now and he still hadn't made any progress with it. The bright sun was beginning to dim a little. He glanced up at the sky, but the eclipse hadn't started yet.

"Maybe the other entrances to the city will be less well guarded that night?" he mused. It was possible, surely, with all eyes on the main gates?

"There *are* no other ways into the city," Karya told him. "Dis has but one door."

"But *you* got out," Henry argued. "You came from Dis. How did *you* get out of the city? You didn't stroll out of the main gates in a pair of nose-glasses and a fake moustache, did you?"

"I stole the flute that Eris used to tie me to her, remember?" Karya replied, sounding wistful. "It freed me to travel and I was able to tear between the worlds. I flipped to the human world, where there was no Dis, just a great, human city. And I ran." She looked a little distant. "My memories from that time are fractured. From before then, even more so. I remember that I flipped back and forth as I fled, but Strife and the others were tracking me all the time."

She looked down at her hands. "There's no way I can tear between the worlds right now," she said. "Not in this state. I could probably tear us across the moors over there, but that might finish me off, to be honest. Who knows?" She shrugged. "But certainly I could not get to the Netherworlde – or back."

Robin was watching Ffoulkes, who was paddling some distance from the shoreline in a small boat, oars flailing ungainly, preparing who-knows-what spectacle for his second lesson.

"What about this serpent thing?" he asked, remembering the oblique reference in the hex message.

No one knew what that referred to. "Plenty of strange snake symbolism in that book at the gallery," Jackalope recalled; but in truth, neither boy had any clue as to its meaning, and the only thing linking the diary to their current need to infiltrate the capital was the mention of a serpent.

"Gran used to say 'snakes and ashes' instead of swearing, when something upset her," Robin mused. "She said a lot of weird things, but now I wonder if it's a saying that comes more from the Netherworlde than this one? Not that that helps us much."

"Your tutor, who is waving frantically for your attention out there on the lake, may know more about Pyrenight than us, Scion." Karya gestured out onto the water.

Ffoulkes was standing up in the small boat, making it rock perilously on the shimmering winter water, waving an oar wildly above his head in an attempt to catch Robin's eye.

"Master Robin!" Ffoulkes' voice echoed across the lake. "A practical experiment today, if you will." His voice was bouncing back and forth across the water's edge. "Would I be correct to assume that you have not yet mastered the lighting of your candle? The cantrip known as Ignimbrite? Are we to take it that, as yet you remain … ahahah … unenlightened?"

Robin waved the hateful candle stub across his head in response, deciding that doing that with his hands was preferable to making a rude gesture.

"They say that necessity is the spark that lights the tinder," Ffoulkes called out. "And so today I aim to fan the flames of your fiery ambition, by introducing a little *urgency* into your learning." He was grinning like a stage magician, playing to the crowd before performing a trick. The next words out of his mouth did nothing to dissuade this impression.

"I shall require an assistant, if one of your associates would be so kind?"

Everyone on the shore exchanged looks. Karya sighed and made to step forward in a resigned manner, but Jackalope shot out and caught her by the wrist.

"Whatever the Panthea has planned, you're not strong enough to go swimming," he reminded her. "In your state, you'd sink like a rock."

Karya glanced down at his hand encircling her arm, frowning a little, but she didn't shake him off.

"I'll go!" Woad said, jumping to his feet and splashing out into the frigid lake, waist deep before anyone could raise a word to stop him.

"Good show, that faun," Ffoulkes said, applauding. "Jolly good. Now, if you could make your merry way over here to the boat, that would be capital! That's the way. Swim, boy! I would say the water is chill enough to turn your skin blue, but …" He shrugged. "I guess that's quite redundant in this case."

"I don't like the look of this, Scion," Karya said, a frown of suspicion on her forehead as they watched Woad splashing his way out across the lake towards the boat. "Ffoulkes is unreliable at best. What nonsense is he plotting?"

"I don't like the look of *any* of this," Henry agreed, pointedly noticing that the girl and Jackalope were still joined, seemingly quite comfortably, at the wrist.

They watched in a mixture of worry and admiration as Woad splashed his way swiftly and with messy exuberance out across the icy lake's surface, towards Ffoulkes and his distant boat. The lake was not glittering now – the light seemed muted and strangely expectant, like a breath withheld.

"I'm sure he's got no nerve endings, that one," Henry frowned, chattering his teeth. "Just watching him is making me feel cold. This water would kill a human in ten minutes flat."

He tucked his chin into his scarf. "It's weird enough that batty old Ffoulkes has scheduled a lesson today, during an eclipse he's arranged just for us. Icy lake swimming in January is just adding silly to strange."

"Ffoulkes didn't arrange an eclipse," Karya explained. "There's simply one due."

"Yeah, Robin said so too, but I checked on the news before breakfast," Henry said. "There's nothing about any eclipse, not anywhere in the northern hemisphere, anyway. I'm sure it would have been in the newspaper or something. How is it only happening here at Erlking?"

Robin had been equally confused, when Ffoulkes had first informed him about Erlking's skies being as tied to places other than the building itself. Knowing a lesson was due today, he had questioned Aunt Irene about this at breakfast, and now explained to Henry what she had explained to him.

"Erlking exists in both worlds, Henry," Robin said, not entirely sure he fully grasped the notion himself, but trying to sound authoritative at least. "The human world and the Netherworlde. That's why there are some Netherworlde plants in the forests around here, and why the house sometimes has wind blowing through it when there's no breeze outside." He glanced up at the wintry sky, which was still covered in shredded clouds, and, at least for the time being, daylight of a strange and unreal type. "It's kind of like an iceberg. Some in the water, some above it, and like anything as big as an iceberg, it makes waves."

"Those waves cause spills," Karya said and nodded in agreement. "Ripples from one world to the other, back and forth. There might not be any eclipse in the human world, but there is one in the Netherworlde. It will reflect in the skies over Erlking, though none other in the human realm will see it." She shrugged. "Of course, we all know from experience that we can flip from one world to the next and find that the day we have left is deepest night over there, or that the summer warmth in the human world is winter's chill in the other. Seasons and days don't exactly line up. So, there's a fair chance that the eclipse we will see today already happened days ago as far as the Netherworlde is concerned. Or maybe it won't for a few more."

Henry was staring at her blankly.

"But we shouldn't get into that," she smirked. "I don't want your head to explode."

Woad had reached the boat and Ffoulkes hauled him up into it, giving him a damp congratulatory pat on the back and happily muttering something which none of them on the shore could hear.

"The reason you have not yet managed to light your candle, Master Robin," Ffoulkes called out, steadying his footing on the side of the tiny craft. "Is because you have not yet felt that you *have* to."

Robin frowned down at his candle stub in confusion.

"Fire is a symphony, as I told you before," his tutor continued, his voice echoing back and forth from the banks and trees. "And yet, you have been paralysed looking in earnest for sheet music. Turning your brain over and over to try to find a melody written down somewhere that you might copy. But this is not a history class. It will not do to bundle up your arms with piles of books and then to copy out the words of others." Foulkes shook his head. "Attempting to sing the tune of another is always a hollow and reedy noise, you see. Fire crackles and flows and consumes. It never makes the same music twice. You must find your *own* song, deep within yourself, and let's face it, you have … ahahah … barely begun to figure out how to hum."

Robin thought this all sounded suspiciously new age, and that any minute now, he would be asked to paint with all the colours of the wind.

"Sometimes, we need a little jogging elbow," Ffoulkes said. "A gentle push to loosen the lungs ... and peril can be a fine and efficient tuning fork."

"Peryl?" Karya narrowed her eyes.

"I think he means *danger*," Jackalope glanced at her, squeezing her hand a little. "Not the maniac Grimm who almost killed you."

"I'm concerned about where this is headed," Robin said quietly. His mana stone had begun to thrum slightly. There seemed to be a thin haze above the small boat containing Woad and Ffoulkes. He hadn't noticed it before. It was like a small moving cloud. It looked like midges. Tiny water flies.

"Are we all familiar with pyreflies?" Ffoulkes called.

Everyone was, of course. Tiny fireflies that glowed golden in great shimmering clouds and which tended to show up after scenes of deadly violence or at battlefields, hence their name. Robin and the others had seen many of these Netherworlde insects in the high branches of the giant tree in the valley of the Undine, back when they were on the trail of the drowned tomb.

"Pyreflies are not simply drawn to places of horror and death, as many believe," Ffoulkes' voice carried across from the boat. "These tiny fire-critters get a terrible reputation for that, but it's only a partial truth. To be more accurate, they are drawn to any place of high emotion. You are as likely to see a cloud of pyreflies at a wedding as you are at a grave. They are as sure a signifier of romance and love as they are of murder and death."

He pointed one hand dramatically to the sky, his frilled cuffs ruffling.

"However!" Ffoulkes yelled with a great degree of drama. "What many also do not know is that, much as bees are benevolent unless you kick their hive, pyreflies are not aggressive unless disturbed. Once angered, however, they will swarm and harass, sting and bite relentlessly. Only drawn away from the subject of their torment by a more tempting distraction. By a brighter light."

He glanced up at the cloudy sky. It had begun to darken significantly. Although it was mid-morning, the unseen birds in the trees all along the lake shore had begun to raise a chorus, twittering and flapping loudly, their calls echoing across the water in their confusion at this unexpected twilight.

"There's a break in the clouds," Henry said. All of them were looking upwards now, as the winter sky deepened and cooled. Through scattered trails of cloud, the sun, a watery coin as pale as shining milk, had emerged. It was already partly covered with shadow. It looked as though someone had taken a bite out of it, turning it into a witch-like waning moon of fiery daylight.

"Is that our world's sun or the Netherworlde's sun we're looking at?" Robin asked. In the eerie and surreal fading light, he had lowered his voice, though he couldn't say why. Other than the birds, the whole world seemed to be hushing itself. The air was growing cooler still.

"There's only one sun, Scion," Karya said, her voice also quiet. "You still misunderstand the Netherworlde. We call it another place, but two opposing faces are still part of the same coin after all, they just never see each other." She shielded her eyes with her hands. "Although they used to ... once ... I think. It's one of the old memories I have. We used to be closer, tighter knit, the two worlds. Now it's all more like a frayed jumper, kind of ... unravelled."

"You shouldn't look directly at an eclipse," Jackalope told the others. "Mesmerising as they are. You can damage your eyes if you do. Look at it in the lake."

Robin saw that the ever-diminishing disc of the sun was indeed reflected in the surface of the water, wobbling and shimmering like a mirage, as the sky and lake both dimmed and darkened further. It had grown cooler still and the birds were quieting down, fooled into thinking it was nightfall.

"Darkness falls, Master Robin!" Ffoulkes' voice carried across from the little boat, filled with portent. "Will you light up the night and rescue your friend?"

Robin, slightly mesmerised by the shimmering and disappearing glow of the sun, broken and dancing on the water, glanced up in confusion. "Wait, what? Rescue?"

Even from this distance, he could see that Ffoulkes was grinning. The happy smirk of one about to pull a practical joke or perform a show-stopping trick. His tutor reached up a hand into the misty swarm hanging above his head and from his palm there issued a flash and a bang, bright as a firework. It echoed around the lake like a gunshot.

The cloud over the distant boat burst immediately into a thousand pinpricks of bright red light. Robin had only ever seen them glow a soft gold before, but this swarm was startled by Ffoulkes' cantrip, as angry as a kicked hornet's nest. They descended on the boat in a glowing and glittering whirlwind, fierce and furious. Bright against the unnatural twilight.

From the shore, they heard Woad yelp in alarm and moments later, the skinny blue boy was flailing his arms around, trying to bat away the swirl of angry pinpoints. The insects ignored Ffoulkes completely, focussing all of their wrath on the hapless faun.

"Is he mad?" Jackalope barked.

"Woad!" Robin yelled, alarmed by the sight of his friend besieged by the angry crush of lights.

"The sun hollows, Master Robin!" Ffoulkes called merrily from somewhere within the seething insects. They could no longer see either of the figures on the boat clearly, lost in a swirl of bright embers. "No larger light in the sky to draw off *these* attackers. No sir. It is down to you and only you."

"Stop them!" Robin shouted, the others staring out at the boat in helpless horror. "Call them off! Are you insane? He's going to …"

There was a loud splash as Woad, still flailing around in a futile attempt to defend himself, stumbled and toppled off the boat completely, sending up a huge plume of foam as he fell into the dark lake.

"*You* stop them, Scion of the Arcania," his tutor instructed. "You, not I." He made no move to help Woad back onto the boat. Indeed, as the faun surfaced, spluttering and choking cold water, the angry swarm left the boat to follow and harass him, their countless angry forms reflecting in the water like a scarlet constellation. Ffoulkes sat down, utterly ignoring the faun's distress and that of his friends, and began rowing away, quite determined to leave Woad to his fate.

"You can't just leave him!" Karya was outraged.

"Why, of course I can," Ffoulkes replied as his boat dwindled into the darkness. "Robin cannot, that would never do. But this is *his* lesson, not mine. Bring the faun back up to the Hall when you are done here. I shall see you all later."

Robin couldn't believe it. He stared aghast. Woad really was being abandoned to the mercy of the angry pyreflies. The cloud of insects, glowing and swooping, would not let up. Every time Woad came up for air, they dive-bombed him, buzzing furiously and driving him back underwater. He could barely break the surface long enough to draw breath. Ffoulkes had always been unreliable, but this was irresponsible, even for him. The light had fallen quickly and shadows had deepened everywhere, pooling like ink and spreading across the sky.

He heard a series of splashes at his side, and Robin, startled out of his frozen shock saw that Henry had run into the lake, kicking up huge waves in the darkness as he waded out, the icy water already deep at his waist.

"Henry, no!" Karya called. "The water's dark and freezing! You'll sink in those clothes. You're only a human, not a faun!"

"We can't just leave him!" Henry shouted back. "He's in trouble! Real trouble." He sounded breathless. The chill of the water had shocked all the air out of his lungs. "He's going to drown out there if those stupid things don't leave him alone!"

"So will *you*!" Karya argued. She stared at Robin, her face almost lost in the gloom as the eclipse now progressed to full darkness. "We need to do something!"

Robin didn't know what to do. He couldn't make out Woad at all, now. It had become so dark. He could only tell where the faun was from the distant glow of the pyreflies, an angry nebula shimmering furiously in the distance.

He stared down at the candle stub clenched hard in his hand. This was the lesson. He had to light it. To draw them away. But how?

Jackalope dropped Karya's hand and ran into the lake too, though she made an angry grab to stop him and missed in the darkness. Unlike Henry, who was forging his way into the ever deeper water, walking with chattering teeth and angrily sweeping his arms in front of him, the Fae dived head first, disappearing underwater entirely like a silver fish.

"Jack!" Karya snapped. "For the sake of the fates! These two!"

Robin held the useless candle in front of him at arm's length, pointing it towards the spot in the cold darkness where he could still hear Woad struggling. The faun was not yelling any longer. They could hear him splashing frantically, but Robin doubted he had time to shout, only coming up for gasps of air before the furious, scarlet pyreflies pushed him back into the icy depths.

He squeezed his eyes shut and focussed on his mana stone, willing all of his energy into it, trying to direct and force his mana down his arm and into the candle. He could hear his own heart beating fast in panic. He'd tried this countless times since Ffoulkes had given him the stub of wax. It didn't work. He knew it didn't work. But what else was he expected to do?

Jack surfaced, a pale shape some distance from the shore, barely visible in the freezing darkness, with Henry close behind, both boys plummeting into the darkness to save their friend. They would reach the swarm, Robin thought, and then what? They would be attacked too. Any second now there would be three bodies struggling with the fire in the darkness, not one.

"I don't know *how* to light this!" he yelled as loudly as he could, calling out to his tutor in the darkness. "I can't! I've tried! I'm trying now! This isn't working! Come back!"

But there was no response from the darkness. The boat had disappeared into the shadows. Ffoulkes truly had gone. Leaving them all to their own fates.

Karya called out after Henry and Jackalope, but neither of them heeded her. It was almost full night and freezing. The clouds above ripped and skittered in the sky, and the sun was nothing but the thinnest sliver of silver-white, a cruel nail hanging in the black sky.

Robin ran into the water until it reached his knees. The cold shocked him, seeping instantly through his jeans and making them heavy and dragging around his legs. He thrust the candle out again like a useless talisman. "Light! Light, damn you, come on!" he said through gritted teeth.

Now would be a really good time to Puck out, he thought frantically. The Puck would know what to do. Where was he when you needed him?

The candle refused to light. He gripped his mana stone with his free hand, holding it tightly in his fist as though he could shake it awake.

Karya was suddenly at his side, a splashing flurry of animal skins as she forged into the darkness. She dropped to a crouch in the water, thrusting her arms deep below the surface, searching for the ground at the shoreline.

"What are you doing?" he stared, teeth chattering.

"I can raise the bed," she grunted, scowling in concentration. "Not all of it, but I can shift the sand, send them all back towards us in a ripple, Woad included."

"You can't tilt the lake bed!" Robin argued, incredulous. "Even at full strength that would be impossible. Making a wave by shaking the earth to bob them all to safety? Your mana isn't …"

"I *can* do it!" she snapped, spitting out water as her hands splashed around. "I can do it because I *have* to do it."

She closed her eyes tightly, arms in the water up to her shoulders and her hair falling over her face into the lake. She had buried her hands in the soft silty sand beneath the black surface, twisting them through the earth. Robin glanced up, trying to make out what was happening on the water, but against the red swarm of pyreflies, darting to and fro close to the surface, he could see only shadows, hear only frantic splashing, and someone shouting in alarm. Whether it was Henry or Jackalope, he couldn't tell.

A shudder ran through the ground, making the water jump and leap beneath his feet. It was like a silent earthquake making Robin struggle for balance. Karya made a pained noise, and he dropped beside her, heedless now of the icy touch of the water. Her face was furious with concentration, her teeth grinding with determination, and from somewhere below the agitated surface, Robin saw a muted flash. A brief, bright amber glow beneath the water. He knew it was Karya's mana stone. The tiger's eye bracelet she wore. It had been dead and dark ever since her injury at the Hive, but now, through sheer bloody mindedness, she was forcing a cantrip – one strong enough to tear her muscles and causing her to emit a low growling scream.

The shock wave came again, larger this time, and the whole surface of the lake seemed to jitter and shimmer as the lake-bed itself bucked like a living thing, arching its back in the darkness.

There was a great rushing noise, and from out of the gloom of the eclipse, a wave barrelled towards the two of them, a furious wall of foam, silver against the blackness, carrying three tumbling forms, tossed like flotsam.

"Karya!" Robin grabbed her by the shoulders, attempting to brace them both, but the wave broke over them, huge and powerful. It dragged him off his feet, casting them backwards up the pebbly shore and right to the grassy edge of Erlking's lawn.

Robin struggled under the water, a confusion of bubbles and noise as he was carried along, still gripping Karya tightly by her soaked animal skin coat as though his life depended on it. It tumbled them head over heels, spitting them onto the ground. When the wave receded, they sat up, spluttering and drenched, coughing up water.

Robin stared around, dizzy and disoriented. He could hear the wave still receding, a rumbling roar, as the lake slopped and wobbled, settling back into place.

Henry was back on the shore, he saw, on his hands and knees and retching up water. Woad was beside him, lying flat on his back in the sand, face up to the eclipse in the sky and motionless. A small, washed-up doll. Robin saw Jackalope, his hair flat to his head, stumbling out of the sudden surf, twice almost losing his footing as he hurried, dazed, towards the faun.

"You did it," Robin gasped breathlessly to Karya, pushing his wet hair back from his forehead. "You brought them to shore!"

Karya had scrambled to her feet, and she grabbed Robin's shoulder for balance. He had never seen her look so pale. Her wild hair was slicked back from her forehead in tangled ropes, and her eyes were barely focussed. "Not … just them …" she panted, staring out at the water, which was still receding into the darkness. Robin followed her gaze. The pyreflies. The large swarm of fury was zooming closer towards them, roaring out of the darkness. Determined still, it seemed, to descend on their target. They would be on the others in seconds. Jack, Henry, Woad. A cloud of stinging violence – and now they had no water's surface to protect them from their stinging fury.

Robin scrambled about in the sand near his feet, searching desperately. The candle stub had been knocked out of his hands when the wave had come. He saw it in the gloom, half buried in the sand, and lunged for it, barely thinking.

There was no time to worry, there was no time to consider that if he had been unable to light it before, that it was even less likely to light it now that it was soaked through. Karya's words made perfect sense. He had been thinking too hard, from too many angles. Trying to approach the exercise as he would a maths equation. Looking for answers in books and lore, other people's answers. As Ffoulkes would have put it, singing other people's songs. With sand caking his hands, Robin gripped the candle stub in freezing, numb fingers, and held it aloft like a beacon. *I can do it, because I have to do it*, as Karya had said.

Robin stared furiously at the cloud of approaching pyreflies. His fear and worry for his friends, his anger at Ffoulkes, his frustration at his own failures so far, they were each discordant notes, jarring one another.

Concentrating, he threaded them together, making his own, unique melody. Telling himself to light up the night. And believing with every ounce of his being that he would. Because he had to.

Mana shot from his core down his arm like magma, red hot and swift. It did not light the candle stub. The blast of sudden heat utterly demolished it. The wax evaporating into the air almost instantaneously with a *whoosh*. The tiny wick floated for a moment, a black thread above his outstretched hand, and then with a flicker, a column of fire shot upwards, bright as lightning. It roared from his palm up into the false night as surely as if he were holding a flamethrower, lighting him in a circle of brilliance, making the sand at his feet glitter and glow. Karya shielded her eyes, knocked off balance by the blast of heat and in the bright illumination, Robin saw Jack and Henry, both boys crouched over Woad. Both boys turned to look, their faces lit up by the blast, and the swarm of pyreflies, which were seconds away from descending on them, swerved and made for Robin instead, drawn helplessly like moths to a flame.

Robin stared, determined, at the column of pure white flame pouring from his hand up into the sky above. It was spinning and whirling like a tornado, slim and swift, flickering spirals of white and yellow, the heat singeing his eyebrows. It roared into the night, guzzling the oxygen around him. To Robin, it felt as though the fire began not in his palm, but somewhere deep inside. He could feel it rushing through his arm like roaring blood, escaping through his fingertips to manifest in the air where it screamed and sang.

It was fierce, and to Robin's surprise, it was utterly joyous.

The pyreflies swarmed around him now, dancing and encircling the column of fire he held aloft, countless living sparks around a bonfire. They swooped in and out of the flames, dancing themselves, like a murmuration of starlings in miniature, hypnotised and controlled by the fire. As they did so, they slowed – little by little – and their furious red glow faded. Moments passed, with Robin lost in a cloud of swirling motion, and soon every last one of the countless tiny airborne bodies was a soft and peaceful gold.

Feeling his mana spent, the fury and joy that had coursed through his body suddenly depleted like adrenaline, Robin shakily dropped his arm. The column of flame disappeared instantly, bringing darkness and quiet down upon them all once more. The pyreflies remained, but they were calm now, casting the lake shore in a soft and ever-moving galaxy of light.

Karya had begun to stumble along the bank, tottering and looking close to collapse after her efforts. Robin followed, light-headed and woozy. The clouds above had parted once more, and the eclipse was at totality, the sun a perfect black disc, crowned with a blazing corona of fire. Beneath this dramatic sky, on the shadowy and frosted lake shore of Erlking, Henry was yelling, and Jackalope was kneeling over Woad, his hands laced and pumping on the faun's chest.

"Woad!" Robin cried hoarsely in panic, blearily realising what he saw. Jackalope was performing CPR. Henry was on his knees next to them, running his fingers through his hair, looking drenched and distraught. The grey-haired Fae lowered his ear to the faun's mouth. He listened, panting a second, then shook his head, his expression grim. He resumed pumping at the blue boy's chest.

"No, no, no …" Robin heard Karya chanting quietly under her breath as they reached the others.

"He's not breathing!" Henry said shakily. "He's just … he was under the water out there when we got to him … and he's not breathing …"

Karya dropped down in the sand beside Woad, her hands shaking with fear or exhaustion or both. "Move!" she snapped. "Let me …"

"Wait!" Jackalope cut her off, refusing to be pushed aside. He was still pumping air, his eyes flashing. Robin had never seen him look so angry. "Just … wait!"

"But …"

"Karya, let him," Henry said, staring wide-eyed down at the unconscious faun.

"He's not leaving," Jackalope grunted, determined. "Wake up! Come on, you little bulletproof smurf! No …" he pushed his laced hands down again rhythmically, "sneaking … away!"

Woad suddenly coughed and spluttered, making everyone jump back. His eyes fluttered open, dazed and unfocussed. Jackalope rolled him onto his side, as the faun vomited water nosily onto the pebbles.

It was the best noise Robin had ever heard. He let out a shuddering breath himself, relief flooding through him like an electric shock.

"Woad!" Karya helped the faun sit up, wrapping her arms around him. "You stupid bloody idiot!"

Woad shook himself like a dog, then sat glaring around at them all, still confused. The pyreflies had followed Robin and Karya, and now they surrounded the circle of children in the wet dark sand, countless tiny lights drifting between them silently and calmly, pinpoints of gold lighting their faces.

"Pinky ..." Woad coughed a little more, blinking up at Robin with something close to triumph. "Did you do it? Did you light the candle?"

Robin stared at him, gobsmacked. "As if that's even remotely important right now!" he gasped. "Woad, you scared us all to death! Just now, I thought ... we thought ..."

Jackalope was almost knocked completely to the floor as Henry gave him a hearty slap on the back, grappling him in an exhausted and awkward hug. Both soaked boys tumbled to the ground, with wet sand caking their hair.

"What are you doing?" the Fae gargled, sounding panicked. "Get off me!"

"You saved Woad!" Henry grinned. "You really *are* an Erlkinger, after all!" He released the sodden Fae, punching him lightly in the arm. It was the first time any of them had ever seen Henry show anything other than scorn to Jackalope.

"You're okay, you are!" Henry proclaimed, shaking sand out of his hair, with the air of one bestowing the highest honour possible. "You're one of us. No point pretending you're not, anymore."

Jackalope scowled as always, but also looked slightly embarrassed. "Shut up," he muttered. "You must have water on your brain." His teeth were chattering.

As Henry scrambled to help steady Woad, Jackalope looked at Robin. "You didn't light your candle, you *incinerated* it," he observed. "Impressive, Scion."

He glanced over at Karya, looking genuinely concerned. "And you, what did you do to the lake? It was like a tsunami. How did you ..."

"I did what I had to," Karya said dismissively, still kneeling in the sand. "We all did." Her voice sounded wobbly and weak. She was looking at Jackalope with clear admiration.

Robin reached down and grabbed Woad's outstretched hand as he and Henry helped him up. The three of them staggered a little, Woad looking up at the sky.

"Wow," the faun breathed, wiping his mouth with the back of his hand, still wobbly on his feet. "Look at the sun. It's gone."

Henry and Robin, still both shivering at either side of Woad, followed his gaze upwards. The sun was a black disc, a wild negative of itself with a blazing corona, magnificent and unreal, an encircling crown of fire.

"What happened to your hair?" Robin heard Jackalope ask Karya behind them. His voice was soft and full of quiet concern. He had never heard Jackalope speak so gently to anyone. There was worry in his voice. "You have a white streak now. You should not have pushed your mana. It was foolish of you."

"You brought Woad back to us," he heard her reply. "Back to me."

"The pyreflies have gone, too," Henry noticed in confusion. And he was right, the cloud of glowing insects had abandoned Robin, leaving the Scion, Henry and Woad in darkness.

The three turned around, searching for the golden swarm, and Robin stopped dead in his tracks. Henry let out an involuntary yelp, which he managed to stifle.

Woad turned as well, rubbing his eyes as he shook off the last of his disorientation. "What are you both ... oh!" His hands whipped up and covered his eyes.

Behind them, still both kneeling in the pebbly sand on the dark shore of the lake, beneath the black sun and surrounded by a glowing cloud of golden pyreflies, Karya and Jack were engaged in a kiss. His pale hands were on the sides of her face, fingers brushing the thick white streak of hair that had appeared. Her hands were wrapped around his wrists. They seemed utterly oblivious to the others.

Robin's face burned with surprise and embarrassment, as he, Henry and Woad all turned swiftly away.

"Well ..." he heard Henry whisper, sounding both winded and scandalised, "all's fair in love and war then, I suppose ..."

Robin's thoughts were not of Karya and Jack. He was focussed on what was going to happen to Ffoulkes when he got back to the Hall. His tutor would have to answer for this. Recklessness. Dangerous. Idiotic.

He looked up the bank, away from the shadows of the lake and towards the distant Hall – and was surprised to see a figure standing, not too far off, in the grass. The nymph Calypso was there, looking like a ghost in the strange gloom of the eclipse, her gown and hair silently flowing around her. Dispassionately, she regarded the three drenched boys with unfathomable eyes, then she glanced at the black lake and up at the sky, where the eclipse was already moving on, the blazing corona shimmering and fading as it progressed. Finally, she looked over at Karya and Jackalope, who were now getting to their feet, surrounded by the soft cloud of lights. Both looked shaky and exhausted, and more than a little awkward.

"Well," the nymph said eventually, in her careless, faraway voice. "This has been interesting, hasn't it?" She walked over to them, barefoot in the sand.

"As you've heard, pyreflies are drawn to emotion. See how they light up the night. Smitten fires." She peered at Karya and Jackalope thoughtfully as she made her way towards the group. "Drawn to moments of happiness, lured by the rhythm of swiftly beating hearts." Robin and Woad both glanced back at the pair. Henry, however, didn't look back, and although no other saw her do it, Calypso reached out a pale hand and smartly brushed a single, stray glowing pyrefly from Henry's shoulder. She swatted it off him like a wasp. "And drawn to despair," she whispered quietly, giving his shoulder a gentle squeeze as the stray pyrefly fell dead at her touch. "Brushed off ... for now."

Henry looked at her, thoughtfully.

"Ffoulkes put everyone in danger!" Robin turned back to face his tutor. "Woad really could have been killed! He almost was! Any of us could have been seriously hurt by that swarm! And have you been here this whole time? Just ... watching?" He spluttered in disbelief. "When Aunt Irene finds out that ..."

"Your aunt," Calypso cut him off, completely unruffled, "was the very person who suggested and arranged this lesson."

Robin gaped. The others stared in disbelief.

Calypso smiled at them all, a little lopsidedly, as though at a subtle joke that no-one else could see. "I think she will be very proud. Danger and helplessness. Sometimes they are the flint and tinder. Struck together to make the spark. And *what a spark.*" She gestured for them to follow her, turning away back towards the house and not bothering to check if they were following. Around them, it had begun to get lighter, the shadows lessening as the moon overhead finally retreated from the face of the sun and the unnatural darkness and chill began to lift. In only a few minutes, it would once again be daylight in full.

"She is waiting for you at the house. Much has been discovered, and much must be discussed."

"Wait!" Jackalope's urgent voice came from behind them. He sounded worried. Robin and the others turned from the nymph.

"Something's wrong," Jackalope said. "Something's *really* wrong."

Karya was slumping, crumpling to her knees, gripping onto him to try and stay upright as she collapsed. As they all stared, a second white streak appeared in her long, wet hair, where moments ago there had been only one. The boy struggled to hold her upright as the others rushed to help.

"Boss!" Woad shouted, scampering to support her as she collapsed in the sand. Where her wrist fell, her mana stone bracelet hissed against the wet floor as though it were hot iron.

"Get the girl to the house. Immediately!" Calypso commanded. All lazy whimsy was gone from her voice. In the curious half-light, staring down at the slumping form of Karya, her face was that of a frozen ghost.

5

Feathers and Scales

"How is she?" Aunt Irene asked quietly. Hestia shook her head, shrugging slightly, looking at something of a loss. They were gathered in the library, where Robin and the others had been summoned.

"The girl sleeps," Hestia explained, having just returned from Karya's room. "I have put her to bed. She has no wounds, she is merely tired. As tired as anyone old Hestia has ever seen." The housekeeper looked very worried indeed. "I do not know how to treat her," she admitted miserably, looking Irene directly in the eye. "She is beyond my knowledge. Her hair is greying and her breath is weak but it is even. Hestia is no hedge-witch, but whatever medicine is needed, it is not berries and lotions, nor poultices or potions. Nothing I have can improve her."

"She is stable?" Irene wanted to know. Hestia nodded.

"For now. But she must rest." The housekeeper shot a look at Robin and the others, who were standing around the large library table. They had changed clothes and dried off as soon as they reached the Hall, while Karya had been spirited away by the adults to be tended to, but their hair was still dripping wet. "No excitement! No attempts at magic!" she snapped at them, as though they were responsible for wilfully goading her on.

"We want to see her," Jackalope said.

"Later," Irene replied calmly, raising her hands as the other boys all voiced their agreement noisily. "Karya needs rest and quiet, not four flapping boys clucking over her like hens." She nodded in thanks to Hestia, who took this as her cue to depart, still looking fretful, closing the library door behind her.

"There are other things that we must discuss right now."

Robin glared past her to where his two tutors stood; Ffoulkes leaning against a bookshelf and Calypso seated by the cold fireplace. He was so angry he was surprised his wet hair wasn't steaming. "Bloody right we do," he said murderously. "These two! What happened out at the lake … That was just … dangerous!" He pointed at Woad, who flinched a little. "He nearly died! Karya has made herself worse, we were all in danger!"

Irene looked at Robin patiently. He had never raised his voice to her before now, not once during all his time at Erlking, and both Henry and Woad gasped a little at his outburst.

"Calm down please, Robin," she said, her voice quiet and controlled. "Erlking never promised to be without risk, and an important lesson was learned here."

"Indeed it was! A rousing success! You lit your candle, you harnessed the fire." Ffoulkes clapped his hands proudly. "Well done that boy. Jolly good show if you ask me."

"Are you kidding me?" Robin spluttered. "You put Woad in danger, used him like an experiment. You – none of you – could have known what was going to happen. He almost drowned."

At that second, he wanted Ffoulkes gone. Ejected from Erlking. He had had enough of the man. It had just been reckless, the whole lesson.

"And as for my other tutor." He looked at Calypso, still disbelieving. "You were there the whole time? Watching? And you didn't help us?"

The nymph shrugged, looking rather bored with the meeting. "I didn't need to. You had the situation under control."

Robin shook his head in frustration, looking back to his aunt, who was still watching him with interest. It was almost as though this were still part of the lesson, with her watching to see how he would react.

"Robin, my young ward. I really must insist that you calm down." She spoke quietly, but very firmly. "You are right to be angry. It is to be expected. You have been so recently filled with fire. One does not channel the element of flame through one's body without it affecting one's equilibrium." She raised her eyebrows. "However, fired up as you may be, I must remind you that these are still your tutors before you, and I am still the steward of Erlking. Respect is important."

Robin swallowed. He leaned on the table and took a deep breath. There was truth in the old woman's words. Inside, he could still feel the fire that had flowed through his mana. His blood felt superheated. He tried to count to ten.

"We chose to hold this lesson during the eclipse precisely *because* you might have failed," she said. "Had this happened at night, and had you failed to summon the fire, the darkness would have remained and Mr Ffoulkes would have been forced to intervene, to conjure himself a light bright enough to draw away the swarm. This day, where a small night falls for minutes only, was safer."

"*Safer?*" Robin looked up at her.

"It was necessary to leave you alone to perform. The demand had to be present, to force your hand. Had you failed, the sun would have come back out regardless. The swarm would have calmed, drawn by the larger light." She laced her fingers together, rings sparkling in the sunlight. "As it happens," she said with faint admiration, "you did not fail. You performed admirably."

"Are we all forgetting the part when Woad actually nearly drowned?" Henry asked, looking confused. He gestured to Jackalope. "If he hadn't been able to resuscitate him …"

"Then *I* would have done so," Calypso interrupted. "Of course. That's precisely why your aunt requested that I watch over proceedings from a distance. Had you not been able to handle the situation, I assure you, I would have stepped in." She gave a lazy shrug with one shoulder. "It is the simplest thing in the world to draw water from a faun's lungs. Simple for a nymph, at least."

"But we didn't know you were there," Robin countered. "We thought we were on our own."

"That was rather the intention, Robin," Irene said. "Every measure was taken to control the circumstances that we needed to engineer in order to awaken the Tower of Fire in you. As others have said, sometimes you cannot believe you can do something until you have no choice *but* to do it."

"What about Karya?" Jackalope said. "She has damaged herself further because of this."

Irene regarded him with a heavy look. "The girl, I am sad to say, is deteriorating regardless."

The truth of her words hung for a few seconds in the air.

"It is no longer wise for any of us to pretend otherwise." Irene sighed when no one else spoke. "She is weak … and worsening." She looked keenly at Robin. "I know you have been looking for a way to fix her, Robin. Searching for a solution to her problem. Although you have certainly not shared your ideas with me."

Robin swallowed.

"Very little happens in Erlking without my knowing about it," she explained softly. "Erlking is full of secrets – yes, this is true. But we have never before kept secrets from one another."

Robin looked back at her evenly. "We've never tricked each other before, either," he said quietly.

"Needs must," Irene replied. She spoke unapologetically. "I know you are growing up. Robin." She glanced at the others. "All of you are. But a balance must be struck between doing things on your own, such as mastering an element, and knowing when collaboration is best, for example to save the life of a dying friend."

"Boss is not dying!" Woad looked terribly affronted.

No one looked at anyone else. The silence in the library was very uncomfortable.

"She is getting worse, Woad," Jackalope said eventually. "Even Hestia doesn't know how to rekindle her, and she a master of healing."

Woad looked outraged. "You don't know that! Just because you were stuck on her face an hour ago doesn't suddenly make you an expert on everything to do with her. This faun has known boss a lot longer than the rest of you."

"Jack's right, Woad," Henry said thickly. "I wish he wasn't. But unless we find a way to fix things, this only goes one way in the end." He looked imploringly at Robin. "Your aunt's right, Rob. This is too important for us to just be making our own schemes."

Robin knew what he was getting at. Irene already knew they were up to something. Whether she guessed that they were trying to make plans to travel to Dis itself, he couldn't imagine, but by some extra sense inherent in grandmothers and great aunts worldwide, she knew he was keeping *something* from her. It was time to admit that he couldn't fix everything on his own.

"I had a message," he confessed with a sigh. "I don't know who sent it or why, but it talked about Pyrenight, and serpents, and I think it might give us a way to find out what is wrong with Karya."

Irene pulled out a chair in the now sunny library, inviting the others to sit also. As they did, pulling up their own chairs as if for a council of war, she laid out some items on the tabletop. The long thin denuded quill they had found in the library and a pile of stapled photographs, print outs of the pictures Robin and Jack had taken from the odd book in Mr Knight's office in London.

"It would appear," she said thoughtfully, that you and I have much information to share with one another."

Robin and the others explained everything. How they knew that Karya had originally come from Dis, and that, though even she didn't really understand or remember her origins, they were all agreed that any answers must lie in the capital, and that if they ever wanted to hope to stop her strange deterioration, a way must be found to get there. Robin told his aunt and tutors about the strange hex message that had come in the night. About the upcoming festival of Pyrenight, and how he had been directed to seek something named Luna in a place known as the agora.

The adults listened intently. Ffoulkes frowned with interest, occasionally twirling his red moustaches artfully. Calypso stared distantly out of the window at the snow covering the grounds outside, but nodded along as Robin spoke, clearly paying attention despite outward appearances.

When they were up to speed, Irene steepled her fingers on the table, giving it all some thought.

"I understand your thinking, Robin," she said. "And I now understand why you have hesitated to tell me of these plans, for you must have guessed that I, as your guardian, would forbid such a foolhardy plan – to walk directly into Eris' city."

She looked around at all of them, eyes piercing, then returned her gaze to Robin. "And of course, you would be correct to think so. I do indeed forbid it. As noble and well-intentioned as your goals may be, driven by friendship or not, I am both Erlking's guardian and yours. The highest of the Fae placed Erlking into my care, and your own grandmother passed the custody of the world's last changeling to me at her death. I do not intend to put either in harm's way unnecessarily."

"We were in harm's way this morning!" Henry blurted out.

Calypso waved a hand at him dismissively. "Hardly in harm's way," she said. "At worst, a little to the left of harm. No need for dramatics."

"My singular duty is to keep the Scion of the Arcania from Eris," Irene said to Robin, just as he opened his mouth to argue. "It is not a duty that I asked for, nor one that I feel qualified to uphold," she pressed. "Before you came here, there were no children at Erlking, and now ..." She glanced around at them all with raised eyebrows. "Well, we appear to be infested."

She smiled. "However, whether I asked for such responsibility or not, I honour it. As I honour your previous guardian, and as I honour the King and Queen of Erlking, and your parents' wishes." She raised a finger to silence him as he opened his mouth again. "I will brook no argument, Robin. You must not expose yourself so recklessly, not even for Karya. Your worth is too great, and your death would end every hope we have, in this world and the other."

"So, what's the alternative? We just let Karya ... fade away? To keep the precious Scion safe and sound? Is that the plan?" Robin spoke desperately. He shook his head. "You know we can't do that. We have a responsibility to help her."

"You have a responsibility to every Fae in the Netherworlde," his aunt said sharply. "Every one of them. You are the Scion. Will you potentially doom countless lives to save one? Could you?"

Robin felt helpless and frustrated. "We can't just do nothing. You can bet Eris and the Grimms won't be just sitting on their hands like we are. They'll be searching for the remaining Shards, getting stronger while we ... flounder."

Irene drew their attention to the photographs on the desk with a sweep of her open palm. "I am not suggesting we do nothing, my nephew. And I am not ruling out answers or help for the girl. Karya has become dear to all of us here, and Erlking does not abandon its people. Not ever."

They looked at one another for a few moments and Robin, apparently persuaded by her earnest expression, finally nodded.

She seemed to take this as her cue to continue. "It may be that all things are connected. While you have been dreaming and scheming of storming the enemy's gates and having cloak and dagger midnight conversations with unknown and dubious informants, I, with the help of your tutor, have been making sense of *this*."

"The journal from knight's office?" Jackalope asked, and Irene nodded. She held up the thin black barb.

"It has taken some time and much research," she said. "But I know now what this is."

"It's a feather," Henry said. "We already knew that. Well, a feather with no ... feathery bits left."

"Not just any feather." The old lady looked at it thoughtfully. "It is, or was, a phoenix feather."

They all stared at it.

"It can't be." Woad raised a hand, as though a student in class. "There aren't any phoenixes left. They used to roam the Black Hills in the Netherworlde long ago. But they're gone now. They were hunted to extinction ages ago."

Robin didn't know much about the creatures of the Netherworlde, but even he had heard of phoenixes. "But don't those birds come back to life?" he asked, confused. "They rise from their own ashes, don't they? How can you kill off an animal that comes back to life?"

"They only rise *once*," Irene clarified. "Kill a phoenix twice and you have a dead phoenix. They have two chances at life. More than most, but even so, what Woad says is true. The birds have passed entirely into myth. It is only a rumour, but it is believed that the forces of Eris had the last one alive, some time ago."

"But whoever owned this journal had one of them?" Henry asked.

"Doubtful, but at the very least, they had one of their feathers," the old lady said. "Phoenix feathers, you see, have tremendous healing properties. They can restore almost anything – if a skilled alchemist knows what they are doing, of course."

Woad's eyes lit up. "So this feather barb could fix boss? Is that what we're saying?"

Irene shook her head. "This particular example has been used up." She dropped it onto the table. "Utterly spent. And there are no more recorded in existence. However, the journal you found was a record of searches ... or should I say hunts ... for someone. And that someone, whoever they may be, may know where another can be found."

"How do you figure that?" Robin wanted to know.

Irene beckoned Ffoulkes over to explain. He tapped the photographs of the journal pages on the table with the air of a master detective. "I have studied these for a while. They are written in very elaborate high tongue, difficult even for one such as myself. You see this coat of arms you have photographed, the one with the entwined serpents? It is the crest of House Calescent."

"Who are they, when they're at home?" Henry frowned.

"A *very* noble and *very* powerful Panthea family." Ffoulkes puffed his chest out. "Extremely wealthy and influential, practically royalty. They rule much of the Black Hills, the region of the Netherworld south-west of Dis. Fire Panthea, all of them."

"Fire Panthea like you," Robin pointed out. "Do you know them?"

A smile flickered across his tutor's bearded face. "Well, naturally," he blustered. "One of my station has been intimate in every section of high society. I have enjoyed the hospitality of House Calescent, although it was long ago."

"It is something of a broken home, rather plagued by misfortune and scandal," Irene stated. "The last patriarch of House Calescent is long dead. Rumours abounded after the war that he had Fae sympathies, that he had conspired with the Fae against Eris. Whether that's true or not, I do not know. I only know that if there *was* any truth in it, then Lord Calescent chose the wrong side. He may have been executed as a traitor." She shrugged. "The entire estate has been governed since by his two offspring, the Lady Tinda and her brother. But according to Mr Ffoulkes here, there has been some further scandal in recent years."

Ffoulkes nodded. "It's a tragic tale, if infuriatingly scant in terms of detail. Lady Tinda died mysteriously. An illness of some kind. The upper classes are ever so close-mouthed about family affairs, so no one seems to know for sure what happened to her, but the long and short of the story is that with her out of the picture, Lord Flint is now the head of House Calescent."

Robin looked down at the photographs. "So, whoever has been doodling in this book we found was interested in phoenix feathers, and was investigating or involved with this posh family?" He scratched his head. "I don't get it. If they thought this Fire Lord guy had whatever they're looking for, why not just go to his house, or mansion or whatever, and ask him directly about it?" He looked up at Ffoulkes. "I mean, we're all agreed right, that this thing has 'Grimm' written all over it? I can't see anyone saying no to Eris, no matter how private and posh their Panthea family is."

"It's possible that it is *not* Lord Calescent who is of interest," Calypso piped up quietly. "There are plenty of whispers in the Netherwolde that would suggest the ambitious and powerful Lord Flint is already very pally with Eris' highest. Practically friendly with the Grimms. He has often been seen at court in their presence." She turned her attention from the snow outside and looked at them. "Whoever is doing the searching, it's entirely possible that their focus is not on Lord Flint at all, but rather his sister."

Robin's confusion deepened. "The dead sister?"

"The *reportedly* dead sister," Ffoulkes corrected him. "That is ... ahahah ... rather an important distinction, young master of the Hall."

He tapped the photograph of the sketch in red ink, which showed twin snakes entwined, one dark, one pale, in an elaborate pattern, circling upwards like a Celtic knot tattoo. Where their heads met at the top, they held something between their twin fangs, apparently a heart-shaped jewel. "See here? This word, *soror*. It means ..."

"Sister," Robin remembered.

"When Karya had her vision on Christmas Eve," Jackalope interjected. "She mentioned something about a sister, remember? Secret sister, she said. You think she could be tapping into the same thing?"

"The fates weave all threads in the tapestry," Irene said, nodding. "We're speculating of course, but it's entirely possible."

"It's certainly indicative that the sister of House Calescent may not be as dead as the official story would have everyone believe," Ffoulkes agreed. "All these maps in the journal, all the notes. Someone appears to be searching very earnestly for the Lady Tinda, and we have no idea why."

"Karya also said in her vision something about half a heart," Jackalope remembered. "She said they had half a heart each." He looked questioningly at Ffoulkes. "Do you think she was talking about this brother and sister? Is that a thing with Fire Panthea?"

Ffoulkes shook his head. "No, no, no," he insisted. "I haven't the foggiest what that is supposed to mean. As a Fire Panthea myself, I can assure you that we have a whole heart each, and the usual amount of kidneys, lungs and other internals."

This was all very vague and frustrating.

"What does any of this have to do with helping Karya?" Robin asked.

"If her mind is filled with visions tied to all of this," Irene explained patiently. "Perhaps it has everything to do with it. We went to Mr Knight's little party on the trail of one mystery, but we appear to have inadvertently stumbled upon an entirely different one. Mr Knight, I feel, is someone with his fingers in many pies. Unravelling the mystery of House Calescent, and finding out what truly happened to Lady Tinda, may well lead us to help for Karya."

"Someone else clearly believes she still alive, and on the run from something or someone," Ffoulkes said. "She's clearly someone of interest to Eris."

"And therefore of interest to us," Irene added. "A person on the run, presumed dead but pursued, through this world and the other. Anyone hiding from Dis is a person who is welcome at Erlking."

Robin thought for a moment. The unknown and unusual hex messenger from the other night – could that have been this mysterious Lady Tinda? But how would she have his old hex paper? And how would she know how to contact him? He shook off the theory. It didn't make sense at all.

"If boss is vision-dreaming of this fiery family, that's good enough for me," Woad said folding his arms. "But even the best tracking faun needs somewhere to start, especially to find someone good at hiding."

Robin looked at his friend. "Are you suggesting we need to go to the Black Hills? That we could go and see this Lord Calescent guy and get some answers?"

Ffoulkes actually laughed, in a harsh bark. "That would be madness, Master Robin! House Calescent, as the good Lady Calypso has already indicated, is unshakably loyal to Eris. Under the rule of the Lord, it would as dangerous a place for you to visit as Dis itself."

"Couldn't you contact them, then?" Henry suggested. "You're a Fire hob-nob too, right?"

Ffoulkes looked uncomfortable. He fiddled with the buttons on his waistcoat as though he suddenly found them vexing. "I have very little desire to rekindle any association with Lord Flint, thank you very much. We did not part last on the best of terms. My departure from the Netherworlde has not left me in the best graces of any of the noble houses."

Irene drummed her fingers on the table. "I plan to travel to the north, in the human world," she informed them. "I have business there with our old friend, Hawthorn of the Fae. He and the Fae resistance that he represents have informants in many places. I have been in correspondence with him this week, and he states that he may have information to give us. More insight into the motives and allegiances of the charming Mr Knight and Sire Holdings."

She looked at each of them. "I must not lose sight of my greater goal, to locate the missing book and gain further information on the Cubiculu-Argentum. That must be my focus, and I cannot delay on it for other matters."

Her eyes came to rest on Robin. "If any further information is to be discovered as to the fate of Lady Calescent, it will fall to the rest of you."

Robin perked up, realising what his aunt was suggesting. "Wait. You *want* me to go to the Netherworlde?" This was certainly a first.

"Not to Dis, certainly," Irene asserted. "Let me be most perfectly clear about that. But yes, I believe a careful and controlled expedition could be arranged. But only under careful supervision. Mr Ffoulkes will accompany you."

Robin considered asking if Ffoulkes was the most appropriate adult for the job, considering his lesson earlier, but he didn't want to say anything that might cause his aunt to change her mind, and so he bit his tongue.

"We must find out more, and so far we have only one thing to go on. One place, as Woad pointed out, to start," Irene said. "The obscure message you received from unknown parties instructed you quite clearly to 'seek out Luna', did it not?"

Robin nodded excitedly.

"Whoever or whatever that may be," Irene continued. "All we have been told is that Luna should be sought at the agora."

"Is that a place in the Netherworlde?" Robin looked between his aunt and tutors.

"It is *many* places in the Netherworlde," Calypso explained. "An agora is simply a marketplace, Robin. Many towns in the Netherworlde have one. Some are larger than others." She rose from her chair and they watched as she pulled a large scroll from the library shelf behind her. Crossing back to the table, as Aunt Irene moved the photographs and quill aside, the nymph unrolled the scroll, revealing a large and detailed map of the Netherworlde, in scratchy black ink on yellowed vellum. Between them all, they smoothed out the edges.

Robin had never seen a map of the Netherworlde before. It looked vaguely like the British Isles, but the proportions were all wrong, slightly askew and everything was larger. As though someone had tried to draw Britain from memory with an unsteady hand and too much ambition. Robin saw names and symbols on the map of places he knew. Up here was the wide sweep of the Gravis Glaciem, the frozen north-east of the map. Over here, the open grassy plains where they had been pursued by centaur on their way to Briar Hill, and here, the vast dark tangle of the Elderhart, the great forest of the dryads. Far to the south was the marker for Dis itself, much further than Robin had ever travelled, and below, stretching to the southern coast, an area marked as the Black Hills. There appeared to be doodled volcanoes.

"I shall attempt to cast a cantrip," Irene said, holding her hand over the map. Between her fingers she held the spike of the phoenix quill. "To narrow perhaps our options in terms of agorae."

Closing her eyes, she concentrated, muttering a few words under her breath as she passed her hand slowly back and forth across the map, divining slowly, just as a planchette moves across the surface of a Ouija board.

Everyone stayed as quiet as possible, watching the old woman move her hand back and forth. Robin felt it grow warmer in the library, although Irene's control and subtlety of mana was so refined and unshowy, it could simply have been the sun coming out from behind a cloud, shifting the shadows in the room. He thought he saw her earrings, tiny teardrops of haematite, flash as they caught the light. She turned her head this way and that, eyes still closed as though listening closely for some small noise.

Suddenly, her hand stopped, hovering high above the map. Her eyes snapped open, blue and clear, and she dropped the quill.

It landed point first like a thrown dart, sticking straight into the map. They all gathered around, looking down where it lay, seemingly atop the meandering line of a wide river.

"Your mana focussing on this 'Luna' brings us to Titania's Tears," Calypso mused with interest.

"Is that a place?" Robin asked her. "Or some kind of Netherworlde curse term, like snakes and ashes?"

"It is a place, Master Robin," Ffoulkes confirmed. "Titania's Tears is a sizeable town. Magnificent once, back in the time of the Fae. It was abandoned after the war, but a sizeable Panthea population lives there now. New buildings in the old ruins at the great waterfalls. A vibrant and busy market town sprang up after the war. It's a capital place for all manner of commerce and trading, positioned as it is on the river."

"The town of Titania's Tears is certainly one of the largest marketplaces in the Netherworlde," Calyspo agreed. "The largest agora. It has another name; the Sorrows. A dangerous place for the Scion. Lots of people from every corner of the Netherworlde travel there to trade. To buy and sell."

"It is perhaps easier to hide in a crowd sometimes, than alone on an exposed moor," Ffoulkes suggested diplomatically. "The Sorrows are a capital place to visit. I've fenced many a ... that is, I've made many profitable transactions at Titania's Tears. I still have many contacts there."

"And it might be where we can find this Luna?" Robin asked. "Somewhere in this market town?"

Irene considered. "It is as good a place as any to begin. A town built over mouth of the great waterfall of Titania, it's certainly a sight to behold. I would, however, urge caution and care. All cities are policed by Eris' peacekeepers. And you must remember that you are the most wanted person in the Netherworlde."

Robin was staring at the map. He had been to the Netherworlde several times now, stealing secretly through deep forests, abandoned villages, open moors and icy mountains, but this ... this was a town. It would be his very first experience of urban life in the other world.

"If Luna is here and can tell us anything about dead-but-not-dead Fire noble, we need to find them ... or it," he said. "For Karya."

"Then it's settled! We shall leave at dawn!" Ffoulkes clapped his hands together. He looked positively merry. "It's been a long time since I had reason to walk the streets of an agora, and I could stand to look up a few old friends." He glanced at Irene. "Discreetly, of course ... ahaha."

Irene stood up. "I too will be leaving soon," she told them. "I cannot keep Hawthorn in the north waiting. None of the resistance stay in one place for too long. It isn't safe for them to do so. All of us, it seems, have some packing to do."

6

Hiking to Dishwater

It is a strange task – Robin mused, as he laid out his belongings on his bed – to be packing for an expedition to another world. Of course, he had travelled to the Netherworlde several times before, but always under somewhat extenuating and rather impromptu circumstances.

His first foray into the world of the Fae and Panthea had been a desperate rescue mission to save kidnapped friends, and his guardian had been unable to stop him – being temporarily and most inconveniently made of stone at the time. His second trip had been one of necessity, tearing a hole between two worlds from a hidden passage deep beneath the city streets of Manchester to find himself flung into the middle of a Netherworlde snowfield, and his third outing, which had at least had some form of adult guidance in the person of Hawthorn the Fae, had been one of duty, and called for him to rid the great forest of the dryads of a dangerous beast, bound by his old oath to the slippery redcaps.

This felt slightly different. His aunt had approved this visit for a start, they were headed to a town, a civilised place, and he would be accompanied by his newest tutor. It seemed unlikely that much could go wrong; all they had to do was locate this mysterious Luna – be that a person or a place – and find out all they could about House Calescent or Pyrenight. It was practically a tourist outing.

Leaving at first light meant getting up in the middle of the night to pack, which made it feel even more like getting ready for a holiday. Into his Swedenborgian satchel, which was always handy for carrying supplies as it contained its own pocket dimension, Robin packed a change of clothes, his battered copy of Hammerhand's *Netherworlde Compendium*, his new book on herbs gifted by Woad, and his hex message parchment – in case he received any further mysterious notes. He also packed the cubic cornucopia gem that Ffoulkes had given to him, the fire-carrier, as he understood it, and Henry's gift – his moral compass. There was no need for Robin to worry about sourcing food supplies. Hestia would already be downstairs preparing enough foil-wrapped sandwiches and strings of cooked sausage to feed a small army.

"It's a shame boss can't come with us this time," Woad said. He was sitting cross-legged on the end of the bed and watching Robin's diligent packing, whilst also being very careful not to help in any way. "I'm coming, of course. Someone has to keep an eye on you, Pinky, and I don't trust old ember-whiskers to be the most responsible guide. He'd probably forget all about you and leave you abandoned in the town while he went off shopping for knock-off powdered unicorn horn. Wouldn't put it past him."

Robin smirked as he tucked things away neatly into the bag. "Unicorns?" he asked. "First extinct phoenix, and now unicorns. Are they a real thing then? In the Netherworlde, I mean."

"Real thing in *any* world," Woad said, nodding knowledgeably. "You don't want to come across a pack though. Bloody-minded things, they are."

Robin looked up, curious. "I thought unicorns were symbols of purity and wisdom and twinkly glittery magic and all that," he said.

Woad spluttered derisively, shaking his head in a world-weary way at the naivety of his clueless companion. "The only glittery thing following a run in with those dark mares would be your insides on the outsides of their horn," he said in a no-nonsense manner. "Dangerous creatures, nothing like your human-world storybooks show."

Robin shook his head in bewilderment. "Nothing about the Netherworlde is ever quite as I expect," he admitted. "You'd think I'd have learned by now, wouldn't you?"

"Ahh." Woad nodded sagely. "But if you only ever expected things to be unexpected, then the unexpected things would be exactly what you had expected, which would make them very expected indeed." He sighed happily. "And where would be the fun in that?"

"Woad?"

"Hmm?"

"You're giving me a headache. Go and see if the Nightingale twins have arm-wrestled their way to any kind of agreement yet, will you? I want a word with Karya before we go, and I can't get near her with those two flapping."

As Woad had said, and everyone agreed, Karya was in no fit state to go wandering the towns of the Netherworlde. She would remain, very much against her grumpy and incredibly vocal wishes, bed-bound and forced into unhappy convalescence by Hestia. Both Jackalope and Henry wished to go to Titania's Tears with Robin, and both Jackalope and Henry also believed they were best suited to remain with Karya. She needed little more looking after with Hestia already on hand, but it just didn't seem right to leave an Erlkinger alone. And after all, this was only one, relatively brief, reconnaissance mission.

"I don't see why *either* of you need to stay. In fact, I don't see any reason why I can't just come along myself." Karya was sitting up in bed, covered in a thick marshmallowy blanket and propped on about ten pillows. She looked quietly furious, but was controlling it admirably.

"Well, chiefly because you look like death warmed up for a start," Henry pointed out with characteristic bluntness from her bedside, where they were all gathered. "You've fainted twice recently, had a mental vision that left you practically foaming at the mouth, and you've now got enough grey streaks in your hair to pass for the Bride of Frankenstein. Of course you can't come. Rob isn't going to carry you around on his back like a pack mule, is he? Have you seen those noodle arms?"

Karya shot Henry a dark look from her nest of plumped-up pillows. "Thanks for that," she muttered. "You're all treating me like I'm made of glass. I've got a little fight left in me yet, you know!"

Robin hoisted his backpack onto his shoulders, checking once more that his mana stone was resting neatly around his neck. "We want a *lot* more fight in you, not a little, that's the point," he told her. "That's the reason we're going at all, to find something to make you better. This is just like ..." He shrugged a little helplessly. "A trip to the chemist to pick up some medicine, that's all. Woad and I would be totally fine on our own, to be honest."

"Oh, definitely not," Karya said with a hint of alarm. "You're not leaving both of these two here, at each other's throats. Not if you insist on me getting any kind of rest."

"Henry should go," Jackalope suggested. "One Fae at large in a world where our kind are outlawed is risky enough. Two of us are bound to draw lots of attention."

Henry scoffed. "Oh, and leave you here?" he snorted. "You'd be a bit of a distraction, don't you think?" His cheeks were a little flushed. "Karya needs rest, not to be wooed by someone fluttering their eyelashes and being all ... lovey dovey."

Jackalope looked aghast. "I have never once in my life fluttered my eyelashes," he snapped. "If you're still sore about what happened at ..."

"I don't care *who* is sore about *what*," Karya interjected, her ears a little pink. "I don't need a nursemaid. And I thought you two had finally decided to be friends, anyway?"

Henry folded his arms. "You *did* save Woad," he grunted to Jack, a grudging allowance. "So yeah, you're a true Erlkinger. I don't ... dislike you, but ..."

"I'm honoured," Jackalope interrupted. "I have chosen not to actively dislike you, also."

"Well, this is very heart-warming." Robin raised his hands, speaking loudly to drown out their bickering. "I'm glad we're all now very-best-no-longer-enemies but the point is, I don't want someone here as a nursemaid, I want someone here as a *contact*." He flung a rolled-up scroll across the bed to Henry, who caught it deftly.

"It's your hex message paper," Robin explained. "I need to know if there's any change to the ... situation ... while were away, that's all."

"You need to know if I deteriorate, you mean," Karya said flatly, looking at him with wary eyes.

"Yes, if you don't want to beat around the bush about it," Robin said. "If you slip into a coma or god knows what else, I want someone telling me about it right away, so we can hightail it back here pronto." He looked at Jack. "And yes, you have a point, two Fae is a risk, but neither of us has horns, not visible ones anyway." He indicated Henry. "Henry, on the other hand, is human and will stick out more. He's known Karya longer, and he and his dad are practically part of Erlking Hall. If no one else is going to make a rational decision, then I will."

He cleared his throat. "Jack, you're coming with. Henry, you stay. Keep me updated."

To Karya, he said: "Henry probably will be less of a distraction." He couldn't resist teasing her slightly about her kiss at the eclipse, it was too much fun.

"Oi! I'll have you know I can be very distracting," Henry argued indignantly, his pride obviously dented. He crumpled the hex message scroll in his hands. "I'm easily as distracting as Silver Top over there."

Jackalope snorted down his nose, looking derisive.

"Fates, give me strength," Karya whispered to herself, laying back and burying her head in her pillows. She had apparently decided that the best course of action was to pretend that none of them were there.

Woad clapped his hands with an air of finality. "The almighty and great and unchallengeable Scion of the Arcania has spoken!" he intoned with great drama. "Henry and boss will stay here, and drink cocoa and play scrabble and absolutely *not ever smooch*, even until the day they die." He gave a well-meaning and reassuring double thumbs up to Jackalope.

"Woad!" Karya snapped hotly.

"And this noble and brave faun shall escort the two clueless and hornless Fae ones to the Netherwolde! Onward to intrigue and mystery. And maybe souvenirs. Sound good?" He glanced up at Robin. "Only … it's nearly first light. We should daddle our skis, Pinky."

"Fine," said Henry and Jackalope at the same time, both looking suspicious and dissatisfied. Robin, with his thumbs in the straps of his backpack, glanced at Karya and gave her a wide grin.

She shook her head at him, eyeing him ruefully. "Power has gone to your head, Scion of the Arcania, pulling rank like that." She sighed and smiled at him, however – and Robin noted with worry that she looked more drawn and tired than ever. "Fine then, go, go! Find out what you can and come back in one piece. Quick in and out, no calamities. No pieces left behind. But if I discover you've been led astray by sneaky messages written in blood, I'll absolutely tan your hide, Scion or not."

Robin crossed his heart with his fingertips. "Puck's honour," he said with great solemnity. "We'll be back before you even know we were gone."

They gathered together by the red door at the end of the corridor in Erlking, the sole Janus Station not controlled by Eris. Robin and Jackalope were both shouldering travelling satchels, and Woad as ever had brought nothing with him but his trousers, his tail and a sense of adventure. This being, he had stated on many occasions, all that was needed for a good expedition – and even then, trousers were optional. The small blue boy was currently explaining in great detail the care and feeding schedule of his pet squid, Inky, to a rather bemused and inattentive Hestia.

Ffoulkes had donned what he proudly declared a "travelling cape" – a crimson affair laced with gold which he slung artfully, and completely impractically, over one shoulder. With his fiery pointed beard and haughty face, it made him look like an own-brand Francis Drake.

"Remember, Robin," Aunt Irene told him, her hand resting on the silver doorknob carved with its ornate letter J, "you are on an information gathering trip *only*." She raised her eyebrows, looking closely at all three of the boys, before sliding her eyes over to Ffoulkes with equal sternness. "This is not an opportunity for japes, high jinks, capers or swashbuckling ... *especially* not swashbuckling. Is that understood?"

"Nary a single buckle swashed, good lady, ahahah," Ffoulkes assured her, fiddling with his lacy cuffs.

Irene looked back to Robin. "Should you encounter any trouble ..."

"I know, I know." Robin nodded, not wishing to say or do anything that would change his guardian's mind about this expedition. "First sign of trouble, we will high tail it back home to Erlking, don't worry."

Irene smiled, the tiniest flicker at the corner of her mouth. "Well, perhaps the *second* sign of trouble," she allowed. "Too much caution and none of us would ever get anywhere." Then, she snapped her fingers, drawing the attention of Woad, who had been chattering away in the background to Hestia. "Now listen, all of you. Erlking's Janus Station is not under my jurisdiction but its own. However, as far as I have any small skill or influence, I have attempted to steer your ... landing coordinates ... in the Netherworlde to the city itself. Titania's Tears is a considerable distance to the east. Much farther from Erlking than you have ever travelled before, Robin. It would be most impractical for you to flip straight over to the Netherworlde Erlking and hike from there. That trip alone would take weeks."

They all nodded to show how attentive they were.

Irene looked momentarily doubtful, but only slightly. "However, I must caution you that I am no great expert in travelling magic, so it may not be your smoothest ride ever." Her eyes glittered. "Therefore, I suggest that you bend your knees when you land."

"Land?" Robin began to ask, but at that moment, his great aunt opened the door. There was a *whoosh* as though a vacuum-sealed chamber had been opened, and a thick and glittering mist shot through with gold poured forth from the door frame.

It carried a strange warmth into the cold and dim January hallway of Erlking's winter, lighting their faces softly like sun reflected off water. The subtle scents of cinnamon, wild spices and heady flowers drifted over them in invisible tendrils. Robin just had time to take a deep and happy lungful of the smell, the scent of the Netherworlde, before he felt Ffoulkes' hand in the small of his back, pushing him forward in a friendly yet rather forceful manner.

"Tally ho then, chaps!" he heard the Panthea say, and then Robin stumbled, slightly off balance with his pack, into the warm golden mist, out of one world and into another.

Tearing between two worlds was not a sensation Robin believed he would ever get used to. There was always a moment, somewhere in the transition, where you felt the floor slip away from you, your stomach flipped, and you could no longer tell which way was up or down. Blinded and disoriented by the mist, Robin felt his stomach lurch as the creaky cold floorboards of Erlking Hall fell away, and for a few seconds, without really knowing where his arms and legs began and ended, he felt as though he had been suspended in a blazing nebula somewhere unfathomably distant in space. The only thing ruining this near-perfect sensation was the distant sound of Woad giggling, clearly enjoying the lurching ride.

Moments later, where hard wood had very recently rested beneath his feet, there was soil and deep grass. Robin hit it at rather more speed than he had been anticipating – it was as though he had stepped nonchalantly from a moving car, and his feet swept gracelessly out from under him, sending him somersaulting head over heels through the mist, his backpack clanking and rattling as the tall grass slapped unseen at him from every direction. When he came to rest, spreadeagled on his back and panting, the golden mist cleared, dissipating in seconds, and he found himself staring up into the widest, bluest sky he had seen in a long time.

"Ugh …" He struggled into a sitting position and hoisted his pack back onto his shoulders. He shook his head, dislodging grass seed and pollen, and waited for his eyes to focus and his head to stop spinning. He was dimly aware of the others around him. Jackalope was a blur to his left, getting unsteadily to his feet and brushing grass off his shoulders. Woad's legs were sticking out of the long grass; the faun was completely upside down, as though someone had attempted to plant him in the ground.

"It's … warm," Robin observed. It was the first thing he noticed. The frigid air of new year had gone. Here in the Netherworlde it was a bright and sunny day, with only a few high and wispy white clouds, and the scented breeze, which rippled the deep grass they sat in, was fresh and welcoming.

"Indeed it is," Ffoulkes said from behind him. "Spring in the Netherworlde, it would seem! These things do lag so from here to there. I must say, it's nice to see a bit of life after such a bare and gloomy winter, what?"

Robin got to his feet, his disorientation fading, and looked around to see where they had landed. They were on the high slopes of what appeared to be a wide and panoramic alpine hill, a vast meadow of long grass that almost reached his shoulders in places, lush and enthusiastically green. Squinting in the suddenly bright sunshine, he shielded his eyes and looked around, expecting to see people in lederhosen, and cows and goats with metal bells clanking around their necks, but the four of them appeared to be completely alone in the landscape. The hills rose around them, a green and verdant ocean rising up in towering peaks. Surrounding them, the sweeping green carpets were broken up by wide patches of swaying purple and red flowers, splashes of bright colour smothering the outcrops. The alpine vegetation climbed as high as it could before giving way to rocky peaks and broken tumbles of scree, mountains shimmering blue in the sunlight.

"Ah, Netherworlde, I've missed you!" Woad said happily. He had righted himself and was spinning around on the hillside like a nun in a musical, bashing through great patches of the red and purple poppy-like flowers and sending their petals surging upwards into the breeze. They were caught like confetti and carried away over the valleys, swept in mountain eddies.

"We could be in Switzerland," Robin observed, enjoying the fresh sunlight on his face. Compared to the human world, everything always seemed more vital here. It was hard to explain exactly how it felt. To Robin, it was as though everything was in high definition – sharper, clearer and more colourful. Even the air tasted better.

Ffoulkes was looking around at the commanding and flora-filled valleys and peaks, clearly searching for landmarks. "We are, to the best of my knowledge, in the Floreo Hills, above the valley along which runs the Dish. Which is exactly where we wish to be."

"The Dish?" Robin asked, clueless.

"One of the major rivers in the Netherworlde," his tutor explained, fussily brushing grass from his travelling cape. "It begins far north of here, fed from goodness knows how many streams up in the Gravis Glaciem, and it grows and swells as it travels south, cutting through many valleys and across many a grassland. Should you follow it far enough, I daresay it takes you right past Dis itself, far to the south, though of course we have ... ahahah ... absolutely no wish to do that." He squinted around in the sunlight, still attempting to get his bearings. "Beyond Dis, it carries on down through the Black Hills, turns into a delta and spills out into the Great Southern Sea."

"Wherever we are," Jackalope pointed out. "Pretty as it is, it's definitely not a market town. We're in the middle of nowhere."

Ffoulkes smiled. "Well naturally, dear Lady Irene is most wise not to drop us straight into the city. There are many strange sights in the Netherworlde, but even I must admit that a dashing chap and three chattering boys simply dropping out of the air in the middle of a market square would be likely to draw attention, and probably of the wrong kind."

"So, we are near this town then? Titania's Tears?" Robin scanned his surroundings. As far as he could see was sweeping meadow, pollen dancing thickly in the air above the carpets of flowers.

"Oh, most certainly," his tutor assured them. "If one wishes to find a river in the steep hills, one simply heads downwards. Water, like most sensible things, will always find the easiest path. We shall descend these bucolic slopes, locate the wondrous majesty of the River Dish, and follow it downstream. There we shall locate our agora. There are many things hidden in the countless valleys of the Floreo Hills, and many places to hide them."

Producing a tall walking stick from somewhere about his person, Ffoulkes set off with a determined spring in his step through the long grass, disturbing a family of small white rabbits which scurried off furiously. His travelling cape, which looked too warm and cumbersome for the bright spring weather, now presented a smattering of rabbit droppings.

"I suppose we should follow him," Jackalope said to Robin, looking around cautiously, as though expecting the forces of Eris to erupt from the large swathes of alpine flowers at any moment.

"For want of any better option," Robin agreed. "Come on, Woad."

"Onwards and upwards!" Woad said, enthusiastically, "Or rather, onwards and downwards, I suppose. No time to yodel, no matter how pretty and bubonic the hills are!"

It took them quite some time to clamber down out of the dizzying hills and find the bottom of the long craggy valley, but it was not, Robin felt, an unpleasant way to spend the morning. The scenery through which they hiked was stunning, the day was bright and warm, and all around them the Netherworlde bloomed with life – in stark contrast to the sleeping and frozen world of winter they had just left. As they tramped onwards and downwards, following the rolling hillsides at a diagonal so as not to tire their legs with too steep a descent, his only complaint was that, in jeans, a jumper and a hoodie, he had dressed too warmly for the journey.

Before long, as they paused for a breather amongst glittering micadashed rocks to sip gratefully from their water flasks, Robin peeled off his winter layers, stashing his hoodie and jumper in his Swedenborgian satchel, and felt the refreshing relief of his mana stone bashing only against his t-shirt with each descending step.

The long grass of the slopes was damp with dew, which soon saturated their trousers from the knees down, and between that, and the position of the bright sun in the sky, Jackalope ventured to suggest that it was still reasonably early in the morning. As they ploughed on through sedges, clumps of wild achillea – that bobbed in the breeze like clouds falling to rest on the ground – and thick, fragrant tangles of wild strawberry, Woad was inclined to agree. Although he judged the time not from their surroundings, but from the occasional rumble of his stomach.

"Being home always makes me hungry," he said happily. "Do you think we should hunt some hare? I've seen plenty darting about here. Little white ones. We could make up a quick stew for lunch."

"We haven't packed for camping, Woad," Robin reminded him.

Woad indicated both Robin and Ffoulkes. "We have two people here with fire magic, we could roast one little beastie on a spit quite easy.

There's nothing like fresh mountain hare to invigorate you, I heard that somewhere."

"I think you're thinking of fresh mountain *air*," Robin laughed.

Woad shrugged as if it were all the same to him, and skipped merrily over a patch of lichen-covered boulders, startling a few small, brightly-coloured birds into flight, each no bigger than his thumb. "Cooking or not," he said. "I'd eat them raw, as nature intended, but I know you Fae can be fussy about these things." He nodded to Jackalope. "Silver Top could probably gut and clean a hare, right? You lived in a cave for ages. I bet you're the master of disembowelling small fluffy things."

Jackalope rolled his eyes, squinting up at the faun with his hand shielding his eyes. "You could make it sound a little less pathetic, you know."

"There will be no need to forage in the wilds like scavengers, survivalists or reality television contestants, thank goodness," Ffoulkes announced brightly from the front of their snaking troupe. "I hear ahead the rush of the river, which leads me to believe that we near the bottom of our healthy but – I must remind Lady Irene when we return – unasked-for constitutional."

He pointed ahead, where the slopes did indeed seem to be finally levelling out below them. Across a meadow of rippling sagebrush, dotted with yellow flowers as tiny as bees, was a screen of dwarf spruce, the trees dense and huddled together against the exposed elements of the wilderness. "Just through here and we will meet the road to civilisation, I assure you. By lunchtime we will be dining in the Tears. I know a dashed good place where one can get a decent freshwater eel Florentine. Positively to die for."

"Or to die from," Robin murmured doubtfully to Jack and Woad. He wasn't overly keen on eels, having not spent a great deal of time as a Victorian cockney orphan. He felt equally dubious at the idea of catching one of the wild rabbits they had seen darting about the hillsides during their trek, unsure if he would be able to sit and eat one with its family members looking on accusingly from the tall grasses nearby. Robin was fervently hoping that Hestia had packed sandwiches. Something sensible like roast beef and Branston pickle, or thick-cut ham and glam-glam jam.

It transpired, however, that Ffoulkes was correct. They passed beneath the shade of the spruce and firs, the brown needles crunching satisfyingly beneath their shoes, and their noses filled with the sharp and fresh tang of pine, finding flat ground on the other side. A wide road of dry and dusty earth stretched off in either direction along the valley floor, a dropped shoelace weaving and meandering as it hugged the great river.

Robin hadn't known what to expect from the Dish. He had vaguely envisioned a babbling country stream, all white foam and leaping salmon, but the waters were wide and full, so swollen in places that he doubted he would be able to swim to the far and distant bank without the aid of water mana. And it flowed quickly as it moved along, tumbling and roaring, deep and clear and foamy.

"You could float a ferry on that," Robin observed. "The river is massive. It's like the Nile or the Amazon."

"I'm not familiar with either of those, but if you think this is a broad river, little lord, I'm happy to tell you it gets larger further south," Ffoulkes told him. "Once out of the highlands and over the great waterfall, the Dish spreads out lazily on the lower ground, like a lion in the sun, but it's lost much of its speed and energy by then. Here high in the Floreo, it's still young, full of energy, vim and vigour!"

"And much more likely to drown you and pull you to your death," Jackalope added. "We follow the flow of the river, right? Downstream will lead us to waterfalls and Titania's Tears."

Their guide nodded in agreement, but he was frowning a little. "That is indeed so," he said. "Lamentably, by my reckoning it is around thirty miles from here to the falls, and that is as the crow flies, not as … ahahah … the boy walks. Youth, vim and vigour notwithstanding. My shoes are, alas, Saville Row, not Reinhold Messner, and I have no wish to walk it. But fear not! The agora at the Tears is a meeting place for all people."

He planted his long walking stick at an angle in the grass at the side of the road, and rested against it as though it were a shooting stick.

"What are we stopping here for?" Robin asked, dropping his pack gratefully from his shoulders. They had only been walking for perhaps two hours, but much of it had been near-vertical.

"We await transport," Ffoulkes replied, by way of explanation. He fished out a frayed-looking rope from his belongings and tossed it casually to Woad, who caught it with quick reflexes. "Pop this around your neck, would you, old sport? There's a decent chap."

"Righty-ho!" Woad nodded happily, slipping the rope around his head.

"Hang on!" Robin interrupted, looking concerned. "What? Why are we tying each other up?"

Ffoulkes looked world weary, as though his student had been placed on earth for the sole purpose of asking ridiculous questions. "Because, dear boy, we are headed to market. And those who head to market do so with the intention to buy or sell. Discretion, if you recall, was the watchword of your estimable aunt. As far as the Netherworlde cares to know, today I am a simple if stylish merchant, off to sell my faun at market, and the two of you are my young apprentices. It will provide us good cover."

"We're not selling Woad!" Robin argued.

"My young, *mute* apprentices," Ffoulkes amended. "And of course, we are not. But fauns are wild creatures and their pelts do indeed fetch a pretty price here in the Netherworlde." He glanced at the faun, who was now happily wearing the rope like a leash. "No offence intended, my cobalt companion."

"None taken," Woad insisted, puffing his blue chest out proudly. "Of course a faun is valuable. We are worth ten of any other, pelted or peltless."

"It's not a bad plan," Jackalope admitted, drawing a wide-eyed look from Robin. "As subterfuge, I mean. You have to admit, Scion, it's a better cover story than 'two illegal and wanted fugitive Fae enter town for nefarious reasons with blueberry blabbermouth and chatty old fop'."

Ffoulkes bristled, but coughed politely, ignoring the "old".

"Although I recall that you did try and kidnap Woad once before," Jackalope continued thoughtfully. "So, I should probably point out that if you try any funny business, Phorbas and I will have sharp words about it with you." He twirled his knife casually, its blade flashing in the bright sun.

Ffoulkes looked scandalised. "I am a changed man!" he insisted, hastily picking up the loose end of Woad's rope. "And, might I add that it is remarkably indecorous to threaten your elders and tutors, even obliquely."

Jackalope shrugged. "You're not *my* tutor," he pointed out. He glanced sidelong at Robin. "Don't worry, Scion. We will keep our eyes on him."

Ffoulkes leapt to his feet. "Look! Here comes a cart right now. Capital! We shall hitch a ride and be at the Sorrows for lunch or I'll eat my hat, you'll see. Just keep quiet and let me do the talking if you please. I am perhaps the sole member of our happy hiking company with even the barest modicum of charm."

There was indeed an open-topped farmer's cart in the distance, being drawn by a small black mule and almost lost in a haze of road dust as it made its bumpy way slowly towards them.

As it got closer, they could make out the driver. He was a short and heavy-set man, bent over the reins with an aspect of familiarity and comfort. He was dressed simply with a cloth cap atop his balding head, and his cart carried two of the largest pigs Robin had ever laid eyes on. One black and glossy, the other spotted pink and brown in a way that reminded him, for some reason, of fairground rock.

The boys stood back as Ffoulkes hailed the farmer and listened warily as Robin's tutor did all the talking, spinning a convincing yarn filled with completely unnecessary embellishments about his career as a mountain trapper of rare and luxurious game. The old farmer, who to Robin appeared almost human, expect perhaps for his eyebrows being unnaturally long, listened gruffly as Ffoulkes yammered on, eyeing them all with a kind of lazy and disinterested suspicion and occasionally leaning forward from his seat to reassuringly pat the flank of his restless mule.

When Ffoulkes had finally stopped talking – about the mountain air, about the beauty and quality of the farmer's pigs, and the daredevil trials of trapping wild fauns, even with the help of hapless and unskilled assistants – the farmer finally removed his cloth cap, revealing a leathery head, which he scratched thoughtfully.

"You'll get a fairer price for a faun up near Worrywart," he said flatly. "Ravens are always patrollin' up there, those dark ones under the Wolf of Eris. Give me the shudders, they do." He shrugged. "But they do like a bit of faun to make a belt or such. Fancy lot."

Woad made a great show of inspecting his own outstretched arm, as though admiring its quality and worth.

"Market at the Sorrows ain't so busy right now," the old Panthea told Ffoulkes. "Wrong season, see? No travellers from distant parts, Only really local folks from the Floreo. Pigs and mutton, the odd chalpie crop. I'll give you a ride, aye, if you're fixed on it, but you're throwin' your coin in the river, if you ask me."

"Capital!" Ffoulkes leapt on this. "Business is business, after all. And sometimes a quick sell is better than a good sell, they say." He glanced at Woad. "Some game is troublesome to keep for too long."

The old man tilted his head to the rear of the cart. "Hop on then, though you'll have to squeeze in with Bess and Clara. They don't bite, but they ain't in the best o' moods. Reckon they know this is the last trip for my old girls. Clever things, pigs, you know."

"Clever *and* delicious," Ffoulkes agreed, beaming. He waved Robin and Jack to the back of the cart, where both boys clambered up, making the whole thing shake and the two very large pigs grunt and snort in indignation.

"Oh, woe!" Woad cried tremulously. "Fie and alack!" He was gripping the rope around his neck with great drama. "What fate befalls this handsome faun? What magnificent end awaits this most glorious creature? As a young faun, I always believed if I lived wild enough and free enough, I could become anything! Oh woe! I didn't mean to become purses and boots! Even those of the highest quality!"

Ffoulkes gave the faun a murderous look, appalled by the amateur theatrics. He gave a tug on the rope, turning Woad's subsequent gruff chuckle into a gurgle.

Robin was glad that he and Jack were hidden behind the pigs, trying as they were not to laugh.

"Hold up, one thing," the old farmer said as Ffoulkes clambered up beside him at the front of the cart. "That little blue menace of yours. He don't have no Skyfire, do he?"

Ffoulkes shook his head emphatically. "Oh, no! No, no, no, no! Not a spark, not a flicker. Hasn't come into it, thank goodness – late bloomer, for a faun."

"Right-o," the farmer said, nodding and then slapping the mule firmly to resume the journey. "S'long as that's the case, cause any o' that, and you'll be buying from me a whole lot o' crispy bacon I can't sell elsewhere, don't you doubt it, sir."

Ffoulkes laughed, sounding extremely false. "Onward then, to the market town," he insisted, stretching out comfortably as he could on the hard plank of the cart's seat. "And as for you …" He pointed at Woad as he scampered up onto the cart with the other boys. "Not another word."

"Quiet life, that's the best." The old farmer nodded amiably in agreement, frowning his long eyebrows. As they pulled off, the rickety cart rumbling and swaying down the road, he glanced back at the two Fae squashed in with the pigs behind him.

"And what about you two? Assistant trappers, eh? You're quiet lads."

Robin saw Ffoulkes give them both a worried look. Woad's overacting was bad enough, clearly his tutor doubted he could recover the situation if either of them said anything to make the old Panthea farmer suspicious.

Jackalope stared the old man dead in the eye.

"We're mute," he said flatly.

The farmer nodded in understanding and faced forward again. "Best way, probably," he muttered philosophically to himself.

It is far easier, Robin learned, to admire and appreciate the grandeur and beauty of nature when passing through it comfortably seated. Although, with the wooden wheels of the cart, the bumpy earthen road, and the alarming immediacy of the enormous pigs right against him, "comfortably" was something of a relative term.

The valleys of the Floreo were a magnificent space, however. As the cart, road and great river wound their ways along, the slopes rose up on both sides, high and wide, rumpled like bedsheets and filled with endless dips and hidden valleys. The bright mountains were draped with jewelled flowers and they passed dark and dense spinneys of huddled firs and stocky fragrant spruce. Birds wheeled in the blue sky above them, dancing in the mountain updraughts, distant specks. And the occasional cry of a hawk rolled down across the rocks, mellowed by the long whispering grasses before it was lost in the ever-present roar of the wide river at the base.

Jackalope had taken to passing the time by carving his initials roughly into the cart's interior with Phorbas, the blade flashing and shining as he busied himself, and Robin wondered briefly if the spirit of Phorbas, trapped in the knife, took offence at being used for such a mundane task, or whether he was simply happy to be of use and leaving a mark, however basic, upon the world.

Ffoulkes attempted to keep up some form of friendly conversation with their Panthea host, which was painful to listen to, as the farmer was clearly a man of few words, whereas Ffoulkes was a man of very many words indeed. Woad busied himself by sometimes riding on the cart and sometimes leaping off and running alongside it, still on his tether, to burn off "excess faun energy". Eventually though, even he grew tired of this and nestled down between the pigs, who graciously accepted him as one of their own, and with the warmth of the animals and the rocking of the cart, he fell into a happy and extremely noisy sleep.

With nothing else to occupy him, Robin leaned on his forearms and peacefully watched the river, fierce and deep and beautiful, as it kept pace with them for mile after mile. Occasionally, silver fish leapt and broke the surface, flashing like spearheads before disappearing back beneath the turbulent surface. He wondered briefly if there were sirens in the river. He had met them once near Erlking and almost died at their hand, succumbing to their deep-sea hypnotic glow. He decided that if there were sirens in the Dish, they would all have been swept away long ago. The current looked fierce, right the way across to the distant shore, which, as the river widened, valley after valley, must surely now be more than a mile away.

Robin searched through his satchel and drew out the strange moral compass that Henry had given him for Christmas, looking it over curiously, simply for something to do. He still wasn't entirely sure how the compass was supposed to work. It had a needle like a regular compass, but where the directional points should have been, there was a confusing procession of faces, tiny and carved, all along the rim, each displaying a different emotion. They reminded him of theatre masks. The kind you always saw laughing and crying.

"Should we be going to this town?" he muttered to himself quietly, so the others didn't hear.

The needle spun in his hands, wavering back and forth, before it finally settled on a direction. The tiny carved face with which it had aligned looked reasonably happy, Robin thought. Although it was hard to be sure what it was trying to convey. Was it a confident face? A small smile and a slightly furrowed brow ... was that supposed to indicate determination? Good judgement? Robin had no clue.

"Will we find this 'Luna' at the agora?" he asked it. Again, after a moment, the needle spun, coming to rest this time in a direction which, on a timepiece, would have been seven o'clock. Robin turned the circular device in his hands to see where it had landed. This tiny carved face looked blank, as though lost in thought. It also had something carved above its eyebrows. Holding it closer, Robin saw that it appeared to be a tiny crescent resting on the forehead. A moon?

"Is it safe for us at Titania's Tears?" he whispered to the device, again ensuring he kept his voice low so that over the clatter of the cart's wheels,

Woad's snoring and the grunting of the pigs, the others wouldn't hear. He didn't want them to think him foolish for worrying.

This time, the needle spun quickly and came to rest with such a jarring shudder, the device almost leapt from his hands. Again, he turned it in his palm so that the needle's resting place was visible, and a strange foreboding ran through him. *This* face didn't even look human. It was wrinkled and open mouthed, like a muzzle full of sharp teeth, and its brow was furrowed, the empty eyes merely slits. It looked to Robin like a wolf or a demon.

A sound had been growing, but in his fascination with his strange new device, he hadn't really registered it. It sounded like distant thunder, rolling and endless, and it was getting steadily louder, providing a menacing growl to accompany the chilling, bestial leer of the face he was inspecting.

But it was not thunder. Jackalope tapped him on his shoulder, making Robin look up, surprised.

"We're here," the grey-eyed Fae told him. "I can hear the falls. We are at Titania's Tears."

7

City of Sorrows

The cart had left off following the river, and the beaten track they followed widened as it meandered away through a deep stretch of trees, looping downhill and around increasingly craggy rocks before doubling back on itself so that, as they approached the falls, their porcine carriage trundled along the lip of the very cliffs themselves. They were joined here by other carts and wagons, this was a busier thoroughfare, where all walks of life headed along the precipitous drop towards the falls. Their modest cart jostled for space on the dusty road with carts laden high with caged birds of every colour, with brightly-painted rickshaws pulled by odd squat Panthea with rough skin the colour of stone and deep blue eyes under heavy brows. Their passengers, dressed in billowing silks of turquoise and aquamarine, shielded themselves from the sun with elaborately decorated paper parasols, swirling with printed images of suns and moons, and seemed to take great pains to ignore the rougher farmers' carts around them.

In the growing crush of traffic on the cliff road, Robin saw caravans pulled by horses of deep blue glass, their innards alive with rolling fire, silent and flickering as their hooves clipped the floor musically. There were fortune-tellers' palanquins, strung with flapping pennants like prayer flags, and odd low transports made of beaten sheets of bronze, rumbling along on thick spiked wheels, their interiors filled with large jars and tanks of giant eels, flicking angrily with the clattering motion of the road.

He had never seen so many Panthea at once, and the rumble of traffic raised dust in clouds from the cliffside road.

Robin had heard that the agora was located at the great waterfall of Titania's Tears. What he had not been prepared for was quite how enormous the waterfall would be, nor that the city itself would be built *across* it. As they curved back around the cliffs, approaching the water once more along the curving scoop of the landscape, the Tears, glittering and shining in the sun, came into view.

He had seen waterfalls in the human world of course, mainly on television. The widest being Niagara Falls in Canada, the tallest being Angel Falls in Venezuela. The Tears, he now saw, as the cart rounded a bend and it came into sight, dwarfed them both. From here high in the Floreo, at the ragged edge of a great cliff, the turbulent and swollen vastness of the River Dish spewed with apocalyptic abandon over the rocks, launching itself out into space and thundering down a sheer drop of dizzying heights in an endless, ever-roiling torrent of whipped white foam. It disappearing into the air to tumble ever downwards to the landscape of the plains that lay far below, spread out to the distant horizons like a patchwork quilt. In the very middle of the wide waterfall there was a natural spur of rock, wider than a street of houses, sticking out into space as proudly and arrogantly as the horn of some gargantuan rhinoceros. The torrid waters parted around this huge outcrop, dividing into two torrents as they flung themselves off the cliffs, before flowing back together as the water fell in huge amounts below. The sky was misted with such a permanent cloud of spray that rainbows danced like spirits, suspended in the tumbling mass.

But the town itself was strange and fascinating to behold. Robin got to his feet, gripping the sides of the cart to steady himself as he strained to get a better look.

A great wide bridge spanned the distance from this bank to the other, leaping across the river, a flattened rib bone of carved stonework. It looked for all the world as though someone had taken London Bridge and stretched it in an arch, distorted like pulled elastic, until it spanned the great waters. It must have been a mile wide, with countless supports and foundations thrusting downward from its underside into the water at the waterfall's edge, like a jumbled mass of toothpicks. They criss-crossed in every direction, being lashed to the bridge and to each other in a thousand places by ropes and pulleys.

On every visible inch of the gentle, shallow curve of the immense bridge, beneath which the Dish flowed unimpeded, there stood buildings;

cheek-by jowl and jostling for space. Constructions of stone and timber soared upwards into the sky, ridiculously and improbably tall. Higgledy-piggledy skyscrapers of swaying shops and houses. To Robin, it looked as though Vikings, in their fondness for log dwellings, had decided to try for Manhattan.

"If Henry was here …" Robin stared at the teetering, jumbled skyline of the town, watching the stacked houses and ramshackle towers sway and wobble in constant motion. "He'd say 'bloody hell!'"

The sky above the teetering, chaotic bridge-town was alive with motion. Huge colourful sails hung in the sky, great kites of canvas, billowing with air, some as large as bedsheets, others as huge as football fields. A multitude of ropes tethered them to the very tops of the many dwellings and structures, making a shifting lacework in the sky as they snapped and swayed in the high air above the town.

"The skykites," Ffoulkes explained, pointing rather redundantly with his walking stick, as though anyone's attention was elsewhere. "It's largely how the buildings stay up, you see? Dashed lack of ground space in the market town. The bridge is long, yes, this bank to that, but it's only half a mile wide, you see, aha." He was shouting a little to be heard above the growing traffic of rumbling market-goers. "So you build upwards, of course. Falls this big? Creates one devil of an updraught. Winds go up, kites never fall, and the Tears stay upright, if a little … unsteady."

"Let's hope there's never a drought," Woad said, grinning. "Whole place would come crashing down!"

They closed in on the vertical jumble of the tight-knit town. Each end of the great bridge was hidden behind a steep, wooden, encircling wall. Countless terraces covered the span, cut into the towering Jenga stacks, linked everywhere by dangerous-looking staircases and rickety rope bridges criss-crossing one another. An endless hodgepodge of rooftops crowned with smoking chimneys peppered the sky, sending smut up into the spray. The wobbling town creaked and groaned in its constant motion, like an old pirate ship at sea.

Here and there amongst the jumble and bustle of the huge bridge, Robin spied the occasional old stone ruin. A crumbling white wall towering over here, a half-crumbled archway of ancient pale stone nestled over there. They stuck out from the ramshackle wooden town like broken old teeth, shining in the bright sun.

Robin knew that the agora town of the Panthea had grown up in the ruins of some ancient, long-gone settlement of the Fae. The chaotic appearance of the newer town made it look like a host of ambitious barnacles clinging to the bones of old stone.

"I know you said the agora town was on the waterfall," Robin said to Ffoulkes, a little lost in disbelief. "But I thought you meant ... you know ... *by the side*. Built on one bank or the other. Not actually *on* the waterfall!"

"A masterful showcase of ancient engineering, isn't it just?" His tutor nodded with a strange kind of personal pride, as though he himself had single-handedly laid every brick of the gargantuan bridge which arced across the river. "It is truly wonderful what the powers of earth and water mana can accomplish together."

The cart had turned finally turned off the road and Robin and his companions leapt down eagerly.

The other carts, wagons and foot traffic flowed around them, leaving the banks and passing out over the wide lip of the falls, and in and out of the town. With a thankful wave of farewell, their ride, with its doomed and grumbling pigs, joined the flow of traffic, leaving them standing in the shadow of the riverbank.

"How does it stay up?" Robin wondered, as Ffoulkes led the way, beginning to climb the steps carved into the road and up towards the gateway of the bridge with Woad in tow on his leash. "I mean, even with all the ropes, and the sails in the sky ... just the force of the river ... this bridge ... massive as it is ... it should be swept away."

His tutor nodded with an expression of infinite wisdom. "Titania's Tears was once a place of pilgrimage for many of your kind, young Master Robin," he explained. "Built by your people as something of a holy site, to honour the distant Elementals. Those who came before the Fae themselves, the primal entities who shaped the very Netherworlde, and who first gifted the king and queen with the Arcania. And of course, the boons of the Elementals with which the Fae were to govern."

"The boons?" Jackalope asked as they left the shore behind, striking out for the town gates. The roar of the waterfall, so loud only moments before, seemed to lull somehow into the background as they made their way across the wide stone path becoming more of a dull and constant background roar.

"You mean, like the Mask of Gaia that we had?" Robin said.

Ffoulkes nodded. "Indeed. Seven Elementals there were, and seven gifts they left the Fae, seven relics, along with the Arcania itself. Even long *after* the Elementals left this world, the Fae have honoured and remembered them. Once, long ago, this wide bridge town was all white stone. The most magnificent carved delicacy, truly a sight to behold." He shrugged. "So I'm told, anyway. That old city is gone now. These spurs and tumbled ruins you see here are there are all that remain."

Now the agora town had blossomed in its place. Like mushrooms growing wild in the skeletal ribcage of some poor forgotten forest creature.

"But hey-ho. That's progress for you, eh?" Ffoulkes winked back at the two Fae following him. "Every bit of the Tears is prime trading real estate now. Hence the properties … ahah …" He jabbed upwards with his stick into the air, "*skyrocketing*, if you'll pardon the expression. You saw the rather large spur of rock sticking out over the very centre of the bridge, I assume? That's the Spit. Divides the waterfall, makes it look like two wide streams of tears, hence the place's name, of course. Well, even that bit of land is covered in shops these days, although technically it's not a part of town any *respectable* person would go." He fussed with his cuffs a little. "Most dubious and disreputable merchants, out there. *Within* the walls … centre of town … is where all the *real* commerce goes on, as you will see."

Ffoulkes gave a little shake of his head. "As to how the place stands against the mighty force of the Dish … who knows? It has always been a favoured spot of the Elementals; perhaps they protect it still with their eternal grace."

"They're gone, though," Woad pointed out. "They've always been gone. Ever since forever."

"True," the Fire Panthea allowed. "But some footprints are so deep they never quite fade from the sand, no matter how many tides come and go."

They had reached the gates of the town, a tall archway with wide wooden doors standing open, carts and carriages of every size, shape and colour passing beneath it busily. On either side large braziers of iron stood unlit, resting on beds of rushes and straw that lay scattered across the cobbles. Robin saw pennants, long flags of green and silver snapping in the breeze, suspended from the town walls. Each was decorated with an embroidered creature, some kind of shadowy and muscular beast, rendered in dark thread and as unidentifiable to Robin as the illuminations from a mediaeval bestiary. The tapestry work looked frayed with age and faded from the sun and the elements.

"Unicorns," Ffoulkes told them. "Down by the distant base of the falls, where the river leaves the Florea and enters the lowlands, there stands One Horn Forest. It's big and *not* a place you would be advised to travel through. Filled with bandits and all manner of ne'er do wells. That's why the blasted animals are the symbol of the town up here."

Carved above the wide wooden archway through which they now passed were the words: *Dolorem Ipsum. Caveat Emptor.*

"Many people call this town 'the Sorrows'," Woad said. "I've heard that before. Because of the Tears and the river."

Ffoulkes laughed. "And because of the chance of losing a fortune here, as well," he added. "Buyer beware *indeed*. One definitely needs one's wits about oneself to turn a profit at the agora."

Robin had never visited a working town in the Netherworlde before. He had made his way through an abandoned ghost town on the Isle of Winds once, and he had explored the banshee-haunted holding of Briar Hill, but the Sorrows was a world of difference. It was *alive*.

Within the walls, his senses were assaulted with all the sights, smells and sounds of hectic life. The town was bustling, with many Panthea making their way through the narrow and twisting streets, dodging carts and driven animals. The wooden buildings, almost every one a shop or tavern, loomed over the people. Ramshackle structures of wood and whitewashed plaster, crammed close together and atop one another, stretching away above them. Robin gazed upwards at the dizzying net of rope bridges and walkways that was swaying in the breeze, linking the gently-wobbling towers above. Peaked roofs shaded the crowded cobbled streets from the morning sun.

They passed a vendor's stall stacked high with a pyramid of shining, iridescent beetles, each as large as Robin's hand and all warbling and singing in high and delicate harmony. The storekeeper, a thin man with oddly elongated mantis-like arms, caught their eye and beckoned them closer to check out his wares. Ffoulkes waved him away politely as the vendor grinned at them, flashing a set of shining golden teeth.

Elsewhere in the street, a sinewy Panthea was juggling globes of slow-moving fire; the baseball orbs of flame flickered red and purple and blue, constantly shifting hues as he tossed them into the air in intricate patterns. A woman with the widest mouth Robin had ever seen sat cross-legged on the floor nearby, accompanying him on a double-barrelled flute.

Ffoulkes led them up a steep flight of stairs to a higher level of the town and jostled them through the crowds, along a narrow and winding street filled with food shops. Some seemed familiar to Robin. Bakeries with windows thrown open wide and their windowsills and doorways piled high with neatly-stacked bread and round, golden rolls, glossy with butter. Others sold stranger fare; dark roasted lizards on skewers, stacked three to a stick, bowls of bubbling soup through which swam tiny fish, glimmering and shining in the steam, and a cheery-looking stall sold multi-coloured ice cream labelled, in looping script, *vanilla regret, blueberry ache* and *chocolate chip foreboding*.

"Can we stop for dessert?" Woad piped up. "I could go for a scoop of liquorice schadenfreude right now." Ffoulkes ignored him, tugging a little sharply at his leash to remind the faun that he was supposed to be produce.

Onwards, upwards, and across they went, weaving through the crowds and up and down rickety wooden staircases that clung to the corners of buildings, and across wide paved terraces suspended between the shaky towers by thin rope bridges.

They travelled along roads where fabric merchants decorated the fronts of their stores with dizzyingly-complicated carpets, the patterns of which seemed to shift and move as Robin passed them, like kaleidoscopes turning. Dyers were laying out great circular tubs of brightly-coloured wares before their stalls; red, blue and green, all steaming in the air. They passed through narrow alleyways that were strung with fluttering ribbons of fabric in every colour, a spider's web rainbow of drying material beneath which they passed. It seemed that everywhere Robin looked there was something to buy and something to sell. An old woman with a tray around her neck, and her hair in a silver handkerchief, tried to get them to buy a selection of eyelashes from those she carried and displayed. "Blue ones would suit your sullen little boy, sir." She nodded at Jackalope as she jostled Ffoulkes' elbow. "Give dreams of hidden treasures, they do. Per'aps these long ones for the skinny lad? One 'undred percent damask camel, they are. One flutter and he'll be seeing through walls, he will."

"No, thank you, madam," Ffoulkes told her politely. "We are all quite satisfied with our current features."

On every teetering corner, it seemed, was a tavern or an ale house, the hearty aromas of beers and wines floating out through their glowing windows, along with the sounds of merriment and music, muffled by the thick walls. Hanging signs declared their names and Robin read them aloud each time they passed one.: "The Unicorns' Watering Hole … The Gravediggers' Arms, The Fox and Banshee."

There was usually a smorgasbord of odd steeds tethered at the tavern doors while their owners rested and drank within. There were lizards the size of Shetland ponies, rolling their eyes in swift reptilian suspicion, their hides shimmering through different colours as their scales bent and tilted against the sun. Dogs the size of mice, sleeping on windowsills with long tongues lolling. And occasionally, a horse, looking surreally normal and boring by comparison.

The Panthea were everywhere. They threaded through the vertical, swaying jumble of streets and bridges; jostling, haggling, trading, shouting. Robin suddenly felt very exposed, as though he had a sign branded on his head that said *Scion of the Arcania. Illegal Fae. Arrest on sight!*

A group of women passed them in one narrow street, their purple and white dresses billowing and floating around them, infused with water mana. A muscular man in trousers that were covered in black and white harlequin patterns was herding a group of roughly spherical rocks along one road, as though they were a flock of sheep. He clacked along behind them with a stick as they rumbled by. He doffed his pork-pie hat to Ffoulkes and the boys as they stepped aside to let him pass, smiling at them through a thick handlebar moustache.

"There are so many people here," Robin said, speaking loudly enough to be heard above the clamour and din as they were carried along through the agora.

"Of course there are," Ffoulkes replied. "Everyone comes to the Sorrows to buy and sell. It is said that there is nothing you cannot find in the Sorrows – except perhaps a moment's peace and quiet, ahaha. Come, this way, stay close and stay together now. There's a square up ahead. There should be a little more room to breathe there. We shall get attempt to get our bearings."

Robin need not have worried too much about being conspicuous amidst so many Panthea. As they fought their way along the wooden streets, ducking snapping guide-ropes and skirting dizzying drops as balconies wound around the tottering heights, few people seemed to pay him any attention. As they wove themselves between customers vying to buy vast strings of smoked sausages, huge grey sacks of what looked suspiciously like flickering thunderclouds, and rolls of brightly-coloured silk by the yard, it was Woad, not Robin, who drew all of the attention. Evidently, a live and captured faun was a rare enough sight, even in such a place of colourful and varied distractions, and many an eye followed their progress with interest. Several of the leather workers, tanners and other dealers in flesh and hide hollered and beckoned to them from their stalls and shopfronts as they passed, but Ffoulkes dismissed them all with polite nods and waves.

Woad himself did not seem remotely perturbed by this attention, despite the hungry gleam evident in many faces. Indeed, he flexed his tiny muscles and struck the occasional dramatic pose as they passed through the crowds, preening like a prize-fighter and loving the attention, even as Ffoulkes made an all too convincing show of pulling his bounty along on its rope.

They eventually tottered along a wide swaying bridge, which spilled out from the busy side streets into a modest square, formed on the flat roof of the buildings below. With more open space, the traffic was less busy here and the town seemed at last to open up and breathe a little. At the heart of the square, a fountain had been erected around a crumbled and ancient-looking carved archway, a remnant of the old city. Ivy, choked with small purple flowers, trailed over it and a gaggle of tiny golden monkeys clambered all over the foliage, scampering like squirrels as they picked at the petals and flowers. Here and there in the square, people sat and rested, laden with goods to buy or sell. Ffoulkes and the boys made their way to the fountain, like drowning folk sighting a piece of flotsam, and in its relative peace and shade, they paused at last.

"Well, we're here," Jackalope said, his eyes constantly darting around, weighing up everyone in the crowds. "What's the plan of action now?"

He looked very uncomfortable being around so many people. Having lived the life of a hermit for years, this assault on the senses was clearly not his happy place, Robin supposed.

All between the high piled buildings, Robin could see little imp-like creatures darting, their iridescent dragonfly wings buzzing as they swooped between the streets, carrying large plates of food, barrels of ale, or sizzling kebabs smelling of honey and spice from one part of the Sorrows to the other. He guessed they were the messengers of the town. Flying was the simplest way to transport food and carry messages. Titania's Tears was such a busy place that even the air beneath the great sails was full of fluttering motion.

"We're here to find Luna, whoever or whatever that is," Robin said, ducking as one of the swift imps zipped just above his head, speedy about its business as it delivered a tray of Cornish pasties. "Though now that we're actually here, I haven't really got a clue where to start. It's going to be like looking for a needle in a haystack." He wished the odd hex message had been more specific.

"Best way to find a needle in a haystack is to jump into it, that's what I think," Woad said, and smiled. "You can always trust the needle to find your butt, no matter how much hay you're hoping for."

Ffoulkes was looking around the square thoughtfully. It was sunny, and the vast sails and skykites high overhead cast ever-moving shadows across the ground. "It may be prudent for the four of us to divide our efforts. Cover a little more ground that way, perhaps."

"You want to split up?" Robin frowned.

"I used to have a lot of contacts here at the Tears." Ffoulkes glanced at him, ignoring his look of mild alarm quite deliberately. "Specialist traders of the Sorrows, all thoroughly reputable and honest folk, of course. If I can locate some of them, I can ask around, perhaps call in a few favours. It is a good thing I am a well-connected man of note, you know."

Robin thought it was about as likely that Ffoulkes was connected to any honest or reputable people as it was that Woad would pursue a quiet life of scholarly self-reflection.

"I don't think it's a good idea for you to take Woad off into the market and leave me and Jack here twiddling our thumbs," he said. "You'd probably come back and find two captured Fae in the town stocks." *If you came back at all*, he added silently to himself.

"I think it's a good idea to split into teams," Jackalope said, unexpectedly. "We will certainly draw less attention than the four of us together."

"Capital!" Ffoulkes clapped his hands together, looking pleased with himself.

"But …" Jackalope waved Phorbas at him in a non-threatening but rather obvious way. "*I* will go with *you*. Woad and the Scion will stay together." He gave Robin a sly look, making it clear that he did not intend to let Ffoulkes out of his sight, for even a moment.

Robin nodded in approval. Ffoulkes looked a little sour, but he attempted to hide his irritation as best he could.

"However we divide our labour," Robin's tutor said warily, fiddling nervously with his cuffs as his eyes strayed suddenly across the square. "we would do best to keep the lowest profile possible." His voice had dropped to a low hiss and the colour had drained from his face. "Look over there."

The others followed his furtive stare and Robin's heart froze. Away through the crowds, making their way out into the bustling square from one of the wider side streets, he spotted a troupe of peacekeepers.

He had encountered Eris' police force before in the dark snows of the north, and they were no less chilling to see here in the bright and busy light of day. Looking like a cross between haunted scarecrows and knights, their thin bodies were boneless patchworks of different coloured materials, and their heads plain sackcloth into which rudimentary eye-slits had been roughly slashed. They had no other features. Their heads bobbed as they travelled through the crowds, which made their long, surreal head-dresses of porcupine quills quiver and shake. They were a creepy, unsettling sight to behold. Every peacekeeper looked the same; a rag doll with elongated arms and legs. They looked like puppets broken free from their strings, which – Robin reasoned – was exactly what they actually were.

Nothing filled the sackcloth heads and bodies of the peacekeepers. They were hollow shells, brought to life and given motion and sentience only by the mana of Mr Ker, one of Eris' most powerful and dangerous Grimms.

"Peacekeepers! What are they doing here?" Robin asked in a low hiss as the Erlking outlaws huddled by the ivy-covered fountain, trying to make themselves as inconspicuous as possible.

"Peacekeepers are *everywhere*," Jackalope said darkly, watching the group make its disjointed and silent way through the swaying square. That group had a dozen members, and the crowds of Panthea were avoiding them, flowing widely around them like a stream around rocks, so that

Eris' creatures seemed to move along in their own invisible bubble of space. Clearly, they were feared even by the lawful folk of the empress' Netherworlde.

"Wherever people are, the peacekeepers tread," Jackalope hissed. "They are the eyes and ears of the empress. The long arm of the Grimms, and they reach into every shadow. My brother and I spent years in their 'care' at the camps. Before they killed him."

"It's true that it's not unusual to see a peacekeeper or two in the Sorrows," Ffoulkes commented. He had positioned himself, without any of them really noticing, so that he had his back to the distant group of scarecrow-men, thereby shielding Robin, Jackalope and Woad, should any of the empty eyes and hollow heads turn across the crowds towards the fountain.

"The empress always ensures that her subjects know they are being watchfully protected from any disloyal or criminal activity, including their own. A peacekeeper presence dissuades dissent. Especially as they have the power and authority to dispense both judgement and punishment on the spot, without trial, and with full force." Ffoulkes stroked his moustache, thoughtfully. "I've never seen them in patrols of more than two or three at a time, though. It's most irregular to see so many together. It … upsets people."

"So they're here in town for a reason, then," Robin stated. "Not just keeping an eye on the townsfolk. We need to keep a low profile. Where there are peacekeepers, you can be sure to find a Grimm."

"Best to split up as planned, then," Woad asserted. "The quicker the better. Me and Pinky on team one. Silver Top and Ginger Beard, team two. Empty-heads can't look in every direction at once, eh?"

Robin still wasn't sure about splitting up, but he certainly didn't want them spending another second out here in the open. It was far too exposed.

Jackalope must have seen the concern in his face, as he patted Robin's back in an uncharacteristic show of reassuring camaraderie. "I'll keep an eye on Ffoulkes," he whispered. "Make sure he doesn't get up to anything too slippery. Stay low, keep Woad out of sight, and we will meet back here in an hour, yes?"

Robin nodded, feeling oddly reassured by the elder Fae's calm and pragmatic presence. There was nothing else for it. They had to slip away, get themselves lost in the maze of the agora, and keep well out of the peacekeepers' sight. He rifled through his satchel until he found his hex message parchment, and tore off a strip, which he pushed into Jackalope's hands.

"If anything happens, send me a hex," he said.

Jackalope instantly handed the parchment to Ffoulkes. "I don't write, numbnuts," he muttered. "What am I going to do, send you a finger painting?" He peered at Ffoulkes as the Fire Panthea took the parchment and tucked it away into his waistcoat. The peacekeepers were still worming their way around the square, like sharks through a large shoal of fish.

"One hour, back here," Robin said firmly to Ffoulkes, who nodded regally.

They waited until the stream of scarecrows was momentarily blocked from view by a lumbering rickshaw, and, with as much decorum as they could manage, they scattered, Ffoulkes tossing Woad's leash to Robin as the Scion and his friend scampered off through the crowds, keeping low and ducking away down a steep street of bobbing, suspended steps, ducking under jumbled stalls and signs, darting swiftly past multi-coloured concoctions and practically sliding along an unstable platform helped up only by ropes attached to something like small grey weather balloons.

Robin looked back as they reached a corner, but Ffoulkes and Jackalope were already gone, lost in the endless commotion of Titania's Tears. He tried to shift the lump of worry that had settled in his stomach. He didn't wholly trust Jackalope not to try something confrontational with the forces of Eris. They had torn his family away from him, long ago. The boy had never recovered from the death of his brother. It was a scar that still wouldn't heal. Robin prayed that he would have the sense to lie low, but dread was nibbling at the edges of his thoughts – a quiet certainty that something terrible was going to happen.

With no knowledge of the Tetris-like geography of the agora town, Robin and Woad didn't stop moving until they had put several twisting streets, and multiple levels of staircases and bridges between themselves and the peacekeepers, heading ever downwards, out of the heights and towards the base of the rock archway that spanned the river. The wooden-board streets and twisting, rickety stairs here were steep, with ladders here and there, and many a sharp turn as the walkways hugged the buildings. Not fit for mules or carts, although the foot traffic was still heavy. Robin took some comfort in the labyrinthine alleys and streets. Even if they were being trailed, it would be easy to shake off a pursuer.

Dropping beneath the awning of a tall thin shop, the emblazoned name of which, above the dark windows, read *O'Hannerhey Tannerhey*, the two boys rested, slightly breathless, against the leaded panes of the mullioned windows.

Woad tugged the rope out of Robin's hands. "I can carry my *own* lead, Pinky," he grinned. "Don't worry, I'm not going to run off and leave you here to fend for yourself."

"This town is a complete maze," Robin considered. "How are we supposed to find anything useful and avoid peacekeepers at the same time?"

Woad shrugged, unconcerned. "We could always ask around?" he suggested. Leaping immediately away from the shop-front, he tugged at the ruffled skirt of a passing woman, making her stop in her tracks. "Oi, missus, do you know where Luna is?"

The woman almost jumped out of her skin. Her hand, the fingers of which were laden with rather gaudy-looking paste jewel rings, fluttered to her chest. She stared down at Woad, who was grinning up at her like a loon, and then over to Robin.

"Boy, is this your faun?" she asked tremulously. Her chins wobbled with distress. She could have passed for human, except for her eyes, which were a glittering red.

"Um … yes … sorry," Robin said apologetically, dragging Woad back. He wondered vaguely what manner of Panthea the large woman was. "He's just … enthusiastic."

"You should learn to control it!" she snapped in a high and scandalised voice. "Leaping out of the shadows and giving people a fright! Wild things from wild places!"

"Sorry, again." Robin grinned sheepishly, trying to give the affronted woman his most winning smile and shove Woad behind him at the same time.

"What is it babbling about?"

"Oh … well, Luna. We're looking for someone called Luna," Robin explained. "I don't suppose you've heard of him? Or her? Maybe a storekeeper or market stall holder around here?"

She shook her head, still looking put out. "I have not!" she snapped, snatching back her skirts, still clutched in the faun's fingers, and storming off into the crowds. "And if I were you, child," she called back tremulously over her shoulder, "I should barter off that beast sooner rather than later! Old Mr Chutton down by the west bank gives a good price by the pound for decent skins, but sooner is best! A chatty beast with snatching fingers is a burden to everyone and a menace to civilised society!"

Robin glared after her as she bustled away. "Don't listen to her, Woad," he muttered. "You're not an animal."

Woad seemed utterly unruffled. He blew on his nails and rubbed then against his chest, polishing them happily. "You can say that again," he agreed, puffing with pride. "I'm a beast!"

Robin jumped slightly as a gnarled hand tapped him most unexpectedly on the shoulder. Both boys whirled to see that the shopkeeper in whose window-bay they currently lurked had emerged from the darkness of his store. He was a small and wrinkled creature with a straggly mop of grey-white hair and rather protuberant eyes. Robin opened his mouth to apologise, expecting to be asked to move along and stop cluttering the tiny man's doorway, but instead, the old Panthea wiped his hands on the leather apron he wore and tilted his chin at them.

"I hear right there, boy?" he rasped. "Looking for Luna, are you?"

Both boys nodded cautiously.

"Yes, that's right," Robin said hopefully. "We don't know the town very well."

The tiny man shook his head, frowning at them both. "Luna ain't no *person*, lad," he told them. "Luna's a *place*. Bone-reader resides there, out by the Spit, though what a young 'un like you and your pet here might want with that kind of mumbo jumbo, I can't begin to guess."

Absolutely nothing he had said made any sense to Robin, who looked to Woad desperately.

"Bone reader?" the faun frowned. "Fortune-teller, you mean?" He flicked his yellow eyes to Robin. "Those who say sooths, that's what he's saying. A soothsayer, so to say."

The shopkeeper nodded. "Aye, that's the shape of it. There's plenty a businessman, merchant and traveller who pay a pretty price to have the blind one at Luna stroke their palm-lines and tell them whatever they want to hear." He didn't sound very approving. "Good harvest, fat cows, safe travels." He snorted down his nose. "Paying to hear what you want to hear, if you ask me, all that smoke and mirrors nonsense. Might as well talk into a well and take your echo's advice when it says to jump."

"What's the Spit?" Robin asked politely.

"The Spit?" the shopkeeper explained. "It's the big old rock down at ground level, of course. Halfway along the span of the Tears. Splits the falls in two, it does. Sticks right out over the edge into space like an eagle's beak." He sniffed, looking unimpressed. "Ain't really a part of the town proper though. Walls of the Sorrows lie up against it, not around it. There's only a few buildings stupid enough to be out on the Spit itself. Those that don't mind spray and thunder, and enough rumble to shake the teeth out of your head." He patted the door frame of his own shop with a kind of affection pride. "Best spots are up here. Not a likely pitch down on the Spit for anyone setting up shop in the Sorrows and hoping to make a penny."

Robin wondered how far it was to the Spit from here. The layout of Titania's Tears was so confusing he could barely tell which way he was facing at the best of times.

"It's all *odd folks* on the Spit," the shopkeeper said and nodded at them warily, clearly not realising how odd he himself seemed to Robin. "There's a shop selling lamps. Rattle away all day they do, hung above the door. Shifty old sod who runs it claims they're genies, one wish left in each, huh!" He grunted, which might have been a humourless laugh, leaning against the frame of his open door. "Though if that were true, the swindling old bugger would have rubbed one himself long ago and asked for a better pitch in town, for a start. Another place sells rings, necklaces, probably all stolen from graves and barrows, and likely cursed, or even worse … fake." He shook his head. "And then … well, there's the house of Luna, danglin' right over the edge of the falls itself and throwin' chicken bones in the air to con good folk out of their money and sense." He fixed Robin with a warning stare. "Nowt but bad deals go down on the Spit. You'd do best to stick in town." His face suddenly brightened up. "Head on up Copperfield Street two rows over and get yourself a pie. Does good pies, the bakery there," he told them enthusiastically. "Or order an imp, save your legs. Uber-imps are a growin' business in the modern world, don't you know."

Robin nodded, not wanting to seem impolite.

"Give your money to a fortune-spinner, and you get nothin' but dreams and mind-fluff, mark my words," the shopkeeper advised them. "Give it to a baker and ... well ..." He hooked his thumbs decisively in the pockets of his apron. "At least that way you know there's pastry in your future, and that's nowt to be sniffed at in this day and age."

He tilted his chin again, this time in the direction of Woad.

"How much you asking for the faun, then?" he asked Robin, attempting to seem disinterested. "Quality tanner, me. Says so on the sign. Got some new brass eyelets in today, good quality, all the way from Spitrot. Those redcaps are devil-good with metals. Could make you a decent belt, help hold your trousers up with all the coin I'll put in your pockets for that fine hide."

Robin waved his hands a little urgently. "Oh, no ... he ... it's not for sale."

The shopkeeper eyed him, confused and suspicious.

"I've decided to keep him ... for a bit." Robin was aware how unconvincing he sounded. "I can hold my own trousers up for now."

"Why'd anyone keep a faun?" the shopkeeper grumbled to himself, but he shrugged, as if it was all the same to him. Clearly, a boy intent on throwing his money at fortune tellers, when he could be throwing them toward a sausage roll, didn't have enough business sense to sell a decent faun pelt when an offer was on the table.

Woad beamed admirably. "I am simply chock full of novelty value!" he declared.

They thanked the old man for his help and advice, and after taking some rather beflaboured directions, they set off once again through the streets, making their way downwards and out, to the edge of town, and the spit of rock and the location of Luna.

Before long, the roads and alleyways they took seemed to grow much quieter and distinctly shabbier. There were far less Panthea on this side of the town, less tumult and hubbub, and it seemed the shopkeeper had been correct. The closer and lower you got to the edge of the falls, the less reputable and desirable the establishments in question became. Before long, the only people occupying the ever-narrowing streets, suspended walkways, tethered steps and rickety alleyways had a distinctly shifty air about them, hurrying along on their business, hoods up and heads down. Lurking and smoking pipes in narrow doorways, or occasionally peeping out from shadowy windows, faces like inquisitive ghosts behind thick and wobbly glass as Robin and Woad padded up and down steps and along grubby cobbles.

"I think we're definitely on the bad side of town here, Woad," Robin said as they passed a narrow shop with dried crocodooms hung on cruel-looking hooks in the windows. "There's barely anyone here, and if there was, I think it would just be the …"

"Slit your throat and cut your purse kind?" Woad said helpfully, skipping ahead.

Robin nodded. The only people he could see in this particular alleyway were a couple of hook-nosed redcaps, their lobster red skin and tiny black eyes giving them the appearance of demonic puppets from a Punch and Judy show. They melted away at the boys' approach. Robin had the distinct feeling that the kind of people who frequented this warren were the kind who did not care for others to see their business. In truth, he was beginning to have serious doubts about the person who had sent him the strange hex message. How trustworthy could someone be, when they wrote to you in blood and directed you to the shabbiest, most unpleasant part of a distant town to have your fortune told in a tumbledown shack? The one positive was that there didn't seem to be any peacekeepers here.

Robin called Woad to a halt at the next grimy street corner, shrugging his pack off his shoulders. He rummaged through it, with the vague idea of seeing if his mysterious messenger had sent any further cryptic instructions, but when he opened his folded sliver of parchment, he found instead a scrawled message from Ffoulkes.

Master Robin. The wolf is in town, it read, in hastily-scrawled letters. *We've seen him. be cautious!!!*

Robin read this aloud to Woad, frowning to himself, as Ffoulkes' words, once read, began to fade. The image of his spinning compass and the bestial maw it had come to rest on loomed in his mind.

"What wolf?" Woad asked. "What are he and Silver Top up to? And is there any real need for quite so many exclamation marks?"

Robin dug around for a pen and began to send a message back asking just that, but before he could put pen to parchment, new words from his tutor appeared.

About time you read this! they said. *Had a blasted run in with peacekeepers. Not to fear! One knows all the back streets here. Haven't found anything useful, per se. Your sombre and glowering friend, I believe, is cramping my usual charm. Although he has gotten a fair few looks from the ladies. Nobody seems to appreciate a well-groomed beard these days, alas! Getting nowhere. Where are you? Will come to you. Rather dangerous with the wolf here, really cannot state that quite strongly enough. Ahaha. We should leave the city post haste.*

As Robin read the words, vaguely astonished that Ffoulkes had taken the time to actually write out his laugh, he heard low voices just around the corner and the shuffling of feet. Someone was talking nearby, quite urgently it seemed. They sounded agitated, afraid even. But it was the second voice that made him freeze. This was a low growl, barely a whisper, but Robin knew it instantly.

He hastily scrawled *Luna, fortune-teller. Out on the Spit. Edge of the falls. On our way there.* Then stuffed his hex message parchment back into his satchel without even bothering to watch the words disappear. With his free hand he had raised a finger to his lips, motioning Woad to be absolutely silent.

That voice … *the wolf*, Robin thought. It wasn't just peacekeepers at Titania's Tears. Strigoi himself was here.

Beckoning Woad closer, Robin edged to the corner of the bare and crumbling brick wall and cautiously peered around, as stealthy as an assassin.

The alleyway beyond was close and twisted, with shops on both sides looking grubby-windowed and closed up. The source of the voices was coming from some way along, where a group of four peacekeepers stood surrounding a short, portly man in tattered clothing. He appeared to have been dragged from his shop; a pawnbroker's, from the look of the assortment of oddities in the small leaded windows. The man looked afraid, as would anyone currently surrounded and held up at the elbows by the creepy scarecrow police of the Netherworlde. But the source of his wide-eyed terror was not the peacekeepers at all, but the figure in their midst, which towered over him with its arms folded.

Strigoi, Wolf of Eris, glared down at the shopkeeper in the quiet abandoned alleyway; his long cloak of black feathers hanging from his shoulders and blending with the shadows. The dark armour he wore glinted in the dusty air, and his face, as ever, was hidden behind the fearsome helmet he wore – fashioned to resemble a grinning wolf, carved from dark steel and topped with horns. It glared down at the hapless man in the doorway like a demon come to take his very soul.

Robin's blood ran cold and the hairs on the back of his neck stood up. What on earth was he doing here?

"I ... I ...swear, my lord," the captive pawnbroker said, his voice filled with a kind of forced, ingratiating laugher. "No one ... no one of that kind, not as far as I can remember. I've no reason to lie, not to the likes of your good self."

Strigoi tilted his head to one side, the shadows from his horns playing across the man's face. His arms, heavy vambraces threaded with twisted iron spikes, were folded against his chest.

"You are certain?" he rasped. "Think carefully, Krook. You have a reputation to uphold. All know that you fence and buy the most *interesting* things in all the Sorrows. If someone wants something, or wants rid of something ... you're the man to come to. Your reputation, however disreputable, precedes you."

The shifty-looking man shook his head desperately. "Haha, my lord is too kind, but I'm sure! I'm most certainly sure. I would remember someone like that. And of course, that kind of thing? Something of such ... value, passing through *my* humble establishment? Why, I'd have notified the authorities right away, I would!"

Strigoi did not seem moved. He stared down at the squirming man, unconvinced. "Would you, I wonder? I hear that your loyalty lies to gold, Krook. To the empress, of course, as with us all, but in *your* case ..." The tiny sliver of sunlight that had managed to penetrate this far down into the lower streets of the town shone from his carved metal face, gazing down in judgement. "Perhaps only when she appears on the face of a coin."

The pawnbroker called Krook looked panicked; he attempted a scandalised expression but failed miserably.

"I swear it!" he insisted. "It's true, Lord Strigoi. Nothin' passes through the Sorrows without old Krook knowin' its value. You're right about that, of course. I've a keen eye, anyone will tell you, and I hear much of everything that happens here ..."

"Which is why I've come to you," Strigoi said, leaning forward a little. The man attempted to scurry backwards like a cornered rat, but was held fast by the boneless arms of the peacekeepers.

"But…but…no one's come to me like what you've said," the man spluttered. "Nothin' like that's passed through my store, not even rested here for a moment, I swear it on my mother's life!"

"Your mother is long dead," Strigoi said dismissively, his voice still low and even. Unmoved by the man's fervent protestations. "And were she not, I have no doubt you would sell her for any piece of silver you could leave tooth marks in."

The man laughed, a little high and hysterically. "Aha, well yes, you've got me there, good and proper. Always admired that about Lord Strigoi, I have. Knows the measure of a man, he does. I say it to anyone, you can ask around…"

Robin crouched in silence, trying desperately to resist the urge to rush out and fire every last cantrip he knew at the Wolf of Eris. Air, earth, water, even try a little of his new fire. Every fibre of his being wanted to assault the creature, to send him reeling down the street on his back like a clattering tin can. Here was the servant of Eris responsible for his parents' death. The fiend who had led the Grimms to the hiding place of the Sidhe-Nobilitas, following the shattering of the Arcania. Eris' bloodhound, who had sniffed out the remaining Fae knights and exposed them, bringing about a massacre that few survived.

Woad must have sensed Robin's tension as, crouching beside him in the shadows of the wall, he had laid a restraining blue hand on his forearm.

"Fools rush in, Pinky," he hissed quietly. "Time will come, but not now. Wolf is too strong for you, for any of us. He'd squish you like a bug, and no one has a use for a squished Scion. We're here for Karya, remember?"

Robin nodded, still scowling at the figure intimidating the shopkeeper with his band of nightmare police. Woad was right of course. Going up against Strigoi would be suicide, but he was still struggling to contain his hatred.

"Ain't no one that fancy comes to this part of town, anyhow," the shopkeeper babbled on. "Person like that would stick in the mind." He rapped the side of his head emphatically. "Even a mind as busy as old Krook's."

"They may not have appeared as you would imagine," Strigoi growled. He seemed to be losing patience with his prey. "They are … elusive. We have sought them for quite some time."

Now a new voice piped up, surprising Robin. From within the shop, pushing out past the peacekeepers and the terrified little man, a new figure appeared.

"*That's* an understatement, I've been hunting this prey all year. More aliases and identities than you could shake a stick at. There's nothing in there, I've looked. No sign of the heart. No trace of the lost one."

He was as impressively wide as he was tall; a large man dressed in a pale blue suit, perfectly tailored and looking rather out of place amongst the surreal peacekeepers and armoured presence of Strigoi. The newcomer's hair was a shock of floppy yellow waves, his skin as waxy white as spoiled milk, and a wide friendly grin above his jowls. Robin's eyes widened. He had recognised the voice before he saw the face, but the way the terrified shopkeeper leapt fearfully out of his way confirmed his suspicions.

"That's Mr Knight!" he hissed to Woad. "From the gallery in London. He's …"

"A Grimm," Woad confirmed as they stared at the two figures squaring off in the alleyway.

Strigoi glared in the direction of the ghastly-white man with the happy smile and the dead black eyes, as the latter dusted off his hands, smoothing his suit in an absent manner over his ample stomach.

"You have been hunting all year, Mr Nyx, yes. And you have *failed*," the wolf said darkly in his low whisper. "That is why I am here. To clean up your mess. The mess left by your futile search, with that hollowed out assistant of yours. Your carelessness has drawn even the attention of Erlking, and now … *they* seek what we seek. This is troublesome for us."

Mr Nyx stared at him. His smile had not dropped, but his eyes were as cold as space. "Accusations are not helpful in service of the empress," he said, any pretence of humanity falling from his voice. He sounded like a cold wind. "My sanctum, my private space in the human world was infiltrated by Fae. Filthy *Fae*. I was making good headway tracking …"

"I have heard enough of your excuses!" Strigoi cut him off, and though the Grimm glared challengingly at the horned mask, his lips remained tight and silent. The chain of command here was clear. "Your journals, your careless notes – all compromised. You had the Scion of the Arcania under your nose, and did you capture him?" His growl was a threat and a warning. "No. Too busy hosting champagne parties and basking in the glow of human admiration. The other world has made you soft, and the empress is displeased."

Mr Nyx folded his arms in a mirror of Strigoi's own pose. He tilted his head at the pawnbroker. "This is a cold trail," he said. "The only place left to search … is in here." With a large pale hand, he reached out and gently, almost affectionately, stroked the little man's head. "And getting inside people's heads … well. That's absolutely my speciality."

"P … please, my lord …" Krook stammered, quivering. "I'm telling the truth … I am! No need to scramble …"

"Take him back inside," Nyx instructed, removing his hand, and the peacekeepers roughly dragged the struggling man back into the darkness of his pawnbroker's shop. The Grimm looked to Strigoi. "I will show you what is in his mind. It is a subtler skill than the bark of an angry dog. And then we will see for sure."

He raised his hands, palms outwards as though in offering. From their hiding place, Robin and Woad stared as they saw shadows begin to form there. Little dots and shimmers of darkness between the man's fat fingers. They seemed to roil and crawl over one another. All of the Grimms had mastery of the Tower of Shadow. Strife had his devil-dogs, Moros his grimgulls. Miss Peryl commanded gloomoths, and even Mr Ker infused his puppet peacekeepers with a shadowy semblance of life. Mr Nyx, formerly the enigmatic Mr Knight, CEO of Sire Holdings, soon had handfuls of fat black spiders, dozens of them, crawling over his fingers and over each other, made from solid shadow. Robin's skin crawled at the sight.

"You will ruin his mind," Strigoi said flatly, apparently unmoved by this macabre display. "Hollow him out, like you did with the noble boy."

Several of the spiders had already dropped from Mr Nyx's hands, landing on the cobbles at his feet with a nauseating series of plops, and were making their way swiftly into the darkness of the shop after the pawnbroker and his peacekeeper guards, scuttling and chittering quietly amongst themselves.

"You have objections to my methods?" Nyx questioned, looking faintly amused, his dark eyes slightly narrowed.

"If the result is fruitful, no," the wolf said dispassionately. "But waste my time, Grimm, and you'll be joining your fellows in the Pits of Dis."

Both men headed inside the store, passing into shadow, Strigoi having to stoop to duck his ghastly horned helmet beneath the lintel. The door closed behind them with an air of horrible finality, and other than the sound of chittering spiders and a muffled cry, Robin and Woad were left staring at an empty alleyway.

Woad breathed out, visibly sagging as the tension left him.

"What are they doing to that man?" Robin stared at the shop.

"He's a bad man," Woad nodded. "Anyone can see that. A liar and a scoundrel."

"But what are they *doing* to him?" Robin asked again.

"Questioning," Woad replied, uncharacteristically serious. He looked at Robin. "Pinky, peacekeepers are bad. Grimms are worse. Strigoi? That's worst of all. But all three together?" He shook his head emphatically. "That's a layer of Eris trifle that I do *not* want to stick my spoon into, that's for sure. We should go now, right now, before we're seen."

"We can't just do nothing," Robin argued, aghast. "I know we can't get involved, but …" He flailed around, "We have to tell someone, tell …"

"The police?" Woad gave Robin a sad little half smile, then rapped his knuckles on Robin's head, quite hard. "Those *are* the police, dumb diplodocus. Welcome to Eris' Netherworlde. There's no one to report corruption to when the ones in power are the rot themselves. Right now, you and I need to find this fortune teller, because I don't need magic powers to read the future we'll have if we hang around here kicking our heels and wringing our hands over some back-alley dodgy dealer who has been stupid enough to get on the wrong side of Eris. Our future will be icky Grimm spider-hands around my throat, and you tossed into a bag and slung over the big bad wolf's shoulder, all the better to eat you with." He dragged Robin to his feet. "Come on. Silver Top and the fop will already be making their way to Luna too after the message you sent. Time to beat it like a red-headed step-chalpie."

Before Robin could argue, Woad had grabbed him by the wrist and dragged him away in the opposite direction. He was always shocked by how very strong the skinny little faun was. He stumbled after him, grabbing at his backpack as they melted away from the dangerous shop and twisted down roads and pathways towards the Spit.

"First sign of trouble, that's what your aunt said," Woad reminded him briskly as they made good their escape. "No swashbuckling. Getting into a bun fight with Team Evil falls into that category. Let's just do what we came here for, and maybe afterwards get a sausage roll like that old man told us to, eh? Sausage rolls are better than death … usually."

Robin knew this made sense, but however shifty and dodgy the little shopkeeper might have been, he didn't think *anyone* deserved to be locked in a room with such a collection of horrible people. He forced himself to focus on their mission. They were here on Aunt Irene's instructions. They were here to help Karya. They couldn't afford to get distracted by whatever shadowy deeds the vile agents of Eris were involved in; which, as ever, seemed many and varied.

8

Grave Memories

Eventually, where the paths and roads gave way to rough rock and the buildings of the town of Titania's Tears petered out, they came to the Spit. The vast arrowhead of curved rock was wide and flat, covered in ramshackle dwellings and stalls. They passed through an archway in the perimeter wall of the Sorrows and left the town behind them, walking out along a well-worn path that had cut a shallow groove into the rock over time. Robin couldn't help but stare at the rushing, tumbling waters of the falls, cascading over the edge of the cliff in wide white foam either side of the protruding rock. They roared like endless thunder here, the spray hanging thickly in the air.

"There! Look!" Robin pointed. One of the lopsided buildings – a two-storey affair, which looked as though it had been hammered together from driftwood and bent nails, clinging to the wide slippery rock by various lashed poles and props – had a wooden sign above the opening. Swinging on its chains, the carved letters, surrounding a cutaway crescent moon, read: *Luna's Rest: Fortunes and Futures*.

"That doesn't look very … stable," Robin observed. Indeed, the shack was built so precariously over the lip of rock that more than half of its bulk was suspended in thin air, a dizzying space stretching away to the misty landscape far below the falls. It seemed to cling to the rock through sheer determination and narrative necessity.

"I've never met a soothsayer who *was* stable," Woad said. "But given the choice of going in there, or …" he wiggled his fingers menacingly in the air, "heading back to spend time with Grimm Mr Spider-Hands, I think we're better off with the devil we *don't* know."

Robin nodded in agreement, glancing back towards town, and what he saw almost made his heart stop. Standing in the gateway through which they had just passed was a peacekeeper.

It was framed by the open wooden gates. Its long, lolloping arms hung motionless at its sides and its slender, patchwork body cast an elongated shadow on the floor. The blank face regarded them dully, empty black eye sockets staring out across the rock through the eternal mist of the waterfall. The sight of it sent chills down Robin's spine.

Woad turned to see what has spooked his friend, but the peacekeeper turned away and disappeared behind the gates, moving with swift and oddly-agitated movement.

"Did you see that?" Robin whispered. Woad nodded.

"Peacekeeper saw us."

"It doesn't know who we are, Pinky." Woad tried to sound reassuring and failed miserably. "We are but humble traders, remember. Nothing shifty about us, no sir."

Robin knew that wasn't true. The peacekeepers were made from Grimm magic, from the mana of Mr Ker himself, and Robin had had the misfortune of meeting him on several occasions. Ker knew his face, which to Robin's mind meant that *all* peacekeepers knew his face. Wherever there were empty peacekeeper eyes in the Netherworlde was no safe place for a Scion.

"I think it's run off to Strigoi," Robin swallowed. "I'm sure of it. Or to that Grimm. We've been rumbled, Woad."

The faun grabbed his wrist and pulled him towards the ramshackle building out on the slippery rock.

"All the more reason for us to get a move on, then," he insisted. "We don't have time …"

"You *only* have time." A voice cut in above them, startling them both. It was a low, female voice.

The door to Luna's Rest before them had opened and two identical Panthea stood there. Slender women with pale skin and willowy arms and legs. There was a slight green tinge to their skin, an odd iridescent sheen, like scales catching the light. Both wore deep purple robes slung across one shoulder, reminding Robin of something from ancient Rome, and their hair, a deep and mossy shade of green, was piled artfully above their heads in pinned ringlets. They looked like mirror images of one another, standing in the doorway.

"Time is all any of us have, little ones," one of the women said. She was smiling down at them, but it didn't seem a particularly warm smile. Her eyes were yellow, the pretty shade of a buttercup, with a snake-like pupil that, in the bright sunlight piercing the spray-mist, was nothing more than a slit.

The other twin nodded in agreement. "Time is the only *true* currency," she added. A thin, forked tongue flicked out and darted about her lips for a split second. "So many people spend it unwisely. And *your* purse is almost empty."

"What are they?" Robin whispered to Woad out of the corner of his mouth. Both women were beautiful, but in a tightly coiled way, like cats about to pounce on mice. Their movements and words were lazy, but the hairs on the back of Robin's neck were standing up, and every animal instinct he had said he was facing a predator. "Some kind of Gorgon?"

Woad shook his head. "Lamia," he explained. "Snake-kin."

"You're *late*, and she is waiting for you," one of the women said to Robin, lazily folding her long arms and peering down at him with an air of faint disappointment, as though she had been expecting a feast and had found only a morsel.

"Are they safe?" Robin hissed, as the two boys, with no other reasonable plan, approached the dark doorway of the hut.

Woad gave an almost imperceptible shrug. "They are more wily than flat-out dangerous," he answered. "Seduce and hypnotise idiots and steal their coin, bewitch and befuddle." He gave Robin a reassuring smile. "I mean, the *rumours* are that they eat the flesh of men and boys, but to be perfectly honest, this faun has always suspected that's just something that men and boys say, to give them an excuse to stay away."

"You needn't worry," the second lamia told them, looking faintly amused. "We've already fed. You are quite safe, and, let us be honest …" She flicked her yellow eyes over them with disdain, "hardly very appetizing to begin with."

They stepped aside, one to each door lintel. "Come inside and spend a little of your time wisely, for once. She has been expecting you."

"How did 'she' know we were coming?" Robin asked, still cautious and resisting the urge to look over his shoulder to see if the agents of Eris were descending on them already.

The two lamia exchanged glances. "He's not too bright, is he?" one said.

The other shook her head, pointing to the sign above the door for Robin's attention. "Fortunes and futures," she explained. "She knows because it's her job to know. Now, come in or leave. Every moment you dally, you are spending more of your time. It slips away from you like coins from a cut pocket."

They melted inside, leaving Robin and Woad to make their own decision.

"Come on, Woad," Robin said. "At least we look unappetizing. Never thought I'd be grateful to be the walking equivalent of overcooked broccoli."

"Speak for yourself," Woad muttered as he followed Robin into the darkness of the hut. "Personally, I'm as delicious as ice cream. I've yet to meet a lamia able to resist eating at least an arm."

The tiny shack was dark within, and it took Robin's eyes a moment to adjust to the gloom. The walls and floor were bare boards but hardly an inch of the wooden floor could be seen under the many scattered and overlapping rugs of every colour and design. The walls were similarly hidden, behind the largest collection of dreamcatchers Robin had ever seen. They were everywhere – vying for space, filling the hut like spiderwebs of thread, jostling against one another on all four walls, and dangling from the ceiling in such abundance that nothing could be seen of the rafters above. The roar of the waterfall thudded through every board around them. It made the hut vibrate, causing every one of the dreamcatchers to be in constant shivering motion. Not one part of the room was empty or still. Shadows leapt from the light cast by a tiny hearth. The two lamia women had retreated here and now sat curled on the floor quite comfortably, either side of the fireplace, watching the boys with interest. No fire burned in the grate, but a cluster of pillar candles, between which were wedged several burning sticks of some deep, earthy incense, gave the illusion of a burning fire.

In the centre of the floor, amidst a pile of tossed cushions, a short woman was sitting cross-legged and peeling an egg.

"Shut the door will, you?" the woman said. "You'll let in the mist, and it plays havoc with my joints."

Woad dutifully kicked the door shut with his heel. It rattled a little in its frame, making the tenuous structure shake even more, and for a second Robin wondered if the whole thing was going to collapse and send them all over the falls. He glanced down, grateful that the floor was covered in rugs and carpets. He knew that if he could see between the bare floorboards, he would glimpse nothing but empty air and a long, long drop to the bottom of Titania's Tears. They were hanging over the edge here.

He couldn't tell if the woman sitting in the middle of the room was young or old, whether she too was a lamia, or some other kind of Panthea, as her face was hidden entirely beneath a gauzy black veil. Around her forehead, a collection of sparkling cut-out moons and stars shimmered on a shoddy looking diadem. Her voice gave nothing away.

"Pay no attention to these two." The woman flicked a thumb across the room at the lamia coiled by the fire, their narrowed yellow eyes glowing in the dim light. "Don't know why I keep them around, half the time. Spend all my life sweeping up shed skins, I do. Dannel and Samanna, stop staring at our guests. You're making them uneasy. Remember, we practised blinking? And anyway ..."

Having finished peeling the egg, she tossed it casually across the room. One of the women struck out, swift as a viper, catching it in mid-air in her mouth and swallowing it whole. The sudden striking motion made both boys jump.

"They've already eaten." It was hard to tell, with the veil obscuring her face, but she seemed amused at Robin and Woad's alarm.

"I am Iucundaque Murmurauoxlunae," the soothsayer said. She gestured broadly. "Known to some as Visionary Vinson." She waved a hand. "But you can call me Luna. The knuckle-heads in town do. Can't get their tongues around a proper name, any of them. Only around a pie or a pint. Muttonheads."

"One needs a forked tongue for your name, Mother Darkmoon," one of the lamia said quietly – though whether it was Dannel or Samanna, Robin had no clue. She flicked her own snakelike tongue out petulantly.

"Keep yours behind your teeth, if you please," Luna replied sternly. "This boy has come some distance to see me." She tilted her hidden face up to Robin, peering at him in the candlelight while the shadows of the dreamcatchers cast an ever-moving web across her veil. "What a curious thing it is," she said, "to travel so far only to see what is in one's own head."

"You knew I was coming?" Robin asked, as she gestured for him to sit with her. He lowered himself down onto the cushions in front of her, while Woad stayed by the door, keeping a watchful eye on the snake-like sisters.

She tapped the side of her head. "Luna's eyes might be dark, but they don't miss a shadow," she nodded.

"Do you know who sent me here?" Robin wanted to know. Perhaps the strange woman could shed some light on the identity of the hex messenger who had brought them this far.

She made a kind of grunt in response. "One who wants, that's who. Always wants and never gets. Shame really, to be starving and never fed. Tragic." She looked over at him. "You know. But it's a bones-know, not a brain-know. Bones are wiser, you can trust them, but they're so quiet, no one ever listens to them … except me."

Robin opened his mouth to argue – he didn't have a clue who the strange messenger had been – but she raised a finger to silence him.

"The twins here speak the truth when they say your time is short," she said. "Even now, the scared old man and the lonely boy approach, and they trail dark shadows with them. Very dark. Spend your time wisely on the right questions, boy. You won't get another chance."

Robin could only assume she was referring to Ffoulkes and Jackalope. They were on their way here? Good.

"Can you … I don't know … read my fortune or something, then?" he asked. "I don't have any Netherworlde coin to pay you with …"

"You'll owe me more than coin for ruining my house anyway," Luna said bluntly with a snort. "Cutting a great hole in my livelihood. That's the thanks the likes of *me* can expect from the Scion of the Arcania." She shook her head, the veil dancing. "You don't need to see your *future*, boy. That's where many want to look when they come to see me. But how can you expect answers for questions that haven't even been asked yet?"

She held out her hands, palms upwards. They were very smooth, Robin noticed. Perhaps she was younger than she sounded through the veil. "You seek a cure, and a mystery lost. Dreams of feathers and fire, sickness and secrets. Those answers are in the *past*. And I can hardly charge you for old memories, can I? What's passed in story already belongs to the world. It isn't mine to sell."

"Our friend is very sick," Robin said, taking her hands. It felt odd and awkward to do so, but it seemed to be what she was expecting. He was half waiting for her to ask him to cross her palm with silver.

"No, she isn't," the soothsayer replied. "She's dying."

Robin felt Woad bristle behind him.

"Can she be cured?" he asked, staring unblinking at her.

"Healed? Mended?" She seemed to think about this for a moment. "No." Robin's heart seemed to plunge into his stomach. Instinctively he went to pull his hands away, but the woman held them firmly.

"I did not say she was done for," the soothsayer clarified. "She was never meant to be here anyway. She cannot be cured. But she can be remade. A bolt in the air, a feather in the heart. Sometimes to unravel the tapestry, you have to go back to the first stitch."

"Do you mean we have to go to Dis? Where she came from?" Robin tried to keep up with the woman's cryptic speech.

"The thing you are seeking is not at Dis, boy," Luna told him, rather impatiently. "But you must take it to Dis once you have found it. I see hooves and books, and a glass ceiling open to the northern lights. Hmm." She shook her head, as though clearing her thoughts. "Useless to you anywhere else, but you're not the one to do it."

"What 'thing'?" Robin asked, confused. "What do I need to find and take to Dis? I don't understand."

Luna turned her head to Woad, and then back to Robin, seeming thoughtful, as though unsure whether to speak or not. "There is a wolf in this city," she said. Her voice had turned very low. "He is also seeking what you seek. The path of the wolf and the path of the Scion are one, perhaps they always have been. Although neither knows it yet."

"If you mean Strigoi," Woad piped up, mention of the name making both the lamia hiss quietly, "we already know that metalhead nightmare is in town. He's bullying shopkeepers and trailing Grimms around for fun."

"Strigoi is looking for something," Robin said to the woman. "We overheard. He and the Grimms seem to be looking for a lost object, or a person."

"Both," the woman said, nodding and peering down at Robin's hands. "The second knows where the first is, and *only* the second knows. Find the person, find what they hid, and where. *That's* what the wolf wants. But if you want to save your friend … you will need to find them first. They're your only way into Dis."

Robin nodded. "This is about the family, isn't it?" he pressed. "We know that Mr Knight…I mean, Mr Nyx was looking into some noble Fire Panthea family, where the girl died and her brother rules alone now. We found his notebook." He peered intently at the veil. "She's not dead, is she? She's just ... missing. And you're saying she has something, or had something, that can get us into the city. And something that Strigoi needs for ... what?"

"That dark one has but one goal." Luna said thoughtfully. "He's been searching forever. He has almost lost himself entirely to the search. It has become all he is, and this has made him more dangerous than even he knows."

Robin felt the woman was talking in circles. He was worried. Worried about the peacekeeper who had seen them, worried about why Jack and Ffoulkes weren't here yet, about Karya getting worse by the day. If time was indeed coins, he could almost feel them slipping between his fingers, one by one, while they beat around the bush here.

"Lady Tinda Calescent is alive," he said firmly. "What does she have that I need? And where can I find her?"

The soothsayer chuckled. "You're sharper than you look, Scion of the Arcania. I will grant you that. Sharp as a fish hook. Where is she?" She shrugged. "Right where she was when last you met her, of course."

Robin was deeply lost now. "No, you've got it wrong," he insisted. "I've never met her. I'd never even *heard* of her until recently."

"Maybe *not* so sharp after all," Luna sighed. "Very well. Time is too pressing. You have things to show yourself. I'm not here to lead you by the hand, little saviour. I'm here to open a door you already hold the key to. It's up to you to walk inside. Remember what you see. And remember that when you walk in memories, you're telling yourself things you already know. Bone-know, not brain-know. Your mind is full of answers, everyone's is. But nobody listens."

She gripped his hands harder, startling him.

"Are you ready?" she asked. "Pay attention. You won't get a second chance."

Robin was about to ask "ready for what?" but before he could speak, a great heat rushed through his hands, up his arms, and filled his entire body. Light flooded the dark room, reducing everything around him to sketches. He could no longer feel him arms or legs, Woad or the others around him. He could no longer feel the hut vibrating and the dreamcatchers shaking, nor hear the endless background roar of the great waterfall outside. There was nothing but the light and the heat, and the world fell away.

* * *

This isn't real.

Robin was floating, seemingly without a body, in a calm, white and silent space.

This is some kind of dream. Did she hypnotise me? Put me into some kind of trance?

No, came a silent voice inside his own head. It was almost his own voice, but much more self-assured. It was the voice he had come to identify as the Puck. *Not a dream. Memories. Thoughts and memories. Some our own. Some others'. Things we need to see.*

The light receded, and Robin found himself in a large room. He didn't feel as though he had any physical presence here, no body to speak of, more that he was an invisible phantom of sorts, floating weightlessly as he stared around.

The room was cavernous and ornate, polished marble floors and high stone walls like a cathedral in long avenues of archways. Tall alabaster statues of Fae knights, their carved hands resting on long shields held before them, lined each soaring arch, and the ceiling above vaulted overhead. Sunlight flooded the clear air from high windows which lined both walls. It felt like a church or ancient temple, but Robin knew, with that strange, unquestionable certainty of dreams, that this was a throne room.

I'm at Erlking, he thought. Long ago Erlking. Netherworlde. Before it was an empty ruin. This is the throne room of Titania and Oberon. The home of the Arcania itself.

Indeed, in the very centre of the end of the room, flanked by two tall carved thrones which stood conspicuously empty, there was a raised dais. A pedestal before a great stained glass window. The dais was an empty stage. It looked – though it was hard for Robin to explain why – horribly empty, almost obscenely so, as though something had stood here for time immemorial and was now gone, and its absence was not only noticeable, but somehow appalling.

Clearly, Robin was not alone in this unshakable feeling of wrongness and loss. There was a group of people gathered by the empty thrones, men and women, and all of them were staring at the horribly empty dais before the stained glass with looks of frozen shock and horror.

Robin approached them. He couldn't feel the floor beneath him, and when he glanced down in confusion, expecting to see his legs, he realised he had no body at all. In this space, he was consciousness only. An observer, as insubstantial and unseen as a ghost. He could direct himself around the room, he discovered, simply by thinking of moving. It seemed the most natural thing in the world. The faces of the group lamenting at the empty thrones and dais were unclear. To look at them was like trying to remember the faces of adults you knew only as a baby. But a few of them seemed more in focus than others, and amongst these clearer shadows, there were some he recognised. Here was Hawthorn, member of the Sidhe-Nobilitas, hale and hearty, and dressed in the knight-garb of old, just as Robin had once glimpsed him when he had used the Mask of Gaia to look back into his memories on Briar Hill. Another two Fae, each with spiralling horns and both wearing the same formal uniform were present in the small crowd. Other members of the Fae guard, clearly.

Robin hoped briefly, with all his heart, that one of the two might be his own father, but he did not seem to be present.

"It's true then," one of the unfamiliar ones said, his voice close to shaking. "They really have gone." His words echoed around the huge room.

"Yes, Nightshade," the memory of Hawthorn replied, sounding hollow. "Both they … and it."

Robin had once been in the tomb of Nightshade, sunken deep below a lake, but he had never seen the Fae alive. Focussing his effort, Robin willed the man's image to focus, becoming clearer through concentration. He was tall and bright, with flowing chestnut hair and eyes like glowing coals. He looked devastated. "It is over, then." He shook his head. "Eris' forces approach Erlking. The king and queen … without them, without the Arcania, what can we do? Erlking will fall."

Three women stood close by the Fae trio, each of them clad in white robes. Robin, turning his attention, noticed with surprise that he recognised them. One was very old, one appeared in her prime, and the third little more than a young child. It was the Oracle. One woman in three bodies.

"Erlking will not fall now," the younger of the two adult women said.

"Might later," the old woman nodded. "That's up to others, but not now. Things are in place. Protections, even from Eris. Erlking will be safe, but none of you can stay here."

"She's right, my love," said a woman who stood by Nightshade. From what Robin could see, she was a nymph. "We must take what we were given to keep safe and flee, all of the Sidhe-Nobilitas must flee. Erlking will be left in safe hands, but it is not safe for any knight of Oberon and Titania to remain here."

"Whose hands?" the third Fae demanded, standing beside Hawthorn and Nightshade. His voice was harsh and commanding and filled with distrust. Robin had never seen this Fae before. He was tallest of them and his twin horns were long. His face, which was thin, with large oval eyes and narrow lips, glared at the rest of them. "Our king and queen gone? The Arcania, gone? And we are to leave Erlking to whom, as we flee with our tails between our legs?"

"To me, Peaseblossom," a voice replied, from somewhere behind Robin. The voice was shockingly familiar, and Robin, bodiless and invisible, turned to see Great Aunt Irene walking the length of the throne room toward the huddled group.

She was dressed in a long, simple gown of dark grey and her hair, which Robin had customarily seen her wear up in elegant control, was loose and flowing long, a silver stream running almost to her knees. She looked very calm, but very sad.

"To … to … her?" The Fae named Peaseblossom stuttered, his eyes flashing at his fellow knights and the Oracle in clear disbelief. "Leave Erlking to a Panthea?"

"I will remind you, Peaseblossom," Nightshade said, his chin jutting, "that my wife is a Panthea." He squeezed the hand of the nymph by his side. "Many of us have found comfort and companionship despite the war, and not all …"

"Not all Panthea belong to Eris." Irene finished for him as she reached the group, bowing politely to the Oracle, all three versions of which seemed to regard her thoughtfully, returning the bow.

"War is here," Peaseblossom said. "Chaos descends, and you all think this is the place for peace, for *order*?" He pointed at Irene.

"This is *exactly* the place for peace and order," the child-like Oracle said. "Indeed, the only fit hands and the only way to keep this place from the uprising."

"We have no magic," Nightshade said. "The Arcania …" He gestured to the horribly empty plinth behind the thrones, "is gone, there is no magic. The Arcania flowed magic through the world. How are we to channel the Towers without it? How are we to defend ourselves?"

"We are working on that," the eldest Oracle said. "Something small, perhaps." She had fished a stone out of her pocket and was regarding it thoughtfully. "Sticks and stones … yes. That might work. Small, portable … enough for everyone."

"I will hold Erlking," Irene assured them. "I have no wish to, but it was the decree of Lady Titania. Before all this."

She cast her eyes around at the assembled Sidhe-Nobilitas. "You all know more than I do, I'm certain. This is no random act. There is no doubt your monarchs left each of you tasks."

Each of the assembled Fae remained silent, apparently not wishing to meet each other's eyes.

"I see," Irene said. "An enlightenment for me another time then, perhaps. But now you must go. Regroup, await strength and defences from the Oracle. Eris does indeed fall upon Erlking, and any Fae found here when that happens will not leave alive, I can assure you of that."

"Most of the castle has been evacuated," the nymph said. "There is only the baby. What is to be done with the baby?"

"He has already been taken," Hawthorn told them. "Lord Wolfsbane is seeing to his departure now. He will be sent away, far from the war. It is too dangerous here, now, for one so young."

"He is taking his son to the other world?" Peaseblossom stared, looking aghast. "We need Wolfsbane here!"

"Another is taking him," Hawthorn reassured his fellow knight, placing a calming hand on the Fae's shoulder. "They left just now. Swift and sure. The boy is in good hands, I have never trusted one so much, and with so precious a burden."

Robin realised, with a kind of wonder, that this was a day in history that he had revisited once before. The day the king and queen vanished, and the Arcania was shattered. They day the Fae lost the war and fled, defenceless before the conceit of mana stones, into hiding. It was the day he had seen before, in a vision, where he had witnessed Hawthorn and his father sending him away as a baby. The memory he now found himself in might be just hours later, maybe only minutes.

"He will return to Erlking when he must," the Oracle said, though which of the three versions of the woman had spoken was impossible to tell. "As will the Puck."

All of the Sidhe-Nobilitas gathered turned to stare at them.

"Wolfsbane's son?" Nightshade whispered.

The Oracle nodded. "Sent away and kept safe," the oldest said. "A key that must not fall into Eris' hands. A burden has been given to one – to carry this."

"Eldest is gone," Hawthorn sighed, disbelieving. "Erlking will become a shell … a ruin."

The doors at the far end of the huge room suddenly opened, banging back against the walls with a noise that echoed back and forth across the archways. Another Fae entered, crossing the room hastily, his boots ringing on the marble floor. By his side was a satyr; half man, half goat.

"Lord Wolfsbane," Nightshade said, nodding in greeting. "Your child is evacuated? If so, we must trust he makes it to the human world safely. The Sidhe-Nobilitas must make haste and leave. Regroup …"

Robin wanted to turn and see his father, but before he had a chance to do so, he heard the man's footsteps falter and stop.

"The babe is safe," he said, and Robin could feel him surveying the room, looking at each one of the assembled company here, one by one. "Where is my wife?"

Nightshade and Peaseblossom exchanged confused looks. The Oracle, in all three of her forms, turned to look at the empty thrones. No-one answered him.

"My lord …" the satyr at his side began, and Robin was shocked to recognise the voice. Phorbas?

Lord Wolfsbane's voice came again, louder, and more desperate, cutting the satyr off as Robin turned to face him. Light flooded the room, blinding as an atom bomb, obliterating the scene of replayed memory like a dropped jigsaw as it fell away from him.

"Somebody answer me! Where is my wife?"

The white light flooded Robin's vision once more, and he was momentarily disoriented. Unable to tell up from down, where, or indeed when he was. He flew through a confusing tornado of memory, before slowing once more.

When another scene came into view, Erlking and that fateful day had vanished, and he found himself instead up on a high grassy moorland somewhere, in the dead of night. The craggy hills reared all around him, great lumpen shadows, black against a cloudy night sky that was full of rain. Somewhere in the distance, beyond the downpour, thunder rumbled menacingly. This was the human world. Robin knew this because looming against the darkness everywhere around him there were wind turbines, colossal black skeletal shadows cutting in constant motion against the deeper darkness and the rain. Their gargantuan blades sliced the wet air and whooshed through the night above him.

Before him Robin – once more an invisible and intangible observer – saw a man on a black horse, a Fae, dressed in the garb of the Sidhe-Nobilitas, its colours darkened and shiny with the heavy rain. His shoulders and face were hidden in the darkness by a long, hooded travelling cloak, which protected him from the downpour and was now cracking and whipping behind him in the wind. The man had just passed a large wicker basket down from the horse to a second figure standing on the grass. This one stood huddled beneath a large umbrella, which he was struggling to keep steady in the storm. From within the depths of the basket and a mass of swaddled blankets, a baby was crying.

"It's true then? The Fae have really fallen?" the man beneath the umbrella asked. His voice was shocked, disbelieving. Robin saw him shake his head in sorrow. "What will become of you all? What'll become of everything?"

"We will regroup," the Fae astride the horse told him calmly, as the restless beast stamped in the mud, thudding its hooves and blowing clouds of breath from its nose. "We will organise, and we will fight back. There is an ark, of sorts. Built in secret. It will take the many Fae far beyond the reach of Eris, and we, the Sidhe-Nobilitas, shall shepherd them. Right now, my brothers and sisters flee to hide, and your mistress holds Erlking. Keep it safe for us, and do not let despair take you."

"The Lady Irene?" the man said, cradling the basket as though it contained the world's most precious treasure. "Well, I'll be blowed. But this little one …?"

"No place in war," the hooded Fae told him flatly. "Safer here. These are his parents' wishes. No harm must come to him. He must be hidden, here in the human world. A changeling."

"I've a lad of my own," the man with the umbrella said. "Only a babe himself, he is. My lovely Olivia, bless her soul, she passed in birthing him, took herself out of the world bringing him into it, she did." He nodded his head, jogging the basket gently to quiet the crying infant. "I ain't sure yet I've the mettle to be the best dad, but a brother I could give to this one here, if ..."

"No," the Fae shook his head. "The task of this child doesn't fall to you, my friend. He must be taken to Elsbeth. She must hide him. She alone must raise him."

Robin watched as the man standing before the horse tilted his umbrella back to stare up in confusion at the mounted Fae. Robin glimpsed his face in the moonlight. He knew him.

The man holding his infant self, here on this empty moor on this terrible stormy night, was Malcom Drover. Henry's father looked younger in this memory, certainly slimmer, with less grey in his much fuller hair and moustache, but it was clearly him. There could be no mistaking it.

"Elsbeth?" Mr Drover stuttered. "Surely not! She won't like that, not after everything ..." He shook his head. "Better for him to come and live with me and my babe Henry. If Lady Irene really is taking Erlking ... why ... he'd be safest there, with us, surely."

The Fae on the horse would brook no argument. "He would be too visible there," he said. "Safe, yes, but caged. The boy must disappear. Elsbeth must hide him, even from himself. He must not know he isn't human; knowing would draw attention. Too young and defenceless. Elsbeth *owes* us this."

"She was only a child back when ..."

"Back when our worlds changed forever?" the Fae said. His voice was sharp. "Yes. But her father turned the wheel, and what was done then cannot be undone now. Look where it has led us all." He looked around at the stormy moors, his face still hidden in the folds of his hood. "To war and ruin! To empty thrones, and the Arcania itself – gone! Shattered and scattered!" The Fae steadied his horse, which had become agitated at his raised voice.

Drover nodded, looking wary, as thunder rolled across the hills again, the rain still lashing down and drowning out the baby's cries.

"A *debt* is owed to the Fae," the rider said. "Elsbeth owe us at least this. For all that is done. Take the boy. Take him safely. But take him to the Graves'."

The sound of the rain stopped abruptly, and what Robin first thought was a flash of lightening filled his vision, but it did not fade. It was not the storm. This memory, this fragment of his past was also fading away, breaking apart. Petals thrown to the wind.

Robin was back in the whiteness, the turbulent nothingness between these little slices of history, as though they were the flip of book pages turning. More images came now, but nothing so coherent. It was now as though, rather than reading, he had his thumb on the pages and was flipping them past his eyes, glimpsing only odd and disjointed things, snatches of thought and images here and there flashing up to pass before him, gone as soon as he saw them.

He saw his thirteen-year-old self, standing in a room at Erlking, surrounded by old statues, some broken, others covered in dust sheets.

He saw himself walking Erlking's corridors, fresh from a bath and wrapped in a robe, finding himself lost in a long portrait gallery of Fae.

Then he was ascending the inside of the tree at Hiernarbos, the secret valley of the Undine, while Karya spoke with the keeper of the tree as though they were very old friends.

He glimpsed himself at Jackalope's bedside, back when he was trapped in his dreaming coma, with the strangely veiled Sisters Eumenides arguing with Karya and declaring that they didn't talk to people who were not real.

He was in Barrowood, in a bric-a-brac shop with Woad and Penny, long before he knew she was Miss Peryl. She was offering to buy him a Hello Kitty keychain and teasing the shopkeeper, who peered at them all suspiciously through her thick glasses.

He saw the court of Princess Ashe, deep in Rowandeepling amongst the dryads, where they treated Karya like royalty, and he prepared to fight the scourge.

And long ago, when he had first channelled the Puck on the Isle of Winds, and had dreamed, after falling unconscious afterwards, that he was in a large dark room, with unseen figures who were sleeping yet not sleeping, talking to him.

Every glimpse, every vision, passed more quickly, and his heart beat faster and faster until they seemed a blur, and all became confusion and noise. A final image rose in his mind, that seemed neither memory nor dream, a fleeting glimpse of a figure standing in a doorway; nothing but a silhouette against a frame of metallic light that was so bright, it seemed burning magnesium. The image made Robin's heart almost stop, there was such sorrow in it, just loneliness and yet a calm pride, a sense of duty flooded over. And then – the slam of a door, firm and final, the light extinguished.

Solid, silent blackness descended.

Robin's eyes shot open as he drew in a gasp like a drowning man. He almost toppled over backwards, shocked and overwhelmed. For a moment he had no idea where he was, but Luna, the hidden soothsayer, released his hands, and the tiny, shaking shack of the fortune-teller at the Sorrows swam back into focus around him.

"Pinky!" Woad dropped to his side and took him by the shoulders. "Are you okay? What happened?"

"He's back," the woman said simply. "He's back from his mind and it's always something of a jolt. I hope he learned something useful."

Robin fought the urge to throw up, shaking his head, the room swimming around him. He had broken out in a cold sweat. "I saw …" He struggled to explain his experience to Woad. "Erlking. That day when everything ended. When the Fae fled, and I had to be sent to the human world … I saw myself being taken to Gran's, and … lots of other things. Things from since … since I've been the Scion." He ran a hand across his face. "But I don't know what any of them mean. What any of them have to do with anything that …" He looked around blearily, coming back to his senses. "How long was I gone for?" he asked.

Woad frowned at him. "Gone? You haven't been gone. You just held that lady's hand and then the next second you jumped out of your skin. Scared the life out of me."

Robin swallowed, rubbing his hands. "It felt like a lot longer to me."

"That's time for you," Luna said, sitting back amongst her cushions. "We think we only have the present, but every moment of the past is wrapped up inside it, layers upon layers, stretching away." She rubbed her hands together. "But even when we dally and play in the past, our future catches up with us. It doesn't wait. Time is relentless." She inclined her head to the door. "Relentless and heartless. And now it has run out. I'm sorry about your friends, Scion, I truly am."

Robin shot her a questioning look, but before he could open his mouth to speak, the whole shack rumbled and shook, more than could be accounted for by the ever-roaring motion of the great waterfall. The lamia by the fireplace hissed, and Woad almost lost his footing. In its frame, the flimsy door rattled violently.

"Scion of the Arcania," a voice called from outside, loud and authoritative.

Robin and Woad exchanged panicked looks.

"We know that you are in there, little Fae," the voice called again. It sounded faintly amused, as though enjoying itself immensely. "So very bold of you, swanning around the decent town of these honest, hard-working Panthea folk! To have such an outlaw in their midst … such a danger to them. What a scandal! Did you honestly believe you would slip by unseen?"

"It's Spider-Hands," Woad hissed to Robin. "The fat Grimm. I know it. That peacekeeper ran and tattled on us."

Robin scrambled to his feet, glancing around the small hut. There were no windows, no other doors. No other way out of this shaking shack dangling over the tremendous waterfall. They were well and truly cornered in this dead end of a place.

"Will you continue to cower in the shadows, I wonder?" The voice sounded just as polite and smarmy as it had back at the gallery in London. "Is this how the so-called champion of the Fae behaves? Like a rat? A cockroach? Hiding in the shadows?"

Robin could hear much shuffling outside. He could already picture the peacekeepers filling the street, flanking the Grimm. It sounded as though a lot of them were out there.

"What do we do?" Woad asked. "Think we can take them? But your aunt wouldn't be happy with swashbuckling."

"On behalf of the Empress of the Netherworlde," Mr Nyx called, his voice merry, "I arrest you, Robin Fellows, for the crimes of being a renegade and of being an unregistered Fae. For your past crimes of desecration to the Temple of Winds, for your acts of thievery from the Tombs of Elders, and your warlike aggression in the valley of Hiernarbos. For the further crimes of disrupting the peace at her Majesty's great correction facility, the Hive, and the rebellious and terrorist activity of releasing from said correction facility great numbers of known traitors to the empress. You have ten seconds to surrender yourself of your own free will, or I shall …" and here his voice practically dripped with relish, "be *forced* to use aggression."

Another voice suddenly yelled from outside. "Scion! Don't! It's a trap!" Robin's eyes flew wide.

"That's Jackalope!" he gasped, staring at Woad. He crossed swiftly to the door.

"Careful, Pinky!" Woad urged him, and Robin's hand froze on the scarred and rough doorknob.

"If they've captured Jack and Ffoulkes on their way here, we *have* to fight!" Robin insisted. "I'm the Scion of the Arcania. I'm not helpless!" He ran through a mental list swiftly, every combat cantrip he knew. "Galestrike, needlepoint, waterwhip, boulderdash … I can take down a blasted Grimm. I don't have as much creepy shadow-spider magic he has, but …"

"Enough!" Now a new voice spoke outside, much quieter than the crowing Grimm. This was a low and angry hiss, a dark whisper, and it made the hairs stand up on Robin's arms.

"Enough of your theatrics, Nyx, I've no time for your tongue-flapping and pantomime. He is merely a boy, not a cornered tiger."

"Strigoi!" Woad hissed, wrinkling his nose in distaste. "Pinky, you might take down a Grimm on a fair day with a following wind, but the Wolf of Eris?" He shook his head insistently. "That one is darker than the darkest shadows. Don't you remember how he tore Hawthorn from the gates at Briar Hill? How he nearly blasted us all to dust at the Hive?"

Before Robin could respond at all, a powerful shock wave thudded through the building, and the door, still gripped in his hand, creaked and shattered into a million toothpicks. Woad covered his face to defend against the explosion and shrapnel, and only an instinctive breezeblock cantrip thrown up by Robin prevented him from being peppered with countless shards of wood. As though sucked out through an airless void into the blackness of space, the busted detritus of the door was pulled away, along with much of the door frame and a large portion of the surrounding wall. An invisible force, tearing at the hut.

Staggered, Robin blinked in the light. Before them, standing amidst the shanty huts of the Spit, a gaggle of peacekeepers filled the misty, open ground. Mr Nyx stood off to one side, with Jackalope and Ffoulkes both kneeling on the rock before him like prisoners of war. Their hands seemed to be tied before them. And in the centre of this macabre display,

Strigoi stood, one arm still outstretched where he had unleashed his mana and torn away the front of the building, littering the rocky street with wooden flotsam.

Robin heard the lamia and Luna moving behind him, tucking themselves into the far corners of what remained of the fortune-teller's shack, which, half-collapsed, swayed ever more alarmingly.

"I'll huff and I'll puff," Strigoi said quietly, his nightmarish metal grin leering up at the two boys steadying themselves in the ruin. "And I'll blow your house down!"

"Such a pleasant coincidence," Mr Nyx called up to Robin, standing between his two prisoners and giving each of them a proprietorial pat on the shoulder with his large hands. "Meeting the infamous Scion himself, here in the Sorrows. We have never yet had the pleasure, little Fae boy. Although I have heard *much* about you from dearest brother Strife, of course."

"Let them go!" Robin shouted down to them, glaring at the black-eyed Grimm and his white, horribly friendly face. "If you've come for *me*, fine! Leave them out of it."

Strigoi tilted his head a little, the shining horns of his helmet catching the sunlight in the mist, but he said nothing. The rumble of the waterfall surrounded them like war drums.

Nyx, on the other hand, shook his head and tutted, as though Robin had misbehaved quite badly. "Oh, but that would not be my civic duty, now, would it, hornspawn? I must say, you keep some *terrible* company. It's really quite reprehensible."

Quick as a flash, his hand shot out and grabbed Ffoulkes' bald skull, tilting it roughly back. "This one here? A traitor to his own kind. A deserter of the war, and an escapee from the Hive to boot! Quite the criminal at large."

"He's a hob-nob!" Woad pointed accusingly. "You can't just grab him like that. Even if you are a Grimm. He's nobility, that one!"

Nyx's eyes danced merrily and he laughed, a harsh and barking sound. "Noble? *This* one?" His grin widened. "What nonsense has he been filling your heads with?' He jerked Ffoulkes' head around to stare at him. Ffoulkes looked murderous, squirming under the Grimm's loathsome touch. "Honestly, Silas Ffoulkes … you *have* got ideas above your station, haven't you?"

Ffoulkes wrenched his head out of the Grimm's grip, blinking up at Robin and Woad. He looked fearful, though whether for his own well-being or theirs, it was difficult to tell.

"I'm afraid ... ahaha ... we seem to have run afoul of these mannerless brutes, young master. Laid in wait, you see? We were rather outnumbered. Most unsporting. You really should *flee*. Right now."

Robin noticed for the first time that both Ffoulkes' and Jackalope's hands were tied not with rope, but with wide grey sashes of what looked like spider-silk.

"This man kneeling in the mud before you, exactly where he belongs," Nyx called up to the boys in the ruined hut with obvious relish, "is no more noble than the filth-encrusted hovel-dwellers who squat in that hut behind you. Did he try to tell you otherwise?" He laughed. "I imagine so. That he was acquainted with all the noble houses of the Panthea, no doubt. That he has mixed in the highest circles."

Robin wanted nothing more than to wipe the slimy grin from the Grimm's face.

"Half-truths, every one," Nyx said, with a rueful shake of his head. "This creature was a servant. Lower than the lowest hearth-scrubber. Oh, he mixed with the great and good, I've no doubt of that, but only when he was serving them dinner, washing their plates and scrubbing out their bedroom fire-grates, that is." He turned his attention back to the kneeling Fire Panthea.

"Boiling bedpans, that's his place. That is, until the day he stole a fortune in silver and tableware from his trusting masters and fled the Netherworlde like a coward. What *shame*! What *dishonour*! What luck of mine to finally be the one to bring him to the empress for justice."

Strigoi had not moved during Nyx's chattering. He stood as still as a statue, his unfathomable face trained on Robin, half hidden in mist as the falls roared about them. He had not taken his eyes off the boy, even for a second.

"The other," he said, speaking at last, "is a Fae, like you. Tell me, Scion. Are you collecting them? Hiding them at Erlking?"

"Not *only* a filthy Fae!" Nyx dropped Ffoulkes like a bag of garbage and grabbed Jackalope's arms instead, still bound at the wrist.

"Get your hands off me, scum!" the boy spat, struggling in the ghastly man's grip. Jackalope had blood on his lip. He had clearly put up a fight, however futile. Nyx ignored him, forcing his hand in the air to expose the inside of his forearm.

"Not only a filthy Fae," he repeated, "but the *stolen property* of the empress. See here."

He indicated the tattoo on Jack's arm, the letters burned into his skin: *MMMMCMXCVIII*. Nyx read out each letter, savouring them, laughter bubbling in his voice. It was the brand Jackalope had received in the prison camps. Where every Fae was reduced to a number, a designation, all liberty and identity stripped from them.

Nyx's gimlet eyes flicked up to Robin. He tossed his ridiculous yellow hair. "An ungrateful refugee. One who scorned the hospitality of the empress, who was benevolent enough to feed and clothe his sorry corpse for years. Gave him a roof over his head, a reason to exist. Hospitality – which he fled from, ungrateful animal! And then you find him. Clearly marked ... and yet you do not return him?" Nyx shook his head as though utterly confused by this idea. "That, little boy, is dealing in stolen property. Yet another crime to add to your list. You are not doing so well, are you? We are painting a rather ugly picture of you."

"I'm no one's property!" Jackalope spat, wrenching his hands from the Grimm viciously. "*Futue te ipsum!*"

"Quite the tongue in this one's head," Nyx's smile faded. "I may cut it out."

"The traitors will be delivered to the empress *whole*," Strigoi warned his companion. "Whole and undamaged. Stay your temper, Nyx, before I do so for you."

Nyx had grabbed Jackalope by the chin, staring down into his face. "My last assistant was all worn out to a husk, weak fellow that he was," he said. "I intend to petition the empress for the use of you. A few spiders in your brain and we will find you much more obedient and respectful, wild dog."

Jackalope wrenched his head away and looked furiously at Robin. "Scion!" he said. "I know you're thinking of doing something stupid and heroic. Don't. You can't beat these. Just do as your tutor says, and run!"

Robin shook his head. There was no way he could leave his tutor and his friend to the mercy of Strigoi and the Grimm.

"The time for running is over, Robin Fellows," Strigoi growled. "Now, will you walk out of that hole and retain a shred of dignity? Or must I drag you?"

"Master Robin." Ffoulkes spoke urgently and. Robin's eyes went to his tutor. He had expected Ffoulkes to beg to be saved, or try to bargain with his captors, but there was nothing but panic in his tutor's eyes, and it shocked Robin to realise that it really wasn't panic about his own capture. It was for his student. The Fire Panthea shook his head urgently. The message was clear. Don't come.

"Bind these two," Strigoi commanded Nyx, waving a hand at the kneeling prisoners and drawing a sullen look from the Grimm. Clearly, the pale man took no pleasure in being ordered around, but he nodded in resentful deference. The gaggle of peacekeepers widened their circle, seeming skittish and unsettled. They melted back to give the ghoul room as Nyx stood between the captured pair and spread his hands as though in benediction. Dark spots formed, hazy globules which swiftly sprouted legs and began to drop from his palms. Shadow spiders, indistinct in the mist. Robin and Woad watched in horror as more and more poured forth from the Grimm's hands, like a flow of dark water. Jackalope and Ffoulkes struggled against their bonds as the large spiders began to crawl on them, swarming over their bodies, heads and faces. In moments, both were nearly covered, hundreds of the loathsome black creatures moving in a writhing mass over each of their forms.

Ffoulkes screamed in panic. Both he and Jackalope fell to the ground, writhing on the floor as the spiders flowed over them. They were spinning, silk ropes everywhere beneath their fat and glistening bodies.

They were cocooning them both.

"Scion. Escape!" Jack gasped, shaking his head furiously, trying to dislodge the creatures crawling through his hair and around his neck.

"We can't leave you!" Robin had already taken a step forward out of the wreckage, horrified by the sight before him.

"Idiot!" Jackalope sounded more angry than afraid, though his voice shook a little. "Don't you understand? If you're taken, she dies!"

Robin froze. Ffoulkes was fully cocooned already, nothing but a lumpen mass of silk and spiders, writhing on the floor. Jackalope's face was fast disappearing beneath sticky silver coverings, but one wild grey eye found Robin, staring urgently. Jackalope was right. If Robin was captured, it was game over for Karya. She would wither at Erlking until the inevitable end.

"The prisoners will be taken to Dis," Strigoi said, as Jackalope disappeared fully beneath bindings, becoming just a second sack of writhing, sticky silk on the floor. He spoke to the Grimm at his side, though his voice was louder than his usual low hiss and carried up to Robin and Woad standing in the wreckage of the hut. "A fitting tribute for the empress, and a fine example of executions on Pyrenight. We have ourselves a centrepiece."

Mr Nyx looked gleeful at the thought of execution.

"It would be a shame to burn both, though," he mused. "When I have need of help in the laboratory."

"Pyrenight is in one week," Strigoi continued. "Petition the Lady Eris for a new toy if you must. But in the dark of the day, we shall have fuel for the bonfires."

"I know when it is!" Nyx snapped in response, frowning ungraciously at the wolf. "You don't need to tell me." He pointed a finger at Robin. "*There* is your centrepiece, wolf. There is the gift for the empress, better than a *hundred* traitors or rogue Fae scum. Shall you collect this prize? Or shall I?"

"Pinky, the spiders ..." Woad said. He had taken a step back into the hut, and when Robin followed his gaze he saw why. Nyx's spiders, done with their gruesome task of wrapping Ffoulkes and Jackalope, were now flowing over the splintered debris of the broken walls towards them, a dark and undulating carpet. They could hear the low whisper of chittering and hissing from them as they approached like a tide.

"There is nowhere to run, Scion," Strigoi said, his voice low and menacing once more. He took a step toward the hut and raised his hand, fingers outstretched before him. Robin could feel the man gathering his mana. It was like electricity in the air and the hairs on the back of his neck stood up. He couldn't beat Strigoi one on one.

"Nowhere left for you to hide," Strigoi continued. "You stand atop Titania's Tears. The only way out is down to death." The empty eye sockets of his helmet seemed to transfix Robin.

"Tell me, saviour of the Netherworlde. Is it cold here, at the edge of hope?"

Robin knew he had only seconds to decide what to do. Any moment, Nyx's spiders would be all over them and they would be bound and trussed like the others. In the next instant, Strigoi's mana would lash out and drag them onto the rock. He could stay and fight and probably lose, leaving Karya to die. No way forward. No way back.

Unless ...

He grabbed Woad firmly by the wrist, dragging him until they were back in the centre of the small room. The faun looked startled and confused, and Nyx's laughter rolled from outside, clearly amused at his cornered prey shrinking back.

"Do you trust me, Woad?" Robin asked, his heart in his mouth.

Woad blinked but nodded immediately. "You have a plan?" he whispered. "A not-get-caught-or-killed plan?"

"The only way out is down," Robin said, echoing Strigoi's words. The Wolf of Eris had approached the ruined wall now, crunching over the broken wood, and Robin looked up to see him standing, a shadow in the doorway, framed like a vengeful demon, as spiders of darkness flowed in through the torn maw of the door frame around him. They scuttled between his armoured boots and across the floor towards them, spreading out like ink on the walls and ceiling, threading their small and scurrying bodies between the many dreamcatchers.

"No plan." Robin made his decision quickly. "Sometimes you just have to go with the flow."

Keeping a tight hold of Woad, he grabbed his mana stone and cast his energy downwards with all his might, at the rugs and thin old boards of the hut beneath them, tapping into the Tower of Earth. With a huge crash, the floor fell away beneath them in a neat circle, as though hole-punched from the world.

Leaving Strigoi, the Grimm and their captured friends behind … leaving Luna and her snakelike charges huddled in the corners, Robin and Woad fell like stones from the hut suspended over the great waterfall and plunged into the horribly empty air below, disappearing instantly into the thunderous depths.

9

Marrowstride

When they had first arrived at Titania's Tears and Robin saw the great waterfall, his mind had, of course, imagined what it would be like to tumble over the edge. The same way that the human mind, when standing on the precipice of a cliff, cannot help but picture itself throwing the body out into space. It is a strange habit of people, a morbid lemming-like curiosity. The call of the void. Looking at the intimidating waterfall, with the town nestled at its spewing mouth like a suicidal suspended salmon, at the time it had been merely a passing thought, hypothetical and safe.

Now though, as he and Woad, having broken through the flimsy floor of the soothsayer's hut, launched themselves into space, it was anything but.

It was like free-falling from an aeroplane with no parachute, so high were the cliffs. The water gushed and roared around them, endless curtains of powerful white foam, surging downwards, heavy and enormous and they fell with it, through endless spray and scattered glimpses of fractured rainbows.

Robin couldn't think. He was deafened and drenched. It was all he could do to hold on to Woad's wrist as they plummeted together through the air. For several seconds the only thought he could form was that he wished the faun would stop screaming so that he *could* think, before he realised that the scream was coming from himself, instinctual and as impossible to stifle as a yawn. The world flipped over and back and over again. Sky, water, forests; the latter so sickeningly far below, as they spun, head over heels, rocketing downwards. He imagined he glimpsed the Spit above them, and the ruined, ragged floor of the soothsayer's hut. He thought he glimpsed two faces peering down through the hole – green hair and surprised yellow eyes – but whether it really was the lamia sisters or simply his own frantic imagination, he would never know. They were falling so fast and spinning so helplessly that in seconds the town, and everything in it, was lost far above them.

Robin wanted to shout to Woad. They were going to reach the bottom of the falls. A drop from this height would surely kill them. It would be like hitting concrete at these speeds, not water. And even if they didn't die instantly, the force of the water at the base of the huge waterfall would push them down into the churning, white fury. Driving them under, rolling them around in its force and current like a crocodile with its prey, until all their bones were broken and they drowned.

He couldn't say a word, of course. He had only just managed to stop screaming, and had only achieved that due to choking on water.

Woad, on the other hand, had managed to grab one of Robin's wrists with both hands, and in the cacophonous din, he heard the boy's high shrill voice scream one word into the fury:

"PUCK!"

That word cleared Robin's mind. The wind was whipping at his face, making his sodden clothes flap furiously around his limbs, but he could also feel it around his horns. He felt them blaze above his temples, the power of the Arcania rising up within him out of sheer self-preservation.

"HOLD STILL!" he yelled, and his voice was the echoey voice of the Puck. Both his and not his. His eyes blazed in the mist and he felt water hissing as it boiled off the surface of his mana stone.

Robin closed his eyes, forcing breath into his lungs, and with pure force of will he thrust an arm into the curtain of water falling by his side, demanding its obedience, certain of his sovereignty over it. The water shone as though lightning had been released from Robin's arm, and he grabbed and pulled. A wave of liquid tore itself from the falling cascade. With a wide loop of his arm, he pulled the water through the air, encircling them both with it. It foamed and glowed, and in seconds they were within a large rolling bubble of water, thick enough to distort the world beyond like deep blue glass, and solid enough to muffle even the apocalyptic roars of the falls of Titania outside.

Robin and Woad slid around helplessly inside the bubble as it careened down the falls. It was far too small a space to scream in, and Robin, feeling the full power of the Puck flowing through his veins, had no time to do anything but concentrate, to bend the Tower of Water to his will and keep them in their tenuous shield, this marble of water. He gasped for breath, watching the world whip by outside their glassy sphere, and was only faintly aware of Woad beginning to giggle, a little helplessly and hysterically, as the shadowy hills and landscape rushed up from beneath to meet them.

"Brace," he heard himself say, his voice devoid of panic or worry, and a second later their bubble finally hit the base of the falls and was enveloped in a cloud of white, blinding foam.

Beneath the water they were buffeted to and fro, spinning around dizzyingly as shoals of bubbles cascaded past the surface of their spherical shield. All went dark for a moment or two of alarmingly loud gurgling and then they broke the surface, skipping out of the river entirely, before crashing back down onto it, carried along on its surface. They bobbed and spun along furious rapids at terrifying speed, the banks of the river, high and distant on both sides, flashing past alarmingly.

"We're alive!" Woad yelled breathlessly, a manic grin splitting his face from ear to ear. His voice sounded muffled and odd in their watery sphere.

Robin stared at him dizzily, the world outside the bubble rotating and bobbing as their odd craft was borne along as surely as a fallen leaf. The faun's sodden hair was plastered to his face, but he looked exhilarated.

Robin couldn't help but laugh. It bubbled up out of him, a mixture of terror and relief and sheer pent-up adrenalin. Woad laughed too, equally hysterically, and to anyone standing on the bank, they would have made quite the unhinged sight. Two boys in a magic bubble, drenched and shaking from head to toe, laughing hysterically as they rolled on by.

Gran had never been one to go for theme parks of any kind, finding it foolish to scare oneself for money, so Robin had never been on a real roller-coaster. But as the Dish bore them swiftly along, it felt exactly how he imagined it would feel to ride one of those "white rapids" rides – little inflatable rubber boats tearing down rivers of fast foaming water, soaking the riders, who whooped and hollered with the sheer giddy joy of it.

The only difference here was that they were not wearing large inflatable life jackets. They were not wearing carefully checked crash helmets, and instead of a sturdy boat of inflatable rubber, the only thing preventing them from becoming a smear of jam on the jagged rocks hidden beneath the foam was a thin shell of liquid, formed from nothing more than willpowered water.

When he got his laughter under control, still shaking a little uncontrollably, Robin bent all his concentration on the rather important task of not dashing them to death on the rapids.

The waters of the Dish on the plains immediately below the Floreo were fast and fierce and they carried the boys for some distance, around many loops and whorls in the meanders of the wide river, before eventually – what seemed to be hours later – and only after a few more hairy waterfalls, the Dish began finally to calm itself.

"We … we need to get to the bank," Robin said. He was kneeling up inside the bubble, as he had been doing for some time now, hands outstretched and touching the surrounding curved wall on both sides, feeling the water flow endlessly over and between his fingers. Sweat was beaded on his forehead, despite both of them shivering from the cold. Their clothes were heavy and drenched, and exhaustion was beginning to set in. He could still feel his invisible horns atop his head, but they seemed to be flickering on and off in his mind, like a faulty neon sign. "I'm not sure how much longer I can do this, Woad." His voice was shaking.

Woad nodded in understanding. Being small in stature, he could get unsteadily to his feet, using his tail for extra balance as they bobbed along at what was now thankfully a rather stately pace.

"I've got an idea," he said. "And it's an excellent one, naturally. Have you heard of zorbing?"

Without waiting for an answer, Woad began to walk against the surface of the ball, hands outstretched to steady himself, and it tilted, almost knocking Robin on his back.

"Get up and help me, Pinky," Woad insisted. "Don't just lie there like a pterosaur."

Robin didn't have the strength to argue with Woad's implication that he had been lazing around enjoying life on the river. He struggled to Woad's side, righting himself as best he could in the cramped space, and together they proceeded to walk the bubble towards the bank on their right, for the simple reason that it seemed nearer than the other.

When they had almost reached the shore, Robin's mana gave out completely. His mana stone had felt as heavy as darkmatter around his neck for a while now, and he had finally reached the point of magical exhaustion. The bubble collapsed around them all at once, drenching them afresh as it lost form and fell back into the water with a crash. They fell too, but the bank was only knee-high in water, and groggily they stumbled ashore.

Robin had never imagined he could be so grateful to stand on solid, dry, non-moving land as he was at that moment, and after a few staggered steps, both he and Woad collapsed completely onto the sand and the grass, lying spread-eagled on their backs and panting up into space.

The sky above them was beginning to turn a soft orange. With the light catching the ends of what thin clouds there were like torch paper lit against their edges. The two stared up at in in breathless silence for a while.

"So," Woad said eventually. "Want to go again?"

Robin sighed and sat up, scooting back off the sand of the wide riverbank and onto the grass proper. "We left them, Woad," he said thickly, still staring up at the sky. "We left Ffoulkes and Jack … with those monsters."

The faun shook himself quickly, like a dog, shedding droplets of water. "Yes, we did," he agreed. "We didn't have a choice." He considered this for a moment. "Well yes … we *did* have a choice, but the other option was 'let's have a brave and heroic fight, which will be for no purpose at all because metal-head-nightmare-face is powerful enough to snap both of our necks at ten paces with a flick of his wrist, and then not only would our friends be captured, cocooned and taken away to be thrown on a bonfire, or worse'." He sighed. "But we would have been captured, cocooned and taken away to be thrown on a bonfire, too."

"We still ran away," Robin countered. Woad held up a finger.

"Fauns never 'run away' and neither do Scions. We beat a tactical retreat. To regroup and regather, that's all." He seemed genuinely unconcerned by all of these events. Robin stared at him, puzzled.

"You really don't feel guilty at all for leaving them?" he asked.

Woad flicked his yellow eyes in Robin's direction, then leaned over and pushed the Fae's soaked hair back from his forehead with almost parental care. He gave his cheek a little patronising pat.

"Blah! What use is guilt?" The faun shrugged, leaping to his feet as though fully reenergised and refreshed already. "It's not a useful emotion. Guilt doesn't help them, or us, or any person. It's a self-indulgent way to feel bad about something you did or didn't do, when all that energy should be going into making better whatever you did or didn't do. Guilt is for poets, not fauns. I feel," he seemed briefly to lapse into careful thought, "excited!"

Robin dragged himself to his feet as well, scrunching his t-shirt in his fists and trying to wring some river water from it. He frowned at his companion.

"Excited?"

"Of course. Because *now* we get to rescue them! That's my best kind of adventure! Didn't you hear? Silly old wolf was stupid enough to let everything slip. Baldilocks and the Silver Sulker are being taken to Dis. They're going to be burned to death on Pyrenight!" He grinned widely.

"Woad!" Robin spluttered helplessly. "How is that a *good* thing?"

"Because it's not Pyrenight for a week," the faun explained. "Which gives us absolutely ages to get there. And an excuse to go to Dis that even your old aunt won't be able to argue with." He brushed his hands together. "We can find a cure for Karya, save our two damsels in distress and still be home in time for crumpets."

"You never fail to amaze me, Woad." Robin shook his head.

"Well, I wouldn't be much of a faun if I did, would I?"

Robin peered around, taking in the landscape. They couldn't even see the falls of Titania's Tears and the high cliffs of the Floreo's borders were lost far back in the landscape they had travelled. The river must have carried them fifty or more miles south from the base of the waterfall. All that lay around them now were hills. Across the river on the distant eastern bank, broken rises of deep grass stole away through the afternoon light, receding one after another to the distant horizon.

He turned to survey their side of the riverbank. The ground sloped upwards from the shore through patchy grass and reeds, and not too far off a screen of tall and close-grown trees formed their vista, stretching away both north and south. The edge of a forest.

"Do you have any idea where we are?" Robin asked, shivering.

Woad looked around thoughtfully. "We're on the riverbank," he said.

"I've never been lost in the Netherworlde before," Robin realised. "We don't have a guide. We don't have Karya with us to tear us back to the human world. I don't even know if there's a town or a village or another living soul a hundred miles in any direction, how about you?"

"Being lost is easy," Woad shrugged. "You just keep moving until you're not lost anymore." He pointed towards the trees. "I vote we head that way, Pinky. If the Grimm, or Strigoi, or any of their scarecrow flunkies are searching for us – which you can bet they are – I reckon they'll be searching around the bottom of the waterfall way back, looking for mangled bodies. I don't think they'll expect us to be this far along the river and quite so not dead, but even so ... better to hide in a forest than out here in the open."

Robin peered around, surveying the grassy hills and watching the tall grass ripple. A breeze had sprung up from the lowlands and everything he was wearing was soaked through. He was already starting to shiver, and the orange glow of the sky suggested there were maybe only a couple of hours left before sunset. The treeline of the forest looked dark and close-knit. It might well be better to be undercover. As well as being out of sight, they would be a little more protected from the elements. But the shadows didn't look hugely inviting.

"We need to get word back to Erlking," he said, squelching off through the grass in slippery trainers. "They need to know what happened to Ffoulkes and Jack. I know Aunt Irene isn't there, but the others ..." He shrugged, hoisting his pack onto his shoulders wearily.

Soon they had left the wide river and grassy hills behind them and found themselves ducking under low branches and into the surprising cool and dimness of the thick woods. The trees around them were tall and knotted, with high branches interlacing widely above to form an almost solid roof overhead. In this dark wood, light reached the ground only in thin shafts and spears, illuminating a forest floor that was thick with boulders swathed in spongy green moss. Almost every tree trunk was thickly laced with a stringy and dark ivy. It covered everything.

"Beware of bogs," Woad muttered sagely. "That moss? It's impbeard. I recognise it from my book ... I mean *your* book. It's everywhere, look. That means there's lots of damp in here. Might be mud, might be swamp, maybe even be quicksand. I've never been a fan of a bubbling bog, myself."

The thick carpet of moss also served to hide the hundreds of jumbled tree roots, rocks and boulders that threatened to turn their ankles with every step. When they had carefully picked their way far enough into the trees that they were in no danger of being spotted from the grasslands, and the open sky with its orange glow was just a memory in the shadowy closeness of the ivy-choked silent woods, Robin stopped and unslung his pack, resting it against a rock. He rifled through it until he found his hex message parchment.

"It's soaked," he said grimly. "Everything's soaked." He considered trying to wring it out, but settled for shaking it gently instead, for fear it might collapse into pulp in his hands.

"Even the sandwiches?" Woad cried in horror, dipping his hands into the Swedenborgian satchel and rummaging around until he withdrew some rather squashed and defeated-looking oblongs of tin foil. He tilted them, watching water pour out from their insides, and made a sad little keening noise.

"I'm a bit more worried about the hex than I am about the ham and cheese, Woad," Robin said. "I wish Ffoulkes had bothered to teach me more of the Tower of Fire, I could at least warm us up and try to dry some of this stuff out then."

"I can make fire," Woad said, and grinned. "A little one, at least." His smile melted into a thoughtful frown. "Might not be the best idea though, not if Eris' goons are combing the lands for us. Nothing says 'Here I am! Come and wrap me up in nightmare spider gunk!' quite like a nice clear smoke signal drifting up through the trees."

Robin considered trying instead to use the Tower of Water to draw some of the liquid out of their belongings, but his mana stone still felt like a dead thing. He needed time and fuel to recharge, and a wet cheese sandwich was simply not going to cut it. They were both exhausted.

Finding a pen, he scrubbed a flattish section of the rock clear of ivy and moss and laid the parchment out carefully.

Henry, he wrote. *Bad news. Ran into Strigoi. Ffoulkes and Jack caught. Woad and me lost. You there?*

Robin and Woad leaned over the paper, waiting for the ink to sink into the surface and disappear, as it always did, before appearing on its sister-slice elsewhere.

Nothing happened.

"Why isn't it disappearing?" Robin frowned. He lifted the paper and shook it a little, as though he were slapping a remote control to make the batteries work again.

"The words are still there."

The only change to the words was that the ink had bled slightly into the wet parchment, making it appear a little blurred.

"Maybe we're in a bad area for signal?" Woad glanced around at the dark, choked woods. "The hex waves, or however it works?"

Robin used his damp sleeve to wipe the ink away and wrote the words again.

For a second time, they watched impatiently as absolutely nothing happened.

"Maybe the hex got washed off?" Robin worried. "What spell is on this thing? I'm guessing they're not designed to be enormous-waterfall-of-death-proof."

Robin wiped the waxy parchment clear again, his sleeve now smeared messily with ink, but before he could lift his pen to try again, panic slowly beginning to set in, words appeared in front of him, red and scratchy.

Have you learned anything?

For a moment, he thought it was Henry. But then, as soon as the words were read, they disappeared and new ones formed, rising up out of the yellowed surface like bloodstains.

Pyrenight approaches. You're wasting time you don't have. It's my one chance to get out.

"That's not Henry," Woad remarked and peered with interest. "I can tell, cause of how I can read the handwriting. It doesn't look like someone spilled a bowl of spaghetti."

"It's our mystery messenger," Robin exclaimed. "The one who sent us on this wild goose chase to Luna in the first place. But how is the message coming through at all?"

"Maybe it's just the long range, between-the-worlds stuff that's gotten scrambled," the faun shrugged. "Looks like we can still make and receive local calls."

As the words faded away again, Robin hastily penned a response.

Eris' people were there, he wrote. *But maybe you knew that already. Leading us into a trap? Is that what your plan was all along?*

There were a few seconds of blankness before a response formed.

Don't be a baby, it said. *Clearly you didn't die.*

I lost some friends! Robin scrawled angrily, while Woad nodded in cross agreement at his shoulder.

Careless, the response came, thoroughly unapologetic. *But did you learn anything useful?*

Robin considered this as the parchment faded to blank once more. He gazed around at the silent forest shadows. What *had* he learned? There had hardly been time to consider the meaning of the visions and memories he had been flooded with in Luna's strange trance. He hadn't had a moment to make sense of them, what with being attacked by peacekeepers and the rest of it.

His pen hesitated, hovering above the paper. He was unsure whether he should reveal the odd visions he had received of the downfall of Erlking to a total stranger.

How do I know I can trust you? he wrote.

The answer came almost immediately, as though impatient.

What choice do you have? More words formed below. *I don't have time to chat with you. Only moments between when we are not watched. So listen well.*

Without waiting for any answer from Robin, the words faded and new ones formed, the handwriting becoming scratchier still with haste.

Pay attention to whatever details you saw. Remember who you're looking for, remember how you know them. Where are you now?

Woad whispered into Robin's ear, as though superstitious that the rather bossy messenger could hear them. "It's just a guess, Pinky," he said. "I don't know this part of the world. But remember what Firebeard said when we were entering the town today, about the countryside around here. He said there was a forest down by the river falls."

Robin nodded. *One Horn Forest,* he wrote on the parchment. *We're just on the eastern border of the woods, I think,* he added, guessing from the position of the sun as they had entered the trees.

Bad luck for you, the messenger replied. *Try not to get run through. Head in and upland through the forest. If you make it, the mountains lie on its western border. Seek sanctuary at the library. Seek swift wings there. Far-sight and a mirror might be useful to cover more ground.*

They looked at each other in confusion. Woad shrugged.

Did you have a sneezing fit while writing that? Robin scrawled. *That makes no sense!*

Not only did he receive no reply, but his own words did not fade away. They sat uselessly on the page, obstinately unread. Clearly their elusive contact in Dis had gone again, for now.

"What did they mean 'run through'. And what library? I doubt there's a library out here in the wilds of the Netherworlde. That makes no sense at all."

"Well, if this really *is* One Horn Forest," Woad considered, watching Robin roll up the parchment and place it back in his satchel. "Then we need to tread carefully and quietly. We don't want to run into a pack of unicorns after all. I've had quite enough entertainment for one day without rounding it off with a lovely gored-to-death finale."

"Have you ever heard of a library in the Netherworlde?" Robin asked him, looking around warily at the deep and tangled shadows of the woods. They seemed very still and quiet, the only movement the occasional rustle of the ivy clinging thickly to the trees.

"Oh, there's just about a ton of things in the Netherworlde that I haven't heard about," Woad declared with pride. "Books are your thing, Pinky, not mine. Unless they're interesting herbarium ones of course."

"Remind me to thoughtfully gift you one for Christmas then," Robin smirked.

Woad gave Robin a sheepish grin. "No library knowledge in this faun. But if we're going anywhere, it's my strongest suggestion that we do it quickly. Every tingling sense in my tail is telling me that I don't think it's healthy to be in this forest all night."

"I've never known you to be scared of the dark, Woad," Robin frowned.

"No, it's not that. It's just that unicorns are nocturnal. They hunt at night, better to find their prey, see? Easier for them."

"Why would that be easier?"

The faun gave him a funny look, as though Robin were the dimmest person he'd ever met. He pushed himself up off the rock and scampered away into the deeper shadows of the trees, leaving Robin to grab his pack and hurry after, deep into the tangled darkness.

"Because they're blind, of course … duh," the faun called back.

With nowhere better to go and no plan to speak of other than to find some way to reach Henry and Karya at Erlking, Robin agreed that it was best to keep moving, even if they were cold and wet and miserable, with no destination in mind other than a vague and unfathomable direction given by a very unreliable guide.

Soon, the forest closed in around them utterly and Woad took the lead, picking the easiest ways through the dense and uneven undergrowth. More than once, they passed patches in the tangled woods where mist seemed to hang in small, suspended patches. Woad explained these were bog patches. Pits of warm mud, hidden between the trees. Tremendously good for the skin, full of revitalising minerals, with only the one small drawback that getting stuck in one would result in being slowly sucked into the earth and suffocated to death. But at least your corpse would have wonderfully clear pores.

They dutifully avoided these misty areas whenever they found them. Woad pointed out various Netherworlde plants as they moved along, filling the time with his newly-acquired encyclopaedic knowledge of fauna.

"Those are bravaberries." He nodded at one twist in the animal track they were following, drawing Robin's attention to what looked like a clump of large, very yellow gooseberries. "Don't eat them, ever. They make you boast. Make you too confident, and then before you know it, you're proving to all your friends how you can take down a gryphon bare-handed, or that you're excellent at doing handstands in a bog."

"What *would* happen if you tried to take down a gryphon bare-handed?" Robin asked, a little breathless from keeping up with his companion's pace.

"You'd have no hands," Woad shrugged.

"That ivy over there, the stuff that's more black than green? We call those fang vines."

Robin asked why, peering off at the tree where thin black tendrils nestled threaded through fatter, green ivy. Woad responded by picking up a small rock and lobbing it at the tree. The dark portion of the ivy shook furiously, making Robin jump in surprise, and slithered off swiftly on a thousand tiny unseen legs.

"Because it's not a plant," Woad explained. "It's an insect. They can grow big enough to cover a whole tree, and their bite is deadly, even for a faun." He glanced back at Robin, who was still staring, mildly horrified, at the bare patch of tree that moments earlier had seemed covered in ivy.

"So, don't ever fall asleep against an ivy-covered tree in the Netherworlde," Woad warned. "Not without checking, or you might wake up tangled in fang vines eating you up like you were a yummy cheeseboard at a Christmas party."

They walked for maybe an hour, deeper and deeper into the forest, without finding any sign of a true path or any clear area that wasn't filled with bog steam. And although Woad kept them entertained, pointing out this herb or that, this deadly or delicious mushroom, Robin couldn't help but notice there were no animals. Deadly and alarming camouflaged insects, yes. But typically, forests were full of birds and deer or rabbits. The stillness and silence of One Horn Forest was cloying; and as the light began to fade and afternoon wore into evening, it only became more smothering and oppressive.

Both boys, by this time, were filthy. Their soaked clothes were spattered with mud, stained with wet moss, smeared with soil and ragged from pushing through the thick undergrowth. Robin's trainers squelched with every step, his ankles sore and aching from the rocky, constantly broken and uneven ground hidden beneath the wet moss and leaves. His hair had dried from the river water at least, but the exertion of lugging his pack through the pathless shadows of the wood meant that sweat had sculpted it into an even grubbier mess.

Now that the adrenalin released by their escape from the agora had leached away, everything hurt. Robin had pulled or maybe torn a muscle somewhere deep in his arm, likely when casting the bubble-sphere during their fall. It ached and burned. Robin noticed that although he didn't say anything about it, his faun companion was limping with every step.

It felt ungrateful to complain about aches and pains, considering they should in theory be dead, killed by the drop from the falls. But the pain in his shoulder was like a hot poker. He tried to ignore it as they trudged onwards, but there was little in their surroundings to relieve the misery.

The forest was full of steep hills, little drops and cliffs, and the occasional precipitous ravine, so the going was slow, and they were often forced to double back on themselves or work around obstacles. Robin, when not listening to his friend's enthusiastic botany lessons, occupied himself by racking his mind regarding the visions he'd had. There must have been something ... even one thing ... that was of some use to him, buried in the strange memories that he had drifted through at the soothsayer's hut. Something that could lead him to Lady Calescent. Nothing from the distant past seemed connected, maybe it was among the more recent memories that had flickered through his mind, faster and faster toward the end of the episode? *Something* that would lead them to the missing noblewoman of the Fire Panthea, or towards a cure for Karya. Or maybe both. There had to be, otherwise Ffoulkes and Jackalope had been captured and were now lost and injured – and all for nothing.

No matter how many times he went over it, though, it was all just a jumble of nonsense. Random and unconnected memories.

Frustrated, Robin called out for Woad, who was merrily scampering ahead, scuttling deftly over fallen branches and ivy-choked rocks, trying his best to ignore his own limp.

"Woad, we're losing the light in this tangled maze. Where are you leading me?"

The faun looked back, a puzzled look on his face.

"I'm not leading you," he said. "You're the leader."

Robin gestured broadly at his companion. "You're literally in front of me, I'm following you!"

Woad shook his head. "No," he insisted. "I'm just beating a path for the route you're taking!"

"Woad, that makes no sense at all!" Robin was exasperated. He rubbed at his face, surprised to find a fresh bruise on his cheekbone which, once noticed, immediately began to hurt. They were both damp, muddy, hot and exhausted. He glanced around at the thick woods. The light was definitely leaching away. There was a soft and continuous patter from the canopy high above that suggested it was raining, though the branches up there made such a thick net, hardly any broke through to the boys below. The patches of fog they kept passing were becoming more frequent and larger, tendrils of mist snaking low through the undergrowth. It was only a matter of time before they stumbled into a bog.

"We could be turning in circles here," Robin rubbed the back of his head, ruffling his itchy hair. "I can barely keep track of which direction we were going in. I've never been in such a knotted forest. It's hardly the whimsical loveliness of the Hundred Acre Wood."

Woad rubbed a finger beneath his nose, sniffing and leaning casually on a tree bole. "I think One Horn Forest is more than a hundred acres, Pinky." He sounded doubtful.

"It's from a story," Robin explained absently, turning around. Something in the deepening shadows had just caught his eye, and by instinct, he had lowered his voice. He was certain he had just seen movement between the dark, ivy-choked trees, from the corner of his eye.

Woad's ears perked up as he noticed Robin's wary expression.

"Pinky?"

Robin held up a hand.

"I thought I saw … something," Robin said. "Over there,"

Both boys stood still as statues, peering into the thick undergrowth, searching the shadows. There was movement, again. Swift and silent. Something had definitely just passed from one shadow to another. Something large.

"Unicorns?" Woad hissed, sounding worried. He looked all around. "If there's one, there's two or three. They never hunt alone."

Robin still couldn't reconcile the idea of a unicorn as a dangerous animal, but there was definitely *something* in the woods with them. Even if they couldn't see anything, there was suddenly a distinct feeling of being watched. Stalked, even.

A twig snapped behind them, some way off, and both boys spun around. Robin's mana stone tingled faintly, though it still felt weak.

"Over there," Robin whispered, the hairs on the back of his neck standing up. This time, he definitely saw movement. Something large and sinewy had slunk past, some way off in the misty skeletons of the trees. He had only glimpsed it for a moment, but it looked a lot bigger than a horse – and it had been fast and fluid.

"Here too," Woad said cautiously, looking in another direction. "Told you. There's never just one." Robin followed his gaze. In another suspended patch of fog, to their right and much closer, there was the faint outline of a humped shadow. It was almost impossible to see because it was standing extremely still.

"What do we do?" Robin's voice was urgent and little more than a whisper. His eyes roved over the dark trees surrounding them in the thickening mist. None had low branches they could grab to climb, and all were strangled in ivy. He didn't fancy trying to shimmy up one anyway, considering they could be covered in those strange and horrible insects.

"Can unicorns climb trees?" he asked. He had never expected to be in a situation where he had to ask that question, let alone that his survival might depend on it.

Woad shook his head. "I don't think so, but it's not like we'd have time to find out anyway. Once they've scented you …" He shrugged, looking like a cat with raised hackles. "You're pretty much guaranteed to end up as a kebab on a stick, either way. We'd be skewered before our backs were even turned."

A far louder crash came from a screen of bushes right behind the faun and he leapt away from the tree instinctively, just as *something* burst forth from the foliage, scattering leaves everywhere.

It wasn't a unicorn of any description. Robin yelled involuntarily in surprise and fell back, tripping over a rock and landing hard on the floor. The figure erupting from the bush was shaped roughly like a man – only toweringly tall, with long, sinewy arms and legs – and it was banging two saucepans together loudly.

"AWAY!" it roared, its voice a loud, gurgling rumble. "Go on … git! Git you away shadows! Away, by Marrow!"

Robin scrambled frantically backwards on his rump, scraping his hands on the ivy and rocks beneath him and kicking his legs out as the massive being waved the huge rusty saucepans around in the twilight, crashing into the clearing and making a deafening din.

Shadows were moving everywhere in the fog now, clearly startled by the sudden ruckus, and amidst the snapping of trees, there was a chorus of angry snorting and growling.

Robin stared agog at the pan-banger. It was twice as tall as a man, with leathery grey skin that looked as rough and mottled as rock, hanging in odd folds. It wore a long, ragged loincloth and enormous fur boots, which were caked in mud. And it was horribly thin, every rib protruding from its grey torso, long arms and legs like knotted ropes. The interloper's head was large with monstrous features; a long, hooked nose and wrinkled puckered mouth beneath eyes so deeply set beneath a single dark brow, that Robin could barely see them in the shadows. From the creature's gnarled skull hung a smattering of long, stringy clumps of hair, looking wet and knotted and hanging around its face like black ropes. Atop its wrinkled head, swaying back and forth on a long neck as it shouted and banged its pans, they saw twin horns – twirling bone like twists of dirty barley sugar – rearing up and away from its ancient-looking face.

"Nothing for you here! Greedy mares! No!" The creature burbled and growled, stamping around the boys. Its huge footfalls were so heavy they shook the ground, making the ivy on the trees shiver. "Marrow's turf, this! Marrow's! Go back to the mist and eat your bugs! Bold as brass! Marrow will tan your hides! Marrow will make new boots from your flanks! Shadows-stank! Be gone!"

Woad had scampered over to Robin in the confusion and dragged him urgently to his feet, both of them backing up against a large rock to avoid being trampled by the gangling grey creature, which was now whirling around like a fury.

"Is it a troll?" Robin gasped, staring at their noisy saviour. Deep in the woods there came further crashes and the swift movement of unseen creatures, but they seemed to be receding, the creatures in the mist frightened off by the din.

"Bog hag," Woad said, his hands over his ears as the tall creature slammed its makeshift drums together, still wheeling around to scare off the stalking predators. "A male one. They're rare, they are!"

The bog hag stopped suddenly, letting the large, filthy saucepans drop to its sides. It stood, monstrous horned head cocked to one side, like a dog listening carefully. Robin and Woad could hear its rattling breath as it turned in a slow circle, sniffing the air wetly.

"Gone! Good!" it rumbled, its voice like a wet landslide of slurry. "Good. Marrow's turf, this. No paths for dark mares here! What brought them? Eh? What temptation? What sweet fancy led blind devil horns into the mist when they know better?"

It whirled, the wet ropes of hair on its largely bald head whipping around, as it stared down at the two boys, wide-eyed and frozen in surprise. They pressed themselves back against the rock.

"Meat! Aha! That's what." The bog hag crumpled its wrinkled face into a slow frown staring down at Robin and Woad from a great height, making its face seem as though it was collapsing in on itself. "Soft, tender faun." It sniffed, a wet and gruesome noise. "Fresh and fine," it grumbled. "No wonder. Bringing them here. This is Marrow's turf." It tilted its head toward Robin. "And what's this?" it muttered to itself loudly. "Smells odd, this one. Don't know it. No forest beast. No town-child. From far away, and full of fear and fire."

Woad stood up, indicating with a flap of his hand for Robin to stay back, he would handle this.

"This is the Scion of the Arcania, swamp-walker," he said, as bravely and loudly as he could manage. "A Fae, from the other world raised. And I am his guardian."

The creature seemed to consider this for a long time, glaring down at them with beetling brows. Then, seeming to reach a conclusion of some slow kind, it tilted its head back, making the shadows of its horns fall across its face in the deepening twilight.

"Hah! Some guardian," it growled. "Leading unicorns where they shouldn't. Good job that Marrow here! Marrow won't let mares of night near!" It banged one of its large pots against its chest, rattling it on its huge, protuberant ribs. "This is Marrow's land. Bogmaster land. You …" it pointed the saucepan at the boys accusingly, "lead the blind ones here with your stink!"

Robin thought this was a bit rich, coming from a creature that both looked and smelled as though it had just crawled out of a peat bog. He stood up, cradling his damaged shoulder and dusting off his jeans.

"We didn't mean to," he apologised. "We were just …"

"Passing through," Woad finished.

The bog hag growled, "Through Marrow's turf?" Both boys swallowed. Clearly, this huge creature was territorial. It bared its teeth, yellow and broken, licking along them with a long tongue as it seemed to consider things. After a few moments, it snorted and leaned back.

"Idiots," it concluded dismissively, letting the huge pan fall back to its sides. "Two morsels of meat walking through the bog-wood, might as well salt and pepper your idiot heads." It stared at them a little longer. Neither Robin nor Woad knew what to do for the best. The bog hag was huge. It could easily crush their heads with one hand. Should they run? How far would they get in the swampy forest anyway in the fog and darkness? And with the unicorns still out there …

"Do you know a way through?" Woad asked. The bog hag tilted its huge head towards him.

"Through the woods, I mean?" The faun gave his most winning smile. "Your lovely … um, *charming* woods. We're trying to get to the mountains on the other side. There's a library, you see."

"Don't know no library," the hag sniffed, curling its lip and sounding the unfamiliar word out carefully. "I is Marrowstride. This is bogmaster turf."

"Yes," Robin nodded, trying to look friendly. "You said that. Um … thank you, Marrowstride. For getting rid of the …"

"Don't know no library, no mountains." The hag cut him off, its voice booming. "Marrow knows these woods though. Every bole and boulder, every bog and pool." It looked proud of itself. "Marrow knows the hot and healing springs. Marrow knows the black mud pits. Marrow knows the magic black rocks, though Marrow don't go *there*. Old magic." It shook its shaggy head, disapproving. "Marrow knows where the dark mares walk, and where they don't. But never seen no fauns or no Scions before in here. And both broken up. That no good. Not whole. Not ... complete."

Robin perked up. "Wait." He held up a hand. "What was that? Magic black rocks?"

The creature folded its oddly long arms, nodding its huge head down at them proudly. "All the old places, Marrow knows."

"These rocks. Are they ... are they in a circle?" Robin asked, hope blooming in his heart. He drew a circle in the air with his finger, the bog hag watching with suspicious interest. "Like this?" He shot Woad a look. Woad's eyebrows shot up.

"A Janus Station?" the faun whispered.

It was possible, Robin thought. If they could find a Janus Station, the doorways between the Netherworlde and the human world, they could flip back. The hex message parchment seemed damaged and unable to send messages back and forth between the worlds, but he had managed to have a conversation with someone here in the same plane of existence. If they could get back to the human world, perhaps their hex message would work there, too. They could get word back to Henry and Karya at Erlking. They could get help.

"Round, they are," Marrowstride grumbled, nodding. "Old and forgotten. Forgotten even by that dark apple on the throne. She don't know 'em. She don't come here. No one does."

"Thank you ... for saving us," Robin said. "Do you remember *where* this circle is? Do you think you could show us?"

Woad gave Robin a cautious look. "Are you really asking a *bog hag* for guidance?" he hissed in Robin's ear. "They're not the sharpest. And they'll squash you underfoot as soon as look at you, even if all the legends about them say they're 'tied to the earth' and full of primal wisdom. Does that thing look wise to you?"

"What's it hissing?" Marrowstride glared suspiciously at Woad. "Little blue kettle, hissing with steam. Rude, that is!"

Robin held up his hands, waving them apologetically. "Sorry, sorry, no, he wasn't being rude," he insisted. "Woad was just saying how ... fearless you are, chasing off the unicorns like that. And how ... clever you must be. You know? To know every tree, like you said." He grinned hopefully. "And every bog. That's all."

The horned monster reflected on this a moment. "Marrow is wise," it grumbled, sounding quite defensive. "Marrow is whole. All things whole. Nothing broken. This is ..."

"Your turf, yes, we know," Woad said quickly. He gave the bog hag a thumbs up. "Great turf! Capital turf, absolutely top-notch."

"Can you show us these stones?" Robin asked. "We will get out of your forest, we promise. We didn't mean to draw the unicorns here. We need to find those stones, then we can go, and stop causing trouble and being ... unwhole, in your forest."

There was a very long pause. It seemed to take quite some time for the enormous creature to process what was said and to mull it over. Its wrinkled face gave very little away. It was like being glared at in the gloom by an angry and very suspicious walnut.

"You come," it grunted eventually, deciding. "Back to Marrow's. You come for dinner." It nodded to Robin. "Marrow has healing waters. Make you whole. Will show you black stones. But too dark now to stay here in mists. Night is coming." It gestured at the trees with a huge, gnarled hand. "More mares out when it's dark. Not safe for little broken morsels. Come for dinner." It sniffed, seeming to regard them both with clear distaste. "And to clean and make whole. Both you stink."

"Charming," Woad whispered, as the bog hag turned away and crashed off through the bushes in long lolloping strides. "Hardly like *it's* the most dapper and well-presented individual this faun has ever seen. I've seen smarter-looking carrion on a battlefield."

"Shush, Woad, come on," Robin said, and, for want of any other option, they scrambled through the mist after the huge, troll-like creature. "We have a chance to get somewhere, as long as we're careful. I'd rather take my chances with the huge bog-monster who scared off the stalking shadows things, than wander around here in the dark alone until we run into them again, wouldn't you?"

Woad made a non-committal noise down his nose, clearly feeling the choice was between a rock and a hard place, but he followed nonetheless, and the two of them stumbled tiredly through the gloom in the wake of their unusual saviour.

Marrowstride led them through the darkness for some time and distance, deeper still into the forest, both Robin and Woad having to scurry to keep up with its long, crashing strides. Night had definitely fallen now and true darkness lay between the trees. The only light seemed to come from the many patches of fog themselves, which glowed like spirits, illuminating the tree trunks and making them still and silent watchers as the three unlikely travellers plunged into the darkness ahead.

Insects had come to life in the gloom and Robin found himself constantly slapping at his arms and the back of his neck as they stumbled onwards. Woad seemed better equipped to fend them off through constant swishing of his long blue tail, and they seemed not to bother the towering bog hag – although Robin reasoned that if *he* was a blood sucking gnat, he would think twice about sinking his teeth into the tall creature's hide. It looked like overcooked meat, boiled until grey. The boy's backpack had rubbed sore red welts into his shoulders by the time Marrowstride finally turned a bend in the dark trees, and, ducking between two thick and overgrown boles, announced they were home.

"Not much," the bog hag grumbled. "But home is home. This is mine. Marrow will heat water, cut herbs, make soup. Not take long. Dark mares not come here so close, or they end up in soup!" It let out a horrible laugh, sounding like someone drowning in a bowl full of jelly, a horribly deep gurgle.

Robin had been expecting some kind of a cave, suitably troll-like, perhaps with skulls on spikes driven into the ground at the entrance. So he was quite surprised to see that, as they found themselves in the shallow bowl of a clearing, there was a long, ramshackle hut. It looked as though someone had tried to make a log cabin, but instead of cutting and stacking the logs, had simply torn them out of the earth and laid them against one another until they formed walls. There was a long sloping roof of twigs and black moss, threaded with a carpet of ivy, and even a stumpy chimney, sticking out of the brush. A door of torn boards lay closed on woven hinges, and before the door, screened by tall bushes, there was a large deep rock pool, filled with water that steamed in the darkness and smelled like minerals.

"Give." The bog hag turned and held out its huge shovel-like hand for Robin's pack. "Marrow cook inside. Will take your things. You two …" It gestured to the steaming pool. "Wash. Heal. Water is full of goodness. Both of you filthy and bloody. No good for supper. Must have manners. No filth in Marrow's house! Clothes first, selves next."

It grabbed the backpack, plucking it away from Robin before he could argue, and turned away, heading in several strides to the long and windowless cabin, where it ducked its tall horned head and dipped inside, letting the door slam behind him and making the roof shiver.

"That's not a muddy bog," Robin observed. "Is that …"

"A hot spring!" Woad chirped. "Who'd have guessed? The old bog hag living the five-star spa-life here in One Horn Forest. No wonder it doesn't want to share with the nasty unicorns. Where there's warm mud pits, there's hot mountain water, too. I should have known, but even a faun can't know everything."

Tired and grubby as he was, Robin still looked around cautiously at the dark forest beyond Marrowstride's clearing. He had seen the intimidating creature scare off the unicorns once, but the bog hag was indoors now and nowhere to be seen. Perhaps the shadowy beasts were still out there, slinking around in the darkness, huge and dark and silent.

The faun, it seemed, had no such reservations, as he barrelled past Robin, almost knocking him to the ground, and swinging his trousers around his head like a flag. With an almighty leap he cannonballed into the steaming water, utterly destroying the calm of the woodland scene. "Last one in is a rotten egg," he called back amidst the huge spray of water. "Which is what you smell like anyway, after tramping through the woods, Pinky," he cackled.

"The phrase 'once in a blue moon' just took on a whole new *horrible* meaning for me, you maniac." Robin shook his head, but Woad swam away, ignoring him completely, and he couldn't help but grin, smiling for perhaps the first time since arriving at Titania's Tears.

The water was indeed hot, he found, and after scrubbing his clothes as best he could against a flat rock, getting out much of the trail muck and soil they had accumulated on their trek, Robin left them out to dry on the grass and gratefully plunged into the water, sinking up to his neck, enjoying the heat and feeling as though all the exhaustion of their escapades since they had tumbled over the waterfall was indeed being leached away by the spring. As Woad swam back and forth, invisible in the steam and mist, nothing but a vague blob of happy blue, Robin trod water in place, looking up at the dark canopy of trees that surrounded Marrowstride's clearing. There was a gap in the foliage above the pool, and he could see a cloudy night sky, and the occasional peeking star, twinkling through in the distance.

"It's not that I'm not grateful," Robin called to Woad, as he lay back and rested his head on a rock, feeling as though he could just close his eyes in the water and sleep for a week. "But we can't stay for supper here. If there really *is* an old, forgotten Janus Station nearby, we need to find it, and let everyone know what happened."

"I don't fancy eating whatever passes for a bog hag dinner, anyway," Woad called back from the mists. "I mean, what's to eat out here? Grubs, roots and tubers? It's not likely to have smoked sausage and half a pig of bacon strung up inside that hut, is it?"

Robin agreed, scrubbing the grime out of his hair. "Jack and Ffoulkes are being taken to Dis right now," he said. "Probably via Janus Station, so chances are they might be there already. Like you said earlier, there's very little time until Pyrenight, and going to see that fortune teller was a complete bust, all it got us was trouble. We don't have time to waste."

The door to the hut on the far side of the pool bashed open, and they heard Marrowstride's rumbling voice in the darkness.

"If not stink now, come drink. Clothes at side of pool for you. Not bogmaster clothes, hur hur, too big for little wanderers. Left long ago from other little lost ones." It sounded amused at its own humour.

"Come drink! Marrow is wise of the forest. Will make whole and unlock. Then guide to black stones."

"Unlock?" Robin mouthed silently to Woad, who shrugged in the water, causing a ripple of splashes, equally clueless as to what the bog hag was talking about.

The strange forest-dweller had indeed left dry clothes at the edge of the pool for them. A rough-spun pair of brown trousers that Woad claimed, and simple handmade trousers and a worn old shirt which fitted Robin well enough, if a little baggily, making him feel like a pirate. When they had dried and dressed, feeling refreshed and less weary, they made their way around the bushes to the cabin.

Robin wondered what had happened to the original owners of these clothes. Had they fallen afoul of the forest unicorns, too? Was the bog hag in the habit of looting the corpses of the dead it stumbled across in the forest? It seemed a grim possibility. There were no shoes, so Robin had slipped back into his own battered trainers, which looked odd combined with the more traditional Netherworlde garb of the rest of his outfit, but which were at least almost dry now.

"I feel a hundred times better." He stretched as he and Woad approached the hut. Woad cracked his knuckles, shaking his still damp hair in an energetic flurry. The faun was no longer limping. "Me too, Pinky. I feel ten times the faun I was."

The bog hag, its long and oddly-proportioned frame folded up on a stool, was sitting outside the door. It sat before a small campfire, over which hung a small cauldron supported by a frame of three sticks. It indicated for the boys to sit on the two other stools awaiting them.

"Ha," it grunted, nodding at the pool. "No normal ground here. Not in the forest. Mud pits good for you, hot water good for you. Everything here good. Make you strong! Whole!" It thumped its own chest. "Make you better! If little morsels lived here ... hur hur ... soon be big and strong as bogmaster themselves!"

Robin wasn't sure whether the bog hag was just oddly proud of its homeland, or whether there really was some restorative property to the mineral springs of One Horn Forest, but he did know that he no longer felt exhausted. His limbs were not aching, his torn shoulder seemed completely healed, and the welts that had rubbed into his shoulders from carrying the pack all this way seemed to have disappeared altogether. Even the bruise on his cheek seemed to have gone.

"If we could bottle your water, Marrowstride, we would make a fortune back in the human world," he said, pulling up a stool.

"Not take from forest," the bog hag growled. "Nothing leaves Marrow's turf. Everything stays."

Robin raised his hands to show that he was only joking. "I just meant ..."

"Is not only water powers that are bottled," the huge creature said. It reached out a thick finger and prodded Woad in the chest, almost knocking the faun off his stool. "Other things bottled up. Stuck. Power inside but can't get out."

"Oi," Woad complained, rubbing his chest. "I'm not bottled!"

The bog hag ignored him, shaking its head slowly to itself. It filled three rough wooden cups with whatever bubbling liquid was slopping about in the pot using a large ladle and passed a cup to each of them.

"Lies. Big lies from little people. All power is trapped in the blue one. Marrow can see!" It tapped where they presumed its eyes might be in its huge, wrinkled face. "Marrow sees the hidden things. Always has. Good eyes for the dark, here in the shadows."

It kicked at the fire beneath the cauldron, causing a flurry of sparks to rise up into the night air around them.

"Bogmasters only deal in things complete and whole. Pure that way. But blue one has no Skyfire. All bottled and trapped inside," it said flatly.

Woad seemed hotly defensive. "Not all fauns come into it at once!" he said, lifting his cup to his lips. "And a faun's Skyfire is a faun's own business!"

Robin didn't feel they should be shouting at the enormous troll-like creature who had them alone in the very dark woods, so he leaned in quickly to stop Woad from yapping.

"What *is* that?" he asked. "I mean, I've heard lots of people mention Skyfire, but I don't know what it means."

"Skyfire is a faun's true strength, diplodocus," Woad said haughtily, taking a deep sip of his drink. "An element all our own, somewhere between the Tower of Fire and the Tower of Light. Neither one nor the other. All fauns can master Skyfire."

"Except for you?" Robin asked, sipping his own drink. It was hot and tasted of liquorice and something peppery. He had half expected anything served by a bog hag to be sludge, but it warmed him inside wonderfully.

Woad narrowed his yellow eyes at him. "I just haven't come into it yet!" he said. "You don't have a hair on your chin yet, Pinky, so you've no room to talk. All fauns get their Skyfire at different times, it's something that is taught from one generation to the next."

"Not you though," the bog hag rumbled bluntly. "Little blue one got no elders. All alone, like Marrow. No one to show you *how* to unlock. No fauns to guide. No lesson, no school."

Robin vaguely remembered Karya saying something in passing, long ago, about Woad being an exile from his tribe. That was how he had ended up with her, with all of them at Erlking. It had never occurred to

Robin for a moment that the blue boy might be missing out on things in the faun world because of it.

"I know lots of tricks," Woad insisted.

"Water makes strong," Marrowstride nodded at the pool again. "Make better." It lifted its cup as though toasting them. "And drink make doors unlock. Marrow can help."

The faun gave him a suspicious look. "How could a bog hag … I mean … bogmaster … help a faun unlock his faun-like potential?"

Robin thought this whole conversation was odd. First the unearthly creature had saved them from the unicorns, then it had led them to safety in the forest. Clothed and healed them, and now seemed to be offering to not only lead Robin to a Janus Station, but to help Woad to reach his full potential, whatever that might be.

"You've offered us a lot of help," he said to the gnarled face, which even sitting, loomed high above them. "What can we do in return?"

The bog hag seemed to consider this for a long time, in its slow, silent way.

"Stay. For supper," it growled eventually.

It looked around the clearing, its wrinkled face flickering in the warm campfire light. "No other bogmasters here in the forest. Not anymore. Marrow is alone. None to share."

Robin felt horribly guilty. He had only just been explaining to Woad how they had to hurry, and here this strange-looking creature, seemed to want nothing from them except a little company.

"What is for supper?" Woad asked, clearly still dubious about the offerings available in a swamp, despite the delicious drink.

"Unlock first," Marrowstride grunted sternly. "Skyfire best. Faun too tightly bottled. Not good for faun to be trapped tight."

"How can you … Robin began, but the bog hag had already reached out a hand, and with one hefty jab, hit Woad in the middle of his forehead.

There was a flash as though static electricity had leapt from one to another. Woad's eyes rolled back in his skull and he toppled from his stool, landing unconscious and spread-eagled on the ground in front of the hut. His dropped cup, contents spilled, rolled away into the bushes.

Robin leapt to his feet, shocked. "What did you just do?" He was already reaching for his mana stone, ready to defend himself and Woad, but Marrowstride pointed its finger up at the sky. From far above, in the clouds of the night, there came a long, low rumble of thunder. It rolled over and around the small hollow of the forest valley.

"Not hurt." The creature scratched absently at one of its gnarled horns. "Just unlocked. Blue morsel fine. Wake up soon. No more tight bottle in chest, just Skyfire. Free and whole. Whole things are best. Best for faun, best for bogmaster."

Robin dropped beside Woad and examined him. He did indeed seem fine, and simply in a deep sleep.

He stared up at the curious creature. "How do you know how to do that? You're not a faun."

"Bogmasters close to earth!" The bog hag stamped its large foot, making the floor shake under Robin and the contents of the cauldron slop. "Fauns close yes, but bogmasters closer." It waved a hand vaguely at the shadows. "Panthea out there, in cities, in towns, far away from the earth. Carts and books and lamps and light, all take them far away. Bad shame."

It pointed at Robin, its crinkled face looking concerned. "You far away too, strange little one. Lots of power in you, yes there is. Earth, water, soil and rock. Even fire." It shook its head. "But no use. You too far away from it." It sneered. "Scared of it, scared of self."

"I'm not afraid of myself," Robin argued, standing up again now he was sure Woad wasn't harmed. "I've mastered three Towers of the Arcania. That's more than most people. And I'm working on the fourth."

"Too far away!" Marrowstride said loudly. Its voice was such a rumble that it sounded like a roar, and Robin found himself taking a step back.

"You have foot in one world, foot in another," the bog hag said. "Marrow close to earth, so can see it." It pointed a thick finger at Robin's eyes; one blue, one green. "You see two worlds from one head even. All about you undecided, unsure. Belong nowhere. Fae … but not Fae. Not whole."

It nodded down at the sleeping faun. "This one is pure," it said. "Better now it's whole faun. Very good. Now … unlocked. More itself. Fuller faun."

Robin swallowed. "When will he wake up?" he asked. Marrowstride stood, pushing himself up with its hands on its knees, until the tall creature loomed over the boy, Robin lost in its primal shadow.

"Soon," it said. It swept something off the floor and tossed it to Robin, who caught it instinctively. It was his backpack. "Come!" The bog hag turned away.

"Come where?" Robin didn't want to leave Woad here by the fire alone. The forest-dwelling giant looked between them, taking a while to understand Robin's hesitance. "Blue morsel will be fine a while. Sleeping and becoming more. Ripe when Marrow gets back. You come with, to black stones behind house. Place of old magic you wanted to find, yes?"

Marrowstride had built its cabin close to the healing springs and mud pits, and, it seemed, also close to the Janus Station it had spoken of. For the creature and Robin had walked less than a hundred steps into the trees behind the house, and down a steep slope full of trailing ivy which threatened to trip the boy at every step, before the trees parted once more, and they spilled out into another low clearing.

Looking back, Robin could still see the firelight outside the long hut at the top of the dark rise behind him, glimmering through the trees. He couldn't explain why, but he felt certain that the unicorns, and any other creature in the forest, wouldn't dare to enter Marrowstride's inner sanctum. Its "turf". Woad would be fine; it was only for a moment.

"Here. See? Old stones. Noisy things in Marrow's head." The bog hag spread its hands, displaying the clearing. Robin saw that there was indeed a wide circle of upright menhirs in the forest. They were each twice as tall as he was, jet black, shiny and craggy, sticking out of the grass and low bushes like a ring of crooked teeth in the moonlight. A couple of them leaned precariously. Two had toppled completely, and lay on their sides almost covered in the choking ivy that wound its way around them and through the grass.

There must have been either another hot spring nearby or another bubbling bog, as thick ground mist crawled across the floor here, filling the clearing and glowing in the darkness.

"Marrow not come inside the circle," the bog hag grumbled. It shook its huge head, horns slicing the mist. "Live close, yes. Lots of power here. Power in the mud, power in the water. But in there?" It pointed slowly inside the circle. "Too thin."

Robin stared into the circle of stones. "The ground is too thin?" he asked.

The bog hag shook his head. "Not ground. Worlds," it said. "Can hear other world sometimes. On wind, comes through circle. Strange noises. Saw rabbit go once. Into circle." It clapped its hands together suddenly, the noise making Robin jump.

"Then gone. To other world. Never back again."

"It's a doorway," Robin explained. "Between the Netherworlde and the human world. All Janus Stations are. Most of them are under control of the empress, though. She watches them like a hawk." He glanced at his companion. "Do you know who that is?"

"Marrow knows of that one, yes. No empress here though," the bog hag said. "Never in One Horn. No place for people like her." It frowned down at the boy. "Or people like you. Only strong live here. People keep away."

I wonder why? Robin thought silently to himself. I mean, between the large deadly unicorns stalking everyone in the darkness, the flesh-eating ivy insects, the bloodsucking gnats, and oh, the constant danger of being sucked into a swampy quicksand muddy death, what's not to love about this place?

"Then she doesn't know it's here," he said out loud. "Eris *doesn't* control them all. I can get to the human world here and back." He stepped into the wide circle, mist and ivy threading around his feet. "Do you know how to … you know, work it?" he asked, looking back to the tall shadow, which loomed in the trees like a towering devil and hadn't stepped inside.

He felt something like scorn roll off the bog hag towards him. "Rabbit can work it. Is thin. Is easy."

"Of course," Robin nodded, bolstered. If a rabbit could cross between worlds unaided, so can the Scion of the Arcania. "I'll be really quick," he called back. "Will you … I mean … stay with Woad? With my friend, the faun. Make sure he's okay? I just need to send a message. I'll be right back."

"Little blue one stay, you go," the bog hag nodded. "Stay for supper. That Marrow's deal. I help you to black rocks."

"Yes, yes," Robin nodded, peering around at the menhirs looming around him. "And we stay and have supper with you, I remember, just … " He reached out and stroked the surface of one of the rocks lightly. Despite its craggy appearance, it felt smooth beneath his fingertips and oddly warm here in the night air. "Let me figure out how … "

A thrum passed through his fingertips, a vibration that shot up his arm. His mana stone flashed like a bulb, and in response, each of the black stones in the circle lit up like floodlights, silent and sudden. They flared into life, one by one until they had come full circle. It was so blinding that Robin was disoriented, and threw up his other arm to shield his face from the glare. It blazed, the light carried by the mist, and the trailing fog on the floor rose up like steam all about him. A shudder ran through the ground at Robin's feet. The earth rippled, and then, as suddenly as it had bloomed, the light faded.

10

Leap of Fae

Robin blinked furiously, trying to clear his vision. It was suddenly cold. A biting chill and a steady wind ruffled through his hair, as though he had stepped right into a freezer. He dropped his hand from the stone and stumbled back a couple of paces, staring around as his vision returned to normal.

He was still in the black circle of stones, but once he had blinked away the swimming after-images of the stone-flare, everything else was different. Gone was the ivy and the mist beneath his trainers. The grass underfoot was short, neatly cut. The stones themselves had not changed, but several of them were now covered in paint, sprayed graffiti, long worn half away. There were a couple of beer cans resting against the base of one of them, and what looked like a chocolate bar wrapper flapping in the icy breeze. Robin looked around.

Close to the circle was a gravel path, lit by yellow street lamps at regular intervals. It wound close to where he stood, before meandering away again and off into a thin line of cedars. The ground all around was covered with thin patches of slushy snow, and beyond the gravel path stood dark and low railings. In the darkness of the night, standing empty and abandoned, a children's playground, the swings and slide deserted and eerie in the dark of the cold night.

"I'm back," he whispered to himself, his teeth chattering in the suddenly icy air. He was in the human world, though where precisely was anyone's guess, and here it was still the middle of winter of course. His breath came before him in little clouds, backlit by the yellowish street lamps.

The great, claustrophobic forest of the Netherworlde was gone. He appeared to be in a town park. There was a bandstand nearby, looming in the shadows, and a fountain some way off. Through the cedar trees he could see the lights of a row of houses nearby, their glimpsed windows lit up cosily against the night, and over all this a thin snow was falling, the tiny flakes whispering to the ground, and visible clearly only in the cones of street light cast down from each lamp.

Robin looked up. The wild dark skies of the Netherworlde were always open and primal in their steadfast refusal to be marked with signs of humanity. Here, the thick clouds above were tinted orange in the reflected glow of this town or city, seeming smaller somehow. Tamer and lower. Muffled in the distance he heard the drone of late-night traffic on a nearby road.

At least it's late, he thought, and there's no-one around here to see me. He could only imagine how alarming it would be for someone to be out walking their dog in the park and suddenly to have a teenage boy drop out of mid-air, dressed like he was on his way to attend a renaissance fair somewhere. Luckily for him, there was nobody in sight.

Shivering in the cold, Robin crossed to the railings, his feet crunching in the thin skin of snow. He deftly vaulted the waist-high fence, crunching across the asphalt of the playground. Sitting on a swing, he laid his satchel on his lap and fished inside for his hex message parchment.

Please let this work now, he thought urgently, as he flattened the crumpled, still damp sheet out, resting on his pack as a makeshift table.

Henry, he scrawled with his pen. *R U there? Msg me back asap u c this.*

For several, heart-sinking minutes, nothing happened. The words sat blankly on the page, staring up at him. Robin stared down, rocking back and forth slightly on the cold swing with a grating squeak, waiting.

"Come on, Henry," he muttered under his breath.

The boy glanced up at the cloudy sky. He had no idea what time it was. If the seasons lagged between here and the Netherworlde, where it was already spring, did the time of day lag too? It was full dark, but it was winter, so that didn't mean much. It could have been anywhere between five in the afternoon and midnight, or later.

From the lack of any other people in the park, it *felt* like the early hours of the morning. Some time after midnight.

The words on the paper suddenly sank away and vanished, and Robin's heart leapt.

"Yes!" he whispered, relieved, gripping the parchment and giving it a little triumphant flutter. He stared in the dark for a few seconds. Nothing happened.

"Don't you dare leave me on read," he muttered through chattering teeth.

Eventually, a reply began to form, in Henry's easily recognisable scrawl.

Rob? Watsup m8? Do u no wat time it is??

Robin was already writing a response before the words faded.

Bad news, he scrawled. *Ran into Strigoi in the NW. Also Mr Knight from the gallery is a Grimm! Ffoulkes and Jack captured. Woad and me lost. Need HELP.*

The next response came much faster. Henry, who Robin imagined must have been woken by his first message, was now clearly awake.

What?!?!

Robin sighed down his nose in frustration.

I'm not going to write it again! he scribbled. *J and F taken to Dis. Need to save them. No leads on the Fire woman. Stuck in dodgy forest. Woad ok tho. Me 2.*

The response came quickly again and was frustratingly short

W8.

"Wait?" Robin stammered out loud. For what? Did Henry need to get out of bed and make himself a nice hot cocoa before he could fully digest that their trip to Titania's Tears had been a complete disaster? That two of Erlking's own had been dragged off to the capital to be served up to Eris, and that the other two were wandering blindly in the woods making strange alliances with very odd creatures.

It was a couple of minutes before any new message came through. Robin jumped up from the swing, unable to stop himself from pacing back and forth across the dark playground. He was restless, but he also needed to get warm. The chill night air was cutting through his Netherworlde clothes and his hair was still damp from the hot spring.

One Horn Forest suddenly seemed very far away to Robin, with its dangerous creatures and Woad lying unconscious on the floor of the woods. He glanced through the trees of the small park, envious of the warmly lit windows of the houses he could see. Regular people would be in there, maybe sleeping soundly, maybe watching late night movies, doing last minute homework. Regular lives without the balance of the fate of the world hanging over their heads. He remembered that life. Living with Gran, going to sleep with no greater worries than any other young boy concerned with the horrors of school. An enviable normal life, he sometimes thought. Something everyone should have.

This made him think of Jackalope, who'd had nothing of the sort. His childhood was a concentration camp. His only family a brother whose death still haunted him so deeply that he had taken his name and forgotten his own.

Robin decided that compared with that, he had no room to complain. He'd had a happy childhood, and his life since coming to Erlking had been at least as wonderful as it was terrifying. If Jack and Ffoulkes needed his help, he couldn't waste time wringing his hands about the terrible burden of being the saviour of the Fae.

There was a sign attached to the railings, a small and instructive map of the larger park, with a "you are here" arrow showing Robin's location in the playground. There were long walks through safe and pretty woods here, what looked like an old open-air amphitheatre, and some kind of ruined castle on a steep hill very nearby. *Clitheroe*, Robin read, shrugging to himself. He had never heard of the place. A village or town, perhaps.

The parchment suddenly vibrated, jittering in his hands. He stopped pacing and stared down at the forming words, tilting the page towards the nearest street light. It wasn't Henry's handwriting this time. It was Karya's. He recognised it at once. That must have been the reason for the delay. Robin could picture Henry leaping out of bed and running through the halls of Erlking in his slippers to wake her and tell her the news.

Scion? The looping handwriting read. *Henry says you lost Jack and your tutor to the Grimms and Strigoi? Are you hurt? Where is Woad?*

Robin ran back to the swing, sat and scrawled a reply.

Not hurt. Escaped with Woad. Got bashed about and flushed a good way downriver, but found someone to help. All healed now. Me and Woad fine. He's still in the NW. I'm here alone.

The reply came swiftly.

What do you mean "alone"? Where are you? You're not in the Netherworlde?

No, Robin replied. *Hex all messed up because it got damaged. Had to come back to human world to msg U. Woad in One Horn Forest. He's okay. With a bog hag. It saved us. Found me a Janus Station.*

There was a long pause, where the parchment remained worryingly blank, and then Karya's words came again, this time all in capitals, with a distinctly shouty vibe.

SCION. V IMPORTANT. WHERE ARE YOU RIGHT NOW?

Robin frowned down at the parchment. *Somewhere called Clitheroe. Near a castle. There's a park with a playground in it. Janus Station here, though I reckon the locals just think it's some old monument.*

DON'T MOVE.

The command was sudden, bleeding up out of the parchment swiftly. As soon as he read it, it faded.

When nothing else appeared, he wrote back.

Karya?

The words didn't fade.

Henry? He wrote next to it. Both names sat on the page. Clearly no one was reading it. What on earth were they doing? He needed them to get Aunt Irene or Calypso. To tell the adults what had happened. They needed help. What on earth were the two of them playing at?

Somewhere far off, a car horn bleated. The snow had begun to fall a little thicker, the flakes fat and soft. Icy kisses. Robin's blinked them off his eyelashes.

After a few minutes of shivering impatiently, he was startled by a loud crack echoing around the park. Out of nowhere, and with a small flash, two figures appeared at the top of the slide, immediately losing their footing and careening down, jumbled up together. They spat out onto the floor, landing in a tangled and ungainly heap.

"Henry? Karya?" Robin's eyes shot wide and he leapt off the swing. His friends had just appeared out of nowhere and were now getting unsteadily to their feet. Henry was wrapped in a thick bubble parka, and Karya too was fully dressed, her familiar animal skin coat bundled around her as they fought to disentangle themselves in a flurry of arms and curses.

"Bloody hellfire," Henry said shakily, staggering a little and looking very dazed indeed. "That was not a smooth ride, even by your standards."

"Get off me!" Karya's muffled and irritated voice came as Henry bent to try and help her to her feet. She blew out her cheeks, looking winded. "That … that really took it out of me."

"How are you here?" Robin rushed towards them, unable to stop a surge of sheer joy. He had never been so grateful to see either of them.

"She insisted!" Henry dusted off the front of his jacket, stamping his feet in the cold and shaking his head. His wild hair was still mussed from bed. "I told her no. Too risky, you're not well." He shrugged. "But *you* try telling this one she can't do something. Like a red rag to a bull."

"I thought …" Karya said shakily, "I had one last tear left in me." She sounded winded, terribly breathless. "And I was right. I could do it. Just! Not between the two worlds. I really think that might actually kill me. But from Erlking to here? Well, it's not like we had any choice. Lucky for you, Scion, you give off a strong signal. Pretty easy to find."

She looked between Robin and Henry, finally noticing that they were both staring at her, wide-eyed and open-mouthed.

She glanced between them. "What?" she demanded to know. "Why are you glaring at me? Okay … yes, it wasn't my *neatest* tear, I admit it. And how was I supposed to know there would be a big bloody metal slide at the end of it? But either of you two try driving with no gas in the tank and see how well you manage, *then* we'll talk about style and finesse, okay?"

Robin shook his head, still staring. "It's not that," he said.

Henry pointed at her, the padded sleeve of his puffa jacket rustling. "Your hair!"

Karya paused, wrinkling her nose in confusion. She seemed unsteady and had gripped the side of the slide for balance. She reached down and grabbed a handful of her hair.

"Karya, your hair has turned *white*," Robin said, peering at her, his face full of worry. It was true. Karya's hair no longer had several grey streaks. Her entire tangled tumble of hair was now as pure white as the snow falling all around them. Her skin was paler than ever, making her seem like a small, strange phantom in the darkness of the playground.

"Well …" she faltered, looking down at her snowy locks in her hand. "That's …" she trailed off.

"You shouldn't have pushed yourself." Henry sounded concerned.

"*Neither* of you should have left Erlking!" Robin insisted. "You were supposed to … I don't know, raise the alarm or something."

Karya dropped her hair, suddenly disinterested in her own appearance, and glared at Robin.

"You knucklehead," she snapped, glaring at him. "As if that's important right now. Who gives a chalpie's aunt about my hair? You said you left Woad in One Horn Forest?"

"There's only old Hestia and my dad at Erlking, Rob," Henry interjected. "Your aunt and Calypso have both gone up north together somewhere to meet Hawthorn and discuss that Mr Knight's company. Did you really say he was one of the Grimms?"

"That's the least of our worries." Karya stalked up to Robin, her freshly white hair streaming out behind her. She was staring all over him, as though assessing damage. "You said something about a bog hag. Are you injured anywhere?"

Robin tried to shake his head and nod at Henry in an effort to answer both their overlapping questions at once.

"Yes, he's a Grimm. A weird one, too," he confirmed. "And no, I'm fine. We're both fine. I mean, we got knocked about a bit when we went over the waterfall, and torn up pretty good in the forest, but the bog hag has this pool, see? And it kind of healed everything."

Henry's eyebrows were in his hairline. "When you went over the *what*?!"

"A pool?" Karya shook her head, grabbing Robin by the chin and turning his face this way and that, evidently not convinced with his insistence that he was fine. He batted her hand away gently.

"Will you leave off?" he said. "I said I'm fine. All healed. Woad is still back there. He … something the bog hag said. He's unlocking his Skyfire." He shrugged. "If that means more to you than me?"

Karya pursed her lips, looking deeply troubled. "I need to know everything that's happened between you leaving Erlking and now," she insisted. "But not right this second. There isn't time. We have to save Woad."

Robin was exasperated. "I just told you Woad was *fine*," he insisted. "Marrowstride, that's the guy we met. It's looking after him while he's on his faun-spiritual-journey or whatever it is, he …"

"That's not a 'guy', Scion!" Karya rubbed her hands across her face. She still looked shaky from tearing herself and Henry all this way from Erlking. Robin wondered if she was about to pass out. "It's a *bog hag*."

"Well, he, or it, has been kind to us!" Robin said. "Saved us from unicorns, invited us for supper …"

Karya dropped her hands from her face, her golden eyes utterly disbelieving. "All the books you've read about the Netherworlde and you're still clueless, aren't you?" She shook her head in disbelief. "You've read the *Netherworlde Bestiary* from Hammerhand. What do you know about bog hags?"

Robin shook his head, his mind blank. He threw his arms up in frustration. "They're hags?" he spluttered. "And they live in bogs?"

"Clue's in the name there, mate," Henry added helpfully, scooting his foot on the asphalt.

Karya glanced heavenwards. "Give me strength. Bog hags are territorial and extremely fussy," she said, straining to keep patience in her voice. "They don't share meals, and they will fight off any other predator to claim their prey, including unicorns. But they only eat whole things, perfectly prepared."

"What *are* you talking about?"

"Listen, a hyena will come across half an animal carcass, left by lions, and feast on the leftover meat and bones, yes? So will a vulture," the girl explained. "Not so bog hags. Even if a deer has just half an antler snapped off they won't touch it. If a rabbit is filthy or missing a tooth, they won't touch it."

"Wait, are you saying this thing is planning on eating Woad?" Henry asked.

Robin shook his head. "No, that can't be right. Marrowstride saved us, healed our wounds …"

"It *claimed its meal*, Scion." Karya cut him off. "And of course it healed you. Got all the grime off. Even Hestia scrubs carrots clean before she cooks them. Why do you think it's trying to unlock Woad's Skyfire?"

Robin swallowed, shaking his head.

"Because he's not a whole faun without it," she continued without waiting for a reply. "It's not been *helping* you, it's been *prepping* you. Nice mineral-bath marinade, scrubbed up clean and ready to eat. Probably even gave you something to drink or eat to flavour and season the meat, and now it has a whole faun. Lovely feast. It wasn't inviting you to join it for supper. It was inviting you to *be* supper."

She glanced around frantically. "Where are these stones? Where's the Janus Station?'

Robin pointed to the circle of rough stones in the shadows. The three of them rushed across the playground through the falling snow, their feet slipping on the surface.

"Can you open it?" Henry asked, as they pushed through the gate of the railings, which squeaked alarmingly in the quiet night. "I mean, in your …"

"If you say 'in your condition' to me one more time, Henry Drover, I swear to the fates, it will be the absolute last thing you say," Karya said, not looking back. "I can't tear us between worlds like usual, no. I can, however, work a damned Janus. Even Robin could do it."

"*Even* Robin?" Robin piped up, a little offended.

"Just checking," Henry grumbled as they entered the stone circle. "No need to bite my head off."

Karya was already passing from stone to stone within the circle, touching them here and there and concentrating. Snow was settling in her white hair.

"I'm more worried about Woad having *his* head bitten off," she said.

Robin felt horrible. He could still see Marrowstride, standing at the edge of the stones as he had left the Netherworlde, insisting that the faun stay "for supper". That had been the deal. How could he have been so stupid?

"I … I didn't know," he shook his head, and Karya glanced at him, her expression softening a little seeing his expression.

"I know," she said, as the stones began to glow softly, snow hissing from their surface where it touched. "There's no time for blame now. We've lost Jack and Ffoulkes to calamity while I've laid in bed like an old maid. We're not losing anyone else. Both of you, stay close."

Robin and Henry shuffled together so that all three of them were standing in the centre of the circle. As the stones grew brighter and the world began to shimmer uncertainly, Robin cast his eyes upwards, at the fat white flakes of snow falling out of the dark wintry sky above. A moment later, they, and the rest of the human world, were gone from his sight.

The world reformed, and Robin found himself still looking upwards, only now it was into a clear, deeply black sky dotted with a thousand stars. Warm night air flowed over him, and the deep rich scents of damp soil, soft earth and woodland rose up to meet him.

They were back in the Netherworlde.

"Spooky," Henry assessed, looking around at the thick ivy-choked trees all around in the darkness and the rolling ground mist. He was already shrugging out of his thick winter parka. It was so much warmer here.

"Where are they?" Karya asked, her eyes urgently scanning the gloom as they got their bearings. Robin pointed off through the trees. He could still see the glimmering light of Marrowstride's strange cabin, floating like a will-o'-the-wisp in the tangled lacework at the top of the steep rise.

"This way, follow me." He set off, Henry and Karya stumbling after him, the last of the snow melting off their shoes and disappearing into the thick vegetation underfoot.

They reached the long low cabin at the top of the hill, stealing out of the trees as carefully as they could. Robin motioned for them to be silent and led them around its perimeter like thieves in the night. Marrowstride, he soon saw, was down by the water's edge at the pool. The bog hag's huge, mottled back was facing them as it squatted on the grass. From what Robin could make out, as they crouched in hiding at the corner of the hut, it was busily engaged in washing roots and tubers. Strange vegetables that Robin had never seen before. Preparing supper, which only gave further weight to Karya's claims. There was no sign of Woad. The boy was not where Robin had left him. The three stools were still in place outside the hut, and the small campfire which had heated their drinks had been put out, now just a charred smear in the grey moonlight shadows.

"He must be inside," Robin hissed. There was only one way into the cabin. It had no windows. Keeping one eye on the industrious creature down by the water of the pool, the three stole to the door, carefully and quiet as mice. Robin pushed it open as slowly and carefully as he could. His hand trembled on the rough boards and he prayed that it didn't creak or make a noise. The bog hag hadn't noticed their arrival. It was humming some mindless tune to itself in a horrible low gurgle, completely engrossed in its meal preparations.

The hut within was lit with the ruddy glow of a large firepit in the centre of the room, above which was strung a huge cauldron, filled with what looked to be a bubbling soup. Wisps of steam rose from it to the rushes and rafters above.

They closed the door softly behind them, shutting out the night, and peered around. Everywhere Robin looked, there were large meat hooks hanging from the ceiling. Several of them strung with cuts of meat. A pig here, a brace of skinned rabbits. The butchery was neat and expert and gruesome to behold, a dangling abattoir in the low and guttering light of the red fire.

Oh yes, well done, Scion. You really do make the best acquaintances, Robin thought to himself, feeling as though they had stumbled into one of those old splatter horror movies about cannibal hillbillies.

"Over there," Henry hissed, drawing Robin's eye away from the bubbling stew-pot and salted carcasses hung up to smoke. They hurried over to where he had pointed. There was a long low table against the far wall, wooden and ravaged with the cuts and scrapes of a hundred knife and cleaver scars. Laid out very neatly atop this huge butcher's block, with his feet bound at the ankles and his hands bound before him at the wrists, lay Woad.

The faun had twigs and herbs twined expertly in his bushy blue hair. Rosemary, thyme and some other stringy root which smelled peppery. His skin looked glossy, for a moment making Robin think the faun was feverish, until he saw the large pat of greyish-yellow butter on a plate nearby, alongside a selection of large and very sharp-looking knifes.

He wasn't feverish. He'd been basted.

"Seasoning the meat." Karya shook her head, as though this was exactly the kind of nonsense she would expect Woad to get up to if let out of her sight.

"Poor little bugger might as well have an apple stuck in his mouth," Henry said. "Bright side though, at least he's not been filleted yet." He glanced back nervously at the door. "Can I just say, this is hands down the worst gingerbread cottage I've ever seen. Let's wake up Hansel and get out of here before we're made into vol au vents too."

Robin leaned down to shake Woad awake. "Ow!" he hissed, jumping back as small bright-white sparks leapt from the unconscious boy's shoulders to his fingertips

"Skyfire," Karya muttered. "Well, the bog hag prepped this dish well, that's for sure." She leaned over the table and lightly slapped the faun on the cheek a few times.

"Woad. Get up," she whispered.

Woad's eyes shot open, making all three of them start a little. For a second, tiny arcs of lightning flickered between his eyelids, making his eyes glow white, then they cleared, and he shook his head, as they returned to their normal yellow tinge. He stared up at them all, looking a little drunk and confused.

"Boss! What are you doing here?" he yelped. He made to sit up, then noticed he was hog-tied and struggled.

Robin put a finger to his lips and motioned for him to be quiet. Henry glanced back at the closed door again.

"Shh! Lie still a second while we cut you free."

Karya was already working at the cooking twine that bound the boy, using one of the sharp knives from the table, and soon had the bonds cut. Woad made to leap heroically to his feet, a dramatic acrobatic feat which was hampered somewhat by him slipping on the table and falling off it completely.

He recovered well, scrambling back to his feet.

"Sorry about that," he said, his voice a little slurred. "I wasn't expecting to be so … greasy." His eyes were darting around the room. They rested on Karya and he looked confused.

"Why is your hair white, boss?"

She shook her head, dismissing the question and flapping her hands at him in an attempt to quiet him down.

"You were nearly stew, mate," Henry hissed. "Bog hag is fixed on cooking you up. Are you okay?"

The faun seemed to take in the situation and his current predicament quickly, and to his credit, to deal with it quite well. He looked around the grisly slaughterhouse of a home. "It's a crying shame," he said quietly. "I would have made the most delicious stew. Fauns are famous for being not only brave and heroic but also tremendously nutritious." He was rubbing at his own head, dislodging the seasoning herbs. "Ooh look, half a pig of bacon. Nice!"

"I'm sorry I left you," Robin said, handing the boy a rag from the table to wipe most of the greasy butter from his face. "You were in a trance. How do you feel?"

Woad considered this a moment. "Bit groggy," he announced with a shrug. "Could have been worse, though, at least I don't have half an onion shoved …"

"It's coming!" Karya snapped. They all stared at the doorway, Robin had already noted that it was the only way in or out of the cabin. He was also only now realising that the fresh clothes which Marrowstride had so kindly given them to wear were no doubt cast offs from a previous "meal". Leftovers, like potato peelings.

Outside, they could hear the heavy footsteps of the huge industrious creature approaching. Every step shook the hut, making the gruesome cuts of meat sway around them and casting leaping shadows on the walls in the flickering light of the firepit.

"Reckon we can take it?" Henry whispered. "I didn't bring my bow. There wasn't time. Barely had time to grab my coat. Pity, really," he babbled. "As when it comes to massive nightmare swamp trolls wanting to eat me, I do tend to prefer a long-range weapon to fisticuffs." He swallowed hard.

Karya shot a look at Robin. "I've no mana to spare," she said quickly. "Tearing from Erlking to you took … everything. There's no more." Her pure white hair looked somehow brittle, as though Robin could have reached out and snap off a handful like dried straw. The girl shook her pitch black mana stone bracelet on her wrist, clearly frustrated with herself. "I don't think I could even move a leaf across the floor anymore."

"Don't worry, boss, I can fight," Woad grinned, his face still oddly shiny in the light. "This is one meal that leaves more than heartburn!" He wobbled a little, and a tiny crackle of electricity leapt from his top lip to his eyebrow, making his mouth twitch and his forehead crinkle quite comically.

"Have you seen the size of it?" Henry frowned at him, shaking his head. The approaching footsteps outside had stopped. "What do you plan to do, a little twig like you? Get stuck in his throat like a chicken bone?"

Karya reached out and steadied Woad as the weaving faun reeled again, unsteady on his feet.

"You've just had your Skyfire unlocked, Woad," she said. "You barely even know where you are, just stand down will you?"

The door rattled as Marrowstride gripped the handle and began to swing inwards.

"All of you stop bickering and get behind me!" Robin snapped. They all stared at him.

Robin sighed down his nose. "I'm the Scion, I'm pulling rank again, get back!"

He had stepped forward, placing himself between the doorway and his friends.

The door swung open and, ducking its huge horned head, the bog hag entered, Marrowstride's massive frame filling the doorway. As it stood upright, the door closing behind it, the bog hag's twisted horns practically scraped the roof. It peered at them all with deep-set eyes under their thick brow. In the leaping firelight and deep shadows, it seemed more monstrous than ever, every wrinkle of its enormous, puckered face thrown into dancing relief by the flames. The knotted grey ropes of muscle and sinew on its shiny arms and legs twitched and bunched as it glared at them all, clearly surprised to see its home so full.

"What this?" Marrowstride rumbled, the timbre of its voice suggesting danger as its gaze rolled over the four children before it. It saw Woad, held up by Karya and Henry on either side behind Robin, and its expression was suddenly furious. "Oi! That's bogmaster supper! Supper stays! That was Marrow's deal!"

"You can't eat him," Robin said, defiantly staring up at the looming figure. "Faun has been taken off the menu."

"That was deal," the bog hag roared, spittle flying from its mouth. It pointed a huge shaking finger at Robin. "Bogmaster shows you old stones! You go. Blue one stays for supper!"

Robin shook his head, his arms out, keeping himself between his three friends and the angry creature before him.

"You wouldn't want him anyway," Henry said, over his shoulder. "He's very stringy. I'm pretty sure he's full of e-numbers and additives too."

The bog hag twisted its head, staring at this newcomer in confusion.

"No I'm not!" Woad argued, offended. "I'm choice cuts, I am! And organic! How dare you!" His eyes crossed a little and he shook his head, trying to clear it.

"Shut up, Woad!" Karya said through gritted teeth. "You're not helping!"

"Who this now?" Marrowstride bared its teeth at Robin. They were huge, like dark flat tombstones. "New morsels? Come to steal Marrow's supper? Liar and double-crosser!"

"You have to let us go," Robin insisted.

"You break deal!" The bog hag sounded outraged by this offence. "When Marrow first saw dark mares stalking, Marrow thinks, good meal here! Feast!" It held up two gnarled fingers. "Two courses!" It shook its head, the wet ropes of thin black hair slapping around its neck. "But no. Marrow is not greedy. Bogmaster is wise! Kind! Close to earth! Choose faun. Only faun can stay for supper. Good meal if made whole first." He stamped his foot on the rushes of the hut's floor. "You, though? You no good! You not whole! Undecided and half of everything! Marrow helped you. Find your black stones!"

"I'm a regular fusion dish, yes," Robin said, slowly moving one hand towards his mana stone, like a gunslinger making for his revolver. "But just because that's not to your taste doesn't mean you can eat …"

"This unwhole one brings more morsels! To steal Marrow's supper! It has no honour! No gratitude!" The bog hag roared, its gurgling voice deafening in this enclosed space. Its frown deepened even more, as its murderous expression roamed over Karya and Henry.

"Now none of you go. None leave forest! Bigger supper." It sniffed the air carefully, sizing them up. "Marrow will wash new ones. Make those two whole. Dry and salt and keep for winter." It nodded to itself, seeming happy with this conclusion. "That one," he nodded at Robin. "No good meat for bogmaster. Make a good jam."

With more speed than any of them would have imagined the lumbering creature capable of, Marrowstride shot out a long arm and snatched a large and cruel-looking cleaver from where it lay embedded in the tabletop. It raised it above its head.

"Rob?" Henry's voice sounded more than a little worried. Robin could hear Woad giggling a little drunkenly behind him. "Pinky jam … yuck."

Robin grabbed his mana stone and cast breezeblock in front of them as hard as he could. The bog hag brought the cleaver down, crashing it against the wall of solid air. Robin's mana stone vibrated on his chest as though struck. The creature was strong.

The bog hag roared in anger, bringing the cleaver back up and hurling it down again, gripped in both hands. The breezeblock shattered, a blast of invisible air exploding in all directions. The wind set the hanging sides of meat swinging wildly like macabre piñatas and scattered the knives and bowls from the tabletop in a metallic cacophony, sending them clattering against the walls and floor. Several of the sharp blades embedded themselves into the wooden walls with a thud. The blast made the fire roar, sending up a flurry of angry orange sparks into the shadows like fireflies.

It's very strong, he thought, swallowing and focussing again, thinking fast. All four of them had been knocked back a step, and Robin dug his heels into the filthy rushes of the floor.

Twisting around at the waist, he struck out his arm towards the hanging cauldron, casting waterwhip. The steaming contents of the bowl sloshed and leapt out of the container like a living snake. Eyes and mana stone flashing, Robin curled his arm around and thrust it at the bog hag, sending the boiling coil of liquid sailing through the air with a hiss. It wrapped around Marrowstride's legs with a hiss, making it roar louder in alarm, as it teetered off balance.

Robin closed his hand into a fist, sweat beading on his forehead, and the waterwhip tightened like rope, drawing his adversary's ankles together. The bog hag stumbled and, as the water boiled and hissed, it fell heavily to the floor, like a tumbling tree.

Robin only avoided being grabbed by the swamp-creature's long fingers by Karya pulling him backwards as it dropped the cleaver and made a snatch for him through the air. Its face was furious now, teeth fully bared, all other features lost in the wrinkled mass of its grey skull.

"You will not leave!" It kicked against the watery restraint as though wrestling a python. "Stay! For supper!"

Robin dropped to his knees before the creature and dug his fingers into the straw and bare soil that made up the floor of the makeshift cabin. He shook his head.

"No," he said. "*You* stay." He twisted his fingers, pushing his mana out and downwards into the earth with all his might.

Roots sprang up, bursting from the ground all around the fallen bog hag. Thick as his waist, black-brown and harder than rock. Robin squeezed his eyes shut, gritting his teeth hard, and the roots flew upwards in a rough circle, slamming into one another at a single point above the bog hag's head. They formed a cage, a rough wigwam of twisting wood and vegetation, and Robin swiftly filled the gaps, as the thick, twining ivy of One Horn Forest, bent to his will, came snaking out of the earth and lacing over and over around the skeleton of the roots, cocooning the bog hag in its cage.

Marrowstride gripped the root-bars, its lumpy knuckles straining as it yelled in outrage, but the roots held, strong as the earth itself. In moments, they could only glimpse the creature, a shifting shadow trapped behind the wood and ivy, a furious, wrinkled brow glaring out at them.

"Wow," Henry breathed, as Robin stood, staring at the captured enemy. "Good going! But it's between us and the only door. How are we supposed ..."

Without taking his eyes off Marrowstride, Robin flicked a hand at the far wall to his left. With a great, tearing roar, the wall burst open away from them in a hail of splintered wood and sawdust, the Tower of Earth peeling back the wood in layers and leaving a gaping hole.

"Oh … okay." Henry nodded approvingly. "That'll do it."

"Let's go!" Karya insisted. "Now, before …"

The cage shook furiously, shedding ivy everywhere. Marrowstride the bog hag, robbed of his hard-earned meal, was yelling some choice obscenities.

"Good idea, we need to leave." Robin nodded enthusiastically. Henry and Woad were already making for the ragged hole, escaping into the dark night air of the forest outside. Karya grabbed Robin by the arm and pulled him away.

"I'm grateful," Robin said, awkwardly. "For the unicorns, I mean. Um … sorry about … everything else. But you really can't eat us. This should wear off soon, okay?"

"Stop apologising to the monster that was going to kill us, and come on!" Henry's voice came from outside.

Robin turned and fled through the ragged broken wall of the hut with Karya. From behind him, Marrowstride sounded betrayed and bitter, its voice coming through the thick foliage of its cocoon as it strained and pushed against it, raging in vain.

"Cheat! Thieves!" it roared horribly. "Nightmares will take you! Take you in the dark! Without Marrow to save you!"

The forest outside seemed darker than ever after the flickering firelight of the bog hag's hut. Robin and the others stumbled over uneven ground, tripping over ivy and tangled roots as they fled the clearing and the pool, steaming in the faint moonlight. Fleet as hares the Erlkingers ran, disappearing under the close and dark trees.

"Where are we going?" Henry asked, breathlessly, a faint smudge in the gloom. They had been scrambling through the dark for several minutes.

"I think away is more important than towards, right now," Robin replied. He felt a little woozy from expending so much mana from so many different Towers at once, but oddly elated at the same time.

"That was impressive, Scion," Karya wheezed at his side, as they scampered over knotted roots and crashed through bushes. With her white hair, she looked like a small ghost passing under the grey latticework of the tree branches. "It doesn't seem forever ago that you were a hornless wonder, struggling to stick a piece of flapping parchment to the ceiling back at

Erlking." It was hard for Robin to see her face, but he had the impression she was smiling grimly. "You're beginning to look like I saw you once … long before we met," she said.

They could still hear Marrowstride's roars of anger in the darkness behind them, but they were growing ever more distant.

"That cantrip back there won't hold forever," Robin said. "We need a plan. Running around aimlessly in the dark is going to get us killed. That bog hag knows these woods far better than we do, and there are deadly mud pits and quicksand everywhere here. Not to mention plenty of cliffs and ravines to run off in the dark."

They scurried unsteadily down a long slope, scattering leaves and vines in the darkness before them. Robin brought them to a breathless halt. Woad tripped, still propelled forward by his momentum and falling face first into a clump of ivy, giggling a little drunkenly. There was a muted flash and crackle of lightning between the fingers of his outstretched hands.

"Our faun is not fully compos mentis," Karya breathed, helping him to his feet. "Coming into Skyfire takes it out of them, I see." She looked to Henry. "I agree with the Scion. If the bog hag doesn't kill us, the forest will."

"I am totally compost mental." Woad assured them, spitting out leaves in a matter-of-fact way.

"Where were you two headed *before* this happened?" Henry panted, leaning forward with his hands on his knees as he struggled to get his breath back. "I'm guessing you weren't just taking a pleasure hike through this lovely beauty spot?"

Robin shook his head, remembering the hex message he had received. "A library. There's supposed to be a hidden library, somewhere secret in the mountains beyond the forest. We were headed there, to find swift wings."

Karya and Henry looked at him in confusion.

"Which direction is the library?" the girl asked. "I don't even know which way we're facing right now, and I'm one of the best trackers there is." She looked down at her hands, frustrated. "Usually."

"West," Woad muttered dreamily. "We entered the forest from the east, but there are no straight lines and now even this faun is dizzy."

Robin had an idea. Shrugging off his pack, he dug out the moral compass. Holding it up so that it caught the faint moonlight drifting down between the deep shadows.

"Where do I go?" he asked, giving it a gentle shake. "Which way to the mountains?"

The small silver needle spun, this way and that, before finally coming to rest pointing over Woad's shoulder. Robin peered closely. The tiny face the needle had aligned with had short nubbin horns and a pointed beard. It looked a little like Phorbas.

"This way, I guess?" he said uncertainly, gesturing behind Woad. Thinking of Phorbas had made him think of the haunted knife. He wondered if Jackalope still had it, or if it had been taken from him by their captors. Spoils of the hunt.

"You *guess*?" Henry said. "Are we really trusting a magic eight-ball to get us out of this place?"

"Do you have a better idea?" Robin asked, irritable. Henry shook his head quickly.

"No, absolutely not," he admitted. He was looking past Robin and seemed suddenly distracted.

"But, you know how you were saying that the bog hag or the swamp pits might kill us all?" He swallowed hard. "I think they might need to get in line. What the hell are *those* things?"

Robin spun, staring back to where Henry was looking. Karya and Woad huddled close to see as well. High on the ridge of the slope they had just descended were large shadows, moving between the trees. Almost silent, save for the occasional careful crunch of leaves. A rank smell rolled down the hill. An animal smell, like the bottom of a lion's cage.

"Unicorns," Karya breathed. And then she swore, quite impressively.

There was a snort above and – as one of the shadows moved again, stalking the children from a distance like a barely glimpsed panther – something caught the light. A long thick horn, dark and shiny, flashing in the moonlight.

"There's … a lot of them," Robin whispered, staying very still, his eyes darting all over the forest. Everywhere he looked, there was movement. Six of them? No, seven?

"Unicorns?" Henry said quietly. "Like … My Little Pony unicorns? You have got to be kidding me."

"They must have been drawn to all the noise at the bog hag's pool," Karya said, ignoring his disbelief. "They wouldn't dare come near with that thing loose, but now it's trussed up and out of the picture …"

"Now, we're fair game," Robin said, and swallowed.

"Let 'em try," Woad said bravely, sticking his chest out. "I'm not scared of night mares!"

"Well, you should be." Karya looked as though she wanted to slap Woad upside the head with the back of her hand. "Unicorns are pack hunters. If they're up there …" She looked around at the rest of the woods. "Then they're over there, too. And there."

"I thought unicorns were supposed to grant wishes or something." Henry sounded nervous. "Magic horses have no business being evil, that's just not playing fair!"

"Dark mares have about as much in common with horses as you do with a fish, Henry," Karya said. "Think more sabre-toothed-beast-of-the-woods, then whatever you're picturing, make it bigger and very angry."

"The only wish these lovely critters would grant is if you wished, *really specifically*, to be impaled to a tree through your heart." Woad nodded, still trying to look bigger than he was and intimidate their prowling stalkers. "And I doubt many people wish that, even on a bad day."

Robin looked seriously to Karya, sliding his compass back into his pack as slowly and carefully as he could. He didn't want to make any sudden movements. He couldn't see the night mares, had never clearly seen one yet, and part of him, he had decided firmly, really didn't want to. But he could *feel* them all coiled like springs of darkness and muscle, just waiting for an excuse to pounce.

"How fast are these things?" he whispered. His hand had moved to his mana stone. He watched her glance down at it as she shook her head imperceptibly.

"Fast. Faster than two feet."

"Faster than four?" Robin asked. He glanced around at them all. "Join hands," he commanded.

Everyone looked at him in confusion.

"Just do it!" he insisted. "I've never done this before, I've only seen it done. But I know it takes a lot of mana and mine is tired. I need to use everyone's."

"I have nothing to cast," Karya told him, but she grabbed Woad and Henry by the wrists, nonetheless.

"I don't have mana, Rob," Henry looked apologetic. "I'm only a human, did you forget?" He held his hand out and Robin took it firmly.

"You have plenty of mana," he said. "Everyone does. You just don't have a mana stone." He had no idea if this was true or not, but it felt true, and he managed to sound very authoritative. He grabbed Woad's free hand with his other.

"Are you focussed?" he asked the faun, who didn't seem to be swaying as much as he had been. He was finally coming out of his stupor.

Woad nodded decisively. "Take what you need, Pinky. We trust you."

Robin glanced at his friends, with a sudden sense of wonder.

They really did. All of them. None of them knew what he was planning to do, but none of them had doubted, not even for a moment. He hoped he didn't let them down. If he did, they would all very soon pay for it on the end of sharp horns.

They believe in me, he thought firmly to himself, trying to ignore the many circling shapes on the slope above, and forcing himself to focus. I don't care what the bog hag said. I'm not undecided. I know exactly who and what I am. I'm the Scion of the Arcania.

He thrust his mana downwards into the earth beneath their feet, at the same time sending it out through both his hands. He felt it travel along his fingers and into those of his friends, roaring around the rough circle they formed like rushing thunder. He felt his energy pick up theirs along the way, streams merging into a torrent. It flowed through Henry and Woad and Karya, a shock wave crashing into itself and rushing back to meet Robin from either side.

His mana stone blazed like a supernova as their energy, mingled with his, flooded through him. It was painful and euphoric at the same time, and he pushed it all downwards into the earth.

I saw Hawthorn do this once, I helped him do it. He was a master of the Tower of Earth, but so am I.

The ground beneath them rumbled and split, a mound of soil spilling upwards between them in a crumbling heap like a monstrous molehill. Shapes began to dig themselves out of the ground, as the children dropped their hands and all staggered backwards.

In the darkness surrounding them was snorting and stamping of feet, as the unicorns drew back warily into the darkness.

"Boulderdash," Robin gasped. His legs felt like water and his heart was pounding. The palms of his hands felt scorched. Erupting from the ivy and muddy soil beneath them, two large and lumbering shapes were clawing their way out of the earth.

When last he had seen this cantrip cast, Hawthorn had conjured great lions made from solid soil and rocks and twigs. The two steeds now shaking off excess soil and dirt were not lions. They had long backs, narrow snouts, and their eyes, burning yellow stones in faces made from roots and ivy, were slits. They looked like two enormous Komodo dragons, long tails whipping back and forth, lizard-like legs digging claws made of rock into the soft churned earth.

Hawthorn told me my father did this, Robin thought in wonder, staring at the forest brought to life, moulded into living creatures. *My father could make dragons.*

"That's some party trick!" Henry goggled at the golem-steeds, and one of them opened its mouth wide and hissed. Its forked tongue was mud, rolling bog slime, black and glossy behind a row of teeth formed from sharp, neat pebbles.

Woad leaped up atop one without hesitation or fear. Robin clambered up behind him quickly, scuttling across the rough broad back of twigs and moss, grabbing the wobbly faun around the waist.

"Come on!" he yelled to the others. Karya and Henry didn't need telling twice. The girl took one last look back at the dark trees, grabbed Henry by the hand and clambered onto the second boulderdash lizard, pulling him up behind her. Henry wrapped his hands around her furry coat, looking terrified, as she sought to find somewhere around the huge lizard's neck to hold on.

There was an almighty crash from the trees above. The dark mares had broken cover. Whether feeling challenged by these new beasts, or simply having decided there were enough of their pack to take the two lizards down, Robin didn't know. He dug his heels into the earthen flanks of their steeds, tilting its head in the direction the compass had shown.

"Go!" he yelled, and with a rattling hiss the two beasts set off, crashing through the darkness and trees with sudden and alarming speed.

Robin glanced back as they sped away, unable to overcome his curiosity, and immediately wished he hadn't. There were a dozen unicorns flying down the slope after them in hot pursuit, and they looked nothing like any storybook creature.

Pitch black, with shaggy fur and muscular bodies, they resembled bears more than anything else, their pounding legs ended not in hooves, but wide flat paws with long, cruel-looking claws digging into the earth and throwing it out behind them in great clumps as they propelled themselves forward. Their heads, on long and thickly-sinewed necks, did have something vaguely equine about them – they were long, with dark snouts, but their wide jaws hinged deeply, and he saw flashes of sharp teeth gnashing in the fur and darkness, like the terrible grin of a shark. A single horn protruded from the crown of their long faces – not long and thin like a rapier, but thick and curved, rhinoceros-like. It covered the whole upper portion of their nightmarish faces, sprouting from where eyes would be. The unicorns were blind.

"Robin! Duck!" Henry called out. He and Karya rushed along behind him on their own thunderous steed. Dragging his eyes away from the horrible creatures flying through the trees, Robin whipped his head around to face forwards, ducking his head just in time to avoid being decapitated by a low tree branch, as his steed slipped beneath it, fleet as a shadow. The ground rolled under them, as the boulderdash steed leapt and sprinted from root to root, dodging trees left and right, crashing through bushes and foliage with wild abandon. He and Woad hunkered down, gripping the stony creature crashing through the brush for dear life and trying not to be battered away and unseated by branches.

The unicorns roared behind them, caught in the frenzy of the hunt as the forest whipped by at speed.

When Robin had last ridden steeds like this, it was on open moorland, and they had flown along under the sky like the wind itself. This time felt more stomach-churning; up and down slopes they fled, the powerful legs of their steeds exploding through ivy, skittering over rocks as tall as him, flowing swiftly through the night. More than once they crashed with great splashes into mud, sending it flying up either side of them in grimy waves, and not for a second did the lizards move in a straight line. Feinting left and right, reptilian and swift. Zig-zagging between trees and crashing through patches of thick mist and fog to burst forth from the other side.

Their pursuers though were fast and relentless, the unicorns threading through the darkness swift as snakes with snorts and grunts, the occasional snapping of jaws punctuating the thundering of their feet. More than once they came close enough to snap and gnash, teeth snapping on air at the flanks of the steeds.

Robin heard Henry yell in alarm as one of the night mares closed in on the beast he and Karya rode; lunging, bit down hard at the boulderdash's tail, which exploded in a hail of soil, twigs and rocks.

The lizard didn't break stride. It rushed onwards unfettered, tailless but otherwise intact.

"We're not losing them, Pinky!" Woad called from his muffled position, practically flat against the heaving back of their steed. "They're as fast as we are!"

Robin glimpsed the forest around in flashes as they flew by, in and out of boles and branches. The moon was out and One Horn was bathed in a silver light. The forest was broken here, deep valleys, choked with trees and mist, and more rocky drops and rises. Gullies and drops. A deep ravine appeared out of the brush before them, the land falling away sharply as their steed altered course, lurching so sharply at the last moment before careening off a cliff edge that both boys were almost thrown clear. Robin held on so tightly his knuckles were white. If they fell, the unicorns would fall upon them like giant wild dogs, he had no doubt of that.

"Look!" he cried. "Up ahead!"

The forest before them seemed to be thinning at last, and a patch of ground stood open to the moonlight. There was a wide, dark scar across it, black as a smear of jet. It spread away to either side, a lightning bolt of darkness in the moonlit grass and ivy. Beyond it, the forest continued.

"That's a ravine," the faun yelled. "They're everywhere here. We've nearly fallen down ten of these already, what's your point?"

Robin grabbed the neck of the stony lizard and twisted it towards the open ground. "We're not avoiding this one," he replied, shouting to be heard over the whipping wind.

With the dark mares in hot pursuit, filling the night air with their keening roars, the stone and earth lizards broke out of the trees, the steeds thundering towards the great gash of darkness. It seemed wider the closer they got. Practically a gorge. Robin tried to see if the opposite side of the canyon was higher or lower than this side, but it was impossible to tell in the dark. There was little time to calculate the physics.

"Scion!" Karya's voice screamed out from behind him as she and Henry followed at full speed. "That's a canyon ahead!"

"I know!" he yelled back as the edge of the ground rushed forward to meet them. The unicorns erupted out of the trees behind them, snapping jaws and flashing horns, roaring their strange cries as they pelted after them. "Hold on tight, Woad," Robin said. He felt the faun tense in front of him, gripping the boulderdash steed as tightly as he could.

"Leap of faith, Pinky?" Woad said, face buried in the lizard's neck.

Something like that, Robin thought, desperately. It was too late for doubts or other plans. The ravine was upon them. Robin dug his heels in harder, making the steed hiss angrily, and they leapt out into space and darkness.

For a horrible, nauseating and weightless moment, the lizard sailed through the air. Looking down in the moonlight, Robin saw empty space beneath them. The ravine was deep, filled far below with sharp rocks and grubby-looking bushes, and the void beneath seemed to suck at them, willing them to tumble into its depths. He held his breath, looking up and forward, seeing the opposite bank closing towards them.

We're not going to make it, he thought, oddly devoid of any emotion but shock.

A moment later, the lizard hurtled towards the cliff side, its riders yelling and clinging on for dear life.

They had cleared the wide gap, leapt the gully, and as they landed by the skins of their teeth on the opposite side, the impact shattered their beast, sending it disintegrating into a thousand pieces and crumbling away from under them.

Momentum carried Robin and Woad forward in a landslide of crumbling soil and rocks, and a great cloud of dust. The noise was enormous. Robin rolled over and over, battered by stones, his arms flung up to protect his face as he somersaulted through the landslide of scree, before finally coming to rest.

Lying coughing and panting in the grass, he heard a second roaring crash. Henry and Karya had cleared the ravine too, their steed disintegrating beneath them on impact in a similarly apocalyptic manner.

"Woad!" Robin sat up shakily, coughing. His face was covered in dust, and he absently wiped blood from a split lip.

"I'm okay!" Woad's voice came, sounding more than a little hoarse. The small blue boy was digging himself out of rubble nearby, shaking his head wildly and dislodging a cloud of dust. He coughed horribly. "I think I swallowed some soil lizard! That's gross!" He laughed – a tad hysterically.

Robin struggled to his feet; his body still so full of adrenalin that nothing hurt yet. He simply felt battered and numb, his heart pounding out of his chest.

Henry and Karya were helping one another up nearby, both unhurt, digging out of a pile of debris. Their steed had etched a long groove from the edge of the cliff where it had landed. They looked as if they were crawling from a meteor strike.

Staggering back towards the canyon's edge on unsteady feet, Robin looked across the deep gap.

It had worked.

The unicorns – he shook his head, that word still felt so *wrong* for what those things were – the night mares, he corrected himself, hadn't followed. They milled around on the far side of the ravine, stamping their feet angrily and shaking their flanks. A dozen of them, large black shadows in the long grass, their thick, cruelly-pointed horns flashing in the light of the moon as they opened their long jaws and keened in anger and frustration, unable to follow their quarry across the gap.

"Hah!" Henry screamed at the absolute top of his lungs. "Take *that*! You stupid … animals!"

Robin's friend was staggering towards him, waving a defiant fist at their frustrated pursuers. He was grey with dust and soil from head to foot. "Not so scary now, are you?" Henry's voice cracked a little with dust. He looked as though he had just crawled out of his own grave. "Bugger off back to the trees! Friendship is bloody well magic, right?"

Robin followed the line of the ravine with his eye, wondering nervously how far it stretched to either side. It went as far as he could see in the dark. At least a mile, maybe more. Could the night mares circle around? Find a place narrow enough to leap, or a place to cross?

"Go home and work on your cutie marks!" Henry yelled. He had grabbed a large stone from the grass, formerly a piece of their now-dismantled steed, and hurled it angrily across the ravine. It didn't reach the other side, not by a long shot, falling away into the darkness, where it seemed to take a long time before they heard it clatter off the rocks below.

Robin put a tired arm around his friend's shoulder, turning him around towards Karya and Woad, who were still dusting themselves off.

"Okay, okay," he coughed. "That'll do. You showed them, Henry. Now let's get out of this bloody forest before they start throwing rocks back, eh?"

He glanced up, beyond the white-haired girl and the blue boy. The trees behind them looked thin and the land they stood on climbed upwards steeply. Beyond them, the darkness seemed solid and high, great hills and thinning cover climbing towards the sky. Blackness stood against a night sky that was slowly giving way to day, the softest blush of grey creeping in at the edges.

Dawn was not far off, and it seemed they had reached the edge of the forest and the foothills of the mountains.

Robin peered up into the wild and rugged landscape ahead and swallowed. With Karya continuing to fade, and Pyrenight fast approaching, he knew there was no time to waste. Lost and alone in the Netherworlde as they were, they couldn't stop moving forward. Not if they hoped to save Jack and Ffoulkes from a fiery death.

The enigma of Lady Tinda had led them here, adrift in the wilderness, pursued by darkness. Answers must lie ahead, and Robin knew he had to find them soon, before the bonfires of Dis were lit.

'Half a heart and half a hope
And dangers still ahead

Embers turn to ashes
As the Glassfire Path we tread'

Continued in The Glassfire Serpent Part Two

Lightning Source UK Ltd.
Milton Keynes UK
UKHW012123051021
391659UK00001B/142